TEMPTATION'S DESIRE

His eyes glowed wildly in the velvet darkness, his breath burning her cheek as his lust intensified. She struggled, gripping his wrist, straining. Then his mouth came down to her lips and she screamed in horror. He pulled back, his eyes widening. Then the instinct to ravage, to satisfy his demanding lust prevailed, sending his hands to her hips, tearing away her nightgown. Writhing, she strained to slip from beneath him, her arm twisted beside her head, her hand digging beneath the pillow, locating the knife, fighting to free it . . .

Tempt Not This Flesh

BARBARA RIEFE

SPHERE BOOKS LIMITED
30-32 Gray's Inn Road, London WC1X 8JL

First published in Great Britain by Sphere Books Ltd 1981
Copyright © Barbara Riefe 1979

TRADE
MARK

Set in Times

Printed and bound in Great Britain by
©ollins, Glasgow

For Leslie,
with love and affection

CONTENTS

CONTENTS

Love is a pearl of purest hue,
But stormy waves are round it;
And dearly may a woman rue,
The hour that she found it.
            —*Letitia Elizabeth Landon*

BOOK ONE

NIGHTMARE PASSAGE

I

She caressed his cheek, tracing the line of his lean jaw lightly, slowly circling his throat. He drew her mouth to his as his arm locked her to him. Savoring sweet passion's renascence, he kissed her soulfully, lingeringly, setting her heart beating like that of a wild creature ensnared. What pride of possession he inspired, how like one living thing they were, how dependably secure the knot binding them. This certainty springing to mind giddied her. Freeing herself, she feasted her eyes upon her prize. Suddenly the hours seemed ages since they had exchanged vows in the little white church in Hanover. She saw again the host of happy faces of friends and relatives, well-wishers all, the rice in the rain, the black blossoms springing into bloom as scores of umbrellas popped up to canopy their way from the church door to the waiting carriage. From carriage to public coach they had tumbled, luggage piled in, the hurried kisses, hugs and handclasps as those who had followed from the church, the shouts of farewell and Godspeed fading, giving way to the rapping of the rain on the coach roof. Then all of a seeming instant, she, Lorna Singleton, had become Lorna Singleton Stone. Mrs. Philip Stone, if you please!

Words and wedlock and wish come true! Said the wise of the world, nothing was ever as wonderful, beautiful or satisfying as imagination anticipated it being. Until this. The harvest of happiness reaped from the crossing of the stars of Philip Stone and Lorna Singleton had outmarveled every expectation. I take thee Philip to be my wedded husband, to have and to hold. Contentment surged within her, flowering, spread-

13

ing, warming her every fiber. To have and to hold.
Fiercely and forever.

The wind worried about the chimneys of the Gray
Dragon Inn, rattling the dormer glass and dirging away
over the rooftops toward the Mill Pond. A draft left
in its wake slipped into the room between the windows
held partially open by top and bottom latches. The
breeze discovered the candle stub in its pressed glass
prison and guttered the flame briefly. The candle flung
its gold up the wall to the shadowed beams and down
upon Philip's nakedness, the edge of the counterpane
double woven in old rose, plum and indigo blue lying
across his thighs. The glow bathed his chest with a
sheen, a cuirass of gold leaf, she fancied. His was such
a magnificent body, so faultlessly sculptured, shoulders,
chest, rib cage gently rising and falling, his stomach
as flat and hard as the top of the oaken chest occupying the corner to the left of the dormer. He smiled at
her, the ends of his mouth probing his cheeks, his
black eyes twinkling. Such a glorious smile.

"What are you thinking about?" he asked.

"Nothing."

"Something, what?"

"You, us, what we've done, now that the rice has
settled; what we've gotten for ourselves. How lucky we
are."

"To have found each other."

She nodded. "I pity all my friends so, having to settle
for so much less in their men. For ordinary men. Little
men. Putterers."

"Mere mortals . . ." He laughed and kissed her.
"Your pedestal for me is much too lofty, darling. If it
totters and falls I'll shatter."

"Never." She sat up, her lovely breasts bouncing behind the ruffled edge of Valenciennes lace at the bosom
of her pale pink silk and satin nightgown.

"And you, Mrs. Stone, are no less perfect."

"Who said anything about perfection? Perfect you're not, my love, not with that temper, with all the patience of a wounded bull. I've never known anyone so incorrigibly impulsive, willful . . ."

"What temper!" he snapped, at once catching the slip and laughing at himself. "Come here, you witch, I'll give you temper and wounded bulls and the rest of it." He seized her roughly, pressing her breasts against his chest, igniting her, setting her flesh tingling.

"Darl . . ."

His mouth upon hers stifled the word. Off flew the covers with a kick of his leg. Gripping her hand he slid it down his hip, over his thigh to his member. It was hardening again, rapidly filling with firmness. The contact with her fingertips sent a great tremor radiating from her breasts, suffusing her and stirring her sex. He gentled, relaxing his hold, easing her down upon her back, lavishing his lips upon her mouth, eyes, and face. Down her neck he slowly ventured, across one pale white shoulder, across and around each heaving breast in turn. She gasped, capitulating heart and soul, reveling in the warm moistness of his mouth upon her flesh, circling and setting tiny fires around the aureoles of her nipples, bringing them to stony hardness. His head lowered, his mouth slipping under her breasts, kissing, kissing, the sound vaguely heard in the shadowed stillness of the room. His tenderness lifted her soul, tearing away all inhibitions, all the bonds of caution and prudence trammeling her emotions.

Now he lay on his side alongside her, their bodies touching full length, his member pressed hard against her thigh, pulsing, throbbing. She yearned so to engorge it with her sex, to lock it inside her. To never let it go. Oh, my blessed Philip, my dear, darling husband, this is, you are, paradise, complete, absolute!

They paused in their foreplay. He raised himself to his knees and grasping the hem of her nightgown removed it. His hands floated upward with such lissome dexterity she felt herself freed of it as if by magic. Then he moved to close the window, returning, once more positioning himself beside her. His tongue flicking tantalizingly roamed about her trembling body. Her excitement intensified and she began to moan softly. This seemed to stimulate him; his ardor increasing, his glorious assault upon her flesh slowed. His fingers found and fondled her hair, casually stroking the lovely auburn waves. Then all at once he stopped short, seizing her, kissing her passionately, their tongues clashing, driving against each other.

"My darling," she whispered.

Once more his tongue set about seeking those secret and sensitive oases of desire upon and around her throat, her burning breasts, her stomach, the inner planes of her thighs . . .

Joining in mute outcry, her mind and body pleaded for an end to play and the mounting and settling of his limbs between her own, spreading them, the first tender tormenting touch that would set her smoldering sex leaping into flame. But she steeled herself, forcibly quelling her hunger, determined to prolong the exquisite agony of anticipation.

An eon passed. Her steel melted, vaporized, down came her defenses, her willpower dashed, overwhelmed by a wave of unbridled lust sweeping over her.

"My darling," she murmured huskily, "take me, take me . . ."

It was as if he did not hear her. The only sounds in the room remained his panting, his teasing tongue and the thunder of her heart.

A delicious shudder wrenched her body. She moaned louder now, a wordless pleading. Then the command: "Now! Now!"

He lifted his body over hers into position. Her hand flew to his member, seizing it, feeling it pulsing powerfully in the coil of her fingers, the head massive, magnificent. Slowly she guided it to her sex and into it

his body lowering over her and easing forward . . .
forward. . . .

They lay dozing atop the counterpane, her nightgown flung carelessly across them. Never had she
known such glorious fulfillment, such extraordinary
satisfaction. His slightest movement inside her had sent
her soaring to the heights. And to the stars at climax,
to ecstasy that defied description, to gratification supreme. Now, lying beside him, reveling in the glow of
repletion, she mulled over the events of this most marvelous day and night. Her mind moved beyond them
to the next thirteen days from now in promised paradise, to their honeymoon in New York City. Two places
had been reserved for Mr. and Mrs. Philip Stone on the
8 A.M. public coach. The journey down the coast would
be interminable, the weather no doubt ghastly, the
coach crowded to the roof rack bolts. But the reward
for their patience would be nearly two weeks honeymoon in New York—two weeks of love's intoxication,
uninterrupted, uninhibited, the fountains filling, gushing forth, draining and filling again. By rights, the rights
of those less free spirited than either of them, she
should feel disgracefully wanton. Instead she delighted
in the prospect, already liberated of all constraints and
so high in heart, so near the point of bursting with happiness she was half persuaded to leap from the bed, fling
wide the windows and shout it out to sleeping Boston!

Their honeymoon concluded, they would return to
New Hampshire to Philip's law practice. Philip Stone,
attorney-at-law. She had painted his shingle herself,
hanging it to announce to the world that in this house
there would henceforth be practicing one uncommonly
brilliant and capable lawyer.

They lay in their room in the Gray Dragon Inn.
Their trip here had been arduous. It had rained all the
way to Boston, a typical June shower, indecently pro-
longed and accompanied by brief blue-white scratches
of lightning and thunder's drums. The downpour had

punished and polished the town, reducing the unpaved streets to quagmires and setting the few cobbled ones gleaming like glass.

Arriving shortly after six they had fled the coach, crammed with the mingled stenches of tobacco smoke, and damp leather and canvas, for the protection of the Gray Dragon Inn here on Ann Street. Over the door of the box-shaped, three-storied, two chimneyed inn was the Gray Dragon's cast iron namesake supported by a single rod. The downstairs tavern proved no less noxious than the coach, but this drawback was more than offset by the presence of good cheer. Dinner at a table shared with fifteen others had been boiled bluefish with oyster sauce, squash, Irish potatoes, and peach pie, burning hot but praiseworthy to palate once its fire was damped. Dinner might as well have been stale bread and tepid water for all the appetite either bride or groom had for food. The hunger gnawing their vitals could scarcely be appeased at table. With the kitchen's offerings, however, had come a worthy chablis, with a bouquet so commendable that Philip had ordered a second bottle delivered to their room.

The rains had rolled out to sea, allowing the full moon to detach itself from the trailing cloud cover. Around it, a rush of stars pricked the darkness, like the clover around the circular pool in the meadow behind their new home. Now the second bottle of wine was empty. Blinking fully awake, grinding his eyes with his knuckles little boy like, Philip sat up, picking the bottle up from the night stand. He held it atilt to the moonlight slanting through the window, the candle having long since gone out.

"Thirsty?" he asked.

"Thirsty," she said, smirking impishly, her right hand stealing around his neck, and pulling his mouth down to her own. "Mmmm, delicious. Definitely a vintage year."

"Seriously, darling . . ." He groped for and found the bell cord, jerking it twice.

"Is anybody still up, I wonder?" she queried.

"My darling, this is Boston, not Hanover. These people drink and loud it and chase the devil's tail 'til dawn. Those that aren't Puritans or Baptists or Methodists or . . ."

"Bother your wine, my Roman god." Playfully, she snatched the empty bottle from him, tossing it to the foot of the bed. "Come down here and love me. It's been ages." Up on her knees, letting the nightgown rustle to the floor in a heap, she threw her arms about his waist. She began kissing his stomach, feeling its firmness under her mouth, and his member relaxed snugging against the curve of her throat.

Again he pulled the cord, then sat on the edge of the bed, cradling her in his arms, kissing her ardently.

"My darling Lorna, my love. I adore you so. I never dreamed I could love anyone so . . . slavishly."

"Mmmm. I wouldn't have it any other way."

He was getting hard rapidly. Once more the ceremony of loveplay began, with determined and dedicated deliberation, the exploring, touching, fondling, the slow sublime and certain ascent to the pinnacle from which together they would hurl themselves upward into the heaven of climax . . .

Somewhere beyond Town Dock Bridge in the direction of the Long Wharf a bell tolled, two lonely rings. Reaching for the night stand, she picked up her watch, its slender silver chain neatly circling it. The hands agreed with the bell. Winding the watch, she slipped the chain about her neck, feeling the cool silver back of the watch as it nestled against her bare flesh. She fingered the casing fondly. The watch was a wedding gift from Grandmother Hastings, her favorite of all the females after her mother on the Hastings side of the family. Heedless of this activity on her part, Philip was sitting up, reaching for his shirt and trousers.

"Darling, what are you doing?" she asked.

"Wine, my love. I thirst for it, I need it, I want it.

Either the bell cord's broken or everybody downstairs is deaf! Imbeciles . . . *Canea!*"

His infrequent lapses into Italian, the words like darts hurled through clenched teeth, always signaled temper. Grown accustomed to the warning, she overlooked such outbursts. They were harmless and never yet had one been directed at her. Why steer it in that direction? Her purposeful avoidance of reaction had an instantaneous effect.

He smiled hesitantly. "Sorry . . ."

"Don't be sorry, it's your privilege."

Chastened, he attempted to cover his embarrassment with annoyance. "For two dollars you might expect a little service," he muttered.

"Blame it on the wine, Philip. If it weren't so tasty you wouldn't be so testy."

He stood up, buttoning his trousers, buckling his belt, pulling on his boots, running a hand through his tousled curls. "I'll be back in five minutes."

"Make it three . . ."

He kissed her. "Lock and bolt the door."

She nodded. He was gone. She did as he advised and pressing her ear to the door heard his steps click down the runnerless hallway. Getting back into bed, propping both pillows up behind her, she sat and stretched, then checked her watch, twisting it about to catch the light of the moon. The minute hand, as slender as a hair, had hardly moved. She glanced about the meagerly furnished room, the crude bench against the wall at right angles to the door, the Normandy armoire, the round-backed spindle chair on the other side of the bed where Philip had laid his clothes, disdaining the armoire. Beside the chair stood a cabinet supporting a wash basin and pitcher, the latter resplendent with an illustration of the *Apotheosis of Washington,* an angel supporting him under blinding rays of heavenly light. Reaching for the night stand drawer she opened it to emptiness, her only reward for her curiosity a musty odor escaping and joining the dampness of the air in the room. Closing the drawer, she propped her chain in her hands and waited.

Waited. And thought. They would have two children, a boy and a girl. Everyone she knew had or wanted two or tons, twelve, fifteen or more. What an abuse of the body and the nerves fifteen children must be! To say nothing of the endless drudgery and exhaustion. Not two children, though, better four. A "six-family," a nice round number. Two boys, two girls. Two small Philips, images of their father.

She stirred, moving her legs, placing her hands on her stomach just above her sex. His seed. Was she to become pregnant this night? Possibly. Hopefully!

"I love you, Philip Stone, with all my heart, all my being. Always and forever."

Two voices floated up from the street below. Two men arguing, their words muffled by the fastened windows. Whatever the problem it was quickly resolved, and the conversation ended in laughter. Silence followed, not even a whisper of wind. Then in the distance she made out the squealing of unoiled coach wheels and the sharp clatter of hooves on cobblestones. Gradually these sounds faded to nothingness. A dog barked, its voice muffled as if, she thought, it were at the ostler's, behind the inn, walls removed from her hearing.

She waited. Five minutes became six and seven. Getting up, she drew on her nightgown, over it her negligee and tied on her cap in concession to the rigid standards of decency of the times. Unlocking and unbolting the door, she was preparing to open it when the sound of scuffling outside stopped her short. A loud grunting followed, unmistakably the sound of pain. Fear's cold hand seized the nape of her neck, descending her spine. Once more she tried to open the door, but fearful of what she might see on the other side, hesitated and leaned against it, her mind whirling. There was more scuffling, a loud jarring sound as if someone's elbow had struck the wall, then running. Now she could hear voices outside, newcomers bustling about. The sound grew louder by the second, then was broken by the shrill voice of a woman.

"Saints preserve us!"

Lorna opened the door. Between two men, their backs to her, she could see a third man lying on the floor. She craned her neck to see his face. It was Philip. He lay twitching hideously, his back arching, his arms and legs jerking. She pushed between the men. A knife protruded from his chest, a crimson circle surrounding the hilt guard. Blood trickled from a corner of his mouth. Beside him, a full bottle of wine lay undisturbed.

"It's murder . . ."

"Quiet, you fool!"

"Somebody get a doctor."

"It's too late, can't you see?"

"Who did it?"

"God only knows!"

She stood stock still, staring transfixed, hearing the words running together, growing hollow and fainter, as if the speakers were drifting away en masse. A sound burst from her throat, a cry to begin a scream. Cut short as she passed out.

II

Everything about him appeared disheveled and askew, his tousled gray hair, his nickel-plated spectacles perched on his nose improperly balanced, the right lens leaning toward his ruddy cheek, his ill-tended moustache at the base of his homely nose. A ridiculous nose, she decided, a gob of pink putty poorly shaped to resemble a nose, the nostrils ludicrously large . . .

But in his gray eyes were warmth and kindliness. And his mouth appeared on the verge of a smile. The sight of it brought her fully awake.

Like a fan snapping open, hope spread across her heart.

"My husband . . ."

His face darkened, his features sagging with sadness. He shook his head.

"I'm terribly sorry, really. I wish . . ." He hesitated and looked away at his bag, battered and crushed-looking, the ear tubes of a stethoscope protruding from it. It sat on the night stand. Alongside it was a candle lamp and a glass tumbler half-filled with a distasteful-looking brownish liquid. His unwillingness to look her in the eye brought home the horrifying reality of the situation. And the patent worthlessness of any hope.

Of course. Hadn't she seen the knife plunged hilt deep into Philip's chest? The blood? Worst of all had been the sight of his horrible twitching as he battled to hold onto precious life, his yielding, the thread released . . .

"No. *No, No, No!*"

"Sssssh . . ."

She tried to rise, but he held her down, his hand

23

firmly against her shoulder. "I'm sorry I was late getting there," he said quietly. "There was nothing I could do for him. Nothing anyone could do. Please try and understand."

She nodded tight-lipped, her throat as dry as stone dust, her body crushed under the weight of aftershock. Oh Lord how she welcomed death here, now, this very moment!

"I must go to him, see him . . ."

"Not now."

"Please . . ."

"There's nothing to see." He studied the floor between his feet, as if reading what had to be said from it. "They've got him on a table downstairs covered with a sheet. By now they may have even taken him away. If you were to see him so soon you'd only faint again. You're the one we've got to tend to now. You must get a grip on yourself."

"My husband is dead, doctor . . . murdered in cold blood. I feel as if I'm breaking into pieces. It's too big, too sudden, too monstrous. It hasn't happened, none of it! It couldn't happen!"

"It's an awful thing to have to face, I realize that but . . ." He paused, angling his homely face, straightening his glasses and staring at her. "What's your name?"

The question so unexpected surprised her. "Lorna Sing . . . Mrs. Philip Stone." She glanced wistfully at her wedding ring.

"And what day is this?"

She deliberated, pushing her tortured and confused mind against the thought. "Tuesday."

"Wednesday now; it's past three in the morning. What month, what year?"

"June 1830. Why the questions?"

"You fell when you passed out. You struck the doorjamb with your head and raised a rather nasty bump. Allow me . . ." He sought it out with his fingertips.

She winced, feeling for the first time a dull soreness. He held up the candle lamp. "Your eyes look clear."

"You examined him?"

"I did."

"And you're absolutely certain . . ."

He nodded. "No pulse, no heartbeat, no sign of life whatsoever."

A pathetic groan escaped her throat, a key unlocking and opening the coffer of her feelings, releasing all her rapidly accumulated wretchedness. Out it poured. She began to cry, the tears streaming down her face, dampening the edge of the sheet clutched tightly in both hands. She twisted about, burying her face in the pillow.

"No, no, *no!*"

"It's a ghastly business, abominable. You have my profound sympathy."

"Who would do such a horrible thing? Why?"

"Heaven only knows. One of the guests on this floor who got there first claims she got a glimpse of someone fleeing down the hall into an empty room at the far end. They searched. One of the rear windows was open."

She turned back to him. "It's insane! Who would want to kill him? He had no enemies. Neither one of us knows a soul in this place."

"Maybe someone followed you here."

"I tell you my husband had no enemies, none!"

"Then it had to be a stranger. We searched Mr. Stone's pockets. He hadn't a penny on him." Once again his eyes drifted to the floor. Picking up the unopened bottle of wine, he set it on the crowded night stand.

The cause of it all, she thought, anger momentarily displacing her wretchedness. If he'd never left the room to get it . . . Out flew her hand, sending the bottle tumbling to the floor. It struck at such an angle that it did not break, instead rolling about briefly, the doctor stopping it with his foot. He set it upright on the floor.

"I want to give you something to relax you, to help you sleep."

"He's dead, dead." Uttering the word was a knife cutting inside her throat. She winced. "My darling Philip . . . God in heaven!"

Her heart was pounding so she imagined that at any moment it would smash through her chest. Like some insidious creature attacking tooth and claw, the awesome reality of the situation was suddenly upon her. No hope, no prayer, no chance, no clutching time and pulling it back. Again she tried to get up, again he restrained her, gently pushing her shoulder back down upon the pillow. Then he slipped his hand under her neck bringing the tumbler to her lips with the other.

"Slowly does it."

"No!"

"Drink it, please. Sleep will do you a world of good."

Too weak to resist, she complied, without even a thought as to what was in the glass or who this kindly, untidy stranger was hovering over her urging her cooperation.

It tasted bitter as gall. She choked, but got most of it down, the remainder dribbling from the corner of her mouth. Almost at once a strange sensation began seeping rapidly through her mind, a fuzziness, relaxation seizing and soothing her.

"My darling . . ." The words were like food filling her mouth, setting the soft inner flesh of her cheeks, her tongue and throat tingling. She floated upward, her arms and legs losing their solidity, the steely tightness at the back of her neck releasing, her body wrapping itself in woolly comfort, floating . . . floating . . .

She awoke, her tongue furry, the inside of her mouth furred, the same taste, but even more acrid. She was in a coach traveling at reckless speed, the horses' hooves hurling gobs of mud up against the underside in a steady tattoo. The canvas window covers were snapped in place, but through a crack in the one closest to her

she could see the darkened buildings fly by like a
zoetrope turning. It was raining again, needling straight
down. Barely conscious, her eyelids leaden, she tried
to speak, to cry out. The effort was beyond her. A
wheel struck a stone or rut jouncing the coach violently.
Out of her corner she lurched, thrown across the seat
against the other occupant. Quickly his arms were
around her, preventing her from falling forward and
helping her back to her place. In the darkness she
could not see his face, not even the profile, his coat
collar standing straight up joining the broad brim of his
hat.

All that she could make out was that he was a much
bigger man than the doctor. He said nothing. Setting
her in her place as if she were no more than a piece of
luggage, he returned to his corner, his face turned away.

Slumped in her place, oblivious of the passing buildings, she gritted her teeth, curled her fingers into fists and
fought to stay awake. She failed.

The coach sped on.

III

The copper sea lamp rode easily from side to side. Lorna's eyes opening to sight of it closed almost at once as a blinding pain struck the center of her forehead, coursing through her brain. Covering her eyes with her fingers, she held her breath, waiting for the pain to dissipate. Its onset could be blamed on the chalk-white brightness of her surroundings combined with the morning-after effects of the morphine or whatever it was given her by the doctor the night before.

Dr. Who? He hadn't even told her his name. And yet in his kindly, gently persuasive way, he had induced her to drink the foul-tasting stuff.

Philip! It came back to her, jolting her senses, twisting her heart in place, the dreadful vision of poor darling Philip lying on the floor dying, the knife, the other lodgers gathering . . . Downstairs on a table with a sheet over him, the doctor had told her, then prevented her from getting up. Back to mind came the coach, the stranger sitting opposite her who would not speak, would not open his mouth. And now here she was aboard ship.

Why? What ship? Heading where? What was this nightmare emerging from the darkness continuing into the day? Gradually her eyes became accustomed to the dazzling whiteness of the cabin. Her hand went to her breast, finding her watch. Five minutes before noon. Through the two portholes she could see the ship's rail. Beyond it the sea rose and fell, its cobalt-blue surface flecked with silver. White-capped waves pushed against one another in patternless profusion. Overhead the wind sang loudly, the masts creaking and groaning, captive to the tautness of their shrouds.

She glanced about the cabin, the pain returning, throbbing dully behind her eyes. The room was sparsely furnished, a rock maple lowboy fastened to the wall between the portholes, the bed in which she lay a crudely carpentered affair, a rectangular box with neither legs nor posts. But it was surprisingly comfortable. Under the pressure of her palms the mattress felt as if it were stuffed with goose down, although her pillow resembled a sack of potatoes.

A double-door washstand of mahogany veneer stood to the left of the door leading, she assumed, out onto the deck. No *Apotheosis of Washington* graced this pitcher standing in its basin, however, nothing but a crooked crack joining the lip to the base.

Outside a bell sounded, four double rings. Again she consulted her watch. Noon, on the dot. Rising slowly, tentatively from the bed, she made her way hand after hand against the wall to a Queen Anne corner chair, plopping down upon the leather seat. Steadying herself, she breathed deeply, continuing the counterattack against her throbbing head, willing away the pain with her scant energies. There was too much to do, too many questions to be asked and answered to bring a halt to this insanity. There was no time for pain, in her head or in her heart where she could feel it taking hold. Enduring pain, for Philip. It was all so hideously cruel, so savage, so horribly unjust. Tears welled. She fought back the urge to cry out loud, drying her eyes with the ribbons of her cap.

Fortunately the legs of the chair in which she sat stood in brass boots bolted to the floor, for at that moment the ship heeled, tilting the floor and jamming her ribs against the chair arm. Getting up, she opened one of the portholes, inhaling the salt air deeply, filling her lungs with it, clearing her senses, soothing her lingering headache. Her range of vision limited by the smallness of the round glass, she was unable to see anyone on deck.

"Is anybody out there?"

Raising her voice brought back pain. She sat down, rubbing her temples, massaging away the discomfort. One consolation raised itself like a flower in a bed of weeds. She hadn't the slightest doubt, there could *be* no doubt but that her presence here was all a stupid mistake. Some blundering fool had assumed her to be someone else, abducting her, carrying her drugged and unconscious aboard this ship. Even bringing along her trunk. For there it was, set in place at the foot of the bed.

A mistake. That's what it had to be, a ridiculous case of mistaken identity; ridiculous and heartless, in light of its timing, coming about so soon after Philip's tragic death. What was she saying? *Murder!* He had been stabbed to death for the nearly two hundred dollars he'd been carrying. The doctor was quite right. Any bridegroom, recognizable as such in a strange town, had to be fair game for a thief-murderer. Leaving the church for wherever, any bridegroom had to be carrying sufficient money to pay for food, lodging and everything else on the honeymoon.

And this was her honeymoon, she reflected sadly, a cabin on a ship she had yet to even see heading God only knows where. Nonsense! She shot to her feet. Heading back to Boston, and without delay!

Stumbling across the heaving floor, she began pounding on the door, and shouting, ignoring her headache and the queasy feeling settling itself in her stomach.

"Open this door! *Open it, I say!*"

"You open it," said a voice behind her. She turned. A bearded face grinned at her through the open porthole. "Just pull down the latches."

"What is this ship?" she snapped irritably.

"The *Anselmo*. Bound for Lisbon with sugar and timber."

"And me, kidnapped, forced on board against my

will. There'll be the devil to pay for this once we're back to Boston! I promise you!"

He laughed, throwing his head back, and showing twin rows of teeth as white as the wave caps. Then he sobered, shook his head and removed it from the circle framing it. Seething, she unlatched and jerked open the door. There he stood, clad in duck trousers, checkered shirt and tarpaulin hat; tall, brawny, the skin of his handsome face visible above his beard even swarthier looking, here in the shadow of the foc'sle head rising in front of him. He stood with his legs spread apart, his fists on his hips, amusement agleam in his eyes.

"Good morning, good afternoon, Sleeping Beauty, *La Belle au Bois dormant, Dornröschen,* whichever language you prefer. I speak several fluently."

"I demand to speak with your captain. At once!"

Doffing his cap, he bowed mockingly. "I shall consider it an honor to escort you to his cabin."

"You will bring him here!"

He gestured, indicating her attire. "Surely not dressed as you are."

Lorna reddened, her hands flying to the V of her nightgown, closing it tightly over her breasts. "I will be prepared to speak with him in ten minutes. Here!"

"Ten." Bowing a second time, he straightened and turned to leave.

"Just a moment . . ."

"Yes?"

"How far have we come from Boston?"

"Charlestown." He thought a moment, scratching his beard. "We dropped the pilot shortly after four. Eight hours, the wind fairly constant; I would guess about a hundred thirty miles. Nautical miles, that is. Do you know the difference between a land mile and a nautical mile?"

"Ten minutes!"

She slammed the door in his grinning face. She made her toilette as well as she was able and determined to appear impressive at the pending confrontation. She put on a white muslin sheath girdled just under the bosom and falling straight to the floor. Then she slipped on white clocked stockings and low-heeled pumps. And, she thought, with the wind up, and masts and yawls and booms chorusing resentment against their servitude to it, there would be a chill in the air, in spite of the bright sun. This decided, she draped her cashmere shawl over one arm, in the event the captain's will prevailed and like it or not she would have to face him in his cabin.

His will became a meaningless factor when within ten minutes two elderly gentlemen in black wool breeches, waistcoats and frock coats draped cape-like from their shoulders, presented themselves at her door. No dandified incroyables these two; to Lorna they looked more like undertakers. Both were well into their sixties, the bulkier of the two extremely pale, the other healthier in appearance, but his face deeply lined. They bowed courteously.

"Signore Valucci," said the pale one indicating the other. He pointed at himself. "Signore Dicostanzo."

"I specifically asked to speak with the captain," burst Lorna petulantly.

"Cap . . . ?" The two exchanged bewildered looks. "Come si chiama questo in Italiano?" asked the one introduced as Valucci. Dicostanzo shrugged.

"The captain, the master of this ship!"

They stared blankly.

"Never mind. Out of my way." Pushing between them, she strode out onto the main deck, stopping, looking about. The ship appeared to be a bark; at least she surmised it was. She had seen scores like it in the harbors of Massachusetts and the bays and inlets up the coast to New Castle. In evidence were the square rigging at her fore and mainmasts, and the fore-and-aft sail bellying at her mizzenmast.

While no fewer than a half-dozen men were occupied aloft, only four were on deck, including the helmsman. The handsome bearded one was at the taf-

frail, squatting on his haunches coiling rope. The other
two were mopping down the afterdeck. All of them
paused in their labors to ogle her. Ignoring them she
once more raised her eyes skyward, shielding them
from the sun standing straight overhead as densely
dazzlingly white as Asiatic ivory. Her two visitors had
followed her out, their perplexed expressions intact.
Spume came arcing over the railing splattering the
deck in a jagged line between her and them. Glaring at
both, she made for the railing, walking along it past
winches and capstans and canvas-covered longboats sitting idly in their chocks. She draped her shawl over
her shoulders, the wind whipping the hanging ends. A
tall individual in the company of a man whom she assumed to be one or another of the *Anselmo's* mates
emerged from the companionway midship. The taller
man's cap, broad four-in-hand tie and jacket stamped
him as the captain. She approached them at a half-run,
instinctively aware of the two men following her at a
distance.

"Captain!"

He nodded, smiling feebly, touching the peak of his
cap and the ends of his pewter-gray moustache affectedly.

"*Signorina . . .*"

"You speak English?"

"*Inglese?*" He shook his head. "*Prego.*" He then addressed the man alongside him. "*C'e qualcuno che parla
inglese?*"

The other shrugged, shaking his head slowly. Up
came her arm pointing past them toward the stern.

"That man coiling rope speaks perfect English. You
there," she called. "Stop what you're doing and come
here."

"That won't be necessary," said a voice behind her.

Valucci and Dicostanzo came up on either side.
Dicostanzo went on. "Captain Saturno is quite right.
He speaks no English."

She bristled. "And why, may I ask, did you two pretend you can't?"

Valucci extended his palms helplessly. "We had, Signore Dicostanzo and I, an idea that by so doing we might be able to avoid any unpleasant conversations. For a time at least."

"There needn't be any unpleasant conversations. What I want is very simple. I want, I demand, that Captain Saturno here order his helmsman to turn around and return to Boston. I haven't the slightest idea who all of you think I am that you felt it necessary to kidnap me, but you've made a ghastly mistake. One for which I mean to make every one of you pay dearly!" Staring at Valucci, she tilted her head at the captain. "Tell him!"

Valucci scratched a crevice in his cheek and turned his eyes seaward. "We would be delighted to do so, but I'm afraid it wouldn't do any good."

"Must I write all this down to make it clear to you!"

"Please," he said mildly, "there's no need to shout. If you are patient, I will be happy to explain everything."

"I'll be happy to listen, *after* we turn around."

"Miss . . ." he began.

"Mrs. Philip Stone."

"Of course, my apologies. And may I say how deeply grieved Signore Dicostanzo and I were to learn of your husband's tragic death."

"Get to the point."

"As you wish. The first thing I must ask you to accept is the fact that you are not, how shall I say it, the 'wrong party'?"

"That's utter nonsense. *And you know it!"*

"This is no case of mistaken identity," said Valucci, continuing to address her in the same insufferably calm, forcibly controlled tone. Everyone involved has been extremely thorough. You are Mrs. Philip Stone nee Singleton of Hanover in New Hampshire. You were married at Grace Church in Hanover yesterday. You traveled by coach to Boston to stay overnight at the Gray Dragon Inn on Ann Street." He paused.

"So? What am I doing here? What do you want with me?"

"Alas, that I cannot say. To tell the truth, not a soul on board knows what is 'wanted of you.' "

He appeared perfectly serious. Dicostanzo picked up the thread.

"Shortly before dawn you were delivered into our hands. And you are now under our protection."

"Why? For what purpose?"

Both shrugged, their eyes blank, their expressions declaring ignorance.

Dicostanzo went on. "Our orders are to escort you as far as the Madeira Islands."

"What then?"

"We are to rendezvous with another ship which will be waiting to take you to your destination."

"Which is? And don't shrug and look as blank as two dead fish!"

"I swear by the Virgin, madam," said Dicostanzo, "the plain, simple, absolute truth is we do not know. We were not told; we did not ask."

"You said you were given orders. By whom?"

The response to this was as unrewarding as all their previous answers. Both maintained that their instructions had come from a gentleman whom neither had ever met before, and who did not introduce himself. Their meeting had taken place in Marseilles one month to the day earlier. She sensed that money had changed hands, but to interrupt with this accusation seemed pointless. She kept silent, though not without reflecting that no small amount would have had to be involved. Kidnapping was a risky activity. In his dreary tone, Valucci went on to explain that while she was "their guest," she should consider herself a first-class passenger. Indeed, she was the only passenger. She was informed, however, that she would have to remain in her quarters after dark. Her door would be unlocked during the day, but locked at night "for your own safety and peace of mind." Capable hands being hard to come by, there were a handful of rather disreputable types among the members of the crew. Dicostanzo was quick to point out that the captain assumed full responsibility for every man's actions. But should any harm come to her, any punishment Saturno might order, which would be issued "after the fact," could hardly be expected to do her any good. The message was clear to Lorna.

Her meals and everything else she desired or needed would be brought to her by the cabin boy. She need only ask the first man passing by her door or a porthole that she required the *ragazzo*. She would be free to stroll the decks any time between sunup and sundown and for as long as she pleased, with or without an escort.

"Your privacy will be respected," said Dicostanzo. "You have my word as a gentleman on it."

Valucci nodded. "Now, if there are no more questions, may we suggest you retire to your cabin. Your lunch awaits you. *Buon appetito!*"

IV

Three days out of the Madeiras the westerly, over-worked and apparently realizing it, quit and began to play, carrying on in the madcap fashion of a spoiled child. It would tease the sails, puffing them fat, or slip by overhead or across the bowsprit narrowly eluding seizure by them, suddenly fill them, then desert them completely, leaving them as limp as rain-soaked flags. Five minutes with the canvas billowing so fearfully full as to threaten bursting would be followed by a whiffet barely able to lift the pennant atop the main truck, let alone flutter it. The howling overhead would reduce to a whisper, then would come flat calm, the air so still that the smoke rising from the captain's pipe stood up as straight as its stem. Movement toward the Madeiras became at times more like drifting than sailing. It was three full days before the westerly resumed its labors, restoring roundness to the sails and keeping it there, pushing the ship at a steady thirteen knots toward its rendezvous point.

Shortly after sunrise on a Monday morning, in compliance with orders given her late the previous evening by Dicostanzo and Valucci, Lorna stood at the rail, her trunk packed and sitting on the deck beside her. Ahead, out of a pale white mist with a faint purplish tint to it, a mountaintop nudged the heavens. The sun rising, rapidly burning away the mist, revealed the mountain's southern slope tightly wrapped in tiers, below them a smudge of white, a settlement spreading out and into the surrounding greenery.

Valucci and Dicostanzo had joined her on deck,

greeting her amiably, both gripping the rail, both beaming in triumph.

"At last," sighed Valucci.

To Lorna the look on his lean face was that of a man who had just gotten word he'd been reprieved from the gallows. She squinted under her hand shielding away the brightening sunlight.

"I see no ship."

"It's waiting on the other side," said Dicostanzo confidently. "Between Madeira and Porto Santo. You'll be traveling in that direction." He pointed eastward.

"You won't?"

Dicostanzo shook his head. "I'm afraid not. Our job is done. We're on our way to Lisbon."

"Of course, I'm forgetting. Your responsibility ends with the kidnapping."

He shrugged. "Call it what you like." He rubbed his hands together briskly and grinned. "This is a gala day for us, and nothing you or anyone else can say can spoil it."

The *Anselmo* continued to close on the island, altering its course two points, intent on rounding its southernmost corner and approaching the opposite side.

Dicostanzo indicated the mountain. "Pico Ruivo. Over six thousand feet high. A volcano, so they say . . ."

"Kindly spare me the geography lesson," she said quietly. "I'm not in the least interested."

His enthusiasm so promptly and properly dampened, he avoided further conversation with her, as did Valucci. The *Anselmo* rounded the island and into sight came a smaller vessel, a two-master, a brigantine bobbing easily at anchor. Spotting the *Anselmo,* men began lining the brig's rail while others scrambled up the ratlines and as they drew closer down came the vessel's mainsails. Fifteen yards from her stern the *Anselmo* hove to, a dory was put over the side and the Jacob's ladder dropped.

Her trunk was carried down by the man who was to

row the dory. She followed, Dicostanzo and Valucci following her.

"I thought I was to be denied your company from here on," she said evenly, staring at one then the other taking their places side by side on the stern seat. "Oh, but you have to get your pay, of course. But why both of you? Couldn't one go over while the other waits? You do trust each other, don't you?"

"It might be wise not to comment on matters that don't concern you," said Valucci, looking away from her, tilting his head and glancing upward at Captain Saturno and the others leaning over the rail.

"Venti minuti. Venti," barked the captain.

"Si, si," responded Valucci.

"Matters that don't concern me," she went on. "That's priceless, that is . . ."

Her eyes turned to the brigantine standing high out of the water. Its holds were empty of cargo, evidently. One passenger only. Men were leaning over the rail staring down at her. On the ship's bow was the name *Iphimedia*. Lorna shook her head and chuckled bitterly, drawing both her abductors' attention. Iphimedia. If memory served, in Greek mythology she had been abducted. Although she was eventually released. Lucky lady.

Her eyes drifted down the length of the ship. Where was it heading, she wondered? Once aboard from here on to what? Dear God, if she only knew. As terrible as her fate might be, at least knowing what to expect would be easier on the nerves than this. Or would it? The prospect of slavery, of torture, of painful death, all were too disturbing and discouraging to even contemplate. Better she continue on in ignorance.

The oars dipped into the green water, roiling it, pulling the boat forward smoothly. In less than a minute the gunwale was thumping against the side of the *Iphimedia*. Greek. A Greek ship? Would that be where they'd be heading? Down came the ladder and Valucci motioned her to start climbing. Grasping it, she turned for one last look at the *Anselmo*.

A lone figure was still standing at the rail, smoke drifting upward from his pipe bowl into the crisp morning air. Captain Saturno.

V

The cabin was smaller than her own on board the *Anselmo,* but much more elegant, with rosewood paneling, ornate brass sconces, a Turkish carpet covering virtually the entire floor and lording it over the other furniture, a flat-top desk of intricately carved black oak, its surface polished to a shine.

Lording it over the desk, rising from his chair behind it was an elderly man in full military uniform. He was short in stature, but impressively broad-shouldered, and full chested and narrow in the hips, although older than either Dicostanzo or Valucci. His sparse hair, like his moustache and beard, was as white as pure snow. Despite his age Lorna could see that his physical condition was far superior to that of either of the two standing to her right, their backs to the door. The man before her was a duplicate of any one of a hundred thousand other overage military officers—in his bearing, in his conceit tinged with arrogance, his love of self-discipline, and that quality peculiar to his sort, undisguisable disdain for men in mufti, for Dicostanzo and Valucci specifically, at the moment.

The gold braid of his epaulets caught the sunlight through the porthole glass, creating the effect of two stemless golden flowers jammed upside down upon his shoulders. His raised collar was emblazoned with gold leaves upon a red background edged with black piping. His tunic, also red with black piping, displayed two vertical rows of seven brass buttons each, the lower two in each row separated by a thick leather belt, at its center a large silver plate. Stamped upon it was an eagle, a crown above its head, a cross in a shield at its

41

breast, a snake in its talons. And assembled over his heart was a motley array of decorations; his personal military history preceding him wherever he walked.

His eyes were dark brown and piercing, staring, impaling her, anchoring her where she stood in front of him. Coming around the desk, rather marching stiffly, he produced a monocle from his pocket, screwed it into his eye and studied her at close range, her face, her hair, her shoulders, her body down to her waist. His first words addressed to her directly were like two darts hurled at a target.

"Turn. Slowly."

"I . . ."

"Turn."

She turned obediently, a complete circle. He stepped back, his glass tumbling from his eye into his hand.

"Yes, yes . . . very good, splendid."

Out of the corner of her eye she could see Valucci and Dicostanzo smiling, more in relief, it appeared, than in triumph. The other man present, younger, also in uniform, though much less impressive looking, stared at her, slowly molding an expression of disapproval on his flat, dark-complexioned face.

"Excellency, with your permission." He had a speech impediment that instantly quashed any impression of authority the sight of him in uniform, his saber dangling from his hip, might convey. It sounded to her as if he were talking with food in his mouth.

"Captain Crespi . . ." began the older man.

"Her hair. It's not blond."

"It's reddish brown," snapped the other. "I can see that, Crespi, even without my glass."

"It's much too long."

The other's patience vanished so swiftly, Lorna could feel her jaw drop.

"You're a fool, Crespi, an ignoramus! Think before you speak. Her hair can be cut. She can wear a wig. Her eyes are the right color, her face surprisingly similar, around the mouth especially. She's the same height." His eyes roamed her body. "Approximately the same weight, perhaps a few pounds lighter . . ."

"What is going on here!" she snapped. "I demand an explanation! *Here and now! This has gone far enough!*"

Valucci and Dicostanzo gaped, the captain's nut-brown complexion appeared to pale a shade and his commanding officer stared.

"Get hold of yourself, child," he said offhandedly. "Your questions will be answered. First things first."

"Exactly. And whoever you are, if you know what's good for you, you'll take me straight to the nearest port, and put me on the first ship sailing for Boston . . ."

"Silence!" he roared. "You will speak when I permit you to. We have important business to conduct here. One more outburst, one more word and you'll spend the rest of your journey locked in a closet!" He moved a chair for her. "Sit."

She did so, reluctantly, forced down by his eyes.

Valucci cleared his throat, drawing them from her. "General . . ." he began.

"His Excellency is Count DeLeone," snapped Crespi heatedly. "You will address him as Your Excellency!"

"Of course, I beg your pardon, Your Excellency." Reaching into a pocket, Valucci brought out a piece of paper folded into quarters. He proferred it to the count who waved it away. The captain snatched it from Valucci, opening and reading it.

"Our bill, Excellency," ventured Dicostanzo, the pitch of his voice heightening with nervousness. "Two thousand gold florins as agreed. Plus expenses . . ."

The word raised the count's left eyebrow. Reaching for the bill, reinserting his monocle with his free hand, he studied the figures.

"One thousand on account," said Valucci. "One thousand due on delivery and 743 florins expenses."

"That seems a bit high," responded the count without looking up. "You were supposed to book passage aboard the *Anselmo,* not buy the ship outright." Crespi snickered. DeLeone cut him short with a stony stare.

"Captain Saturno's fee alone was two hundred," hastened Dicostanzo. "Which we feel is reasonable. He did come nearly a thousand miles out of his way."

"Practically a blood sacrifice. Are you two normally this free with other people's money?"

Both smiled self-consciously. He seemed determined to make them look ridiculous, she thought.

"You'll note, Excellency," said Valucci tapping the paper, "each individual expenditure is clearly described. The total is accurate . . ."

The older man grunted and tossed the bill on the desk. Reaching around his desk, pulling open a drawer he brought out a leather sack, its drawstrings tightly wound, dropping it onto the desk with a loud clunk.

"Pay them the balance," he muttered to the captain

"One moment," said Lorna. "Before you do there is something you ought to know. Something they've neglected to mention. On the way over here I was raped."

This disclosure had all the impact she could have wished for. The bored look on DeLeone's face slowly altered, the muscles tightening, his mouth taking on the appearance of a knife slit.

"Excellency, the woman is a congenital liar," said Valucci curtly. "From Charlestown to this cabin she has been consistently uncooperative."

"Would you expect her to be otherwise?"

She eyed Valucci and Dicostanzo, then addressed the count. "Your Excellency, may I speak with you privately?"

He hesitated, deciding, then nodded. At this Dicostanzo lost control, hurling his hands high, reddening trembling visibly. "See here, Your Excellency, with all due respect, we have discharged our assignment. You've accepted her, you approve. Is it too much to ask that we be paid our balance so we can be on our way? Captain Saturno is waiting."

"Let him wait," said the count.

"He expects us back in twenty minutes. He was very specific. It's already getting onto half an hour." Dicostanzo flung a worried glance out the porthole. "He's discharged his obligation, he'll leave without us."

"If it's a question of our expenses . . ." began Valucci lamely.

"It's obviously not. Not now." Back went the money sack into the drawer. Sight of this panicked Valucci as much as his partner.

"Your Excellency, this is most unfair! The woman's lying; she was not touched. I swear by all that's holy . . ."

"Two minutes, Your Excellency," said Lorna quietly.

"Two minutes it is. You can spare it, gentlemen. Captain, show our friends outside."

"Yes, Your Excellency." Crespi clicked his heels and saluted.

"You'll have what's due you shortly," went on DeLeone. "For the moment, a little patience."

Crespi opened the door and herded them out, both protesting volubly.

The door closed muffled their indignation. They passed the porthole heading for the bow.

"I said I was raped," she murmured.

"That is most unfortunate. However, I trust you've recovered."

She touched her stomach with her fingertips. "I could very easily be pregnant."

DeLeone frowned. "That would complicate things . . ."

"You could be buying damaged goods."

A bemused look clouded his features, but only for a moment. "The agreement our people made with your two friends outside was not contingent on your being a virgin."

You say you were raped, they say you're lying." He shrugged. "Who am I to believe?"

They stared at one another in silence. The count was

preparing to continue when shouting outside was heard
on the other side of the wall behind his desk.

"Come," he rasped.

He pulled open the door and pushed her outside
ahead of him. The first sight to meet her eyes was that
of the sailor who had rowed them over sitting in the
dory, casually rowing back to the *Anselmo*. Captain
Saturno and others were elbowing the rail watching
him. At the same time the street anchor was being
hauled up, two crewmen bending their backs to the
capstan bars, circling slowly. To her surprise, she felt
a sudden tug at her heart at the thought of the *Anselmo*
sailing out of her life. But speedily downed it as absurd.
After all, hadn't she simply exchanged that floating
prison for this one? What earthly difference was there
between the two?

She looked away. To her left forward, Dicostanzo
was climbing the railing, shaking his fist at the depart-
ing doryman. Roaring, going absolutely wild.

"Come back, you bastard!"

As she gaped at him he lost his grip. Valucci standing
inside the railing lunged for him, but away he fell into
the water, raising a sheet of it that splashed down the
bow.

"Throw him a rope!" called DeLeone. Crespi stood
dumbstruck, frozen, gawking in disbelief. Two crewmen rushed up, a rope was tossed, but Dicostanzo
floundering below, slowly drifting away, splashing frantically, screaming for help, did not even reach for it.
When he did see it, it was too late; he sank like a
stone.

"My God!" roared Valucci. Bubbles issued upward
from the spot where Dicostanzo had gone down. One
of the crew had kicked off his boots and was getting
ready to dive in after him.

"Stop where you are!" bellowed the count.

Snapping out of his trance, Crespi shouted the obvious:

"He's drowning, Excellency!"

"Save him somebody!" screamed Valucci. *"He can't swim a stroke!"*

Up bobbed Dicostanzo sputtering, fighting for breath, his face purple, his thrashing feebler now. And again down he went.

The man about to dive in after him turned to the count with a puzzled expression. As did Crespi and the other man. DeLeone responded to their stares with a lackadaisical wave of his hand, dismissing the drowning man, turning his back on the scene. Valucci continued to scream, running up and down the railing, nearly insane with frustration. Catching himself short, he whirled about and began cursing DeLeone.

"Captain," called the count, "shut him up."

Lorna gaped, unable to utter a sound, incapable of accepting what her eyes saw. As Dicostanzo's rounded back broke the surface of the water and his body rolled over, Crespi drew his sword, gripped it under the hilt, raised it high and brought it down hard upon Valucci's head. Stopped in mid-yell, up rolled the man's eyes and down he went, knees first, falling forward, landing on his face with a sickening thud.

"Come, child," said the count calmly. "There is somebody I must introduce you to."

VI

DeLeone's comments in reaction to first sight of her made it obvious that they planned to substitute her for somebody whom she resembled. But who, why, how, and under what circumstances remained a mystery. The count would answer her questions when he felt like it, and not before. That much he had already made clear to her. Turning his own and her back on the grisly goings-on at the bow, he escorted her to a cabin door midships. Her trunk stood on end just outside, leading her to assume that this was to be her cabin.

She turned for a last look at the *Anselmo,* her anchor up and her bowsprit leading her across the *Iphimedia*'s bow in the direction of Lisbon. DeLeone was knocking and opening the door to the odor of stale scent, lilac, and to sight of a man sitting up in his bunk rubbing his eyes, smearing his dark blue mascara. A pallid-looking and sorry excuse for a man, she decided, with or without mascara. She sank into a convenient chair, still somewhat shaken by the scene she had just witnessed. The fellow fairly leaped out of bed, his nightshirt swishing down to his knees, his cheeks rosying with embarrassment.

"Your Excellency . . ."

His voice was as effeminate as she expected, as were his walk and his gestures.

Disregarding the embarrassment their intrusion had caused, DeLeone introduced them. The man studied her, his pale brow knitting in concentration. Looking away from him she glanced about the interior. The bunk, the chair in which she sat, and a washstand in one corner appeared to be the only furnishings. Instead

48

of chairs or tables or dressers, the floor was crowded with large trunks. Two wig stands stood at the foot of the bunk duplicated in a full-length mirror fastened to the wall.

"She's perfect, Excellency. The bone structure's surprisingly similar, the cheeks and around the mouth."

"The same color eyes."

"Yes, but the lids and brows will need a little work. And the outer canthus."

"Don't be alarmed," said the count to her with a chuckle. "Tallot here is not a surgeon, only our specialist in makeup and costume. He knows all the little tricks and techniques to make you look exactly like Her Highness." He laughed. "To make you fit for a queen."

"What queen?" asked Lorna flatly.

Tallot rummaged under his bunk, bringing forth a leather folder, opening it on the rumpled bedcovers. He turned page after page revealing sketches—full-face, profile, enlarged details, full-length portraits, seated, standing, every conceivable pose of a woman who did indeed look a great deal like her.

"Queen of what, where?"

DeLeone cleared his throat, adjusting his vocal chords as it were for the sober, almost reverential pronouncement that was to follow: "You are looking at Her Royal Highness, Queen Caroline-Louisa of Savoy."

"Savoy? Never heard of it."

This visibly unsettled both men, DeLeone in particular. His aplomb deserted him, his fierce eyes narrowing to slits.

"Savoy," he said.

"I said I've never heard of it."

"Your education has been sadly neglected."

"The United States," muttered Tallot scornfully, making a face that suggested he was smelling something putrid. "The United Primitives."

"Don't be such a snob," snapped the count. "Very well, my child, pay attention, and do not interrupt.

Savoy is a duchy, an extremely powerful duchy, the most important state in the Kingdom of Sardinia. Along with the island itself, the kingdom also includes Piedmont." He began pacing a circle around the largest trunk, his hands folded behind his back, his voice gaining eloquence as he warmed to his subject.

"The House of Savoy was founded in the year 1034 by His Excellency Humbert the Whitehanded. Ours is the oldest-ruling house in all of Europe. In all the world. Shortly to begin its ninth century." He paused for effect. "The House of Savoy has been in power longer than was the Shang dynasty in China, longer than the rule of the pharaohs of the Old Kingdom." Once more he stopped and stared at her, inflating his chest with pride, lifting his hand for emphasis, his eyes glittering. "And according to the calculations in the second Book of Kings, longer than the House of David!"

She yawned and excused herself, but he was not about to be discouraged. On he plunged, explaining that the duchy abutted the northwest corner of Piedmont and was also bordered by France and Switzerland.

"We will pass through the Straits of Gibraltar and into the Mediterranean. We will be putting in at Port-St.-Louis-du-Rhône. And traveling the rest of the way by coach up the Rhône Valley."

"All of which is fascinating," she said tightly.

"Any questions?" asked DeLeone. "Ask away . . ."

"I have no questions. I'm not curious. I can't be bothered. You amaze me, both of you, all of you; to go to all this trouble just because I bear a superficial resemblance to this . . ."

"To Her Majesty," interrupted Tallot. "Caroline-Louisa."

"You really think you can pass me off as her? And that she'll go along with it?"

"We have reason to believe so," said the count smirking. "Inasmuch as it's Her Majesty's idea."

"I don't care whose idea it was, it's ridiculous! I don't speak French, I don't speak Italian."

"You speak only English, correct?" DeLeone did not pause for her to nod. "Queen Caroline-Louisa speaks German and English. Her mother, the Duchess of Rothesay, was half-English."

Lorna shot to her feet. "Can't you get this through your heads. I don't care about her mother, or her, or any of you! You say we're landing at . . ."

"Port-St.-Louis-du-Rhône," said Tallot.

"Wherever. The first chance I get, I'm leaving. Crawling on my hands and knees, if necessary. I should be laughing in your faces, but there's nothing funny about this . . . idiocy. It's too outrageous. I couldn't care less how old Savoy is or that this queen of yours happens to look like me or what you have in mind for me to do that she won't or is afraid to do. You'll have to count me out of your future plans. You dare to murder my husband, abduct a United States citizen, subject me to humiliation and abuse, hold me captive. By God in Heaven, I'll see your barbaric little duchy blown off the map by American cannon! When I get home I'll raise the roof! I'll . . ."

"Silence!" The word was a snake striking. She winced, convinced that DeLeone was about to slap her across the face. "You will keep your mouth shut and listen," he said coldly, freezing her with a withering glare. "From this moment on you will do what you are told. And only what you are told. You will cooperate with us completely, without hesitation, without protest or question." He softened his tone. "Failure to cooperate will be tantamount to suicide. We have a great deal at stake here. To be blunt, the immediate future of the kingdom."

"But it's insane, it'll never work. I wouldn't fool anybody!"

"You'll fool everybody by the time I'm through with you," boasted Tallot. He smiled at the count. "They'll look like twin sisters."

"As to your duties, they'll be very simple," said De-Leone. "For the most part boringly so." He resumed pacing, circling the trunk as before, and toying with one of his decorations with his left hand. "You will stand on the palace balcony and wave to your subjects on holidays, feast days, and other special occasions." He stopped and pantomimed acknowledgment of the silent cheers, gesturing with one hand, bowing his head. Then he resumed pacing. "You will travel about the countryside to see and and mingle with your subjects. You will award medals, certificates of merit, you will be seen in the right places with the right people. And understand this, you will at all times conduct yourself accordingly. Every inch a queen."

"What is the problem in Savoy?" she asked evenly, holding herself in check.

His face darkened. As did Tallot's. "Problem?" De-Leone's tone affected innocent failure to understand the question.

"Exactly. I may be in the dark, but I'm not stupid."

"Eh?"

"Your Caroline-Louisa is afraid to show her face. She'd rather show mine. Obviously, someone's tried to assassinate her."

The two exchanged glances, the count pulling at the ends of his moustache, avoiding her eyes.

"I see no reason why you shouldn't know the facts of the matter," he said.

"The facts of the matter? I've hit the nail on the head, haven't I? Now you need me for a target. I'm flattered, but no thank you. I'm overdue for some good luck. With a little I'll get away before I ever see your precious duchy. Yes, I know, you'll chase me. But to catch me, not to kill me." She walked to the bunk and picked up one of the sketches of Caroline-Louisa, studying it, touching her own face, glancing at herself in the glass. "I'm much too valuable."

"The facts are," went on DeLeone, pretending he hadn't heard a word, "no one has attempted to assassinate Her Majesty. Nor do we know of any threat. And in Savoy we monarchists know everything that goes on."

"A spy under every bed, is that it?"

"It was His Majesty, Charles Felix. He, alas, was the victim of a would-be assassin's bullet."

"Was he really?"

"I said would-be. He was not killed; he was wounded in the head." He indicated the side of his own forehead. As a consequence he suffers from periodic headaches. Occasionally his reason is somewhat affected."

"Somewhat affected. You mean he's crazy. You and your monarchist friends can't depend on him so you've got her running things."

He sighed. "My child, you do have a most annoying proclivity for reducing serious matters to the bluntest terms possible. His Highness's misfortune has been a grave blow to Savoy. The queen has been a tower of strength in his stead."

"Good for her."

His hand whipped out, slapping her soundly. "Enough of your sarcasm! The next time you'll feel my fist."

Her cheek stinging furiously, rage boiling up inside her mingling with her mounting frustration, she reacted instinctively, a retaliation she had never resorted to before. She spat in his face. The instant it struck his cheek she blanched and retreated a step fearing he would draw his sword and run her through!

He did not. Instead he calmly produced his handkerchief, wiped his face, restored the handkerchief to his pocket and drove the tip of his index finger into Tallot's scrawny chest.

"Get busy."

He then marched three steps to the door, jerking it wide, and turning back to Tallot. "First wash that filthy stuff off your eyes. It disgusts me! And open your porthole. Get some of this perfume stink out of here."

The door slammed behind him. Tallot made a face at it and stuck out his tongue.

VII

For all his affectations, his mincing and prattling, she felt relaxed with Tallot, far less nervous than with either DeLeone or Captain Crespi. The former's moods were too unpredictable, his temper too quick to erupt; he frightened her. His cold-blooded decision to let Dicostanzo drown summoned up all she felt she need know about the man. As for his aide, him she classified as a typical junior officer toady. Capable of bashing a man over the head with the hilt of his sword without so much as a wink of hesitation. Not that she felt sorry for Valucci. He'd obviously lost his head; knocking him out had probably kept him from falling overboard as well.

No sooner had DeLeone departed than Tallot opened the door and dragged in her trunk. He asked her to open it and she did so using the key on the watch chain around her neck. Sight of her wardrobe brought a disdainful reaction to his face.

"What absolute rags you do wear!" he practically squealed, tisking and sputtering as he held up her white muslin sheath and spencer, turning them this way and that and letting them drop in a heap.

"I'm perfectly satisfied with my 'absolute rags'!" she exclaimed. "I don't happen to have a royal treasury to dip into for shopping money." She sat down hard in the chair. Thought of what lay ahead brought tears to her eyes, and touched Tallot's heart. Slamming the trunk lid, he held up her chin and began stroking her hair, staring down at her, his eyes warming with compassion.

54

"Here now, Yankee, you're not going to go all to pieces, are you?"

"Why me?"

"What a silly question, look in the mirror, look at my sketches."

"Why must I die?"

"It's not going to come to that. For heaven's sake, buck up. You'll get through it in fine fettle."

"You make it sound temporary; it isn't, it can't be. She and her husband will reign for years and years. If anything, I'm only the first of a long line of targets. I'll bet you that at this very moment another DeLeone is out looking for my replacement after I'm shot!"

"Poppycock! Look at the bright side, the two of them could be overthrown in six months, even less. There's a revolutionary movement in Savoy. It's small now, but it's growing every day."

"Is that supposed to cheer me up?"

"She could be dethroned in a bloodless coup."

"Wouldn't it be easier to shoot her? You know it would!"

He shrugged. "Who knows what's going to happen? Certainly not Adelbert, your friend DeLeone. He didn't tell you much about her, did he? She's an absolute bitch, practically everybody despises her. The poor maids run and hide when they hear her coming."

"You're full of good news."

"Oh, you needn't worry on that score. She'll treat you like a queen." He laughed at his little joke. She buried her face in her hands. Meaning to reassure her, he placed a hand on her shoulder. "Now, now . . . listen to me, you mustn't get down. You could easily come out of this with nothing more to show than a suntan for your summer vacation in our pleasant little land. May I give you some friendly advice?"

She nodded, suddenly trusting him, feeling she had found what she needed most at the moment, a friend. Then a second notion followed the first. Here she was again, throwing herself upon the mercy of a stranger, as she had at the Gray Dragon. Still, what option did she have?

"What advice?" she asked.

"Don't get into the habit of crossing his nibs . . ." Tallot nodded at the door. "He's a very important man. And despite what you think, he does have a heart. He feels sorry for you."

"Oh, I'm sure . . ." She touched the cheek DeLeone had slapped.

"He does, he told me so before you ever set foot on board. He's only doing his duty, carrying out his assignment, not a particularly enjoyable one, I imagine, for a man with his military record. He happens to be our national hero. All those medals and ribbons and things are honestly earned. He's one of only two men in the world to be awarded the Emblem of the Black Eagle. And the other one's been dead two hundred years. Adelbert saved King Charles Felix's life four years ago, throwing himself in front of His Majesty and taking a terrorist's knife in the chest. A lesser man would have died on the spot. Not Adelbert. There was a rumor at the time that Death came to claim him and he spit in his eye and kicked him down the stairs." He threw up his hands in exaggerated impatience. "Listen to me, you've got me beating all about the bush. What I started to say was that he can be your protector. Or your most dangerous enemy."

"He makes me nervous."

"He makes everybody nervous, even the king. Not Caroline-Louisa, of course. The only thing she's afraid of is the dark, voices in the night, ghosts. . . ."

"And assassins."

"She's a religious fanatic. And as I said, an absolute bitch." Tallot took her hands in his, squeezing them fondly. "Be nice to Adelbert, Lorna. May I call you Lorna?" She nodded smiling. He wiped her eyes with a hanky. "And you must call me René."

"You're French?"

"No, a Savoyard. Adelbert, Crespi, and I are the only

ones on board. The captain and most of the crew are
Greek." He extended his hands helping her up from
the chair. "Now to work. Before Old Moustache and
Medals comes back to check up on us." Letting her
hands drop, he snapped his fingers and pointed at her.
"But first, I've something to show you, scads of
things . . ."

Whipping open one of his trunks with an exaggerated
sweep of his arm, he disclosed a half-dozen hats perched
on wooden stands, each stand anchored to the bottom.
Up came a huge Leghorn hat, the brim cut at the back
and caught up with an overlarge bow of white silk
ribbon with a rosette displayed over the right ear. He
plunked it on her head, tying the strings under her
chin and moving her to the mirror to look.

"It's darling," she said quietly.

"It's identical to one of her favorites. It's nothing.
I'm saving the best 'til last."

"I would have thought she wore a crown and ermine
robes and such."

"She does, and the latest fashions from Paris. She
adores clothes, she has hundreds of outfits."

In turn she tried on a hat of sage green taffeta with a
cross-bar of salmon pink, corded and bound with pink
satin ribbon, a cabriolet bonnet faced with contrasting
silk and trimmed with huge ribbon bows and all the
other hats and bonnets, each lovelier than the one
preceding, including a spring hat of rice straw trimmed
with bunches of pink azalea, the ribbons light green,
shaded á mille rayes, the stripes as slender as straws and
shot with white. The last hat, offered for her appraisal
with all the flamboyance of a sleight-of-hand artist,
proved to be a darling carriage bonnet of straw gauze
edged with transparent net, embossed with delicate pink
ornaments and finished with a curtain of blond. The
crown was ornamented to match the pattern of the embossed border, and trimmed with a full plume of white
uncurled feathers mixed with three pink ones.

Out of another trunk came pale blue ribbed silk

slippers with satin rosettes, white kid slippers as soft as "a warm breeze" to René, his enthusiasm mounting, his pale face all smiles. She tried on dozens of slippers and gaiters and shoes and boots. And gloves, long, short, and in between.

But it was the gowns that he handed her one by one to hold up in front of her at the mirror that took her breath away. Small wonder he had dismissed the contents of her little trunk as absolute rags. For here was a graceful pelisse dress fashioned to clear the instep and opening over a false petticoat trimmed to match the gown, a perfectly lovely carriage dress made of *gros de Naples* of prismatic rose, its lights bright lilac. The corsage was made with large horizontal plaits gathered at the front with a band. The shoulders were trimmed with three falls of silk, the edges worked in loose floss silk into small points, the falls appearing one behind the other meeting at the front of the belt, itself broad and made of the same material as the dress. The outstanding feature was an enormous pocket. Out of it, with appropriate *voilàs!* René produced a pair of little silk shoes, silk stockings, a scarf, lace mitts, a gold chain and other jewelry, all the accessories she needed to equip herself for dinner or evening company.

There were blouses with enormous leg-of-mutton sleeves, capes and perelines and shawls and underclothing. She gasped aloud when he produced a ball dress of white gauze lisse, gathered in front of the corsage with full loose folds, the underdress a deep rose-colored satin *á la Reine*. The epaulet and the bottom of the lisse robe were cut into square dents; the upper dress was looped up on the left side to the knees *à la Taglioni*, with bouquets of gold barley. The rose-colored satin skirt was finished with a border of full puffs at the feet.

"Lovely, no?" he asked slyly.

"Lovely, yes . . ."

"You'll wear it with white kid gloves, carry a fan embossed with gold and, to catch the eye, behold, the *pièce de résistance!*" He held up a necklace of gold medallions and placed it around her neck. "This you shall keep on for a while and enjoy. It shall be your, how shall I say, spirits' lifter. Now, we must go to work on your face. And your hair." He held up a handful. "God, why so long—to keep your neck warm? Are the winters that cold in New England?"

She was preparing to counter this sarcasm with some of her own when a knock sounded.

"Adelbert!" burst René.

Fortunately the door opened and in strode Captain Crespi. René's sigh of relief was so obvious, in spite of her gloom, she nearly burst out laughing. The captain looked around; the place was a shambles, the trunks open, their contents scattered about.

"What do you want?" shrilled René.

"Nothing with you, dear, another time perhaps." Crespi fixed Lorna with a glare aping his superior. "You, Mrs. Stone, I have news for. Bad news, I'm afraid."

"What else am I to expect in this company?"

"His Excellency has instructed me to inform you that your friend has met with a fatal accident."

"He was no friend of mine, and I saw him drown." She turned her back on him, picking up the Leghorn hat and tying it on a second time.

"I'm talking about the other one."

She whirled. "You fractured his skull. So he's died, has he?"

"That love tap, don't be silly. That was just hard enough to shut him up. No, I'm afraid he too fell overboard."

"Or perhaps after you gagged him and tied his hands you pushed him over . . ."

"I can't say, I was not there when it happened." He shrugged. "His Excellency just thought you'd like to know."

"You can tell His Excellency I'm not surprised. After all, drowning them is cheaper than paying them."

Again he shrugged and left, René closing and this time latching the door.

"You're not thinking, Lorna, you're missing the point."

"What?"

"They didn't drown those two to save money but to save Adelbert worrying over the possibility that once he and they are quits they might one day talk to the wrong people about this little state secret."

"If that's so, what about the captain and the crew of this ship? And the *Anselmo* . . ."

"That's not the same thing. The captain of the *Anselmo* hasn't the remotest idea who you're with now or where you're going. As for our Captain Grigorides, he's an old and trusted friend of Adelbert's. He'll be sailing for home after he drops us off at Port-St.-Louis-du-Rhône. With nobody but the three of us and himself knowing why we picked you up."

She studied him. "Tell me, René, if I had a chance to get away, would you help me?"

"Possibly, under certain conditions."

"What conditions?"

"I might help you get away at Adelbert's funeral. But not while he's alive and breathing fire down our necks."

"You're more afraid of him than I am, aren't you?"

"I know him better than you do. Now sit down and we'll try on some wigs. If I don't have to cut your hair, I won't."

This promise, intended to bring some small measure of comfort to her increasingly uncomfortable situation, was to prove worthless. Within minutes DeLeone reappeared and practically his first words were:

"Cut her hair to one inch in length."

She gasped and protested.

"Your Excellency," ventured Tallot, accepting the scissors thrust into his hand, "that won't be necessary. Her hair can be piled under any one of the wigs. We've tried them all."

"Do as you're told."

"No!" she roared, covering the top of her head with both hands and backing away.

"You will sit down and let him do it, or I shall summon Crespi, who will sit you down and tie you there!"

She gave it up and slumped down into the chair, turning it away from the mirror. Tallot muttered something under his breath and began cutting.

DeLeone drew in his breath sharply. "I said one inch . . ."

"Yes, Your Excellency."

It took all of two minutes. Her hair littered the floor, forming a circle around the chair.

"No," snapped DeLeone.

"Excellency?"

The count had positioned himself directly in front of her, his left elbow in his right hand, his other hand clasping his beard. "I have changed my mind . . ."

"You've what!" She jumped up seething. "It's a bit late, wouldn't you say?"

Pushing her down he held her there. "I want you to shave her head." She screamed and began pounding him in the chest, his medals jumping and clinking against each other. She protested so loudly, Tallot backed away, covering his ears. DeLeone ignored her. "Then if by some miracle you manage to slip away from us one day, the farthest you'll get will be the nearest nunnery. Ha, ha, ha . . ."

VIII

One look in the mirror was enough to make her scream and faint. But she gritted her teeth, set her jaw, and did neither; she'd be damned if she'd give him the satisfaction! This was his way of getting even with her for spitting in his face, an action that spoke louder than his loudest threats, a visible reminder that he could do anything he liked with her. From his expression he was immensely pleased with himself. Pleased or not, it was his first blunder; its effect upon her quite the antithesis of that intended. If anything it buttressed her resolve to seize her first chance to get away and in the process see to it that he paid dearly for this.

For a time the clothes and everything else Tallot had shown her had lured her attention from her dilemma. But scissors and razor had fetched them back with a speed and an intensity of focus that made her head ache. She could feel her flesh burn with hatred. Staring at herself in the glass, embarrassment rosying her cheeks, she vowed to outwit them; by subterfuge, by deceit, with sheer luck, resourcefulness, and courage summoned from every reserve in her being. With help or without it.

Her life up to the night in the Gray Dragon Inn had been as cloistered as that of any princess. Living with the protection and help of her parents and her brothers, she had never encountered a problem, a setback, a heartache, any unhappy experience she'd been unable to confront and deal with. But in this, by far the worst, most dangerous situation of her life, she would not have their help, nor likely anyone else's. Nevertheless, she

could not bring herself to meekly submit, to knuckle
under without a fight. The Singletons had always been
fighters. Where the battle was bloodiest, a Singleton
could be found. Her grandfather had been at Breed's
Hill and Bunker Hill, and had served heroically at
Brandywine, Philadelphia, and elsewhere. Singleton
men had fought for their country in both wars, as had
the Hastings men on her mother's side. Her own father
had fought with distinction as a junior officer under
General William Henry Harrison in the battle of the
Thames, in which Commodore Perry had gained all the
territory west of the Niagara peninsula. And later her
father had earned his captain's bars with General Jacob
Brown for his valor in the battles of Chippewa and
Lundy's Lane. Both families' histories were inextricably
linked with that of the nation. In her veins ran the
blood of heroes; in her mind rose the proud recollection of half a dozen gallant exploits. Were she to strike
her colors, the rumble of Singletons and Hastings spinning in their graves would surely deafen her!

If this cocksure, arrogant old man, this overaged
specialist in blood spilling and violence wanted war,
war it would be!

She turned to him, his dark eyes glistening in triumph, and held them with her own without blinking.

"Your Excellency," she said quietly. "I leave it to
you to decide. You select the proper wig."

"You flatter me, Mrs. Stone." Her request had had
the effect she sought, however, his eyes assuming a
puzzled look.

He picked among the wigs, selected one, and handed
it to Tallot, who had been standing by in silence, his
razor still in hand, his pale face even paler at the sight
of his handiwork. He helped her adjust the wig, stepping back, sighing relief, and bringing color back to
his cheeks.

DeLeone nodded approvingly. "Now, get to work on
her face."

"Yes, Your Excellency."

The count left, Talot's shoulders sagging perceptibly as he latched the door.

"I'm sorry," he said lamely.

"It's not your fault. You tried to tell him."

"Now that you've seen the real Adelbert, what do you think your chances are of getting out of this thing alive?"

"Surely no worse than they were before this."

"You're being very foolish, Lorna. You'll be risking your life for nothing."

"I couldn't agree with that before, I can't now. Let's not talk about it. This wig is hot." She touched the sides gingerly, then straightened a curl above her forehead. "Hot or not, from now on I shall live in it."

Tallot sat her down and opened a small trunk revealing a number of trays which he proceeded to remove one after the other. They contained the materials and the implements with which he would alter her features to conform more closely to those of Caroline-Louisa. The changes he effected were subtle—subduing the sinking of her temples, slightly darkening the rim of each eye to create the illusion of enlarging them, accentuating the natural oval shape of her jaw with rouge—these three, along with the blond wig and the thinning and lightening in color of her eyebrows to match it created an uncanny similarity to the face in his sketches.

"You're very talented," she remarked, appraising his finished work in the mirror.

A melancholy look saddened his features. "I was in the theater at one time. My specialty, my first love was the characters in Delavigne's tragedies. And I was very proud of my Lear. Yes, with all modesty, my Lear was exceptional."

"Why did you leave the theater?"

"I found myself in the eye of the storm of a scandal. I was disgraced. It's a fairly sordid story. Let's talk about something else. Let's talk about you, while you practice putting on your makeup until you're perfect at it."

She was given the cabin next door to DeLeone's, a cubicle half the size of her quarters on board the *Anselmo*. Alone for the first time since coming aboard, she considered matters up to the moment. Things could be worse, she reflected, although how bad they were destined to get defied prediction. Still, there were some bright spots, if not bright at least not wholly black. The duchy of Savoy was small, the nearest border probably no more than fifteen or twenty miles away from the castle. Once across it, she would be one seven league stride down the way home. In addition to her other duties, she had been told she would be traveling about the duchy "mingling with the people." Would this be her last chance for escape? Probably. And DeLeone and his underlings had to be well aware of it, too. It came down to four essentials: the opportunity, the means—some sort of transportation other than a shanks' mare—perfect timing, and that unreliable and maddeningly elusive lackey luck. The last she would have no control over, the other three very little. Nevertheless, she had to attempt it. To remain, to bide her time, to see the thing through, could be calamitous. She would either be taken for the queen and assassinated or she would survive until the revolutionists took over the government. If this happened, Caroline-Louisa and Charles Felix would surely be tried and hanged. But as long as the wily queen had a double behind whom she could hide there would be no need to place her own neck in the noose.

Lying in bed, staring at the ceiling bathed in a roseate glow by the rays of the sun immersing itself in the sea to the west, her thoughts drifted back to Philip, envisioning him lying on the floor, the knife hilt protruding from his chest. She imagined the knife plunged into her own chest, the point magnetically drawing the life from the limits of her extremities. Life ascending the blade, leaving with the outrush of blood, escaping, creating a passageway for death patiently waiting to enter. Death rushing in, all of it happening so quickly there'd be no time to fight it, no chance to even voice protest.

To be alive and within a minute to be dead. One minute, the last of the millions he had lived. How horrible! How barbarously unjust . . . What was this life; to be given it, blessed with the power to breathe, to grow, to learn, to laugh, to love, only to have it all snatched away in one's very prime! The poor darling, to never see the sun again, to be denied the future and all the promise it held. To leave her arms, taking her heart with him.

Her eyes became misty, single tears taking shape in each, loosed and running down at an angle as she turned her left cheek to her pillow.

"I love you, my darling, dearest Philip. Only you, forever."

IX

Rain came during the night, a savage downpour that scourged the ship, rattling with a strange metallic sound against the bulging lower sails and thumping the decks. She awoke in the morning to the sounds, peering out the porthole at the black sea heaving restlessly, its surface pebbled, a slate-gray curtain attaching it to the heavens. Despite the rain's arrival, the wind had not yet risen, the seas were fairly placid, the motion of the vessel continuing its measured lifting and lowering of its fair weather progress toward its destination.

The rain fell all day, all night, and all the next day. The dampness invaded her cabin, permeating the bedclothes and her own clothing, rendering everything clammy to the touch. It was impossible to venture outside for more than a few seconds without becoming soaked through, so she remained in her cabin listening to the depressing sounds and suffering the sadness they encouraged.

The *Iphimedia,* meanwhile, had gained and slipped through the Straits of Gibraltar, under the forbidding, glistening gray cliffs. Once into the Mediterranean, the coast of Spain could be seen in dim outline off the port beam, and in time the islands of Formentera and Ibiza outlined their presence. The ship had altered course from east to east-north-east, then northeast, putting distant Sardinia balancing Corsica atop the Strait of Bonifacio off its starboard beam. Late in the afternoon DeLeone and Captain Crespi looked in on her, the count announcing that they would be reaching port sometime early the following morning.

"A coach will be waiting to take us north up the

valley," he said jauntily. "We hope to reach Montélimar by nightfall. If this sorry weather persists that far north, the going will be difficult and slow. But let us cross our fingers and hope for the best. The first leg is close to a hundred miles. We'll be changing teams in Avignon and as I mentioned, staying the night in Montélimar. Before sunup the next morning we'll be on our way to San Marcellin on the Isère River. Before noon we'll be starting up into the mountains. The scenery is magnificent. With another fresh team hopefully we'll reach Chambéry by sundown. Wait 'til you see the castle turned to gold by the setting sun. An incredible sight!" He laughed and clapped his hands like a child suddenly struck by the antics of a clown, all but dancing a jig in place. Then he became serious.

"It will be a long and fairly arduous trek, Mrs. Stone. You'll be wearing that . . ." He pointed past her. She turned and saw Crespi holding up a hooded merino cloak, cocoa brown and lined with silk. "Whenever you step out of the coach until you are behind closed doors, you will wear the hood up and drawn at the throat," continued the count. "Is that understood?" She nodded. "You'll also need a veil and a different wig. You choose, any color except blond."

Her mind raced. So they would be stopping at least twice, possibly three or four times before reaching Chambéry. Possibly more if the rain kept up and the road became the quagmire DeLeone anticipated. Opportunity, first of the four essentials, suddenly began to loom large.

His eyes were boring into her.

"I shouldn't if I were you," he said in a bored tone.

"What?"

"Dwell on getting away. We'll be by your side every foot of the way and Captain Crespi will be sitting outside your locked door in Montélimar. If you're as bright as I think you are, you'll put such thoughts aside and keep them there. Why get up hope when you haven't a chance? Why live day to day at the ends of your nerves? For what? Certain disappointment, that I can assure you. Enough of that." He cocked his head and grinned. "I really must hand the palm to Tallot. He's positively ingenious. A touch here, a touch there, and he's made you the image of her."

"She's still too thin," barked Crespi, his tone cocksure.

"Oh, shut up, Rudolf!"

Crespi clicked his heels, bowing from the waist and holding it. "Forgive me, Your Excellency, I could not restrain myself."

"You have all the self-discipline, all the restraint, of a witling. You could learn from this lady. Tallot shaves her head, she sees herself in the mirror, and she never so much as blinks an eye.

"Well, Mrs. Stone, until tomorrow morning. Please see that you are packed and ready to disembark. Tallot will be at your door at five sharp to lend a hand. Sorry about the weather, but we'll just have to put up with it."

He had moved to the door and was standing at the latches. He snapped his fingers and Crespi bolted forward, opening the door for him. And they were gone.

The *Iphimedia* continued northward heading into the Gulf of Lions toward Port-St.-Louis-du-Rhône at the river's mouth. And the rain persisted, drenching the world, drowning Lorna's spirits, setting the small candle of hope burning within her to guttering, threatening to extinguish. Protect it she must, shield and shelter it from all the alien elements. Hope, the last refuge of the lost.

X

Montélimar, the capital of an arrondissement in the department of Drome, was situated near the left bank of the Rhône. A picture-book town, with its comfortably thatched cottages and narrow winding streets, it was beset on its three land sides by groves of chestnut trees and pines.

Rising above its houses and public buildings was the ancient castle. Its front wall and its towers threatened imminent collapse, but the side and the rear ramparts and four of the old gates had been diligently preserved by the Montélimarions.

Possibly the least imposing of all the unthatched buildings in town was the local inn, the Croix d'Or, up to the door of which the mud-spattered mares trotted, dragging the rocking coach behind. In keeping with the count's instructions, Lorna wore an auburn-colored wig, Tallot's choice and almost identical in shade to her natural hair long since swept up from the floor of his cabin and tossed overboard with the trash. The rain had begun to let up within sight of the town and had stopped altogether as twilight nestled over the area and as DeLeone and the captain escorted her and her trunk up the stairs to a cramped little room. Its single window overlooked a walled-in sty crammed with fat, grunting pigs, and reeking of the mingled stenches of rotten garbage and excrement. At her door Crespi pressed a silver coin into the landlord's red hand and moments later a younger man appeared with a tool box. Under the captain's interested eye, the man removed the bolt from inside the door, reinstalling it outside.

DeLeone had conversed with the landlord in French,

Lorna standing within earshot but unable to understand a single word. Yet another obstacle in her pathway to freedom, she reflected, her inability to speak or understand any foreign language.

Tallot joined the three of them for dinner served downstairs at a corner table. The *potage* was delicious, the *moules* superb, but the *caneton* overroasted and dry as old wood. Seated at the table, her back to the wall, she was briefly tempted to jump up and run for the door located diagonally opposite their corner. Run and run and run! And pray that she might get away into a pine grove and the dense woods beyond, perhaps circle the town and cross the river in the confusion certain to ensue. She repeatedly raised her eyes from her food to glance at the door. Until DeLeone caught her. He made no comment other than to smile and shake his head.

They retired early, Crespi escorting her to her door, his chair in hand, positioning it, ushering her inside, bolting the door, turning the key in the lock and leaving it there. Seconds later he changed his mind. She could hear him remove it and assumed he was pocketing it.

She stood at the window, the lower sash propped up by a stick permitting the loathsome odor from below access to the room. Better to sleep in stuffiness, she decided, than to leave the window open and suffer *that* all night long. She was about to remove the stick when curiosity induced her to lean out and look down. The pigs were snoring contentedly, a soft nasal drone in chorus. Tightly snugged against one another they formed a carelessly designed pattern. It occurred to her that if one more were to be forced into their midst, the walls enclosing them must surely collapse. Not particularly high walls, she noted; in the light of the three-quarter moon she estimated them at less than five feet. High enough to keep pigs in, not too high to pull oneself over. While standing on a sleeping pig's back? Hardly. She could tie her bed blanket, the single sheet, and the mattress tick end to end, fasten one end to a bedpost and drop the other out the window. But coming down onto the backs of sleeping pigs would raise a racket to rouse the town.

All the same, beyond the far wall stood the stables, in darkness at this hour, with no one about except the horses and mules belonging to the guests. Would it be possible to let herself down to as far as the height of the wall and push her feet against the building? Inch herself to the wall, throw one arm over and pull herself onto it?

That was one way. Was there a better one? She cast about. The tall poster-bed with its painted wooden cornice had been placed against the window wall, its near headpost within inches of the window itself. A handsome paneled and grained armoire stood in the opposite corner beside an ogee mirror desperately in need of dusting. On one side of the door a washstand had been placed; to balance it on the other, a slat-back chair. Footing the bed was a small dropleaf table. On the table stood a brass candle holder, the candle reduced to barely an inch, its perimeter encrusted with drippings.

It was not the candle that held her eye, however, rather the holder. She hefted it. It was solid, heavy, better than a pound. And seven or eight inches in height.

Her mind whirled, groping desperately for the perfect plan; the most practical, with maximum potential for success and minimum risk. She nearly cried out with joy when it sprang to mind. Quickly she set about making the necessary preparations, taking care to first remove her shoes. She then stripped the tick from the mattress and joined it corner to corner with the blanket and sheet. Tying one end to the headpost, she leaned out the window and swung the other back and forth like a pendulum, gradually widening the arc, trying and failing to sling the free end over the wall to the left. On the seventh try it flopped over.

Stealing to the door, she set the chair to one side as

quietly as possible, placed the candle on the table, returned to the window, pushed out the stick propping up the sash, and fairly flew back toward the spot earlier occupied by the chair. The sash came slamming down before she was halfway there. She could hear Crespi jump up on the other side of the door.

"Hey in there . . . what are you up to! Answer me!"

The bolt thrown, the key out, fumbled into the lock, turned, the door flung open. Down on his head came the candlestick, hammering him to his knees. He rolled over on his back, out cold. Dropping the candlestick and pulling his legs out of the way, she quickly closed the door. Then running to the armoire, she climbed inside, pulling the doors closed behind her.

Almost at once the air became so close she could scarcely breathe. She fought to quiet her pounding heart, to calm her nerves, to catch her breath and stop gasping. She waited, straining to hear. She didn't have long. Within a few minutes there came the muffled sound of footsteps, boots pounding. She could hear the door open and familiar voices.

"Crespi!" shrilled Tallot. "My God, he's dead!"

"He's not dead. Never mind him!" rasped DeLeone impatiently. "Look there, she's gone out the window. Downstairs, hurry!"

Away they ran, charging down the hall, down the stairs. A chill raced down her spine. What a thoughtless idiot she was! She hadn't even considered her next move! But she certainly couldn't stay here . . .

Throwing open the doors, she filled her lungs, snatched up her shoes, hesitated at the sight of the cloak DeLeone had ordered her to wear now lying at the foot of the bed, passed it up and, pulling her shoes on, ran out. Down the hall she flew, past a door slightly ajar. Stopping short, she retraced her steps. It was a closet filled with buckets and brooms and other cleaning essentials. Entering, turning over a bucket, she sat down on it, pulling the door closed in front of her, plunging the closet into darkness. Near darkness. At her feet she spied a horizontal band of light where the door stopped short of the floor and immediately felt a draft swirling lightly about her ankles. She sighed relief; even with the door closed, she'd get enough air. She pondered her situation, thinking ahead. She would stay here the night, while Adelbert raised the alarm and roused the town. She pictured him gathering the locals about him, describing her in detail, promising a hundred gold florins' reward for her recapture. Then separating them into small hunting parties and sending them scampering off in all directions. Let them search, let them roam about till their legs gave out and their patience, let them scour the countryside, all they'd find for their trouble would be each other!

Before dawn, between catnaps to restore her energy, she would devise an inspired plan of escape, a foolproof means of getting out to the stables behind the sty and onto a horse. And be miles away in minutes.

Steps, boots pounding down the hall. A very familiar thumping. DeLeone! They were coming back. Why? It made no sense . . . She heard them pass, pursed her lips and mutely whistled in relief.

"Captain Crespi," DeLeone snapped, "back among the living, eh?"

"My head, ooooooo. . . ."

"I must commend you, Rudolf. What a superb job of bodyguarding . . ."

"She got away . . ."

DeLeone's tone in response was that of a man comfortably sure of himself. "I don't think so." She heard a door open and close, then another. They were coming back. A hand was on the knob of her door, turning it, opening it.

"Here we are, Rudolf, safe and sound . . ."

He had high praise for her escape strategy, describing it as ingenious, inspired: "And almost perfectly executed. You made but one little mistake. The armoire in your room . . ."

"What about it?"

"The doors were closed when we burst in and found the captain enjoying his nap, and you nowhere to be seen. We ran downstairs and out back to the stables. You'd want a horse, naturally. But none seemed to be missing. Tallot suggested you might have fled on foot, but that seemed most unlikely, not with an animal so easy to come by.

"Then it struck me that possibly you hadn't left us after all. Sure enough, just now going by your door I noticed both your armoire doors open. So obviously you'd at least delayed leaving the room, and possibly had yet to leave the floor. Which, had it worked, would have sent us chasing off after the wild goose. Much better than chasing you, eh? My dear, it wouldn't have worked, it's a trick much too old and abused. Right, Rudolf?"

Captain Crespi was preoccupied, leaning against the wall, caressing the hump on his head with the tips of his fingers, muttering under his breath and glaring at her. At the sound of his name he braced to attention.

"I beg your pardon, Your Excellency?"

DeLeone turned back to her. "My dear, you should have remembered to close those doors when you popped out. Everything peace and quiet down in the stables sent us running back up here. Seeing those doors open . . . Tsk, tsk, isn't it always the little things that trip us up? Better luck next time, eh? All right, let's get to bed now. We've a long jaunt ahead of us tomorrow."

XI

They crossed the border in the middle of the afternoon
the following day. Less than three kilometers from Pont
Beauvoisin, at the lifeless little village of Domessin,
the coach deserted the twisting slough of ruts and
rubble that served as the high road to Les Échelles
and took to a narrow road leading over a hill and down
onto a sun-drenched plain extending to the distant lime-
stone precipices, the ridge of the immense rock barrier
in service as protection to Les Échelles. They drew
closer and closer to the base, reaching a steep road
which zigzagged up the talus. The horses pulled with
all their strength, but near the top the driver advised
his passengers to get out. They walked ahead of the
team. The footing was treacherous and the way soon
became so narrow that she could reach out and touch
the face of the precipice while at the same time gaze
down with awe and her heart in her throat at the
valley below. Getting back into the coach at the summit,
they waited while their driver let the horses catch their
breaths before starting down the opposite side. The next
village along the route was Bridoire, a small, undistin-
guished but quaint assemblage of cottages and water-
mills. Beyond Bridoire the road once more began to
ascend, crossing a ridge and coming upon a densely
wooded valley, the basin of Lac d'Aiguebelette.
Through impressive stands of walnut trees they passed,
through the village of Lepin, the scenery superb under
a perfectly glorious sun. According to DeLeone the lake
was three miles long by two miles wide and filled with
trout and carp. It was surrounded by fertile fields and

lush meadows themselves enclosed by the wooded slopes of the nearby mountains.

Beyond Aiguebelette they were obliged to climb yet another height. In addition to more lovely scenery spread out below and the point of view of a bird in flight to appreciate it, the driver was presented with a choice of two routes by which to descend from the col. One, the old Roman road, however, promised dangerous footing for the horses. Following the other road it took them precisely one hour by her watch to regain the plain and reach the village of Vimine. Beyond, less than two miles distant, lay Chambéry.

"Home at last," sighed DeLeone, his customarily stern face assuming a pleased expression. "Look there, Mrs. Stone, look and be properly impressed, it's the Castle of La Bathie et de Monterminod."

First sight of the castle, her prison to be, its towers, its finials and merlons rising into the pale blue sky, the setting sun flinging its fire across the face of the outer curtain, its solidity, its presumptuous trespass upon the lovely green landscape, and panic seized her heart. The little town squatting below it, like insignificant rubble swept up to its foundations, scarcely deserved a glance. It was the massive presence uplifting itself, thrusting itself against the heavens, that gripped her attention.

"Your mouth is open, Mrs. Stone. An impressive sight, no? Satisfy an old soldier's curiosity, tell me how would you escape from such formidable surroundings? The walls are eight feet thick, the towers fifty feet high. Four gates guarded day and night . . ."

She did not answer, letting him gloat and savor his success. Which it undeniably was; his assignment had been to bring her from the Madeiras to here and this he had done. Calling out to the driver to stop the coach, the count then got out and climbed agiley up beside him. They went on. The guards at the main gate saluted as they passed through into the outer ward. Through the inner gate they headed, into the inner ward where the coach again stopped. She and Tallot got out and the count descended to join them. Crespi took his place beside the driver and the horses pulled to the right, the whip snapping over their rumps, the coach rumbling off toward the barracks and the stables below. Seemingly enjoying the opportunity to perform the role of tour guide, DeLeone pointed as he explained:

"The great hall and the kitchens. Over there the apartments. More apartments upstairs, including yours in the east area, the royal offices, chapel, blacksmith's shop, storerooms." He indicated downward, between his feet. "Dungeon, torture chamber, all the comforts of the Croix d'or. Of course none of those nasty rooms are used nowadays." He smiled. "Still there they are if they're needed, eh?"

Her eyes drifted upward, scaling the wall, moving from tower to tower, passing the second only to be drawn back to it and the narrow vertical window cut into its wall halfway up to the turret. Someone was in the window looking down at them. As Lorna discovered him he moved away out of sight. He, she wondered, or had it been she? She'd only caught a glimpse. Had that been blond hair catching the sun's rays slanting down over the wall?

A squad of uniformed guards materialized, coming from the barracks, the corner around which they tramped partially concealed by the inner gatehouse tower. Their uniforms and weapons were much too modern for their medieval surroundings. No chain mail, no greaves or brassards, shields or broadswords or pikes. Instead they wore black crop-tailed red jackets trimmed with black collars, epaulets, fronts, cuffs and tails. All their red, save their collars, displayed brass buttons as brightly polished as their boots and the brims and bands of their shakos. They carried muskets and their sabers swung jauntily at their hips as they neared. Their lieutenant ordered them to a halt, they stomped still, tucked in their chins and thrust out their chests as one. The officer stepped forward, drew his saber and saluted the count.

"Welcome home, Your Excellency. Their majesties await you."

"Thank you, Lieutenant Calini."

"We missed you, Excellency."

"It is good to be back. On time to the hour, I might add."

"Extraordinary punctuality, Excellency."

"Not at all. Nothing but sensible planning coupled with faultless execution."

"Indeed, Your Excellency. With your permission, I shall escort you to Her Highness. She has been nervously anticipating your return since early this morning."

DeLeone's tightly sealed mouth collapsed at the corners. "Mmmm, I wonder what she did with the schedule I gave her?" He considered his own answer to this, shook his head, and flung out his hand the way they were to go. "Lead on."

XII

The beauty of the room all but stole Lorna's breath, the finely cut exotic marbles inlaying the tops of tables, their ebony and mahogany legs monopodial, animal legs, each surmounted by the creature's head; bizarre creatures, winged caryatids, griffins, mermaids. Gracing the walls were girandole mirrors in pine and gesso with gold leaf, enormous tapestries depicting medieval scenes, and sculptured sconces already aflame as twilight's shadows gathered over the castle.

Her glance drifted to an exquisitely carved secretary stenciled with gilt and from it to a flounced dressing table decorated with brass inlay and ormolu mounts—wreaths and swans—and to one after another individual urns and vases, delicately fashioned and painted, and to a bed. A bed wider, more elegant, more cozily comfortable looking, more inviting than any she had ever seen. A bed to swallow one in softness, with silken swaths of gold falling from its crowned canopy, the queen's family crest sharing the canopy's center with the black eagle of Savoy.

A bedchamber for a queen. The thought prompted her arrival. The double doors held open for her by two maids, in she floated with her ladies-in-waiting, the hem of her violet-colored silk gown gliding over the parquet floor. Their eyes met. Lorna gasped. Even knowing, expecting it, the sight of her own face staring at her was startling, the resemblance astonishing, though not the hair, nor the look in the eyes, the haughty, imperious stare of grudging approval.

Caroline-Louisa nodded casually, acknowledging Count DeLeone's sweeping bow, straightening him with a flip of her hand, her eyes still fastened on Lorna. The two maids stood stiffly by, both, Lorna noted, scarcely daring to look at the queen, who circled her slowly, her gown rustling, the only sound in the room. Stopping in front of her, she made a face.

"What is your name?" The effort to imbue her voice with as much arrogance as possible was almost ludicrous.

"Lorna Singleton Stone."

"Lorrr-na?" Lorna nodded. Caroline-Louisa wrinkled her nose in disapproval. "It is not pretty. We don't like your name. We shall call you Yankee. You come from Massachusetts . . ."

"New Hampshire."

"The same thing."

"Not to a New Hampshireite."

DeLeone cleared his throat. "Mrs. Stone, you will address Her Highness as Your Majesty."

"Your Majesty," began Lorna, her anger thus far held in check beginning to rise in her throat, tighten it, and harshen her voice. "I will say this once. That's all that's necessary. You know very well that I have been brought here against my will. The reason is obvious, but now that we have come face to face I'll remind you that I am an American citizen. A free citizen of a free and independent country. My country has very strict laws against kidnapping."

"Indeed?"

The count took a step forward, his face gray with fury. Caroline-Louisa motioned him to stay where he was.

"In America kidnapping is a hanging offense."

"In America."

"Yes, Your Majesty. This is a very serious mistake, serious for you and for Savoy!"

"Oh, my. Ah, but aren't you overlooking something? You are not in America. You are in Savoy. Here our laws prevail. And do you know what our laws are?

They are expressions of the will of the rulers. Their majesties."

"With all due respect, Your Majesty, you are not *my* ruler. I don't know you, I don't know your country or your laws. Nor do I wish to know them. Unless and until you release me, provide me with a proper escort to Port-St.-Louis-du-Rhône, and arrange passage for me aboard a ship sailing for Boston . . ."

"You'll do what? What, tell us."

DeLeone laughed. "She'll fly over the wall, Highness."

"Oh? This we must see . . ."

"And fly to America and bring back men and cannon," added the count.

"For shame, Adelbert, you're frightening us!"

"Enjoy yourselves, by all means!" snapped Lorna, "but understand this, you may be able to keep me here, but you can't force me to so much as lift a finger for you. You can beat me, you can torture me, you can bury me in a cell, you can starve me, but *you will not use me!*"

Caroline-Louisa threw back her head and laughed uproariously. Then glowered at her. Turning, her diamond and sapphire coronet catching the light of the sconces nearest her, she waved one of the maids to her, a child-eyed, narrow-shouldered little thing, her hair pulled tightly back in a bun, her lace cap perched absurdly atop her head and pinned in place. Padding toward the queen, passing Lorna, she threw a glance at her out of the corner of her eye.

"We wouldn't beat you, torture you, bury you in a cell or starve you," said the queen mildly. "What could we possibly gain by such brutality?" Her hands on the maid's shoulders, she guided her into position in front of her, turning her so that she faced Lorna. "Tell us your name, dear, your full name." The maid opened her mouth. Out came a guttural sound, as if unseen hands were choking her, crushing her larynx. "Once more." The sound was repeated. "Did you understand that?"

asked Caroline-Louisa. "That was her name, Teresa Zuccola. It is very hard for her to say it. Shall we show you why? Open your mouth wide, dear." The girl did so. "See for yourself . . ."

At the back of her throat lay the healed stump of her tongue. Lorna recoiled in revulsion.

"Now, show us your tongue, Teresa . . ."

Around the girl's neck was a slender black ribbon. Taking hold of the V it formed at the front, she pulled a small velvet sachet up and out of her blouse. Loosening the ribbons and opening the sachet she turned it upside down. Into her palm tumbled a wrinkled object, dark brown, almost black in color. It looked like a dried date.

It was all Lorna could do to keep from retching.

"Animals!" she hissed, holding her eyes away from the loathsome sight. "Animals, all of you!"

"Everyone out!" burst the queen, clapping her hands and gesturing dismissal, sitting down on a Dante chair as she did so. DeLeone clicked his heels, bowed, and backed away out the door, the ladies-in-waiting and the two maids following him. "Now, Yankee, we shall have a heart-to-heart talk. Rather we shall talk and you will listen. Teresa is a sweet child and an excellent maid; she has but one weakness of character. Had. She chatted like a magpie. She talked too much to the other maids and to the kitchen help about matters that did not concern her. This created a problem. She was warned, but was incapable of bridling her tongue. How were we to deal with the situation? What were we to do?

"We could have disposed of her one way or another, but why burn a tree to kill a pestiferous crow? Why deprive ourselves of a first-rate maid? *Voilà,* the solution. Perfect, don't you agree?" She leaned forward, pointing her hand at her listener. "The same solution could solve any problem we might have with you, Yankee. We don't need your voice, your temper, your whining, your defiance . . . You and your face are all we need." She motioned her closer. Almost without realizing it Lorna narrowed the distance separating them, drawn by the woman's eyes as by a tether. "You do as you're told, you obey without question, without hesitation, and you will keep your tongue where it belongs. You disobey, you make things difficult for us in any way and you will carry your tongue around your neck. Do you understand?"

"I understand, Your Majesty."

"Excellent. Somehow we knew you would. Now, step back and disrobe. Everything off. We wish to see what you look like from the neck down."

BOOK TWO

CASTLE MAD

I

She had been examined by the queen, commanded to put her clothes back on, and dismissed. Two guards had escorted her to her own apartment, three turnings removed from the royal bed chamber through corridors crowded with shadows cast by sconces placed every ten feet. As she anticipated, her bedroom was much less elegant than Caroline-Louisa's but the furnishings were attractive and feminine and the bed itself comfortable, she found, testing it. The room was luxurious compared to the one in the Gray Dragon; all that had had to recommend it was its geographic location.

Two arched and mullioned windows looked out upon the rear wall of the castle, and the night-clad mountain peaks distributed along the top of the wall like pastries set out to cool. A field cricket lodged somewhere in the wall chirped softly, monotonously affirming its presence, king, queen, company, captive, and cricket all sharing the house of the House of Savoy.

Her bed was painted and gilded ebony, the silken sheets snugged in place by a counterpane littered with legions of violets and surmounted by a canopy of tulle, lighter blue in color than the violets, Italian blue, the transparent curtain falling as lightly as beams of sunlight.

She was sitting at the foot of the bed gazing out the window at the wall and listening to the cricket's baleful plea for attention when a knock sounded and, in response to her query, the door opened. It was a maid, a squat round little creature with cheeks as red as pippins, and missing two front teeth, turning her smile into a ludicrous leer that nearly made Lorna laugh aloud. Her reddish-blond hair was bound in pigtails springing from the nape of her neck and circling her head up under her cap in the fashion of the Germans. Her colors were German, Lorna thought, reddish-blond hair, cerulean blue eyes, pink skin, red cheeks, and the down dressing her upper lip matching her eyebrows.

She curtsied as delicately as her bulk permitted. "I am Maria, your maid, madam. I am happy to be of service to you." Waddling soundlessly to first one window, then the other, she whipped the drapes closed, turning and curtsying again. "Do you wish me to bring you something to eat before you retire?"

"I'm not hungry, thank you. And I'm not going to bed yet." Lorna indicated the vanity bench behind the girl. "Sit down, I want to talk to you. Perhaps you can tell me a few things."

Maria pursed her lips, a tiny wrinkled pink bud, her face sagging under her worried eyes.

"Don't be afraid," said Lorna, "nothing that's going to get you into trouble. Whatever we talk about stays in this room. Trust me."

Teresa Zuccola's experience was evidently proving a useful object lesson for her sisters in service to their majesties. Regardless, keeping secrets, juicy bits and pieces of gossip, accumulating them, holding them in, was a challenge few can resist, somewhat like holding one's breath. And there is a limit to how much and how long one can hold. Somehow Lorna knew intuitively that this chubby creature would welcome her confidence, would love to pour out all she knew, ignoring the risk that Teresa Zuccola had run and lost to. It would be all in the approach . . .

"Do you know who I am, how I come to be here and why?" asked Lorna. Maria nodded. "Then you know I was kidnapped." A second nod. "There's not a soul here I can call my friend. I need a friend badly, Maria. I've never needed one more. Will you be my friend, someone I can confide in, someone I can trust?"

Maria hesitated before answering, searching Lorna's

eyes. Whatever she was looking for she evidently saw, for almost as quickly as worry had seized her she dismissed it, relaxing and displaying her toothless grin.

"If you want me . . ."

"I do, with all my heart." She had risen from the bed, walking to the girl, grasping her hands and squeezing them affectionately. Maria got up from the bench, padding softly to the door, opening it, glancing outside, then closing it and turning the key in the lock.

"What do you want to know?"

"About her, this dreadful place, this . . . Savoy."

"Oh my, we shall be up all night!" She laughed, then cocked her head and stared grimly. "Mistress, believe me when I say I need you as much as you me. Serving you will keep me busy and away from her." She effected a mock shudder. "We have to trust each other. We have no choice."

As she watched her plump herself down on the bench, the serpent of suspicion slithered across Lorna's mind, its arrival prompted by her experience with the nameless doctor in the room at the Gray Dragon. Was the girl being too willing to confide in her? Too cooperative too soon? Too eager to pledge her loyalty? Would she, in spite of all her outward warmth and friendliness, even sympathy, in her benign blue eyes, turn out to be Caroline-Louisa's favorite tattletale, brought with her from her native Germany for just such a service? It was the sort of craftiness that suited the queen's warped nature admirably.

She'd have to be on her guard.

"Every servant, every guard hates her with a passion," began Maria. "She's cruel, she's petty, she's a tyrant and the very vainest creature alive. She's the world's biggest hypocrite, pretending to be religious and sinning constantly, as badly as the wildest wanton." This disclosed, Maria crossed herself before going on. "Worst of all, you never know what she's going to do from one minute to the next."

"How do her subjects feel about her?"

"They hate her. Why shouldn't they, she treats them like dirt. Him they hate even more. Even though they feel sorry for him because he's mad, and can't help himself. He really is mad, you know. Andrea Fusselli overheard the doctor come right out and say that 'His Majesty is quite mad and there's nothing I or anyone else can do to allev . . .'"

"Alleviate?"

"'His condition.' That's what Dr. Brabossi said. Andrea swears to it."

"You say they hate him as well? Why?"

"The taxes. They're terrible. Taxes on everything. Taxes on taxes. Everyone lives from hand to mouth. He could lower them to where they were before Victor Emmanual was king, before Napoleon. He started them when he conquered Savoy. They say now that there's plenty of money in the Royal Treasury, but His Majesty refuses to lower the taxes."

"Then he actually still rules."

"No, she does, but the people don't know. It's what we call a castle secret, though how well it's kept who can say? We've hundreds of castle secrets. The people don't know how bad off he is. They only know he was wounded."

"What sort of man is he?"

"All horses and guns and marching and chasing the *pupu.*"

"What?"

Maria winked. "You know, the ladies, the pretty maids, those she calls her ladies-in-waiting, la de da. Sick or well, he chases them and rides and hunts and all . . . sometimes with Clothilde."

"Who's she?"

"The queen's sister. She lives here. She's a man; she even dresses like a man most of the time. She's a witch, in league with the Red Devil."

"I'm sure. Is she mean like her sister?"

"She's spoiled and childish, but not cruel. There's nobody like the queen, nobody in the world."

"She's really that bad?"

"Worse. She's so heartless. When she was little I'm sure she was the sort who pulled the wings off butterflies. She once ordered a serving maid hung up by the thumbs for a day and a night. For spilling soup. And if she so much as imagines you looked at her funny, in a way to displease her, she'll order you whipped; even the guards are whipped. The only two who can handle her are Count DeLeone and Paul, Captain Torzzini." Maria smiled and rolled her eyes.

"Who's he?"

"Her lover. And what a lover. They say his thing is as big as a club."

"She has a lover? Here in the castle? Right under her husband's nose?" Maria nodded. "Incredible, how do they get away with it?"

"Oh, the king doesn't know. She sleeps with him, too. She sleeps with guards. They say she's even slept with Dominic, the stableboy. She's not afraid; the king would never catch her, he's out of his head for days at a time. He sleeps in a room without windows no bigger than your bed. He likes to."

"Does he get violent?"

"Sometimes."

"What do they do with him then?"

"Lock him up in his room. Count DeLeone and the doctor take care of him."

"The count I've met," said Lorna grimly.

"He's to be made prime minister and will get a medal. They're always pinning medals on him."

"This one for landing the prize fish." Lorna frowned and shook her head. "You say they're making him prime minister?"

"Yes, General de Boigne, the old prime minister, died just before you got here. He was very sick. He looked like an old lion. He was sweet and jolly. Everyone loved him."

Maria talked until very late; her new mistress interjecting a question now and then. The overall picture brushed into clarity by the girl was as colorful as it was shocking. The castle was a viper pit of intrigue, of duplicity and blatant deceit. The monarchists were firmly in control of the duchy, but mistrust and jealousy flourished. The circle of the queen's favor was a small one, with far too many constantly pushing and shoving their way into it, driving others out in the process. The result was a never-ending change of faces, a situation ostensibly encouraged by Her Majesty. Overlooked and neglected in all this internal activity were the needs of the people of Savoy, the farmers, merchants, the men of the duchy's meager industry, the soldiers and students, the brutally overtaxed lower and middle classes, the majority populace who had served the House of Savoy in its innumerable petty wars, who had respected and honored their rulers through eight centuries. These people might as well not have existed for all the interest Caroline-Louisa and Charles Felix accorded them, other than to systematically empty their pockets and purses.

So Savoy was two duchies, the Savoy of the monarchists and the Savoy of the common people outside the walls, the faceless mass whose welfare and wellbeing came last on their rulers' list of priorities.

And beginning to emerge was a third Savoy, that of the *risorgimento,* whose aim, whose only reason for existence, was the elimination of the first Savoy in order to preserve the second.

II

Lorna slept fitfully, in spite of her exhaustion. Too much had happened in too short a time to dismiss with a yawn and the closing of her eyes. It was almost like a four-hour circus telescoped into twenty minutes, with all the performers seen too quickly to judge their skills, to appreciate and enjoy them. There was in this circus, however, little to appreciate and enjoy, and promise of far less in the future.

She was awakened before daylight by Maria to the sight of none other than the royal monitor of her plight hovering over the bed like the Angel of Death. Count DeLeone looked as if he'd been up for hours, particularly bright-eyed and cheerful and pleased with himself. Probably, she mused, sitting up, stifling a yawn and dispelling the cobwebs in order to grasp what he was saying, due to his promotion and the shiny new gray, white and gold medal joining the collection hanging from his chest. He pushed aside the bed hangings.

"Good morning, good morning. You have a busy morning ahead of you. Listen closely: While we were en route, shortly after we passed through the Straits of Gibraltar, a most unfortunate incident occurred here in Chambéry. General de Boigne, our most illustrious statesman and for nine years prime minister, passed away. The general was Chambéry's most generous benefactor. Some years ago he was in the British East Indian service where he amassed a great fortune." DeLeone let the curtain drop and began pacing as she stifled another yawn. "He founded two hospitals and gave generously to the poor and to civic improvements. De Boigne Street is named after him, and their High-

93

nesses plan to erect a monument in his honor. This morning his funeral will be held at the cathedral. At the cemetery a wreath will be placed on his casket. Queen Caroline-Louisa will place that wreath."

Lorna pointed to herself. "Queen Caroline-Louisa."

"Precisely. Her Highness has urgent matters of state to attend to. It's merely a conflict of priorities. Of course she's desolate at having to miss his funeral. Still, it does present you with an opportunity to wet your feet. You merely place the wreath on top of the closed casket, cross yourself so, fold your hands, and bow your head as in prayer." He finished miming the four actions then turned to Maria standing by. "You, maid, fetch your mistress's dress, hat, and shawl. Everything black, naturally, and don't forget a veil. No jewels, perhaps a ring, but that's all."

"Yes, Your Excellency." Off flew Maria to the closet in the other room.

"Tell me something," said Lorna, "what have you done with René?"

"Tallot? He'll be leaving for Paris shortly, while you're at the funeral."

"A vacation? Or do you feel safer with him miles away from me?"

"Do you seriously imagine I worry about a mincing homosexual? He's too innocuous, too pathetic to worry anyone. Forget him, you'll never see him again."

"I was becoming very fond of him."

"Mrs. Stone, don't do this."

"Do what?"

"That. You're tempting me to anger again. You are deliberately ignoring my title in this conversation. I've warned you before, you are to address me as Your Excellency."

"And if I don't, what will you do, order my head shaved again?"

"Your Excellency. Let me hear you say it."

"Old man, with your temper and your loud mouth

and all those jingling toys on your chest you frightened me at first . . ."

He took a step forward, seizing the curtains, ripping them away, his face black with fury. Maria stood in the doorway to the other room, her arms heaped with clothing, her eyes wide and staring fearfully. Seething, DeLeone smashed at Lorna with his fist, but she saw it coming and dodged it easily. Then she jumped out of bed.

"Punch me and you punch your precious queen! It's this bruised cheek your Savoyards will see at the funeral!"

He was trembling all over, his jaw tightly locked, his face purple. "You mind your tongue," he hissed. "Or you'll earn yourself more than punishment. I'm warning you for the last time!" Getting control of himself, he backed away, turning from her, crossing to the door.

"As to your first public appearance, you will conduct yourself as befits your station. With dignity, the royal air, that highborn haughtiness the common people expect in their betters; it's immensely effective. It reminds them of their status so that they better appreciate the status of all those with superior blood." He chuckled. "Don't misunderstand, I love them one and all, even the rabble, down to the flea-bitten beggars and thieving Gypsies." He studied her, smirking, malevolence firing the pupils of his eyes, setting them gleaming. "My instincts tell me you will play your role splendidly. You had better. You mustn't disappoint me or their majesties. We needn't go into the consequences if you do. Oh, yes, you will be escorted to the funeral and the graveside by Captain Torzzini. You'll like Paul, he's tall, handsome, one might even say beautiful, the sort that turns all the girls' heads, young and old. A charmer. Now get dressed. He'll be by shortly to pick you up."

DeLeone left, leaving the door open, Maria closing it.

"Mother of God," she cried, rushing to the bed and

tumbling the clothes down on it. "Why did you do that? Deliberately provoke him!"

"I did, didn't I." Lorna sat down on the bench tiredly. "Why? I expect because I had to. I'm the loser in this game, at least so far. The least I can get out of it is the satisfaction of seeing him worry about me, just a little bit. He keeps insisting on how much is at stake. Do you think I worry him, Maria?"

"He'll break your neck. He has a vile temper!"

"Don't I know. Yes, Your Excellency; no, Your Excellency."

"Is that so hard to say?"

"For this Yankee it's impossible! We fought a war to rid our vocabularies of such archaic nonsense."

"You're asking for it, begging . . ."

Lorna sighed and, turning about facing the mirror, set up her elbows and dropped her chin into her palms. "Perhaps, but I did it. It feels good. I'll probably do it again. Maybe because I don't care anymore."

"Are you giving up so soon?"

"Giving up what?"

"You know perfectly well. Getting out, getting away. Oh, you haven't said anything, I know, but that has to be what you want." Pity flooded the girl's round pink face. "Heaven only knows how you'll do it."

A flowing mane of jet black hair salted with premature gray, a face from brow to jaw to arouse any man's envy and any woman's fascination, shoulders broad enough "to serve tea from," as Grandmother Hastings had once described a man similarly endowed. Captain Paul Torzzini was even more attractive than the picture jointly etched upon her imagination by Maria and the count. Unhappily, the captain knew all too well how handsome he was; from the moment he took her hand at the door and brushed it with his lips, he posed and prattled and pranced and played upon her intrinsic detestation of male conceit in the manner of the most ridiculous fop in the most ridiculous

English novel ever to flow from a quill. She'd never met anyone so self-centered, so certain of his gifts, so utterly, unabashedly disgusting. By the time they departed the cathedral following the funeral cortege to the cemetery outside of town, she found herself reduced to two options. She could either fling open the carriage door and leap from it to get away from him or render herself deaf by ramming her index fingers into her ears up to their respective second knuckles.

"Will you kindly shut your mouth! *Please!*"

"Oh, dear me, did I say something to offend Your Highness? I surely didn't intend . . . I mean I pride myself on my superb manners, my gentility. I come from a long line of gentlemen soldiers; I'm often complimented on my passion for courtesy."

"I, I, I, I, I, I . . ."

She closed her ears and suffered through it, half-suspecting that DeLeone's selection of escort was either the old man's idea of a joke or his way of heaping additional coals upon the fires of her frustration. Torzzini was an absolute ass, the sort whom either of her brothers, though not as big, would dearly love to smash in the jaw and push in the creek to spare their sister the burden of his boring companionship.

The priest had finished consigning General de Boigne's soul to the keeping of Almighty God and had nodded at her, the signal to place the wreath. Captain Torzzini sidled closer to her and whispered.

"You are to say 'By the grace of God we herewith honor and esteem Chambéry's most generous benefactor and most illustrious son.' "

"Please . . ."

"Say it!" he hissed. "His Excellency's orders." He prompted her, whispering phrase by phrase in Italian. She repeated each in turn, injecting little sincerity in her tone, placing the wreath, crossing herself, bowing her head, pretending a few words of prayer, then stepping back. Suddenly there descended upon her the chilling awareness of hundreds of eyes boring into her back. She could not resist confirming her suspicions; turning, she caught a glimpse of the large crowd of townspeople drawn up in a semi-circle, all of whom had bowed their heads, thereby hiding their faces as Torzzini had walked her up to the grave. Now in every pair of eyes was the identical glare of pure loathing. Directed straight at her, invisible daggers thrusting into and through her. For one whom they despised to say anything, however eulogistic, over the remains of one whom they respected and loved, had seemingly opened the floodgates of their hostility.

Her heart began beating unnaturally loudly and her throat was suddenly dry. If she had ever seen abhorrence in her life, she was seeing it now, so bitter, so sharply focused, so penetrating she had to look away and down. The captain took her by the forearm, steering her back toward the carriage waiting in the shadow of a grove of pines. The gathering was breaking up, only the priest and the pallbearers remaining by the grave. She loosened her veil, letting it fall and dangle by one loop.

"What on earth is the matter, Your Highness?" he asked.

"Nothing."

"You're pale as old wax . . ."

"Nothing." Everything, none of it this simpering fool's concern. Maria had been right, though possibly guilty of understatement. These people didn't hate their queen—hate wasn't the word for it. There was no word to accurately describe what she'd seen in their eyes.

"Are you sure nothing's wrong?" He would press her and press her until she satisfied his curiosity with some explanation, however farfetched.

"Why did you make me say that?"

The footman had bounded up to the carriage door before them, whipping it open, bowing low, the meticulously brushed top of his hat reflecting the sun's glare.

"Is that what's upsetting you? You had to say it."

"However awkwardly?"

"You did passably well. It's to be quoted on the monument that's going to be erected for de Boigne. A direct quotation of Her Majesty's 'By the grace of God we herewith honor and esteem Chambéry's most generous benefactor and most illustrious son.' I thought it up! Adelbert positively adored it. Aren't I the cleverest dog you've ever met? Say I am, admit it!"

She pretended not to hear. Back in the carriage she was conscious of a wave of relief passing through her body, dissipating her anxiety. There had been no attempt on her life, no guns, no knives, no screaming fanatic throwing himself at her throat. Surely an opportunity the enemy had let slip by. Why—because of de Boigne? Because such a bloody act on such an occasion as this would be unseemly? What would the next occasion be, she wondered? Would it be somewhat more suitable to the deadly drama of assassination?

III

All afternoon was spent under Caroline-Louisa's critical eye in her chambers. The queen insisted on personally coaching her substitute in "the walk of a queen, the stance, rising, sitting, posing, gesturing . . ."

"Her face . . ." Caroline-Louisa clucked in exasperation and threw up her hands.

"It's perfect, Your Majesty," said DeLeone with the closest thing to genuine alarm Lorna had yet seen darkening his features. He was standing by, ramrod straight as usual, taking it all in, his shako under his arm, his medals in preposterously neat alignment, the ends of his moustache as sharply pointed as stilettos.

"It's not the face of a queen, Adelbert. Look, can't you see? Are you blind?"

"Her Majesty is right, Mrs. Stone. You should have a prouder, more regal look about you," said the count, nodding.

"More disdainful? More arrogant?"

Caroline-Louisa's hand flashed forward, slapping her soundly. So fast did it find her cheek, she hadn't even time to begin raising her own hand to protect herself.

"Mind your tongue, Yankee! No one gave you permission to speak. You just listen and obey."

The slap was the least of her humiliation. The afternoon dragged on, the sun lowering, the shadows lengthening and Caroline-Louisa reveling in her role of teacher. Again and again she corrected her, snapping at her, cursing her and eventually ordering her out with instructions to: "Practice, practice, practice. You'll see, we'll turn a sow's ear into a silk purse yet. Nothing's impossible."

That evening after dinner, served with neither monarch present, in the aftermath of her recovery from her introduction to Captain Torzzini, she made a decision that struck her as relentlessly logical, though not in the least encouraging. She came to it by putting herself in her assassin's shoes. When would he do the deed? What would be the best possible time, the ideal circumstances? When might he derive the maximum benefit from the taking of her life? Assassination of Queen Caroline-Louisa should trigger the revolution. What more appropriate signal to the people to cast off the shackles of their poverty and degradation, rise up and overthrow the monarchists? Ferment was in the air. She had felt it at the funeral. Or perhaps imagined she had. Her problem was that she had so little to go on, next to no knowledge of the *risorgimento* and those at work underground preparing to light the fuses.

In one respect her plight was a maddening contradiction of elements. The very people who planned to murder her were those she must find and convince of her innocence. Maria was sympathetic and surprisingly understanding for one unschooled in anything but fetching and carrying and otherwise waiting on her betters. But she was no revolutionary, indeed she was as apolitical as the stump the politician stands upon. To whom could she turn, who could she approach for help, advice?

The second night had arrived, cloaking the castle in its starless expanse, the wind rising in the east threatening rain. Perhaps another two-day storm to plunge her deeper into the melancholy nurtured by her dilemma? There was a knock at the door.

"Maria?"

"His Excellency," said a muffled voice.

Oh, Lord, she thought, DeLeone and his petulance, his nastiness. He was the last thing she needed at this stage.

"Just a moment."

She opened the door. He came barging in laughing, reeking of rum. Not the count, but Torzzini.

"Get out of here! *Out!*"

"I beg your pardon, Your Highness." He leaned back against the door closing it, slipping one hand behind him, and turning the key. "Is that any way to welcome a new friend? Pretty good imitation of Adelbert, no?"

His voice was somehow different, and his manner. More manly, without affectation, with none of the sissified inflections she'd found so annoying earlier in the day.

"What do you want?"

"To talk."

His tunic bulged. He brought out a half-filled bottle. "Do we have two glasses?"

"We don't have any!"

"Then we shall drink from the bottle. Like the renegade Neopolitan Mammone and his men. Did you know that Mammone actually drank his liquor from a human skull? They claim he never ate a meal without a freshly severed human head gracing the table."

"You're drunk. Please leave, I want to be alone."

"Oh, dear, what a blow to my ego. You must swear by the Virgin that you'll never repeat that outside this room. Think of my reputation!"

"What do you want, Captain?"

"Paul, please. And you are Lorna, Lorna Singleton Stone. You see, I've checked up on you. May I sit down? Thank you." He dropped down upon the vanity bench, throwing a glance into the mirror and running a hand through his hair. "We must talk, you and I."

"There's nothing I want to talk to you about."

"Then go to your door, yell for a guard, and tell him to throw me out."

"I would hope you'd have tact and intelligence enough not to stay where you're not wanted."

"Seriously, I do want to talk." He proferred the bottle, shook his head when she shook hers, took a swig, and wiped his mouth with the back of his hand, staining the lace on his cuff. "You're in quite a fix, you know that?"

"I'd have to be deaf, dumb, and blind not to."

"You need help."

"No! Whatever makes you think so?"

"Where's your maid?"

"In the kitchen eating a late supper. She'll be back shortly."

"Not too shortly, I hope."

"Aren't you running a risk coming here this time of night? What if somebody sees you and tells her?"

He shrugged. "I like living dangerously."

"I don't. I have troubles enough."

"Living dangerously is one of the character traits that makes me an excellent soldier."

"What's another, modesty?"

He laughed. Again he offered her the bottle, again she refused it. He downed a deep draught, lowering the level of the rum to within an inch of the bottom. He'd had too much drink already; his face was red and beginning to puff under the eyes. And they were slightly glazed.

"We've got to get you out of here. Out of Savoy," he said. He made an absurd face, bobbing his handsome head from side to side. "Over the border into France. Better yet down to the sea."

Her heart beat faster. "Why would you want to help me? What's in it for you?"

"My, my, such a suspicious nature. Why does there have to be something in it for me?" Reaching out he touched her arm sending a tremor up it into her shoulder. She pulled away. "Pay attention. I am not drunk. I'm too full of the fever to let myself get drunk."

"What fever?" she asked, her tone scoffing.

"The fever of revolution. It's in the air, you breathe it in, it seeps in through your pores, it fills your brain with its fire. Don't tell me you didn't see the looks on the faces at the funeral, their eyes . . ."

"I saw."

"It must have given you quite a turn."

"It scared the life out of me."

"It is impossible to plumb the depths of their hatred.
There never has been such hatred, not against the
French, not even the Austrians. Conditions in Savoy,
Piedmont, throughout Sardinia, are the worst ever. If
ever a nation were ripe for revolt. Picture it, Lorna,
two and a half million Savoyards under the thumbs of a
few hundred blue bloods whose veins need only be
pricked to prove them the liars and frauds they really
are. Pricked with bayonets and swords." His pewter-
gray eyes took on the wild look of the vengeance-
seeker, blade in hand, oppressor at his mercy. "Do you
know what lies beyond the Alps?" She shook her head,
mesmerized by his tone, his look, his patently fanatical
dedication to the cause he was preparing to expound,
his detestation of its adversaries, those whose actions
served to fuel the flames of dissent. "Beyond the Alps
is light. The people have come out of the Dark Ages,
out of the caves of ignorance and superstition into the
light. Why not the same for Savoy? Why not indeed?
Who shutters the entrances to our caves and keeps
us in darkness and poverty and despair? Who but the
monarchists, the royal gang. The collar around our
necks is the *macinato,* the soak-the-poor tax on bread,
on wine, on everything on the plate and in the cup of
the malnourished masses. And do you know what
makes the whole black picture even blacker?

"Go on."

"Napoleon. The little corporal with his *liberté, égalité,
fraternité.* With all the havoc he wreaked up and down
our territories the very worst calamity was his legacy,
the Code Napoléon. You see, it broke the iron hold of
the old nobility, temporarily, that is. And temporarily
elevated the cave dwellers to *égalité.* Our elders got a
taste of liberalism, just enough to whet their appetites
for more before Napoleon fell and the Old Order was
restored. Back came business as usual, down to the last
brutal regulation, the wholesale deprivation of liberties,

the taxes, the abuses . . . Overnight life became harsher even than before. But here now, perhaps I'm wrong." He laughed hollowly. "Perhaps Napoleon is to be hailed rather than damned. Perhaps his Code, our peoples' introduction to it, provides a more powerful prod to action than the *macinato,* the cruel neglect, their hatred for Caroline-Louisa and Charles Felix. Perhaps. Oh, and that's something else, our puny savior, Charles Felix, did you know that before he was shot he had actually started preaching liberalism? It was all wind to be sure; he still practiced the old despotism, the despotism she doles out to this day."

"Why are you telling me all this?"

"Because you're entitled to know how cold the water is before you venture in."

"I'm not in the least interested in your politics."

"You'd better be. There's no way you can stand apart and survive. You're either with us or against us. And against us you're doomed."

"How do you know that the moment you leave here I won't go running to her or to DeLeone and repeat every word you've said?"

"I know. I know you. That's the last thing you'd do. There's no currying favor with that scum."

She began pacing, her printed cashmere dressing gown gliding over the parquet floor. There was a knock. Maria called out. Lorna opened the door. Astonishment ignited the girl's features at the sight of Torzzini. She looked from one to the other mystified.

"Come in, quick, before someone sees you," said Lorna.

"No!" burst Torzzini. "Forgive me, Maria, I must ask you to give us a few more minutes of privacy."

Maria looked to Lorna for agreement. "Five minutes, dear. And for God's sakes, don't tell anyone he's here, not your dearest friend, promise?"

"I promise."

The girl went out closing the door. He strode forward, his saber scabbard clacking against his side buttons. He seized her hands. "You're with us. I can tell by your face!"

"With who? With what."

"The *carbonari,* the charcoal burners, the heart and soul of the *risorgimento.*"

"This is all very confusing. What on earth are you doing in this place? Surrounded by your enemies . . ."

"Don't be naïve. I was placed here by my superiors, of course."

"To spy."

He nodded. "Among other duties."

"You mean sleeping with her."

"Not a particularly unpleasant task."

"I'm sure."

"You're jealous. You are, aren't you?"

"Me? That's the stupidest thing I've ever heard. I couldn't care less what you two do. Probably because I don't know you from Adam!"

"You'll get to know me. We'll be seeing a great deal of each other. We're living refutation of the old saw, you and I. In this instance politics doesn't make strange bedfellows at all."

"A poor choice of words."

He grinned, a look calculated to set her heart beating faster, she was sure. It did just that.

"Is it?" he asked, feigning disbelief.

"Don't press your luck," she said quietly.

"You don't find me attractive?"

"You were anything but at the funeral; you were disgusting."

"I was playing my role. Who would suspect a simpering fop, the queen's bedwarmer, of treason?"

"Is that the way you carry on with her?"

"My God, no!" He eyed her with an amused look. I was just teasing you. But see here, would you like a step-by-step recapitulation of our most recent get together?"

"I'm not interested."

He sighed heavily. "A man does a lot for his country, believe me. Talk about above and beyond the call . . ."

"Poor man, what sort of sympathy do you prefer, a reassuring pat on the cheek, words of consolation? Are you trying to say you don't enjoy sleeping with her?"

He thought about this before answering, crinkling his brow and chin. "I suppose I don't. But she does . . ."

"I'm sure. Let's be serious," she said, sobering and searching his eyes. "What do you want with me in your revolution?"

He shrugged. "Who can say? How could we use the queen's double?" He grinned impishly. "I've a thought. We spirit you out of here and day after tomorrow, with the start of Holy Week we produce you at mass in the cathedral and you announce the abolishment of the *macinato*."

"I said be serious!"

"No joke, you could be helpful to us. And to yourself in the process. We could help you . . ."

"How?"

"Time will tell."

"That's discouragingly vague. How about when?"

"When we surface. As soon as Charles Felix and Caroline-Louisa are either assassinated or overthrown."

"You know very well who'll be assassinated."

"Not necessarily."

"You do inspire optimism. It's the words you choose . . ."

"When the sun sets on the great day you'll be alive, and free to leave."

"That could be months, years . . ."

"Months maybe, not years."

"I must be stupid, but I don't see any advantage for me on either side. They use me, you'd use me . . ."

"We'd protect you. Am I not protecting you? I'm grateful for the job."

"Just be alert and competent. Every time I step out of that carriage and face a crowd I'm taking my life in my hands."

"You're very brave."

"Don't be funny. I was shaking in my shoes this morning. I only do it because I know what Adelbert will do to me if I don't."

"Ah, yes, *poco gallo*.* Him I plan to deal with personally when our great day dawns."

"I asked you before, when?"

"I answered, I can't give you an exact date."

"Then it's all just talk, if and when. It's been that way since Napoleon, hasn't it? How long since Napoleon, Paul, how many years?"

"Fifteen." It was a grudging admission uttered in a subdued voice. "It'll be soon," he added, striving to reassure her. Every day we grow stronger. Every day more flock to our banner. Every day their majesties' hold on the people and on the throne weakens. You can see it, you can feel it. You know it in your heart, you just know it!"

"I know what wishful thinking is, too. I've indulged in it a great deal lately."

His hands holding hers had moved to her shoulders. He had been staring down at her, as if striving to solidify his image in her memory. Now he let his hands drop, releasing her.

"I'll see you day after tomorrow. I'll be escorting you to Conflans near Albertville, a few miles from here. You're to attend a dedication ceremony, the laying of the cornerstone of the new hospital, Her Majesty's latest bone tossed to the masses. You, Your Highness, will splatter a bit of mortar onto the stone and smile and wave."

"And will the crowd be instructed to bow and cheer for me?"

"Naturally. A simple display of heartfelt affection for their beloved queen."

"It's not only dangerous, it's nauseating. It's so sordid. I can't stand their eyes, their faces."

---

* little rooster.

"It's not their fault."

"I didn't say it was."

Maria knocked and called out. "Mistress?"

"Come in," said Torzzini, pulling open the door. Once again he took hold of Lorna's hands. "Courage, Lorna, everything will turn out beautifully."

"I'm sure it will. I only hope I live to see it."

IV

She had no idea how long she had been asleep when she was awakened, fighting for breath and terrified by a clammy hand covering her mouth. She could not make out his features in the darkness, but he was a big man, taller and broader even than Paul Torzzini. A thin sheet of ice spread between her shoulder blades and down her spine. Her heart thundered as she struggled frantically for breath and to free herself. Into her mind unclouding itself from sleep sprang the logical, ominous thought.

But he did not attack her. Instead he gagged her with a napkin, wrapped her in the counterpane and carried her out. Without sound or syllable. Down the corridor dotted with feebly burning sconces he bore her, through doors, down circular stairs, his boot heels clicking metallically on the granite steps. Down, down to an arched wooden door belted with cast-iron straps. Setting her on her feet, he pulled the counterpane from her trembling body. She tried to run, but he grabbed her by the arm, opening the door and pushing her through ahead of him.

The wall torches burned brightly, clearly illuminating the frightening sight. It was a medieval torture chamber. So low was the ceiling she could almost reach up and touch the stones glistening with moisture. An iron maiden stood ajar in one corner, its spikes mutely declaring its evil purpose. In front of her was the rack, the bed, the rollers at each end, their ropes wound neatly around them. Fastened to the wall at the right was a large frame, in it pincers, barbed hooks suspended from chains, and knotted ropes in various sizes.

A forge with more pincers and irons thrust into its unfired coal bed stood opposite the iron maiden. Pulleys hung from the ceiling; thumbscrews and iron boots were lined up along the walls on either side of the door. Under the arch leading to cells in the rear was a whipping post, and conveniently at hand, a revolving metal stand from which leather whips dangled.

She gasped, backing against the door, but the guard who had brought her down and was now standing beside her slipped his hand behind her back and pushed her forward. She stumbled over the stone floor, catching the edge of the rack to keep from falling.

A man emerged from the shadows, a small man, his complexion dark, a brooding look on his face. He was beginning to bald, his widow's peak wedging down his forehead, clinging to life there, stalling the full retreat of his brow and lending him a Satanic look, although he wore only the merest trace of a moustache and his chin was barren of beard. An ugly scar disfigured the side of his brow. He motioned to the rack.

"Tie her."

"*No!*"

The loudness of her own voice in the confined space pounded her eardrums.

"Tie her."

"What have I done?" she asked breathlessly, half-sobbing. "Why must you torture me?"

"Do it!"

"At once, Your Majesty . . ."

Your Majesty! Charles Felix. This little, insignificant looking boy-man playing at soldier in his red tunic and black belt, his brass buttons and white gloves jauntily thrust under one epaulet board, was he. She protested loudly, struggling, pounding the guard with her small fists, scratching at his jacket in a vain effort to reach his face. It was useless. In moments she lay on the bed of the rack, wrists and ankles securely fastened to the rollers.

"Now get out," rasped Charles Felix.

"Yes, Your Majesty." The guard clicked his heels and bowed.

"Stay outside, see that we're not disturbed."

"Yes, Your Majesty."

The door creaked closed behind the man and the king threw the upper and lower bolts securing it. Then he returned to his captive, hovering over her, his dark eyes blazing with the madness that possessed him.

"Don't look so, I'm not going to hurt you."

"Please untie me. Let me go, please . . ."

"I can't."

"I beg you . . ."

"Beg all you please. I can't. I won't. You can't make me."

A wild thought needled through the stark terror filling her mind. "I'm your wife, don't you recognize me? Release me, I command you!"

"I'm king. You can't command me. Besides, you're not Caroline. You're too slender. I know all about you. Do you know where you are? Thirty feet below the ground." He pointed upward. "My castle's up there. She's up there. She can't see us, I've locked the door."

"Untie me, please, I'll do anything you say, but don't do this, don't . . ."

"Do what?"

"Torture me. God in heaven no!"

"Of course I won't torture you. What do you take me for, de Torquemada, Nicholas Emyerico? I'd never dream of doing such a beastly thing. Ha, not that I wouldn't enjoy watching somebody being tortured; it would be fascinating, crushing a helpless traitor's thumbs, stretching his limbs. They say a shoulder dislocated makes a popping sound. Pop. Pop. But you're not here to be tortured, never."

"Then untie me. Please untie me."

"I can't. I surely cannot. Not until we're done." He moved up to the rack and gripping the top of her nightgown ripped it apart the full length of her body. The madness gleaming in his eyes brightened perceptibly at the sight of her nakedness, her full breasts beaded with nervous perspiration rising and falling, the shining concavity of her stomach, the soft mound of pubic hair nestling between her thighs.

"You look so helpless, your eyes. You're terror-stricken, aren't you?"

"Please don't. She'll find out, she'll have me killed. You wouldn't want that."

He wasn't listening; it was as if he had closed his ears. He neither heard her beseech him nor saw her anguish. The more she pleaded, the more intense became her preoccupation with her nakedness. He ran his little-boy hands up and down her body, then began kissing her breasts and stomach and thighs and legs, slavering over her like a rabid dog, setting her heart hammering. He was gradually working himself into a frenzy. She could see his lust develop, enlarge, engorge him and drive the last remnants of sanity out of his mind, reddening his dark face, his pupils dilating enormously, setting his forehead and cheeks and the palms of his hands sweating, the perspiration pouring from them. Most ghastly of all was the sound rising from his throat, the guttural voice of his carnal lust. It so filled her with horror she began to scream, her voice slamming against the stones surrounding her, reverberating, fanning the flames of his bestiality.

He pulled himself up onto the rack, dropping down upon her, his member hard, driving forward between her trembling thighs, penetrating, knives of excruciating pain radiating outward from her sex, exploding, piercing her thighs and her stomach. And cutting off her anguished scream, reducing it to a pathetic sobbing.

V

Drifting along the edge of sleep wrapped in the cloak of languor induced by Dr. Brabossi's sedative seemed to soften the impact of the horror. Until her visitors pulled her back to full awareness. Count DeLeone stood stiffly at the door, his face rigid with concern while Caroline-Louisa sat at her bedside babbling, carrying on like a solicitous big sister.

"You'll be relieved to hear that the guard who dragged you down to that dreadful place and . . . Well, he has confessed and will be severely punished."

"Who cares about the guard? What about your . . ."

No, she thought, catching herself. The queen knew, she had to. Correcting her, reminding her of the truth in front of DeLeone, was pointless. It could only infuriate her. She, Lorna, might even find herself accused of seducing Charles Felix. From brief past experience with the imperious-looking creature shadowing the coverlet she recognized it as the sort of convoluted reasoning at which the queen was extraordinarily adept.

"His Highness will be seeing to it personally."

"To what?" Lorna asked, having lost the thread of the conversation.

"Punishing the fellow, of course. You can be sure any man who dares take advantage of a defenseless woman under this roof had better be prepared to pay in hard coin. We've heard the king say it, and we couldn't agree more."

DeLeone approached the bed. Out of the corner of her eye Lorna caught a glimpse of Maria in the doorway to the other room showing her face and vanishing, closing the door quietly. The count seemed genuinely sympathetic, sincerity in his eyes and in his voice. She fleetingly imagined he'd had a complete change of heart toward her, that what the king had done was beyond his tolerance, and he'd at last had his fill of the whole foul business. Could that be possible, or was she once again slipping into the comfortable snare of wishful thinking?

"May I add my own wishes for your speedy recovery," he said in a chastened tone, almost as if he blamed himself for what had happened. "A sorry business this, very sorry indeed."

"I'll be all right," she said quietly. "I appreciate your concern, Your Excellency."

He liked that; it pleased him so he almost fell victim to the temptation to smile.

"Rest today," said Caroline-Louisa. "We want you to be all well again for tomorrow."

"Conflans?"

The queen nodded. "In the afternoon. A dedication ceremony. You'll love the old town, the Chateau du Manuel, the Ramparts, the Tarine Gate and Sarrazine Tower. You must get Captain Torzzini to show you the view from the Esplanade de la Grande Roche."

"I shall, Your Majesty."

Caroline-Louisa smiled. Lorna wondered what thoughts were racing through the queen's mind. This sudden willingness to cooperate must come as a complete surprise.

"Tell me," continued the queen, "what was your impression of Paul, er, Captain Torzzini?"

"He seems very nice."

Caroline-Louisa smiled strangely. "Very nice. Do you think he's handsome?"

"Very."

The queen nodded, the same enigmatic look on her face. She rose from her chair.

"You stay in bed. You need rest more than anything."

"Yes, Your Majesty."

They left. No sooner had the door closed behind them that she found herself fighting off the impulse to laugh out loud. Unhappily she ached too severely to enjoy a good laugh. She'd been so polite their jaws had practically dropped out of their faces. Though why shouldn't she be polite? Why not play their game? There'd be little to fear after tomorrow, with Paul spreading the word that she was an imposter, and that murdering her would accomplish nothing.

Now she must think about escape, with his help. Would he help her? The question stirred an uneasy feeling. She'd seen the look in his eyes and the eyes of other men, even poor dear Philip's. The telltale narrowing of the lids, the look of lust as it roused itself in his brain, the uncontrollable craving. . . .

Paul. He was more than handsome, outrageously beautiful seemed more apt a description. Little wonder Caroline-Louisa kept him on a leash.

Her imagination rose on its wings, circled, and flew swiftly off, easily outdistancing her common sense. To feel his arms about her, his warm lips pressing hers, their tongues meeting, thrashing, the masculine odors of his body intoxicating her, unleashing her passion. The foreplay, and fondling, the finding. Thrusting her hips upward she captured him; he began to move inside her, explore her, slowly, gently, tenderly, then faster, bucking. . . .

Great God, what was she thinking! Here, but a few hours ago she'd been brutally ravished, her most intimate areas pummeled and bruised. Intercourse with any man should be the farthest thing from her mind. With the doctor's sedative now all but worn off completely and the discomfort returning, the dimmest thought of lovemaking should repel her!

But it did not. Blame Captain Paul Torzzini. Blame the look in his gray eyes, the sensuous way he worked his mouth to form his words, the deep, sultry tone of his voice, his hand touching her forearm, sending that tremor up to her shoulder. Being attracted to a man was one thing; being attracted to one whom you clearly impressed, who looked at you, drank you in, and could not begin to conceal his reaction was something else.

Would he help her to get away? Would he willingly deprive himself of what he believed was a certain conquest? Would any man? Or woman?

Her thoughts flew back to the dungeon. First sight of it had been almost as frightening as what had followed. Charles Felix was surely as mad as Bedlam's best, a wild animal. In his madness he had ravaged her; in the period of lucidity that followed he had accused the guard and ordered him imprisoned and punished. Was that the reaction of a sane man, or was it his twisted brain twisting logic, his conscience demanding punishment for the deed. For anyone but the culprit.

She called to Maria who came hurrying in, her pigtails down, her skirts rustling softly.

"Can I get you something?"

"Yes, a knife."

"Knife?"

"A small one." She held up her fingers five inches apart. "No longer than this. Too long and it'll be hard to carry and conceal."

"Just long enough to kill."

"That's it. I intend to wear it. What happened last night will never happen again. Go down to the kitchen, find one, and sneak it out."

Maria nodded, but the look on her face said she disapproved. Lorna could hardly let that dissuade her. She'd get it and when she was up and about, tie it around her leg with a ribbon or bit of cloth. At night she'd sleep with it under her pillow next to her hand. And the next time, if there was a next time, she'd use it, she would drown him in his own blood!

"King or no king!"

She slept and ate and recovered as fully as she could expect by the following morning but for an overall achiness and a well-distributed collection of yellowing bruises that would be visiting her flesh for a week or more. After her midday meal Paul looked in on her. He found her standing at the window staring out at the snow-capped mountains.

"I didn't even hear about it until this morning," he said after they'd greeted one another. "I'm probably the last person in the whole place to know."

"It's over, I'm all right now. I'd really rather not talk about it."

"I understand." She laughed mirthlessly. "What's funny?"

"You understand. Not you, Paul, any man. Can any man understand rape? Can you know something you haven't experienced? Do you know what the worst of it is? Not the shock, not the pain, not even the fear of being killed. No, worse than anything is the feeling of utter helplessness that seizes you. You struggle, you become weaker and weaker, then exhausted. His eyes light up with triumph and he takes you. You're as helpless as a rag doll. He's reduced you to a pliant slave to his lust. And you're left with one thought only in mind, get it over with."

"I thought you didn't want to talk about it."

"I don't."

He shook his head. "Amazing."

"What?"

"The flexibility of feminine logic. By the way, you'd better do what you usually do with your face. And get dressed, the royal coach will be at the outer gatehouse in half an hour."

"You haven't forgotten your promise."

"To let everyone know you're not the real queen? Certainly not. If I can, if there's a chance, I'll get somebody's ear in Conflans. We'll get you through this one and from now on there'll be no need to worry about that."

A knock sounded. "Yes?" she asked.

"His Excellency Prime Minister DeLeone," said a voice not the count's but somehow familiar. It was

Captain Crespi accompanied by DeLeone in civilian clothes, bereft of his medals, as unimpressive and innocuous-looking as a footman. He smiled at Torzzini and nodded.

"Captain, there's been a change in plans. Captain Crespi here will be accompanying Mrs. Stone to Conflans."

"What?" Lorna glanced at Paul.

"I don't understand, Your Excellency," began Paul.

"It's very simple, you stay, Rudolph goes. Her Majesty's orders."

Lorna's heart sank. So the royal jealousy had been aroused, had it? Fortunately for her, DeLeone appeared to have overlooked her stifled gasp in reaction. Paul managed to conceal his disappointment from the two men, although not from her. It was obviously pointless for either of them to question the decision. To do so would only raise DeLeone's suspicions which would have been communicated to Caroline-Louisa within minutes.

Crespi remained as DeLeone and Paul departed. The captain waited in the other room as she put on makeup and a gown of white velvet with a train covered with lace and a design of rosebuds. Maria brought her slippers with small bows ornamenting the insteps. She limited her jewelry to four strands of pearls and a coronet of brilliants. Captain Crespi helped her put on her satin dust cloak.

The coach that was to take them to Conflans awaiting them at the outer gate was Caroline-Louisa's favorite, the carriage and body richly ornamented with laurel and carvings, beautifully gilt. Four large tritons supported the body with four braces covered with green morocco leather and decorated with gilt buckles. The two tritons placed at the front of the carriage supported the driver, and, like those at the rear, were carved with the imperial fasces, surmounted by tridents. The driver's footboard was a large scallop shell, the nautical motif consistent in the overall design. The panels and doors were adorned with the royal coat of arms and other emblems and the interior linings of the carriage were of scarlet velvet.

The vehicle far outstripped comparison with the somewhat common-looking victoria that had taken her to and from the funeral two days earlier. This ornate contraption had to be one of a kind, she decided worriedly, stepping into it. Certainly in the duchy. And easily recognizable for miles on this lovely, unusually clear day. A perfectly splendid target wheeling along the road snaking through the mountains and crossing the valleys on the way to their destination.

An army could hide in these peaks, she thought, nervously staring out the window, her thumping heart keeping time with the clopping of the horses. And riddle this lovely creation, in seconds convert the scarlet velvet-lined coach into a scarlet velvet-lined coffin.

Crespi sitting beside her seemed to be prey to the same fears, from the look on his face. He kept glancing out the window and once, within yards of a col, stuck his head out and called to the driver to pull up and brake. The footmen seated at the rear and the eight dragoons escorting them got down as Crespi got out. He walked ahead a few paces to the col, peering out from under his hand in all directions, then got back in and ordered them on their way.

He didn't seem to think it necessary to explain his actions, not that she needed any explanation. They passed through a valley green with spring and sown with a galaxy of wild daisies. A huddled mass of sheep moved slowly over the grass, a great woolly wave undulating toward them. A marmot raced for cover and here and there white partridge revealed their presence. The breeze curling down from the snow-mantled heights behind them sang spiritedly through the poplars stretching down both sides of the road. Scrubbed-looking, gleaming pink and white with thatched and tiled roofs, Conflans lay directly ahead.

The sun shone as white as the plume in the captain's

shako as he helped her out of the coach in front of a large crowd bowing as one, straightening and staring at her. She had stiffened in apprehension, but the look in their eyes was not at all like that in evidence at de Boigne's funeral. The women stood with their kerchiefs tied tightly under their chins, their shoulders drooping, all but frozen at attention, their hands folded beneath their cotton aprons. Their eyes seemed to be almost pleading for reprieve from their miserable lot. The small children clinging to their skirts and ogling her were for the most part scrawny and unhealthy looking, their curious eyes darkly shadowed in their sunken faces. The men, like their women clad in peasant black, studied her inquiringly, stoically.

They presented a pitiful sight that tugged so at her heart she almost ran to the two little girls nearest her, arms outstretched to embrace and comfort them. A symbolic gesture, as if she were embracing and comforting one and all.

These people were starving, not for food, she knew, but for something just as essential to nurture and sustain them. Perhaps it was the assurance that their queen recognized them as living, feeling, suffering, poverty-shackled, discouraged and disheartened human beings, and that she honestly cared, that she was grateful for their loyalty and respect in spite of their condition and loved them as a mother loves her children, apart from and more devotedly than all other things. It was this affection to which they felt entitled, and therefore craved; it and their religion affording the buoyancy that kept them from drowning in their despair.

A brass band, seven men in bedraggled and ill-fitting uniforms, struck up a march, appropriately sadly out of tune.

The bells of the brass instruments captured the brilliance of the sun as the little town broiled under its remorseless assault. Perspiration gathered on the band leader's broad pink brow and ran down his face, catching in his moustache, causing it to droop pathetically.

His musicians struggled through the tune. Across the street a tall coral-colored building stood high above those on either side of it. Its façade was Moorish, three pairs of slender columns rising to arches, the center and largest arch surmounting double front doors. Above the arches the building was being refurbished and repainted, a scaffold running laterally across it, a large canvas hanging from the roof concealing the uncompleted work.

The band plodded on. A group of neatly but uncomfortably dressed officials, including the mayor, bowed and scraped, Lorna rewarding them with the warmest smile the heat and her depressed state of mind could permit her to display. It had to be 130 degrees in the sun, she thought; it almost burned the lungs just to breathe, and the mountain breeze had yet to wander down from the heights and bring even temporary relief to the town. A stout stone fountain topped by a wrought-iron crucifix stood in the center of the cobbled street some distance down the way in the direction of the church. From its many spigots spewed slender rivulets of water that looked to be ice cold and as sweet to the taste as fine wine. She ran the tip of her tongue over her lips in unqueenly fashion and turned her eyes from the sight.

The crowd pressed forward as the mayor and his committee circled Lorna and Captain Crespi and escorted them a dozen steps to the dedication site. The foundation of the hospital had been laid out and staked and excavation begun. A tarpaulin was whisked away revealing a rectangular block of granite inscribed Anno Domini MDCCCXXX. It sat upon wooden rollers; alongside it was its permanent position squarely atop the foundation stone. She was handed a trowel, on it a small portion of mortar; the mayor spoke briefly, bowed to her for the dozenth time, swinging his hat forward as her cue. The single snare drum in the band rolled briskly, and she mumbled a few words in dedication and flung the mortar onto the foundation stone. A mason kneeling behind it skillfully added more mortar and screeded it as the band struck up another tune. The crowd cheered with all the enthusiasm it could generate and four other workers held two crowbars over the bed of mortar. The cornerstone was pushed onto them, they positioned it above its place, rolling out the bars, and letting it drop neatly.

It was all seemingly well rehearsed, smoothly carried out, and mercifully brief. But the moment the stone was set in place, even before the mason could set about scraping the excess mortar from the joint there came the sound of a gunshot. Across the street on the roof of the pink, white-arched building, stood a man with a hood over his head, holes cut for his eyes, waving the flag of Savoy in one hand and wielding a shining two-edged sword in the other, bringing it down onto the first rope, then the second holding the canvas in place. Away it fell revealing six words crudely lettered in red paint:

FREE SAVOY!
DEATH TO THE MONARCHISTS!

"Viva Savoy! Viva Savoy!" he shouted.

She had gasped, her voice joining that of the crowd even before Crespi translated for her. The mayor reacted shamefaced, mopping his fat cheeks, flinging his hands in embarrassment, apologizing verbosely.

"We will capture the wretch. He'll be behind bars shortly, I promise you, Your Highness. I'm so sorry. This is terrible, shocking! What must you think of Conflans?"

Crespi responded to this before Lorna could, displaying a presence of mind she never would have attributed to him. He assured the mayor that the incident was of small moment, and that his honor's embarrassment was understandable, but uncalled for. This seemed to relieve the mayor and all the others within earshot. Meanwhile, at the captain's direction, her escort had mounted up and ridden off to assist in apprehending the man, since vanished from the roof of the building.

"Are you all right, Your Majesty?" asked Crespi.

"I'm still alive, Captain," she replied airily. "Let's hope I stay that way until your soldiers decide to come back."

His face clouded; it wasn't the response he expected. It only worried him; precisely her intention.

"Perhaps we'd best get back into the coach." His nervousness was aggravating his speech impediment, thickening his tongue.

She nodded. He waved to the driver high up on his scallop shell sitting talking to the footmen some ten yards away. He snapped his reins starting the horses toward them. The eight dragoons came thundering out from behind the arch-fronted building, returning from the chase.

"They got him!" called the one in the lead to Crespi.

If indeed "they" had, she had no wish to stay and wait for them to return. One of her footmen dropped the step and Crespi assisted her up into the coach. The band struck up another march, the driver swung his stallions about and off they rolled, sent away by the cheers of the crowd, the dragoons snugging their chin straps with their faces, staring impassively straight ahead, following at a trot, forming a protective barrier between the coach and their queen, and Conflans and its zealous *carbonari*.

A quarter of a mile down the dusty road four of the dragoons galloped by, two skirting the ditches on either side and taking up positions in front of the coach horses.

It was over, she reflected wearily. With nothing like a close call, only a melodramatic reminder that the monarchists' opposition was as active as ever.

"Relax, Mrs. Stone," said Crespi jauntily. "In less than two hours we shall be inside the circle of mountains surrounding Chambéry, within sight of the town. Twenty minutes after that you'll be in your rooms."

"I can't wait."

"Come now, they're more comfortable than the inn in Montélimar. At least you don't have pigs under your windows."

"Quite right, Captain, now they come in through the door."

"Really, Mrs. Stone, is that fair? What harm have I done you personally? Be specific."

"I think I'll nap. It's been rather a tiring afternoon."

"It's the sun. It's much hotter up in the mountains; we're closer to it up there you know."

"Of course." She almost laughed in his face, but settled for a pitying shake of the head. Such a consistently thoroughgoing ass he was! René Tallot had pegged him perfectly. Adelbert's puppy . . . wet nose, panting tongue, wagging tail and all. She missed René, and the thought that she would never see him again saddened her.

Propping herself in the corner, jouncing along, she hesitated to surrender to sleep, her thoughts rushing back to Conflans and the incident. The poor man; actually he'd done nothing, beyond interrupting the ceremony, startling everyone with his gun, and cutting a couple of old ropes. Disclosing his message had been, his only serious crime.

She would be happy to see this day end. By the time her next public appearance came around, even if they were to send her out tomorrow, by then Paul would have alerted the *carbonari*.

What would the people say, she wondered, when they learned that the queen to whom they bowed was no more than a conscripted imposter? What could they say that would make any difference in the monarchists' scheme of things? What the opposition declared, the monarchists would simply deny. Everything was that easy, every problem that simple to deal with when the throne was yours.

The coach rumbled along, slowing as it climbed into the mountains. The saddle over which they would be passing beckoned less than twenty yards ahead. She turned her attention to the scenery. It was magnificent, even more beautiful than that stretching from before Pont-de-Beauvoisin to Lac d'Aiguebelette and its surroundings. A score of different shades of green created a patchwork deepened here and there by the shadows spilled from the heights. Below and behind them lay Conflans, which continued to shrink as they climbed, all pink and white, like pale amethysts and white diamonds cut, arranged, and set in the emerald brooch of the valley.

The sun turned the snow-capped peaks into white fire, so dazzling it hurt the eyes. She drew her duster tightly about her against the chill and reflected on her companion's senseless explanation of why it was hotter in the mountains than below. With the wind up and swirling about the peaks it had to be one hundred degrees cooler. It certainly felt it!

The coach gained the summit and started down, the road twisting sharply, pulling sheer drops of a thousand feet and more up perilously close to the wheels. Down they rocked and rattled, the driver holding the brakes against the front wheels, slowing their descent, keeping the horses tightly reined, minding the treacherous going, easing them down, down, down onto level ground. They reached the foot of the mountain without mishap. He cracked his whip and away they flew, rounding a corner, all but hurling her and Crespi, seated opposite, clear across their respective seats.

"Slow down, you fool!" yelled the captain out the window. The driver obeyed; not a moment too soon. They had barely come out of the turn into a straight stretch running clear to the base of the next set of peaks when the coach suddenly lurched frightfully, all but toppling over, careening and screeching to a stop, the right front corner crashing down hard, tumbling Lorna and the captain into it. She landed on top of him. He helped her off, sitting her back on her seat atilt, both of

them somewhat dazed. He held her by the shoulders to keep her from falling back onto him.

"Grab the strap! Hold on tight . . ."

"You've bumped your head."

He rubbed the back of it, wincing, shaking it. The wheel slipping off the axletree had rolled ahead of the coach, slowing gradually, flopping down into the ditch. One of the footmen, both of whom had by some miracle managed to keep their places, unlatched the door and helped her out.

"Are you all right?" asked Crespi.

"All right. You? Your head?"

"It's the very spot where you hit me with that candlestick at the inn, thank you, but I'll live."

She almost said, What a pity.

Deprived of the wheel, the arm of the axletree had come down so hard it was, as Crespi observed: "A miracle it didn't snap clean off."

The dragoons had dismounted, two of them running ahead to recover the wheel. The others, along with the driver and the two footmen, set about raising the corner of the coach readying the arm to receive the wheel. Crespi barked orders, making his presence and his rank felt and unappreciated, she noted.

She wandered off, moving into the tall grass sprinkled with daisies, their yellow eyes gawking, their white ruffs bobbing in the breeze, the grass itself leaning in great wide waves, reflecting the glistening sun on its smooth inner surface.

"Not too far there," called Crespi, waving and coming away from the coach toward her. By now the wheel had been brought up and restored to the axletree. The driver was poking through the box under his seat looking for a pin to cotter the wheel in place. She pretended she didn't hear Crespi, raising her face to the sun, feeling its glorious warmth against her cheeks. Sitting, she held her arms out to the sides and let herself fall backward into the grass. It was as soft as a bed of down and smelled so fresh, so clean, the air filling her lungs all but intoxicated her.

Suddenly beneath her the world exploded, the ground shuddering violently, the sound so deafening it smashed against her eardrums nearly ripping them and splitting her brain in two. She winced and cried out in pain and dared to raise her head and look. A great orange plume undercushioned by a cloud of black smoke rose from the spot where the coach had stood, lifting pieces of it as well as rock, clods of earth, hats and limbs, twenty feet in the air. Bodies ascended half that height, backs arching, bowing grotesquely. Down they plummeted like bales of hay tossed from the loft to the floor of a barn. The horses whinnied and died, men called feebly, crying out, dying before her eyes, the carnage becoming visible as the settling smoke cleared.

Only she and Crespi had survived, the captain having crossed the ditch and entered the field, and she lying on her back in the grass escaping the full brunt of the blast. Two of thirteen.

Crespi, however, appeared seriously injured, blood spurting from a jagged cut down his cheek where in falling he had apparently struck a rock. He was also severely shaken, possibly suffering concussion, even internal injuries.

"You . . . ?" he rasped, his voice taut with pain.

So stunned she was unable to speak, she could only nod. She had risen to her knees, her tiara coming loose tumbling into the grass. Retrieving it she restored it to her head, getting to her feet and starting toward him. She helped him up, her eyes drawn past him to the gory sight, the corpses flung about in confusion, the coach reduced to blackened kindling, the dead horses littering the road.

"Great God," she murmured.

He had flattened the palm of his hand against his cheek, stanching the blood. In his eyes was the look of a wild man, the look of Charles Felix, as if concussion had snapped his brain. But he spoke coherently.

"That was meant for you."

"You don't have to say it. The wheel . . ."

"It saved your life, falling off when it did."

"Look at them, look!"

"How could such a thing happen? We come all the way from Chambéry, we stand in full view of hundreds of people, the coach . . ." He seemed bewildered.

"Don't you understand?" He stared at her dull-eyed, thoroughly mystified. "The man on the roof with the flag and sword. It was a diversion; all eyes turned to him when we heard the gun."

"Yes, yes, and somebody got under the coach . . ."

"Either then or when you sent your men riding off after him."

He started to defend his actions, then hesitated and for a moment looked as if he were about to collapse altogether. His round, dark face was becoming ashen. She helped him to sit in the grass, and made a pad of one of his gloves and gave it to him to hold against his cheek.

"You've lost a lot of blood."

"I . . . I must get help. We must get back . . ."

"Where, back over the mountains to Conflans or to Chambéry?"

"Chambéry, of course."

She shook her head. "In your condition you'd never make it."

"I will, I must . . ."

Shading her eyes from the sun, she glanced up and down the road. Back toward Chambéry, the view was blocked by the mountains and a cloud of dust that rose from a spot midway down the slope. Horses, she thought hopefully, fearing the wild chamois that frequented the mountains feeding on blue gentian and saxifrage. Crespi looked ready to pass out. He was bracing himself upright with both hands, his eyes glazed with pain, his breathing rapid, the sweat rolling down his face.

"I'm so thirsty . . ."

"Hang on, I think somebody's coming." She nodded toward the tiny dust cloud.

He brightened. "Perhaps from Albigny. It's closest, we bypassed it on the way." He tried to rise, but she restrained him gently.

"Stay where you are, save your strength."

"I must look to the others, I am in command . . ."

"There's nothing to look to, they're all dead. Even the horses."

"What a pity." He looked worried, fearful that he would be held personally responsible for the deaths of the eleven, she guessed. Again she glanced about. Conflans lay northeast of Chambéry, which meant that the French border was west, under the sun in roughly the opposite direction. How far? she wondered. Reachable on foot? The land seemed to flatten to the west and south, but the border could be a hundred miles away. With no horse, no money, dressed as she was, it might just as well be a thousand. To the north lay Switzerland, probably closer, but rugged going through the mountains on foot. Either way she would have to wait until nightfall. In daylight, looking as she did, dressed as she was, she'd be begging attention, and with it trouble.

She took off her tiara and examined it. She could loosen the brilliants with a rock, use them to buy transportation to either border and sneak across. Then what? How far would the stones take her? They were diamonds, they could take her around the world, if she could find someone avaricious or bold enough to do business with their queen. And keep their mouths shut about it. The situation was becoming more bizarre by the minute. If only she knew something about the countryside, where to head, what to look for. In two hours the sun would begin to set . . .

While she pondered, the cloud of dust reached the base of the mountains to the southwest. There were riders, at least three, possibly more.

Attempting to reach the French border would be difficult if not impossible, she decided reluctantly, certainly under these circumstances—lacking proper clothing, a horse and money, florins and French francs. There was one more problem; Crespi was far from finished. Were she to leave him he would betray her to the first person who came along. His uniform and the wreckage in the road would be sure to impress anyone of the validity of his explanation. They would be certain to catch up with her long before she reached either border, and drag her back to the castle to face Caroline-Louisa's wrath.

To make a try was tempting, but her intelligence overruled the thought. Four riders defined themselves far down the road, shimmering perceptibly as waves of heat undulated straight upward in front of them.

Very soon now they would reach them.

VI

She threw herself onto the bed exhausted in mind and body. The riders had taken the two of them into Albigny, where Crespi was treated by a doctor. Afterward, the local police had provided an escort to Chambéry.

"It was dreadful, Maria, hideous. Only a minute earlier the two of us had been sitting in the coach . . ."

"The *carbonari* will not stop until they have assassinated you."

"Paul has promised to explain to them."

"Captain Torzzini? Oh, forgive me, I forgot. He sent you a message by Teresa Zuccola."

"What message?"

"He told her, she came here and wrote it down. I hid it in the pocket of your dressing gown."

The message was brief. He wanted her to meet him at midnight in the chapel.

"Why so late, I wonder?" she mused aloud, crumpling the paper, handing it to Maria. "Burn it."

"Yes, yes . . ."

"Perhaps Her Highness is keeping him, ah, occupied around the clock."

"That must be it, mistress. Holy week is almost upon us."

"What does that have to do with it?"

"She is piling up sins for confession. Poor Father Asquino, what an earful he will get. And him with a weak heart."

"Maria, you're priceless."

Maria helped her undress and then went for fresh water for her toilette.

"I'll bring you supper. You rest. You could sleep, I'll wake you before midnight."

"Get me a bit of bread and cheese. And maybe some tea."

Wrapped in her white muslin nightdress she dined somewhat Spartanly on freshly baked bread and a brie. She was finishing her tea when DeLeone appeared. He was extremely upset over the explosion and demanded her version of what had happened. He made little effort to conceal his desire to pin down Crespi's behavior during their time in Conflans. She saw no pressing reason why she should position the blame on the captain's shoulders, although at the time and even now she had no doubt that his dispatching the dragoons in pursuit of the *carbonari* had been thoughtless. Doing so had created the opportunity to place the explosive. All the same, she wasn't about to kick the downed dog; let the count draw his own conclusions. Besides, making it sound as if the captain were blameless might be in her own best interests. Crespi would owe her a favor, one she might find of value when the time came to put it to work.

Unfortunately, DeLeone was not about to absolve the captain. It was clear that his mind had been made up long before coming to her.

"Do you know the mark of a good officer, Mrs. Stone?"

"Loyalty, unquestioning obedience, courage under fire, what?"

"All are important, but I hold preeminent the ability to think intelligently on one's feet, or in one's saddle, as the situation dictates. The incident on the rooftop surprised everybody, Rudolf included. That much he's admitted. But, in my view, he ought to have sent four men in pursuit, not all eight. Eight men to capture one? Eight men plus the local police? This was not one of your Virginia fox hunts where a hundred riders chase down one fox. It was very stupid, unforgivably stupid."

She took him at his word. He wasn't about to forgive his favorite whipping boy.

"How could the man on the roof be certain he would draw all eight men after him?"

"He wouldn't have to be. There must have been half a dozen chances to place the charge long before that. When he first showed himself, for example. If his idiotic display attracted your attention and Rudolf's and the mayor's, it attracted everybody's, not excepting the dragoons. It was at that point Rudolf should have acted, surrounded the coach with all eight. Anybody tries to get through . . . Poof. He claims that when the gun went off he was ready to give the order to encircle you but saw that there was no intention to shoot you. Did he mention that to you?"

"It's possible. He was very conscientious about protecting me."

"Don't overdo it, Mrs. Stone."

"I beg your pardon?"

"You're bending over backward for him." DeLeone settled himself on the vanity bench. "Let's go back over it. By the time the man showed himself on the roof he'd thrown away his gun and was holding the flag and the sword.

"Right there, realizing as the captain did that the shot was not meant for you, and that there would be no second shot . . ."

"You think he should have ordered the coach encircled?"

"Absolutely!"

"You mean he should have *assumed* it was only a distraction?"

"Most definitely."

"I wouldn't, I didn't. Would you have?"

"Of course. I would have done what was logical. Standing there thinking on my feet, what would have been more logical than that?"

"How very astute you are, Your Excellency," she said dryly. "I'm impressed. And do you think the wheel falling off was an accident?"

DeLeone considered this. "If it wasn't it was unnecessary. With or without the wheel the coach would have blown up."

"Wouldn't it seem that breaking down like that could have dislodged the explosives?"

"I doubt it. Accident or not, the first thing after you stopped would have been to get you out."

"Which they did, thank God."

"Lucky you, eh?"

"How is Captain Crespi?"

"The doctor is still with him. He's a rugged sort, he should be fit in a day or so, in time for the inquiry."

"He's to be tried? And what, hanged?"

"I said inquiry, a military board, not a tribunal. An inquiry is normal procedure in cases such as this. Hanged indeed! Why, dear lady, must you always think the worst of us?"

"Why, Your Excellency?"

Maria gave her directions to the chapel tower, advising her that Paul had selected it as the best place to meet, since it offered one of the few unguarded doors in the entire castle. The towers, the battlements, and gatehouses were crawling with men, particularly between nightfall and sunup. Charles Felix and Caroline-Louisa seemed positively paranoid over the possibility of the *carbonari* sneaking in and murdering them in their beds. Or friends of the *carbonari* infiltrating the household staff and living, practically, in their very laps!

The chapel door was never locked, according to Maria. Lorna found her to be right. The chapel itself was Gothic, over four hundred years old, a single room two stories high. The altar had been built into a large window recess, the stone window frame cut and fitted with stained glass scenes, among them a copy of Schaeufelein's *The Agony in the Garden* and Raphael's

Madonna della Tenda. Opposite the altar a second recess had been cut out of the tower wall, this one on the
second-story level. It was from there, Lorna assumed,
that the royal couple could look down upon the services
in privacy while the rest of the worshipers stood on the
wooden floor below. Votive candles flickered, gently
casting shadows up the walls and across the vaulted
ceiling, creating a congregation of phantoms. She sat
in the center arched niche, looking out upon the candle
show and the solemn cryptlike emptiness of the chapel . . . waiting.

Waiting. Twice she nearly dozed off, snapping fully
awake the second time. She had opened the madonna
and child window for air. The sky was beginning to
lighten, the stars steadily losing their brilliance. And
still she waited, wondering what was delaying him. Had
anything happened during her absence in Conflans?
Caroline-Louisa was so infuriatingly unpredictable. On
purely a whim, with a sweep of her hand she could
create or destroy, deliver or doom, enrich or ruin. Had
she made Paul a general, she wondered, or broken him
to foot soldier? Or worse . . .

As she floundered in conjecture, the door creaked
open, startling her. She straightened, nearly cracking
the back of her head against the window frame. It
was Paul, a grim look spreading over his handsome
features, his eyes darting about as if he expected an
ambush.

"Lorna . . ." He rushed to her, taking her hands,
then putting his arms around her, holding her close.
"Thank God!"

"You've heard."

He nodded. "The captain of the guard. His men took
care of Rudolf Crespi when you two got back here. The
captain went straight to her."

"She must have been overjoyed at the news."

"She was livid! I've never seen her get so angry so
fast. She raged, carried on, flinging things about . . ."

"Eleven dead."

"That wasn't what upset her. She couldn't care less about the men or the horses. It was losing her favorite coach. It cost half the treasury. She had to wait a year for delivery. Porsaiy Brothers in Paris made it for her. She'd only had it four or five months. But forget that . . ."

"Gladly, let's talk about your damned *carbonari!*"

"You're not going to blame them, they had no way of knowing you were an imposter."

"Not until you tell them."

He sighed, shook his head, and released her. Turning away, he pounded his fist into his palm in frustration. "God only knows when I'll be able to. I've been restricted."

"No!"

"Her Majesty's orders."

"But why?"

"Do you suppose I had the temerity to ask? She's done it before, she'll do it again. In a week she'll relent. It's her way of reminding me who I belong to. Come Holy Week she'll be up to her neck in mass and confession, doing penance, wearing out her beads. A compulsory respite from her wicked ways."

"You're sure of that, I mean a week and you'll be free to come and go . . ."

"What's the matter, do you think I'm under suspicion? I'm not, Lorna, I've enough friends in here to warn me if I were."

"Warn you before they arrest you?" He paused before answering, smiling thinly. "You hope, is that it?"

"We are in a black mood tonight, aren't we?" he asked.

"It's been a long day and a long night."

"I'm sorry I kept you waiting. She . . ." He shrugged.

"She certainly enjoys your company, doesn't she?"

"She's forbidden me to see you anymore."

"That's no surprise."

"She's just jealous. It's no big problem, we can meet here. The door is always open. Nobody comes around this time of night." He drew her close to him, cradling her chin in his hand. "Don't look so glum. Tell me about Conflans and the explosion."

She recounted their every move from Chambéry to Conflans to the accident and the explosion.

"What baffles me is how they could time it so conveniently? How, Paul, some kind of mechanical device? A clock?"

"Nothing that sophisticated. Black powder in a small sack and three sticks of touchwood inserted in the sack and lit. It's hung underneath at an angle so the touchwood can't fall out."

"Touchwood?"

"Decayed wood, softened, rolled into a stick, dipped in saltpeter and dried. It burns slowly with very little smoke. An ideal fuse."

"Why three sticks?"

"Sometimes when the ash drops it takes the fire with it. Three sticks and at least one is certain to burn down to the powder. It's ironic . . ."

"What are you talking about?"

"Me. It was I who probably taught the man who set it. I taught our man—the one in Conflans; either he or somebody he taught set it. And nearly killed you. I'd never have forgiven myself."

"I should hope not."

"I'm falling in love with you, Lorna."

"Don't, please . . ."

"I can't help myself."

"You feel sorry for me, you're sympathetic, but you don't love me."

"You're so wrong."

"Paul, we can't let it happen."

"How can we stop it?" He read her eyes. "You say 'we'; you feel exactly as I do. Why deny it? My darling . . ."

He tried to kiss her, his breath warm on her mouth, her heart suddenly thundering. She steeled herself to resist. Dear God, how she wished she might melt in his arms! To kiss and kiss and kiss. . . .

"Lorna, my darling."

"Don't, please."

"It's him, isn't it, your husband."

"No. I don't know . . ."

"Darling, he's dead."

"I'm not pretending he's not, Paul, it's just that there's a part of my heart that won't let go, that refuses to give him up."

"That's not love, Lorna, it's pity. It was all so brutally unfair, you feel so sorry for him. The sympathy you'd feel for anyone close to you."

"You can't say it's not love; I adored him. I can't close a door on that, not in so short a time. It sounds childish, I suppose, but there it is. I'm still reeling, still torn up inside. I need time, Paul."

"It's loyalty, too, devotion to his memory . . ." He seemed set on severing her last links with love. To clear the field for his own assault on her heart. She sensed his mounting eagerness for just such an effort.

"Please don't examine my feelings. They're not insect parts under a glass."

"Have you considered sackcloth and ashes?" His voice was becoming strained with bitterness. He had no weapon to sunder her emotional ties to the past; none existed. She alone could drive Philip Stone out of mind, out of memory.

Touched by the hurt look in his eyes, she moved to him, kissing his cheek with sisterly affection. And managing a smile.

"I'm hurting you. I'm sorry, I don't mean to."

"It's you who's hurting, trying to relight a candle with a burnt-out match!"

"I suppose I am."

"Look at me, Lorna, pull your heart out of your mind and think. How long must you hold off giving us a chance? Given this snake pit of a place, these times, these traps and tangles, with so much against the two of us, we need each other so."

How right he was, she thought, and she yearned so to give in, to concede his logic, to yield to his embrace, to surrender body and soul, as she was already fast surrendering her heart. But avoiding his smoldering eyes and closing her own, all she could see lodged and locked in her imagination was the same ineffaceable scene, the dimly lit corridor, the flickering sconces, the guests gathered; and Philip lying there helpless, dying. Her poor darling, how senseless, how unbearably cruel . . .

Once more Paul's arms encircled her, once more his mouth was close, finding her lips, kissing her tenderly, infusing her with a cool fire that flushed her cheeks and made her weak all over. His hands caressed her back, her shoulders, his lips explored her eyes, her cheeks, the line of her jaws, her pulsing throat . . .

"No, no . . ." Her voice sounded so pathetically feeble, as if the very last thing she wanted was for him to stop. And it was.

His chest heaving pressed hard against her breasts, she could feel his manhood becoming rigid, immense. Oh, to engorge him, to feel and to fill with him! With a desperate effort of will she broke free, pushing away, running down the steps to the chapel, turning, raising her hands, imploring him to stay where he was.

"No, Paul, please . . ."

His shoulders slumped dejectedly. "Forgive me."

"No. I'm the one who should be asking forgiveness."

"It's her, too, isn't it?"

"The queen? Not at all. She doesn't even exist, not in this, not between us."

"Then it's only the ghost of your husband. Come back to haunt us both, to stand like a stone wall between us. Incredible. How does one deal with a phantom? Is there any weapon, some inspired strategy?"

"Patience, Paul. Help me, hold me up, give me the strength I need with your understanding." She glanced past him at the open window. "It's almost sunup, I must get back. Maria will be frantic."

He pursed his lips thoughtfully and sat down in the niche she had vacated. "Not just yet. There's something else. You tell her everything, don't you?"

"I trust her. You and she are the only ones I can trust."

"You know, of course, she's German."

"I guessed she was the first time I saw her. Her accent, her features . . ."

"I just heard this afternoon what I should have suspected all along. Caroline-Louisa brought her and three or four other girls down here with her."

"Who told you that?"

"Does it matter? It's true. You didn't know it though, did you? The girl never told you."

"No. Paul, if you're implying Maria was assigned to spy on me, I can't believe that. I refuse to."

"You may be making a mistake."

The suggestion that she could have misjudged Maria sent a chill streaking across her shoulders. She could feel herself pale. She'd taken the girl into her confidence without so much as two hours back to back to examine her, properly feel her out, to assess her with detachment. She recalled at the time her intuition warning her to go slowly, and how she'd ignored that warning. To be told that the girl had accompanied Caroline-Louisa to Chambéry was disquieting; there could be no denying that. Still, in itself that was no proof that she'd been delegated to spy on her. Almost the first words out of Maria's mouth had been to down and damn the queen. It was possible, now that Lorna thought about it, that that could have been the very first trap set and triggered to snare her.

Still, how could anyone so unreservedly candid, warm-hearted, and loyal wear two faces? A talented spy could.

Yes, sad to say, it was possible. Better they'd given her tongueless Teresa Zuccola for a maid. Better yet she learn to keep her own mouth shut! For that it was a trifle late.

"Mind you," he went on, "I'm not saying she has to be Caroline-Louisa's eyes and ears. Her Majesty has a rare gift for inspiring hatred. Maria could have turned against her ages ago."

"She's done nothing to make me believe she's a spy," said Lorna flatly, consciously striving for conviction in her voice.

"If she's as skillful as she should be she wouldn't."

"You waver back and forth like a reed in the wind." Her voice sounded so lame to her; how could he help but assume that she was worried?

"What have you told her about me?" he asked.

"We've never talked about you."

"Not even a little bit?"

"I beg your pardon, Captain." She swept her hand in an absurdly low bow. "I wasn't thinking. How could any two females talk twenty seconds without your name cropping up?"

"Lorna, I'm serious."

"I neglected to mention that you're with the *carbonari*. I'm green and I suppose discouragingly naïve, but not simpleminded."

"Forgive me. It's just that neither of us can be too careful."

She turned from him, walking away toward the door. Rising from the niche seat, he followed her at a distance so that they might continue to talk without raising their voices.

"Have you considered how very little any of them has to know to put together the pieces?" she asked. "Everybody in this castle is convinced I want to get away. They know I'll need help. Obviously Her Royal Arrogance has assumed that you and I have talked; doesn't it follow that I've turned to you for help? Could that be why she's split us up and restricted you to the castle?"

"Possibly."

"Probably. Another thing: Has it occurred to you that they may already know you're a *carbonari?*"

"That's impossible!"

"Nothing's impossible, Paul. DeLeone doesn't need Maria to trick me into exposing you. You're Daniel in the lions' den here; you could be betrayed on suspicion only. When you were permitted outside you could have been seen with known revolutionists half a dozen times, weeks ago, months ago."

"You don't have to remind me that I'm playing a dangerous game."

"What I'm trying to tell you is that it's just possible that *they know you're on the other side.* And they're letting you go on playing your game regardless. They have to know the *carbonari* is planning to try to take over. What they don't know is when."

"Or where. None of us knows yet."

"But before that happens, you'll have to show your hand. You'll have to do something to get unhooked from her leash, to get out of this place."

"No, I'm more valuable in here than outside taking an active part in the fighting. At least at the start. Eventually, my commanding officer, Colonel Haproux, will order me to join my regiment, but until then there's nothing I have to do that might arouse DeLeone's or anybody else's suspicions. I have one job only: to keep the up-to-date deployment of their troops in here (he tapped his head). When that deployment is most advantageous to us, when other factors appear favorable, we strike. In the meantime, keep my name out of your conversations. With the girl, DeLeone, everybody."

"Damn you, what do you take me for!"

"Please, keep your voice down . . ."

"Must I give you a blood oath? Can't you take me at my word?"

"I can, I do."

"Thank you!"

"Don't be angry."

"Not angry, just discouraged. While you're stuck in here I'm out there shaking in my shoes wondering how much longer your friends are going to give me."

"Are you going back now?"

"Yes. You'd better close that window. It was closed when I got here."

"Be careful, Lorna. Give Charles Felix a wide berth."

"You might tell him to keep clear of me. The next time he comes after me he'll be in for the surprise of his life!"

She lifted her skirts, revealing the knife tied to her thigh.

"Splendid! On top of everything else, that's what we really need, a knife in the poor fool's brisket."

"Would you rather I meekly submit, like one of the maids?"

"What I would rather is that you avoid putting a rope around your neck. You stick that in Charles Felix and that's what you'll get! That or a garrote."

"I wore it to Conflans, I'm wearing it from now on. If it worries you that much, maybe you'd better warn him."

"Very amusing. Come, I'll walk you back to your rooms."

"To the end of the corridor within sight of my door will be far enough. There's no sense giving the guards something with which to go running to their captain or Lieutenant Calini. When will I see you again?"

"I'll have to let you know through Teresa. I must get word out that you're posing as the queen. Discrediting her could be extremely valuable to our cause. Obviously, any queen who's afraid to face her own people . . . Still, this is not going to be easy."

"Is anything, for either of us? Let's go."

VII

Maria woke her just as the gilt and porcelain clock on the dressing table chimed eleven, ordinarily a pleasing, even delightful sound but one that at the moment cut into her slumber like a razor.

"You must get up, mistress, at once!"

"Go away." She rolled over burying her face in the pillow, shutting out a dazzling sunlight pouring in through both windows.

"Her Majesty commands you to appear before her. You've less than ten minutes before the guards get here. Hurry!"

Lorna sat upright, grinding her fists into her eyes, yawning, groaning. "What the devil . . ."

"The Devil is a woman with a crown and a temper as short as your hair."

"Thank you for the reminder. What's got her nibs's feathers up now?"

Maria shrugged. "They just give me the orders, they don't explain. Except they said you're not to make up like her. And you're to wear one of the dark wigs, any color but blond. Shall I get the auburn one?"

"Whatever. So they're giving me back my identity, are they? What a surprise. What's the occasion, I wonder?"

"Hurry! Hurry!"

The throne room rose to a sturdily arched ceiling crowded with cherubim and seraphim. The walls were hung with lovely tapestries separated by drapes of mauve velvet into which intricate gold patterns had been woven. Above the twin thrones hung a shield emblazoned with the coat-of-arms of the House of Savoy, with golden banners sweeping outward from either side of it.

King and queen sat side by side; rather Charles Felix slouched, his small spare frame angled awkwardly, his chin pedestaled by his right fist and forearm, his elbow firmly set on the arm of his throne, his face screwed into a scowl. Caroline-Louisa sat stiltedly erect, posing, inviting the stares of the small gathering of court officials. Among those present were her corpulent, bowlegged Lord Chamberlain; Maggio, her heavy drinking, loud-mouthed, but spineless minister of war; her newly appointed prime minister and, by all appearances completely recovered and restored to favor, Captain Rudolf Crespi, clad in a new, crisp, bright-buttoned red and black uniform. All eyes turned to Lorna as the white-stockinged, gaudily uniformed, white-wigged doormen closed the doors behind her. Hastily tutored by Marie, Lorna bowed low, focusing her eyes on the floor and keeping them there, absently studying the blurred reflection of the gathering in the polished marble.

"You may rise . . ."

Caroline-Louisa flipped up her hand. She was wearing a white silk robe decorated with delicate lace workings and a necklace of rubies complementing her dark red gown. Her hair was piled in a pompadour and laced with strands of pearls; her crown was set with rubies and more pearls. She motioned Lorna to approach, the others making way for her.

"You look well." The queen stood up and clapped her hands, the signal for everyone to bow and begin backing away. Charles Felix continued staring at his feet, one ankle over the other, examining the shine on his boots ostensibly as if under the impression that he was alone in the room. "Leave us," said the queen. "You . . ." She nodded at Lorna. "Stay."

Once more everyone bowed, Lorna joining them, more a reflex action than conscious courtesy. The doors were thrown open and the room cleared of all save she, the king and queen, and a tall, broad-shouldered woman, with the posture and bearing of a man, her dark hair lopped severely short, her skin tanned, her face without cosmetics, save for a touch of lipstick. She wore riding clothes, a crop in her hand, her gloves tucked into her belt, her black boots shining like glass.

"Mrs. Stone, this is our sister, Clothilde Georgianna Von Schuppe. Clotee, Mrs. Singleton Stone."

Lorna nodded to the girl and in return got a scrutinizing stare. Charles Felix yawned loudly and shifted his feet, his eyes still fixed on his boots. Then he sighed, affectedly, Ajax under the weight of the world, slouched lower in his throne, closed his eyes, and feigned sleep. His wife ignored all of this.

"It has been brought to our attention," she went on, "that you have conducted yourself conscientiously in your ah, duties."

A duty was it? To be blown up? Again the carriage exploded, violently, silently before Lorna's mind's eye. Duty indeed!

"You have earned a few hours of relaxation. Do you ride?"

"Yes, Your Majesty."

"Excellent. Our sister Clotee is the finest horsewoman in Savoy."

"We shall meet at the stables in half an hour," said Clothilde. "Do you ride like a woman?"

"I prefer astride."

"Splendid! So do I."

"I don't have any clothes . . ."

"Everything you'll need will be sent up to your rooms," said Clothilde brightly. "For astride, a long full skirt over gray cloth trousers, patent leather boots with high heels and spurs."

"I don't use spurs."

"As you wish. Shall it be a stallion or a mare?"

"It doesn't matter."

"We'll get you Bayard. You'll love him; he's an

absolute monster, the most powerful mount in the duchy."

"And the most unpredictable," interposed the queen. "See that she gets one of the gentler mares. We want no accidents. And no wild riding down the Montagnole Road. It's too easy to slip into those ditches and break the poor creature's leg, not to mention your necks." Caroline-Louisa's eyes saddened as she looked from one to the other. "My, but we envy you two, getting outside these walls, galloping about the countryside. Would that we might go along. Oh, to break the fetters of state, fly over the wall into the lovely green world outside. It's been so long, too long. Which reminds us. Holy Week begins in two short days. You, Mrs. Stone, will be attending High Mass at the cathedral. Before and after Easter there will be other services and ceremonies, traditional affairs. On Holy Thursday His Majesty will take part in a ritual inaugurated by the Green Count in the year 1353. The king will be required to wash the feet of twelve impoverished peasants and give them supper money. The main gates are opened to the townspeople; the ceremony takes place in the outer ward." Her eyes strayed to Charles Felix; from the absent look in his dark brooding eyes he was still stranded in another world. "If His Majesty feels up to it. Unfortunately his health has been rather poor lately. Should he be unable to take part, we are expected to take his place. Do you follow?"

"Yes, Your Majesty." "We" are not about to dirty "our" hands on the feet of peasants, thought Lorna. Not to mention set the stage for any would-be assassin.

"So much for duties. For now put them out of mind and enjoy yourselves, both of you. You, Mrs. Stone, that auburn wig will do and see that you wear a scarf, something to cover your face in case any strangers happen to pass you on the road. Enjoy yourselves."

The stables situated under the barracks at the eastern end of the inner ward were extensive, with more than a hundred stalls. But the place was poorly ventilated, the narrow windows cut in the rear wall of each individual stall admitting little air. The stench of manure was so powerful it brought tears to Lorna's eyes and the paucity of fresh air, she knew, had to be unhealthy for the horses, obliged as they were to stand idle sometimes for days waiting to be taken out. Torches burned constantly, further reducing what little air found its way through the windows.

Lorna was given a small but sturdy-looking mare badly in want of grooming, her mane askew and knotted, her hair tangled in the hollows of her chest. Her upper legs, withers and croup had not been curry-combed in ages, but in spite of her patchy appearance she seemed spirited and eager to leg, and her rich hazel-colored eyes were bright and clear. Gentling her with soothing tones, Lorna got her tongue out the side of her mouth and examined her teeth.

"What are you doing?" asked Clothilde.

"Her teeth need to be floated."

"What?"

"Ground down so that they meet evenly."

"They don't do that here; they don't have to, she can still eat and drink."

Lorna glanced about the stable. The feeding troughs stretching end to end like open coffins in the semidarkness reeked of bran and old timothy. The watering troughs were abuzz with flies, and the stone floor littered with sprigs of hay and squashed oats desperately needed washing down. The beady red eyes of rats and other vermin gleamed around the corners of the troughs and from out of the darkened recesses of the stalls. With summer coming botflies and other pests would commandeer this squalor and begin breeding in abundance; but the stablemen and boys, the guards loitering about, hiding out from their superiors, even Clothilde, seemed determinedly apathetic regarding the conditions. It was, Lorna knew, a philosophy that separated horse users from horse lovers. To the former, if a horse died, whatever the cause, there was always another to fill its stall.

An English saddle was placed on the mare's back, the cotton girth drawn and securely cinched. The stable-boy led the creature out into the sunlight, holding her motionless as Lorna prepared to mount. Clothilde, busy repositioning her own saddle, meanwhile, stood with her back to Lorna. Pausing, she turned around.

"Let me see under your wig!" she burst. Before Lorna could move to protect herself, Clothilde had snatched the wig cleanly off her head.

"Oh, God, look! It's like a burr, a chestnut burr! *How hideous! Hid . . ."*

Furious, Lorna wheeled, snatching back her wig, and slapping the girl so soundly it startled both horses. Looking on, a dirty-faced stableman and a young guard, his shako set on a nearby ring post, had burst into laughter. But Lorna's rage and the swiftness of her retaliation sobered them. They gawked and gasped as Clothilde went crashing against the post under the force of a second blow, Lorna screaming at her.

Catching herself, regaining her balance, Clothilde charged at her, slashing the air with her crop. Down it arced missing Lorna's cheek by a hair, her upraised forearm fending off a second effort. Then snatching the crop from her, Lorna threw it aside.

"You cut me, you witch, and you'll answer to her!" Livid, Clothilde came at her, but Lorna's upraised knee caught her full in the stomach, driving her slamming back into the post, the wind knocked out of her, staggering her. Her eyes blazed, and cursing loudly she flew at Lorna's throat. But by now the guard pushed forward, shouldering his way between them, holding them back at arm's length.

"Ladies, ladies . . ."

"Yankee bitch, I'll rip your eyes out!" Clothilde screamed.

Seething, burning with embarrassment, Lorna slapped

her horse's rump sending her cantering back into the stable.

"Ride alone, you sow!" she rasped, and spinning about strode off across the inner ward toward the apartments, feeling their eyes burning into her neck. The heartless animal! The despicable, rotten hellhag!

Continuing to revile her, fighting back tears, Lorna stormed down the corridor flinging open her door to the sight of Maria, her hair down, her clothes in disarray, the guiltiest look a troubled conscience ever etched on human features gripping hers.

"Mistress . . ."

Lorna stared at her. "What's the matter with you? Look at you!" The girl smoothed her apron and poked embarrassedly at her hair. "What's going on here?"

Maria could not look her in the eye, her pink face becoming crimson. Lorna's hand went instinctively to her wig, straightening it, feeling her own cheeks flush. Clothilde! The contemptible witch! The heartless sow! Again she glared at Maria, unconsciously focusing all her considerable frustration upon the poor befuddled creature.

"Forgive me, mistress, I beg you." She fell to her knees, throwing her arms around Lorna's legs, pressing her face against her thigh, pleading incoherently, lapsing into German.

"Forgive what? What are you talking about?" A sudden chill gripped Lorna's heart tightly. Something was terribly wrong, something done or come about since she had left the apartment barely twenty minutes earlier, after coming back to change her clothes. What in God's name . . .

Breaking the girl's grip on her legs, she pulled her to her feet, shaking her. "Talk, damn you! What have you done? *Say something!*"

The sound of a man clearing his throat nervously drew her attention from Maria—her lower lip quivering ridiculously, her whole body trembling in Lorna's grasp

—to the inner doorway. A dragoon appeared, his hair askew, his uniform looking as if he'd slept in it.

"Oh, my," said Lorna, more in relief than surprise. "So that's it . . ."

"I . . . we didn't know you were coming back so soon," ventured Maria, her voice subdued with shame, her eyes lowered.

"I was just leaving, mistress," mumbled the dragoon.

Fumbling with his buttons, his saber rattling, the heel guard of his scabbard clicking noisily as he struggled to buckle his trousers, he fled, leaving his Maria flustered, but Lorna immensely relieved. A dalliance, even a romp in her bed she could condone, but the look on Maria's face when she'd first come in, the irrefragable guilt capturing the girl's features had been like a clammy fist clutching her throat. Paul had sown the seeds of suspicion and there they lay in the furrows of her mind, fast rooting, preparing to bud and blossom, the flowers of calamity. She could never recall feeling so relieved in her entire life. Setting Maria down on the vanity bench, she helped her get control of herself.

"You won't tell on me, mistress, please don't . . ."

"Of course not. What do you take me for? Only next time find a spot where nobody can walk in on you. You ninny, you didn't even bother to lock the door!"

"We must have forgot . . ."

"You're lucky I wasn't the captain of the guard come storming in." Maria looked gray and crossed herself. "Help me out of these riding things."

"Mrs. Stone . . ." The two of them turned at the voice in the doorway. It was Lieutenant Calini, beside him a scrawny, scrubbed-cheeked private who looked all of thirteen. The Lieutenant doffed his cap with a flourish, clicked his heels, and bowed. "Her Majesty's sister is waiting for you at the main gate."

"You can tell Her Majesty's sister that I am in bed asleep. And that I've left orders not to be disturbed."

"Quite so, ahem, but my orders are to escort you to her."

"I'm not in the mood for riding. Not today. Not ever, with that one!"

Calini nodded, cleared his throat, glanced at the private, and looked back at Lorna appealingly.

"I would be pleased to convey your message, but unfortunately it will carry no weight. They will send me straight back here with orders to bring you by force, if necessary. It would be easier for all concerned . . ."

Lorna sighed wearily.

"Tell him to tell them you're ill," suggested Maria.

"What's the use? I may as well get it over with. You two wait outside. I'll be out in a minute." She closed the door in their faces, hiked her right trouser leg out of her boot, assured herself that her knife was still firmly tied to her calf—the blade lodged in the boot—restored the cuff to conceal the hilt, and departed with them.

Clothilde was sitting astride a coal black stallion with eyes as white as polished China eggs, its luxuriant tail swishing flies away with the energy and determination of a thresher punishing wheat. Clothilde's eyes wore a sheepish look. A stableboy was bringing up the mare, saddled and ready, handing Lorna the reins, bowing, backing away.

"She pulls to the right, mum," he said softly. "A pat on the neck straightens her right enough. And if you cross grasslands you must mind the marmot burrows."

"I shall." She mounted, bringing her eye to eye with Clothilde.

"I apologize," she said. "I should not have done that. It was nasty of me. You were right to be angry."

"If you ever touch me again . . ."

Clothilde nodded, repeating her apology, as if by rote. Lorna made no response the second time, not so much as a nod to acknowledge she was even listening. Let her stew, let her conscience nettle her, if conscience she had. If there was such a faculty in the meager moral arsenal of the Von Schuppes. She did, however, seem sincerely sorry for what she had done.

They rode off in silence, Clothilde leading the way up

into the mountains, dropping the castle and Chambéry behind them. The plain spread its sun-drenched loveliness southward toward the snow-shrouded mountains, beyond which lay Grenoble. But when they rounded a sharp turn, all this disappeared, as did the white blotches of snugly massed sheep, the mules and bullocks with their carts and herds of goats straggling indolently along. The area's industry, a paper manufactory situated at the entrance of the district, lay hidden behind a wall of trees, but the roar of the torrent that turned the machinery could be heard flinging itself into the chasm. Toward Chartreuse flower-filled fields rose almost perpendicularly to the foot of the inaccessible rocks or plunged to the sharp zigzagging trough forming the bottom of the valley. On the far side lay gentler slopes, a small plain with high-backed mountains squeezing the horizon like the bellows of an accordion.

Leafy vines abounded, ensnarling the landscape, acacias and stately poplars and firs highest up challenging the wind and the ice storms where nothing else tried to grow. The horses were tiring, the mare's flanks heavily caked with sweat. Swinging her off the road into the slender shadow of a poplar, Lorna dismounted, stretched her legs and, shading her eyes, looked about her in a circle. A chamois, its horns and upraised ears forming a four-pronged crown designating it as king of its mountain, gazed down upon them. Then returned to inspecting its realm.

"Are you hungry?" asked Clothilde.

The question was asked just as Lorna's wandering glance discovered two dragoons riding side by side far below.

"Who are those two, our bodyguards?"

"Caroline-Louisa insists. They have a basket with cold smoked grouse, cheese, fruit, wine. I'm famished, aren't you?"

"I could eat."

They sat with their backs to the tree, watching the

soldiers approaching. They cut off the road into the meadow, dismounting and bringing up the basket.

"I'm thirsty," snapped Clothilde.

"There's wine," ventured one of the men.

"It's warm. Fetch us water from the streams up at the top."

"At once, miss."

"Please hurry, I'm thirsty as a camel."

They nibbled on the grouse and the cheese, an uncommonly tasty camembert, and watched a sparrow whirl and dart about above the treetop. Above it a hawk, black as night, its silhouette sharply outlined against the burning sky, hung motionless, waiting. Then it hurled itself down, the hammer of Thor flung unerringly, with uncanny accuracy, striking the little creature, loosing and scattering feathers that floated slowly earthward. The hunter, its prey locked in its talons, soared off, its beak cocked, preparing to strip the flesh.

Lorna turned her eyes from the sight in disgust.

With lunch came questions, in the main friendly curiosity—America, New Hampshire, childhood, family, red Indians, but cleverly interjected were questions having to do with de Boigne's funeral and Conflans.

"Were the people pleased to see you? Were they properly respectful? Was there any sign of, ah, disapproval, dislike? One can see so much in faces without a word spoken. Don't you agree?"

"Is Her Majesty popular with her subjects? That's what you want to know, isn't it?"

"Of course she's popular. They love her. Everybody knows that." Suddenly in Clothilde's eyes was a look that suggested she might better be a bit more realistic. "Of course there are always troublemakers. You know some people, they're impossible to win over, whatever one does for them. Did you see anyone like that at General de Boigne's funeral?"

"Heavens, no. The furthest thing from it," lied Lorna. She paused for effect. "How can I describe the way they looked? There was a sort of veneration in their eyes.

You know, as if they were being treated to the company of a saint, one they truly idolized."

"You don't mean it!"

"I do. Of course I can only give you my impression. Still, they were drawn up close. I could see very clearly."

"Marvelous! And did they bow and curtsy with enthusiasm? You know, the way they compete to impress, to get attention."

"Oh, yes, definitely. The queen would have been touched and so pleased."

"What about Conflans?"

"If anything, they were even more impressed. As delightful as children. They even threw flowers. And when that fellow showed himself on the roof everybody was torn . . ."

"Torn? What do you mean?" Clothilde downed a mouthful or grouse, reaching for the half-filled bottle of rosé resting in the corner of the basket, pulling the cork and swagging a mouthful, washing down the food.

"Undecided whether to surround me or chase after him."

"And in their eyes?"

"The usual worshipful look. Her people really do idolize her."

Clothilde paused in her assault on a wedge of cheese, appraising Lorna archly. "You're not exaggerating . . ."

"Why would I do that? I must tell you, Clothilde, nobody in this world could have been more relieved than I when I first saw their eyes. If they felt any animosity at all, wouldn't I be the one to suffer for it? Wasn't I in effect the queen?"

"They did try to kill you."

"Not the people. Only a handful of crazy radicals."

"More than a handful, Lorna, hundreds, perhaps thousands." She smiled. "Do you know, you're very, very pretty."

"Oh?"

"I mean it. That's why Carrie's jealous of you. I

mean, here, now, when you're not made up to look like her with your blond wig and all. That color suits you much better. She's not pretty and fresh looking anymore. Oh, she used to be quite lovely; she looked just like Mother. But she's become so high-strung, so hot tempered and bitter, those little lines around her mouth harden her so and there's a coldness in her eyes that was never there before."

She got up, dusting off her clothing. She circled the tree, moving toward the rocks, picking delicate pine adrosace, disturbing a hovering group of butterflies who veered about and fled for the higher rocks.

"Will they try to kill me in the cathedral?"

"At High Mass? Never . . . well."

"You can't say for certain one way or the other, is that it? Clothilde, what if I were to be killed? What happens then?"

"If you're dead, what would it matter to you?"

"Seriously. Will there be a state funeral with all the trappings? Will I be regally laid to rest and the duchy plunged into mourning while she runs off to Sardinia or Piedmont or home to Germany?"

"There's a plan of some sort, but I don't know what. They don't tell me. She says it's none of my business."

"I don't understand." Lorna looked past her at the two soldiers grazing their horses.

"What?"

"I can't imagine what she's worried about. The people worship her."

"I know, you said. Not the republicans, though."

"I suppose. Well . . ." Lorna got up and stretched. "If that's all the questions, can we start back? I'm tired, I'd like to take a nap."

"You . . ." Clothilde called to the two dragoons standing on the opposite side of the road talking, passing the time. The one who had brought up the water saluted. "We're going back now. Come clean up."

"At once, miss."

They returned to Chambéry and the castle with

scarcely a word passing between them. Clothilde had learned what her sister had instructed her to find out. Lorna smiled inwardly. Not quite the truth, perhaps, but if Caroline-Louisa were fool enough to swallow it that was her problem.

VIII

Tired from lack of sleep and already beginning to ache from the little mare's jouncing, Lorna put aside thoughts of Holy Week and the crammed schedule that would again place her on the pedestal of public display. Two days hence, by that time, hopefully, Paul would have hit upon a means of disclosing Caroline-Louisa's deceit.

All very well and welcome, but this turn in Lorna's fortunes while solving one problem could initiate others. What, for instance, would the queen decide to do with her imposter when said imposter's usefulness was at an end? Send her home with her blessing and expressions of queenly gratitude? Not likely. Dispensing with this Yankee's services wouldn't be nearly as practicable as dispensing with her altogether. What could Paul do to prevent that? What could anyone do?

Mulling over these new complications, she happened to be passing Count DeLeone's rooms. His double doors were open, his familiar sonorous voice easily recognizable, although he was out of her line of sight as she walked by. Ahead of her was the dogleg double corner, at its farther end the beginning of the long corridor dividing the upper-level apartments. Her own apartment was the last in the line. Passing DeLeone's doors she could hear the sound of liquid being poured, a decanter stopper clicking back into place, glasses clinking in a toast.

"To the continued health of the House of Savoy," said DeLeone expansively. "And to your own, Captain Sasso. You look healthy, rested, fit, ready . . ."

"For action, Excellency."

Lorna had passed the open doors, little interested in

DeLeone, his toast or his guest, intent on getting back to her rooms. The other voice, the three words stopped her approach to the corner. She froze, one hand against the wall bracing herself. Petrified with astonishment, her mouth gaping, she turned like one slowly becoming seized with paralysis. Her ears were playing tricks on her; they had to be. She had not heard that voice! Retracing her steps, reaching the open doors, she pushed them wide and entered.

DeLeone was seated at a small black marble table veined with white streaks, upon it a half-filled brandy decanter. At the sight of her he shot to his feet.

"Mrs. . . ." He paused, his eyes straying to his companion. Seated across from him wearing the familiar red and black uniform of a Savoyard officer was a familiar figure, his glass raised to his lips, preparing to sample his brandy.

Captain Sasso was Philip Stone.

IX

Even as they looked at her, Philip's beautiful dark eyes brightening with embarrassment, she wanted to scream and throw herself upon him. Claw those enchanting, mesmerizing eyes out of their sockets, rip his handsome face. Sight of him, recognition communicating itself to her brain snapped a switch that set her wild. No astonishment, no confusion, no bewilderment, only stabbing pain, like a knife thrust to the heart that comes with the consciousness that one has been used, cruelly duped, your love used as a weapon against you, your most delicate sensibilities trampled upon like so many weeds. To have so freely given her love, to have flung her heart at his feet, and to have suffered through the dreadful charade of his murder staged solely for her benefit. And the sequence of events and circumstances that followed.

"You bastard," she rasped, "you heartless snake!"

"Mrs. Stone," began DeLeone, his cheeks reddening.

"Stay out of this! You . . ." She turned back to Philip. "You contemptible . . ."

"Guilty," said Philip flatly, without the slightest semblance of emotion, lifting his hands in capitulation.

"Bastard, canaille, lowest of the low . . ."

"How could you?"

"Do such a heinous thing? Lorna, my darling, there's an explanation."

"I'm sure . . ."

"You would prefer privacy." DeLeone started toward the door.

She gestured, staying him. "Don't bother leaving. We've nothing to talk about. Isn't that so, Philip? Husband? What explanation is there but that you needed a fool, you found her, you poured out your heart to her, pledged your undying love, trapped her as neatly as a hare in a springe, staged your grisly little melodrama and withdrew from the picture. Your contribution to this insane farce completed."

"It's more complicated than that," Philip said, pretending to study the pattern of the rug at her feet.

"Spare me."

"You're overlooking a very important detail."

A second time DeLeone started for the doors. "You'll excuse me, I have urgent business elsewhere. Captain, Mrs. Stone . . ."

Before she could stop him he was gone, the sound of both doors bringing a servant to the inner door, a curious look on his sallow face. Philip closed that door before the man could get a word out.

"He called you Sasso . . ."

"Italian for Stone." He had taken a stance behind a chair and was staring at her, exploring her eyes, searching for some trace of curiosity, a willingness, however grudging, to hear him out. "I love you, Lorna. As God is my witness, by all that's holy, I love you."

It was the last straw; she hurled herself at him, wrenching the chair out of his grasp, hurling it aside, her free hand flashing toward him, closing in a fist, smashing his cheek. Though it was powered by all the hatred and frustration she could summon, he neither winced nor even blinked. Screaming like a madwoman, she began pummeling his face. He took blow after blow, then, gripping her wrists and stretching her arms outward, brought his mouth down upon hers, attempting to kiss her. She bit him, drawing blood. Twisting and wrenching with all her strength, she jerked free. Raising her hand she brought it down, her nails gouging his cheek, opening slender troughs that quickly filled with blood.

He did not even attempt to defend himself, standing as still as sculptured marble gazing at her. Dropping to her knees, she began sobbing into her hands, her shoulders and upper back shuddering. He reached forward taking hold of her, but again she pulled free and up on her feet rushed to the doors and out.

Down the corridor she ran sobbing hysterically, passing two guards and a maid loaded with linens, the three of them gaping at her, standing to one side, giving her room to pass.

Into her room she rushed, throwing herself down onto the bed sobbing, pounding her pillow. Bringing Maria running.

"Mistress . . ."

Plumping down beside her, Maria eased her over onto her back, bringing a handkerchief out of the pocket of her skirt and daubing at her eyes and cheeks. Talking soothingly to her, gradually calming her down, and getting the story out bit by bit.

"You should have pushed your knife into his belly! Men, curse them all for the heartless pigs they are!" She stopped abruptly, puzzled. "But how could he be dead, lying there outside your room with a knife in him, blood all over and now . . ."

"There was no knife, only the hilt glued to, somehow stuck to the cloth and red paint or chicken blood spread around it. While he pretended he was suffering, dying."

"You did the suffering!"

"Too long, Maria, too many hours of misery, too many sleepless nights and nightmares. How sorry I felt for that man. My heart was so clenched and twisted with pity it ached interminably. The times I prayed to God to make it all a dream. Turn the clock back to Hanover and our wedding day. Given a second chance we'd never have left there, never have seen Boston or the Gray Dragon. That horrible night would never have existed. Yes, I prayed to God and all the while my beloved husband was alive and laughing at me. I've been such a fool, such a blind simpleton! How right you are, I ought to have pulled my knife and killed him back there in DeLeone's room."

Maria's eyes narrowed. "There has to be a better way,

slower, more painful. If you could only make him suffer as you've suffered."

"He's to blame for all of this . . ." Lorna's eyes strayed to her hand and her wedding ring. Pulling it off she flung it across the room. Maria retrieved it and held it up between them.

"This you must keep."

"Take it out and bury it, and don't tell me where. Better yet throw it down the nearest garderobe into a cesspit."

"No. Listen to me, there's an old Gypsy curse. If your man has wronged you or abused you, if you've given him your heart and he breaks it, when he dies and his corpse is laid out, you approach the coffin and place your wedding ring on his sealed lips. It will lock his soul in his body; prevent it from escaping and rising to heaven. Then when he's buried and his flesh molders, his soul molders along with it. And down to hell he goes."

"Intact. Fascinating." Lorna managed a feeble smile. Then sobered. What pained her more than anything else back in DeLeone's room had been Philip's declaration of love. The mere word coming from his lips had infuriated her! If he'd never said it, if he'd been honest enough to admit that he'd lied about loving her, she could understand his willingness to help weave the web that had entangled her. To play, in fact, the leading role. Pretending to love her so as to lure her into their trap was one thing, unconscionably callous and cruel, but their need for her she could understand. But now, with it all out in the open, to have the brazen audacity to calmly claim that he actually loved her and worse that he clearly expected her to believe him was intolerable! It was as if even with his part in it completed he saw it as necessary to prolong DeLeone's and Caroline-Louisa's immorality play. It amused him, he enjoyed it, why not continue it?

The door burst open. Philip stood, his hand flat against his cheek, his passionate eyes gleaming like stars

rangement that might prove helpful beyo

ation."

"Including marrying me."

He nodded. "From the moment

gan to explain my part in the aff

idea. I felt it repugnant,"

"I'm sure."

"I did! May God st

fessional soldier, no

someone who res

under consider

able. But, a

"Who

motive

said   with a scowl that intimated
that she was going back to load a weapon. She withdrew.

"I do not want to hear the word love," said Lorna, her tone belligerent, "not from your lips. It's a beautiful word, but you make it a poison . . . dripping acid. And don't come any closer. Just say what you have to and get out. Five minutes." She nodded toward the clock on the vanity.

"May I sit?"

"Better you get to the point."

"Very well. To begin with, I am a major in the Imperial Guard of Savoy, the most prestigious fighting unit in the Kingdom of Sardinia. We are the elite corps. When Valucci and Dicostanzo, with the help of other agents, found you in Hanover, I was ordered by my commanding officer to a private audience before their majesties. I was assigned by them to bring you here by whatever means necessary. No expense spared, no ard consider-

Count DeLeone be-
air I was repelled by the

ike me dead if I lie! I'm a pro-
a kidnapper. I felt that abducting
embled Her Highness for the purpose
ation was criminal. Thoroughly deplor-
I say, I am a soldier, a loyal monarchist."
wouldn't dream of questioning his superior's
."

Not for an instant. I do not exaggerate when I say
at I am perhaps the most fiercely loyal officer in the
entire army. Were my king and queen to order me to
leap from the North Tower to the rocks below, I would
not hesitate to do so."

"The ultimate patriot, that's you. A pity your friend,
Adelbert, can't spare you a medal. He must have half a
hundred."

His eyes drifted to the vanity, glancing over the
bottles and tins and tiny boxes scattered across it. Seeing his reflection, his face hardened as his hand instinctively went to his cheek.

"That's the gulf that separates your way of life from
mine. You can afford to be flippant, lighthearted. You
don't know the meaning of obligation to one's superiors.
Of life long dedication to a cause. You come from a
country where freedoms thrive like the wild flowers in
the valley from Chambéry to Aix. A young country,
still in the throes of development. A constitutional democracy." He picked up a tin of blush from the vanity,
flipped it like a coin, and dropped it back in place clattering softly to rest. "Savoy too has a constitution, but
we are the furthest thing from a democracy. The law of
our land is the law of our monarchs, never to be questioned, certainly never to be overruled. So has it been

for nine hundred years, and will be for the next nine hundred, when all of us are gone, but the House of Savoy continues to survive and to rule."*

He began pacing. "It may help you to understand if I pose a theoretical situation. Let us pretend that I may not like Charles Felix or Caroline-Louisa as individuals. I may not respect them. I may differ with them in a hundred ways. But they are my king and my queen and not they, but what they represent, is to me more sacred than my religion. The House of Savoy is the supreme commander of my destiny. To it I have sworn life-long allegiance and devotion. My oath obliges me to protect my king and queen with my life. Bound by such an oath how could I possibly hesitate to carry out an imperial order such as the one that brought you here?

"In my heart I am not proud of my part in this. It is not an achievement I gloat over. Furthermore, I had no intention of falling in love with you. As Almighty God is my witness I exerted every effort to avoid it. Nevertheless, it happened, I did."

Tears dimmed her sight and she turned away to prevent his seeing her eyes. "I asked you not to talk about that."

"You did, forgive me. But I can't help myself." He started toward her.

"Stop right there. Maria!" The girl appeared in the inner doorway. "Call the guard. Our uninvited guest is leaving. If he refuses to leave quietly, I want him removed."

Philip sighed and shook his head. "Don't talk nonsense. Any guard shows his face at the door and I'll order him to leave. In God's name be reasonable! All I ask is a chance to explain!"

"All you want is a chance to placate your conscience."

"No!"

---

* The House of Savoy ceased to exist in 1946.

"Get on with it, then get out. And don't show your face in here again."

"As you wish. I suppose that's all of it. Rather a lame explanation, I agree. Certainly no excuse, but I said it before and I have to say it again. In the face of everything, my common sense, my willpower, the iron the army has forged into my spine, I fell in love with you. You're the only woman I've ever loved, or ever will. No man alive can hate himself more than I hate myself for what I've done to you. I would give both my hands on the block under a broadax to undo this rotten business. . . ."

"Would you really?" He nodded, his eyes keen as knives, as relentless as the incessancy of a guilty conscience. "Very well, since you obviously can't 'undo it,' why not cut off your hands as a gesture of atonement? I'd be very impressed."

"I'm serious!"

"I'm not?"

"You really think I got a kind of twisted satisfaction out of this, don't you?"

"I don't think there's anything twisted about it. I think you're as pleased as punch with yourself. Let me give you a bit of advice, Philip. You can stand here all day and all night filling this room up to our necks with excuses, alibis, rationalizations, your soul-stirring avowals of allegiance to those two maniacs—you only did your duty—so you say. You and the hangman. Words, Philip, words and more words. But if your conscience really is as troubled as you want me to believe, there's one sure way to relieve it. Get me out of this god-forsaken place before somebody kills me!"

"You're asking the impossible."

"I rather imagined you'd say that."

"How can I?"

"You tricked *me* to get me in, how about tricking *them* to get me out?"

"I'd better go now."

"Those are the most welcome words you've said since you got here."

"You really despise me, don't you?"

"There has to be a stronger word than that."

"I deserve it."

"How very noble."

"All the same, I'll never stop loving you, saying it, meaning it. With all my heart. We're still man and wife."

"We are, aren't we . . ."

"You can't make me believe you didn't enjoy our lovemaking as much as I. That's something you might think about. Could any man pretend to love as I loved you? In each other's arms, our bodies joined, surrendering, our hearts beating wildly, did you ever once for even a split second doubt me?"

"Whether I did or not doesn't matter two pins now, does it?"

"You've no idea of the torture this has put me through."

"Get out. And stay out."

"Lorna . . ."

"*Out!*"

She pushed him out the door, locking it. And sat down on the edge of the bed. But tears did not come. There was no longer any need for tears, not now, not when she was suddenly so consumed with loathing and anger she felt about to burst. Maria approached her with the ring.

"What shall I do with this?" she asked.

She took it from her, holding it, examining it. "This we keep. There's an old Gypsy curse . . ."

Maria smiled through beginning tears, leaned over, and kissed her on the forehead.

BOOK THREE

THE COUNTERFEIT QUEEN

I

Moonlight poured through the partially opened stained glass window, silvering the chapel floor. The field cricket which had taken residence outside Lorna's windows chirped softly from that direction this night, his song, as she commented, less aggressive than that announcing his triumphant albeit unopposed conquest of the north wall.

"He sounds in a romantic mood," said Paul, cocking one ear and listening. "Probably showing off for some female he's got his eye on. Good for him. What a simple, pleasant way to begin a relationship."

"What makes you so sure he's interested in a relationship?" she asked morosely. She was standing leaning against the altar wall, her arms folded, her eyes red-rimmed from lack of sleep, her thoughts and hopes joined and plunged into the depths by his news. And ill-prepared to permit her spirits to be lifted by irrelevant remarks.

"I can tell you something about male crickets," she went on. "He may sound romantic, but he's probably only singing for his own amusement. And pity the poor female so inconsiderate as to interrupt him."

"Pity this poor male for being so inconsiderate as to bring up the subject."

"If we could save the small talk and stick to more important matters . . ."

"Of course."

"I don't mean to be rude, but this has been a trying day for me. On top of my beloved husband's return from the dead, you get me down here to this mauso-

173

leum you call a chapel and set a bomb off right under my nose!"

"Nothing like a bomb, Lorna. I know it's disappointing news, but would you rather I beat about the bush or lie to you outright?"

"I'm sorry." She crossed four short steps to the center rear of the altar and sat beside him. "It just doesn't make any sense. You say you didn't even have to tell your senior officers that I'm posing as the queen, that they already knew. And yet they choose to drop it into a trunk, lock the lid, and sit on it. In heaven's name why?"

"It could create a problem for our people . . ."

"Lest we forget, I too have a problem that nobody seems to give a damn about!"

"I do. I gave you my word I'd protect you and I will."

She rewarded this with an indulgent smile, but bitterness burdened her words.

"Paul, I know you're sincere. But isn't it perfectly obvious that your hands are as tightly tied as mine? By your own people?"

He made no attempt to deny this, and she was grateful. She had no desire nor any energy left for any more arguing this day. A spider came slowly down the wall against which she had been leaning. She followed its progress.

Paul had managed to slip out of the castle just after nightfall, while Charles Felix and Caroline-Louisa were at dinner. He'd gotten to a friend who in turn had reached Colonel Falcone, the local ranking officer in the *carbonari*, a life-long republican and a long-time friend of Paul's. Joined by two other important insurgents in a closely guarded hideout outside of town, they had discussed Caroline-Louisa's scheme, or rather wrangled, about it. According to Paul, the three men were touched by Lorna's plight and were genuinely sympathetic:

"But Colonel Falcone feels and the others agree that

to reveal to the people that you are posing as the queen would be little or no help to our cause."

"The cause! The cause! That's all I ever hear, that's all you care about." Reaching the floor, the spider picked its way across it. She thrust her foot forward to squash it, but changed her mind, not having the heart to, despite boiling over with frustration. "Let them finish me off tomorrow for all any of you care!"

"Lorna, try and see it from their point of view. If we accused you of being an imposter, how many people would believe us?"

"If I stood up at High Mass day after tomorrow, whipped off my wig, and started spouting English at them they'd believe all right . . ."

"And you'd be dead in fifteen minutes! She'd order DeLeone to order Ascoyne, the commander-in-chief, to order Major Philip Sasso to put two bullets into the back of your head!"

"Why can't your precious *carbonari* waylay my carriage next time they send me out, take me into protective custody, and denounce the queen for forcing me to pose as her?"

"Because she'd simply issue a decree denying the whole thing, branding it a republican plot against the House of Savoy and the people. DeLeone, Father Asquino and sixteen other monarchists would stand up and make their usual impassioned speeches supporting her and denouncing us and that would be that."

"So I'm to be the sacrificial lamb in this stupid tug of war."

"Unfortunately, in every political struggle the rights, the privileges, the justice due the individual must be subordinated to the needs . . ."

"Of the majority, I know. Who doesn't know that old chestnut? But I'm not talking about rights or privileges or even justice. I'm talking about my life."

"You've got to trust me, Lorna."

"Oh, I trust you. It's your friends I don't trust. My problem is you do."

"Nothing's going to happen to you."

"Just how do you propose to guarantee that?"

"We've got to take this thing step by step. I can ease your mind in one respect. Nothing can possibly happen to you during Holy Week."

"You're sure . . ."

He nodded. "We liberals and the monarchists may be at swords points politically, but we are all Savoyards. And in all of Europe there's no nation more deeply religious. No Savoyard in his right mind would attempt to assassinate the queen during Holy Week."

"And somebody not in his right mind? Captain, from what I've seen in the short time I've been a guest in this delightful little duchy, your queen has made more enemies than Caligula and Genghis Khan together! High Mass, Low Mass, no Mass, it'll only take one to do the job. He or she may end up a hero, or be hanged, but I won't be here to see it."

"Calm down and listen. We can't expose you for another reason. Knowing you exist gives us an advantage Caroline-Louisa doesn't suspect. As long as she thinks she can continue using you without risk of detection, she'll go on tightening the screws on the people. The tighter she turns them, the more burdensome the taxes, the more brutal her tyranny, the better the *carbonari*'s chances of gaining the support we need to overthrow her. It isn't just the masses we need; it's the middle class, the merchants, the professional people, the small landed proprietors. Day after day she's pushing them further and further from her."

"What happens when Holy Week is over?"

"I've told you before a dozen times, I don't know when we're to make our move. When I hear, you'll be the first outsider to know."

She walked away from him, down the chapel, her slippers softly slapping the stone floor. She continued to talk, her back to him, her words directed at the arches, their keystones directly over her head.

"Well, that settles it."

"What?"

"What I have to do I will do myself. Oh, Maria will help. We've grown so close I think she'd stick her hand into the fire for me."

"You don't think I would?"

"With what you've told me tonight you've pushed me past caring whether you would or not. Understand this." She turned and glared stonily at him. "Since that noon I woke up on board the *Anselmo* I've done a complete about-face. Somebody once said adversity has certain advantages. They're right. You toughen yourself; you see things a bit more clearly . . . I'm no longer the trusting, patient, come-hell-or-high-water loyal soul I used to be. I've become very cynical and relentlessly suspicious. I've taken on a whole new nature, the way a snake takes on a new skin. I feel inclined to keep a wary eye on you, Captain Torzzini. You claim you've fallen in love with me. Maybe you have, but you were in love with your *carbonari* and its dream long before I left Hanover."

"Lorna . . ."

"So please feel free to remove your conscience from the hook. Forget about me, go back to work on your revolution. It sounds like it needs lots of work. As for me, I'll make it out of here all right. At the moment I haven't the wildest idea how, but there has to be a way and I'll find it. We Yankees are a resourceful lot. We turned a dim-witted king's stubbornness and a harbor full of tea to our advantage and ended up with a nation that in these few years is making this comic opera shambles of a duchy look as ridiculous as DeLeone's medals. Good luck to you, Captain, and good night."

She started for the door. He ran after her, catching up, seizing her by the arm, whirling her around, drawing her close, and kissing her.

"Don't!" Wriggling free, she raised her hand to slap his face. But the anger in her eyes faded quickly, the fire lost its fury and perceiving this, he once more took her in his arms and kissed her. Passionately. She had neither the will nor the desire to resist. It was too heavenly to stop; after Philip she needed it badly.

"You dare do anything to get yourself killed and I'll kill you," he muttered smirking. "I love you, Lorna Yankee Singleton Stone . . ."

"Please, no more Stone."

"Right, we bury the Stone."

"I'd love to, preferably alive. He goes to the top of my hate list," she added coldly, "ahead of sweet Caroline-Louisa, Charles Felix, Adelbert, the whole crew. On second thought, what earthly right has Philip to go on living?"

Releasing her, Paul threw up his hands. "In God's name, either give me that precious pig sticker of yours or toss the damned thing into the nearest cesspit and be done with it!"

"Not a chance." She stifled a yawn with the back of her hand. "Excuse me, blame the hour. I'm going to bed. And it goes with me, under my pillow."

"See that you don't roll over and stab your cheek . . ."

II

Wearing the funeral black of imperial bombazine—
beautiful to the eye, but irritating to the touch—a lace
scarf drawn through a ring over her bosom, black satin
sandal slippers, with her black kid gloves clutched in
one hand and carrying an exquisitely carved ivory fan
in the other, Lorna made sure that the simple silver tiara
supported by her wig was tilted ever so slightly forward
in place and nodded to the manservant who had escorted her from her rooms. He reached for Count De-
Leone's door, knocked, and withdrew with the most
subservient of bows.

Not one whit the wiser that she wasn't the queen, she
mused. Her imposture did have its moments. In one
hour she would be attending the Pontifical High Mass
at the cathedral, celebrated by none other than the
bishop himself. She herself would be on display with her
supporting cast of stiffly collared, spined and mannered
lords and their bombazine-bound ladies. Charles Felix,
according to the latest word reaching Maria, was having
one of his increasingly frequent "poorer days" and
would not be accompanying her. Lorna could only hope
that come Holy Thursday His Majesty would be feeling
sufficiently improved to be able to wash the feet of the
twelve poor men. Religious obligation or no, this
seemed a distasteful job of work, for even a counterfeit
queen.

Ushered into DeLeone's apartments, she passed the
small marble-topped table at which Philip had been
sitting with the prime minister and was bowed through
lustrously polished mahogany double doors with silver-
plated locks. Over her head in a round niche of Carrara

179

marble sat a bust of the count, minus, she noted, his galaxy of decorations. His face had been rendered considerably younger and more handsome looking by the sculptor in stone than by Him who had fashioned him in flesh; younger, better looking, leaner down his cheeks and around his jaw and, if such were possible, even more authoritarian looking, in the set of his mouth and the positioning of his eyelids in relationship of upper to lower.

DeLeone sat enveloped in the folds of a silk robe sizes too large for him. He was at his window looking down the hill at the entanglement of narrow streets, walkways and alleyways and the buildings around which they coursed. Chambéry, founded and fixed at the foot of the Chateaux de la Bathie et de Monterminod. Coffee and green tea were set out in company with dainty pastries and muffins and balls of butter on silver platters, arranged upon a perfectly lovely glass and bronze caddy. DeLeone rose as she entered.

"Good morning, Mrs. Stone."

"Good morning, Your Excellency. You wanted to see me? I shall be leaving for the cathedral for services in an hour."

"I know. Please sit. This won't take long." Moving spryly he arranged a chair for her, then wrapping himself back into his silken folds again took his own chair by the window. "Isn't it a lovely day?" She nodded. "Do you take coffee or tea?"

"Coffee, thank you."

As if actuated by some inaudible bell, a servant materialized at the inner door, stepping smartly to the caddy, pouring her coffee into a china cup so delicately thin the liquid was plainly visible darkening its conchlike pinkness. In an interchange of eye intelligence only, the servant then added cream and a single teaspoonful of sugar. The count went on talking.

"I myself drink neither tea nor coffee. My digestive system is not what it once was. I make a sip of brandy now and then my limit."

"May I ask what it was you wanted to see me about?" asked Lorna.

"A number of things. Try a honey burl, why don't you? They're quite delicious." She did so as he studied her, impatient, for her reaction, which she took to pains to make favorable. He beamed. "Joseph . . ."

"Excellency?" The servant who had been hovering about like a great bird of prey waiting to pounce into further service lowered his head so suddenly she marvelled that his neck failed to snap.

"Let us know when it is fifteen minutes before the hour."

"Yes, Your Excellency."

Joseph withdrew, closing his door. The count's request, as simple as it was, struck her nevertheless as incredible. Just the sort of absurdity that typified life among the lofty in the castle. For at the end of the room not twelve feet from where they sat was a clock with a case of intricate Boulle-work hanging from the wall. Clearly, it was keeping perfect time. To look at it, the count need turn his head less then three inches to the left.

"I must begin by apologizing for what happened here, the other day," he said somberly. "The outer doors should have been closed; your overhearing Major Sasso was most regrettable. His fault and mine. Embarrassing and unnecessary."

"Your Excellency, I would be grateful if you see to it that he keeps away from me." She sipped her coffee, eyeing him over the rim of the cup.

"Is the coffee to your taste?"

"Yes, thank you."

He turned in his chair to gaze out the window at the town below. "The major has already been instructed to stay away from you. From your rooms, your maid."

"If we pass one another in the corridor, I don't want him to speak to me or even look at me. If he pesters me, I must warn you I shall not be responsible for my actions."

Her threat brought the trace of a smile to his lips, but he nodded. "I will see that your wishes are respected. This does, however, raise a slight problem."

"What?"

"Please, finish your coffee. Let me pour you some more."

"No, thank you."

"You're letting it get cold. These cups are paper thin. More sugar, perhaps?"

"It's fine."

"Major Sasso had requested his commanding officer that he be permitted to act as your personal bodyguard at the mass this morning."

"No!"

"He claims he feels responsible for you."

"I said no! I don't want him within a hundred feet of me."

"As you wish. You will need someone, however."

"Then you are expecting trouble."

"An ounce of prevention . . . Isn't that what the doctor says?"

"You know something you're not telling me. What is it?"

"As usual, you're extraordinarily perceptive. Do my eyes give me away?" He leaned forward, lowering his voice. "Listen to me, there is this fellow, a vagabond, actually a paid assassin. We have heard that he has arrived in Savoy. Whether he has reached Chambéry yet or not we cannot be sure. The word is that the republicans have hired him."

"To kill me."

"He is reputed to be an expert marksman, extremely adept with a knife, and a master of disguise."

"Wonderful . . ."

"Now, now . . . Certain things are in your favor. We know of this scum. We know, for example, that he's no fanatic. He's not prepared to barter his life for yours."

"He's a professional; he knows what he's doing."

"Just the same, he'll need to plan carefully, to . . ."

"To do the job right." Dear God, her heart suddenly felt as if it were sinking down, down, down inside her, dropping to the pit of her stomach. "You say he's a master of disguise. So how can a bodyguard, anybody, be on the alert for him?"

"All of us will be looking for suspicious characters. We'll have spies all around. We will pick him out of the crowd like a bad cherry in a basket and hustle him out before anybody even realizes what's going on."

"You hope." She set down her cup, picked up a muffin, and put it back down. "One way or another I won't last out the week, will I? All the odds are against me. All the bodyguards and precautions and the sanctity of the church and Holy Week won't stop them. They tried, they failed, and they'll keep trying till they kill me. Isn't that so? Well, isn't it? *Say something!*"

"Now see here, young lady, get a grip on yourself and pay attention. You don't want Sasso protecting you, he won't. But you're going to need somebody. I've been giving the matter some thought. I hesitate to give you Rudolf again. Tsk, Tsk, he's such a sorry excuse for a soldier. A born buffoon. Yet he tries so hard it's unsporting to fault him for his ways. I don't expect it's occurred to you, but it was you who saved his life coming back from there. If you hadn't wandered off into the field he wouldn't have come after you." He paused, fingered the ends of his moustache and thought a moment. "Not Rudolf, and not the royal *pompa.**"

"Who?"

"Excuse my vulgarity. Her Highness's handsome favorite, Captain Torzzini. No, perhaps Lieutenant Calini. Yes, Calini. From now on there'll be at least two good men in civilian clothes with concealed weapons to stick as close to you as your shadow outside these walls."

"It all sounds very impressive. You'd be doing me a

* pump.

favor by pushing me into your bedroom and smothering me with a pillow," she said, avoiding his eyes.

He had inclined his head to one side and was staring at her. "You are brighter than that, much brighter. Do you think after going to all this trouble to get you here we're about to let you be snuffed out like a candle?

"Tell me something, child, do you hate me as much as you hate him? Knowing as you do that I engineered this sorry business?"

She glanced at the clock. "I could be dead in an hour, and you sit here worrying about what I think of you. I swear to God you men are all the same, all asses! You should have long ears, eat oats, bray, and pull things. Instead of trying to run them."

He shot to his feet, nearly upsetting the breakfast things, glowering vehemently. "Stop the sarcasm and the nonsense! You won't be dead in an hour, in a week, or a month. You'll die of old age at eighty-seven in your beloved Hanover, Massachusetts!"

"New Hampshire. Sit down, please, you make me nervous. I'm fidgity enough already."

"You are addressing His Excellency the prime minister!" Joseph came running to the door. DeLeone waved him back into the other room without even looking at him.

She set her jaw and narrowed her eyes at him. "If you want an answer to your question, sit down."

To her astonishment, he sat. "Well?"

"Do I hate you more than Sasso? I could have clawed your eyes out when you ordered René to shave my head. Better you brand me on the cheek than to do such a despicable thing, so hateful, so utterly demeaning. You know well enough what a woman's hair means to her. I saw your face in the mirror as he worked on me; you enjoyed every stroke immensely. I should despise you—you've insulted me, abused my dignity, treated me like dirt, humiliated me in front of others. . . ."

"But you don't classify me with Philip Sasso. I'm

glad to know it. Now there are a few things I would like you to know. Not excuses for my part in this, of that you can be sure. An explanation. My side of the story. Even a condemned murderer gets the chance to tell his side, eh?"

Old man, she thought, *why did you do it? Oh, yes, out of loyalty and duty; for the black eagle, your precious House of Savoy. You and Philip. I could kill him. I hate him that much, but you? In spite of your contemptible ways, your swaggering, your insults, that slap you gave me on board the ship that I feel again every time I remember, you who I thank for this loathsome-looking scalp of mine . . . In the face of all of it, I must be the stupidest mortal alive because much as I'd love to, I can't hate you. On the contrary, old man, God help me, I guess I even like you. Don't ask me to explain it, I wouldn't know how to begin. Maybe it's comparing you with him that polishes you, makes you less of a beast, more of a man. Ha! As if I'd ever tell you any of this; you're pompous and conceited enough already without my adding to it and easing whatever you have in you that passes for a conscience.*

Oh, yes, old man, another thing I can't tell you is that no carbonari-*hired killer will be coming after me. Thanks to Paul, his people may not be willing to rescue me, but they'll be the last ones to kill me. Not while they're after the real article.*

DeLeone's dark eyes had taken on a weary look, as if he'd unleashed his thoughts like dogs to run across a meadow chasing the wind.

"When I was Sasso's age, I wanted to be prime minister. I promised myself I would be in my mirror every morning when I got out of bed and every night before I blew out the candle and got in. General de Boigne's death and our success in bringing you here was fortuitous timing and suddenly," he snapped his fingers, "look who's prime minister! Off comes my uniform, on goes a suit as stiff as English armor with a red sash slanting down my shirt front. Behold, I *am* my country's prime minister!" He broke off a piece of muffin and disdaining the butter began nibbling it dry, his moustaches rising and falling like the wings of a lazy bird riding the mountain wind. "But having arrived now, able to put my hard-working ambition up on the shelf for a much-deserved rest, I find myself in a bit of a quandary. Where is the satisfaction I'm supposed to feel, the sense of triumph, the elation? Where are the wings on my heels?

"Is it because my office is not so much an honor, but is a bone tossed to me in payment for successfully abducting you, that noble accomplishment added to the death of my best friend who emptied the chair?"

First Philip and now this one, she thought, egged on by some inner compulsion to make her know how conscience-stricken they felt over what they had done to her. Who would be next in the confessional booth, she wondered, Caroline-Louisa? No, impossible. Inconceivable.

But she let him run on, not, she told herself, because he offered anything particularly original in the way of apology or attempt at justification for his black deed, but that she found herself incapable of bitterness toward him this lovely morning. She was not up to snapping back with sarcasm. Not even the clock on the end wall dispatching the minutes, sending them one by one into eternity, drawing her closer and closer to her rendezvous with threatened disaster, could alter her feelings for the man.

For all his pigheadedness, his consistently obnoxious behavior, his delight in demeaning her, his occasional forays into sadism, now, at this time, sitting across from him, seeing what could pass for pleading in his eyes, hearing the humility in his voice, she hadn't the heart to stop his running on.

He backtracked into his life. He assumed that she had taken it for granted he was a bachelor; but he had been married, fairly late in life. He'd been fifty-one, his wife thirty; she had died in childbirth. The baby, a girl, had survived, but had died at eight of rheumatic fever. Doctor Brabossi had tried his utmost to save her, but had failed.

"Her name was Cecilia, her mother's name. Had she lived she would have been just about your age." He paused, fixing his glance questioningly.

"Twenty-three."

"It may not be easy for you to make the connection, but it is for her, among other reasons, that I must confess how deeply ashamed I am of my part in this affair. It's as if I'd . . . well, you know, my own daughter. The order was given me; I obeyed. To command one as duty-bound as this old dog, for me to even fleetingly think to question that command, let alone disobey it, well . . ."

"Major Sasso alibied his part in it in much the same way," she said. "Duty called and he answered."

"I've called this my explanation, but it is an alibi, isn't it." He paused, cutting off discussion of the point and permitting him to bring up another. "It is not for me to say, because it is none of my business what goes on between you and the major, but I think you judge him too harshly. He is deeply in love with you, in spite of himself. For him to succeed in this mission carrying such a burden on his heart does say something for the man's character. Doesn't it, eh?"

"I can say a lot of other things for his character that tip the scales low enough to bend the bottom pan."

"I suppose. I understand."

"I believe you think you understand, Your Excellency; I don't know as you do. You imagine that I'm bitter. It's much more than bitterness that I'm carrying around inside me. You would have done better to gag me, tie my hands behind my back, and toss me into Charlestown Harbor to drown. Would that you had given me the choice."

He nodded mechanically from the start to the finish of this, while the visible portions of his cheeks above his flowing moustache colored. The nerve ends sprouting from his conscience seemed particularly sensitive this morning, she thought. Wonderful!

"All I have left to say without repeating myself is a promise. I can give you my sacred word of honor as a soldier and a Christian gentleman. Your life will be protected as if you were my own flesh and blood, as conscientiously as that of Her Majesty. And Charles Felix. There will be no more incidents like Conflans."

"Charles Felix has already come close to losing his life. Charles Felix . . ." She rolled the syllables around in her mouth as if they were foul-tasting food she was finding it impossible to swallow. "If he ever comes near me again he very well may."

"I'm sure you mean that, and who's to blame you? More coffee?"

"No, thank you."

Joseph appeared. "I beg your pardon, Your Excellency, it is fifteen minutes before ten."

DeLeone's eyes exchanged the man for the clock.

"So it is." He got up, extending his hand to assist her to rise. "May I have the privilege of riding with you and Lieutenant Calini to the cathedral, Your Highness?"

A crude and uncalled for attempt at humor, she thought. Still there was something in the way he said it that conveyed sincerity. As if his esteem for her had reached its pinnacle and there he intended to keep it. Like a climber's flag affixed to the top of a mountain.

The pathway of his alibi—for all its rambling—was paved with good intentions. No doubt of it. Her real enemy, as with Philip, was not this man, but his inflexible devotion to duty.

Duty, the catchall excuse for every crime in the book of human behavior.

III

The sun searched among the Alpine peaks for the aerie of Savoy. Finding it, it focused on Chambéry, drilling its most withering ray straight to the target circle of Lorna's tiara, as she rode along in the royal victoria, its calash down to give the populace an unshadowed view of their queen, the prime minister by her side, and Calini sharing the driver's seat. Hot and uncomfortable on the coolest evening, her wig was all but intolerable this stifling Sunday morning.

Dragoons led and followed the victoria, guarding its occupants on both sides as down a boulevard they moved, trundling slowly toward the cathedral, passing streets barely wider than footpaths. Circling the fountain of the four elephants, they came within sight of their destination, its immense and extraordinarily impressive exterior, the fortress of the Lord set lower upon His world than the castle which overlooked everything in the area but the mountain peaks.

They had traveled practically the length of Chambéry. Tired and tense, her nerves unraveling, she had been all but oblivious of the sights and the crowds, the devout caught up in the pious fervor of Holy Week. The town having been raised from a bishopric to the seat of an archbishop only thirteen years earlier (according to DeLeone), would see the celebration of this week of weeks orchestrated by no less a personage than His Holiness* Archbishop Umberto Falcone.

Falcone. Would he, she wondered, be related to Paul's Colonel Falcone, Chambéry's leader of the up-

---

* A title today bestowed upon the Pope exclusively, but in 1830 designating among others, archbishops.

rising to come? To come when? Thinking about Paul
sparked another question, one that troubled her. Why
hadn't *he* mentioned this man purportedly being paid
by the *carbonari* to assassinate the queen? He must
know about him. Why hadn't he warned her? It was
all becoming increasingly confusing, a lengthening chain
of "ifs" with no discernible final link. If DeLeone, sitting
beside her waving and nodding to the crowd, had told
her the truth, he was warning *her,* not Caroline-Louisa,
sitting safely surrounded by her castle. Obviously,
DeLeone had no possible way of knowing what Lorna
knew regarding the *carbonari.* Nor that Paul was keeping her abreast of every intriguing turn.

Or was he? The *carbonari* knew she was an imposter;
by now everyone in their organization throughout Savoy
had to know. Was bringing in this professional killer
intended as some sort of diversionary tactic? Was it an
out-and-out lie only designed to disquiet the monarchists? Or was the killer coming after the real Caroline-
Louisa? How would he get to her inside the castle?
The *carbonari* knew she never showed her face outside
the walls. At least they did now. . . .

Questions, questions, with only guesses, each one
wilder than the one preceding, for answers. But the
biggest question of all touched on Paul. Again and
again her concentration cut through the morass of confusion to find its way back to him. Was he being completely honest with her?

Her own words came back to her. Faced with a
choice that inevitably he would have to make, would
he throw her to the wolves? At that, was it possible,
would it make any sense at all for the *carbonari* to kill
her, *knowing as they did that she was an imposter?*
What could her death do for their cause, except to
reveal her as a fraud? No. Eliminating her would gain
the *carbonari* nothing. But lurking like a snake in a
dark and remote corner of her mind was one inescapable
truth: the *carbonari* weren't the only opposition to the
monarchists. At least half a dozen smaller but equally

dedicated factions were organized and prepared to join any effort to overthrow their majesties.

Only this morning Maria had awakened Lorna with the up-to-the-hour rumor. The republicans were stirring in neighboring Piedmont, an uprising appeared imminent, and according to Maria's informant, the troops would be called out to trample the malcontents into submission and ferret out their leaders for the government to try and then hang.

And yet in Lorna's meeting with Paul only hours earlier he had made no reference to this, either. Did he know about it, and was he either for reasons of his own or on orders from his superiors keeping it from her? Or had the news reached Chambéry *after* she and Paul had parted and she'd gone to bed? Could a ladies' maid obtain firsthand information before a professional spy could?

The victoria drew up before the cathedral and the crowd gathered around staring curiously, held away from the royal party by soldiers. Lieutenant Calini helped her down and she entered the cathedral between the two men, the dragoons marching in before and after them one by one pausing to touch the holy water, kneel, and cross themselves before ascending the twisting staircase to the king and queen's private box.

Was Maria's informant right about the situation in Piedmont? Or was it all just a rumor; the girl seemed to have an endless supply. Still, if there were to be an uprising, it could easily climb the alps separating Piedmont and Savoy, rush down the slopes and flood Savoy with *liberté, égalité* and *fraternité*. Even if the monarchist forces contained the "revolution," restricted it to Piedmont, Paul would probably still be ordered back to his unit, as for that matter, would Philip, loafing about the castle basking in the lingering glow of his success.

Seated on a velvet cushion, she lifted her veil and gazed down upon the altar aglow with candles, the altar table spread with the consecrated elements of the Lord's supper. The chanting of the choir rising to the great vaulted ceiling was stilled and Archbishop Falcone, his pinched and puckered little face lodged under his miter, called the faithful to prayer. Seated in their straight-backed chairs shoulder to shoulder row upon row, the worshipers dropped to their knees as one, heads bowed, the bald ones among them looking like globe turnips cropped and set upside down.

She must get through this service and the events of this day and meet with Paul that night. She had to know the latest turn of things and whether it would help or hinder her escape. There was no sign of him in the cathedral, upstairs or down on the floor with the host of army officers gathered in attendance near the apse. Then, out of the corner of her eye, she caught sight of Philip arriving at the top of the stairs, pausing, looking about. DeLeone spied him also and with a stony glare and a wave of his hand, dismissed him, sending him back down.

The Mass lasted until just before noon. The victoria took her back to the castle, and once inside the gate she sighed relief as she heard the portals thundering closed behind her. Still, it was such a perfectly splendid day— the burning sun that had accompanied her to the cathedral diminishing in intensity while she had been inside— she was tempted to send word to Clothilde and suggest they go riding. Off with her Caroline-Louisa makeup, on with her auburn wig, dress, and away! Up in the higher valleys the restless breeze was as cool as spring water, there was no dust, and one could escape the sun by the simple expedient of dismounting, and sprawling out, stealing the shade of the nearest tree. Pleasant conjecture, but there would be no time for riding or any other relaxation today or throughout the week. The queen's schedule was as full as the cathedral.

Following the twisting corridors to her apartment, accompanied by the lieutenant, they passed Captain Crespi, who appeared dusty and disheveled looking, as if he'd just come down off his horse after riding all morning. Excusing himself, he tugged Calini aside and the two began talking in low voices. She could make out only occasional bits and pieces, but one phrase in particular aroused her interest. "Piedmontese rabble."

She couldn't wait to get back to her rooms and Maria to find out if any further news had come from Piedmont during her absence. Brusquely thanking Calini for walking her this far, she announced:

"You two want to talk, I'll go on alone."

"*Signora,*" began Calini, a worried look forming itself around his aqualine nose.

"Let her go," remarked Crespi, goodnaturedly. "She knows her way back."

"But I'm supposed . . ."

"Go ahead, Mrs. Stone," Crespi said, waving her on.

Maria was waiting, all of a dither, all but exploding with news.

"Captain Torzzini, mistress, he stopped by here. He said to tell you he is leaving. He has been ordered back to his unit. I think it's the trouble in Piedmont. It's spreading, so they say . . ."

"So who says?"

"Everybody, the other maids, the guards. Francesca Cloynes comes from there. She got a letter from her mother. There is much unrest."

"Did Paul tell you that's why he's being called back?"

Maria shook her head. "He gave no reason. Only that I was to tell you he was leaving."

"When?"

"He's already gone."

"*Damn!*"

His regiment is camped near the Roman Station, the rock of Lémenc north of town."

"What did he say? Am I supposed to go to him there? That's stupid. How does he expect . . ."

"No, mistress, please." Crossing swiftly to the door, the girl opened it, made certain no one was lingering in the corridor, and closed the door. "Everyone is to be restricted to the camp, but he is going to get out tonight somehow and come back here."

"To the chapel?"

"No, here, this room."

"He's insane! To get to the chapel is nothing— through the inner gatehouse, across the inner ward— but these rooms are stuck back here in the corner past dozens of doors!" Suddenly overcome by the seeming stupidity of it all, she plumped down on the edge of the bed, scowling dejectedly. "They'll see him, they'll know he's supposed to be with his company . . ."

"He knows what he's doing."

"I doubt that. The whole thing's crazy; why would Caroline-Louisa let her favorite leave here? Even if there is an uprising, surely the army can spare one man, even a captain."

"Who knows what goes through that one's mind?" said Maria.

Lorna pictured Paul's and the queen's parting and laughed. "He's a born actor: He probably begged her on bended knee for the chance to go riding out on a white charger and play hero for her. It wouldn't surprise me if she's given him her favor to tie at his belt." Maria did not understand and said so with her expression. "You know, the way the knights of old wore their lady love's ribbon or hanky on their helmet or somewhere or other."

"Mistress . . ." Maria beamed, her eyes sparkling, her bosom heaving restlessly, preparing to pour out the last and best of her secrets. "He's coming back to take you with him . . ."

Lorna gasped and jumped up. *Dear God, at last! Why didn't you say so right off?"*

"Sssssh, somebody will hear . . ."

"Pack me everything I can use."

"No, he will be bringing a uniform. He wants you to disguise yourself as a dragoon."

"Me a dragoon? With this shape? He's crazy!"

"In the dark, with your riding cloak held around you, nobody will look that closely."

Grasping the girl's hands, Lorna began dancing a circle, her heart beating madly, happiness surging inside her, filling her, overflowing into her smile and gay laughter. *"Maria, Maria, Maria, I'm getting out!"*

"Sssssh!" Maria crossed herself. "Be still. I'll have to gag you if you keep up so . . ."

"What time did he say he was coming?"

"He didn't say exactly, only after midnight. The later, the safer."

"Oh, dearest Maria, I can't believe it! There've been nothing but darkness and driving rain in my heart ever since my wedding night. Wedding night . . . that disgusting charade *he* worked up for my benefit . . . Now suddenly the sun bursts through!"

Maria went to the bottom drawer of the highboy and kneeling, reached as far back as she could, bringing out a small, furry object.

"Take this for luck."

"A rabbit's foot? Ugh, no thank you."

"A rabbit's foot is always lucky."

"It isn't luck we'll need tonight, dear, it's grit and timing and . . ."

"Luck!" Maria shoved the rabbit's foot so hard into her midsection that Lorna grunted. And laughed. And accepted it.

IV

A clock in the town tolled midnight, mournful-sounding recognition of the hour unheard by the slumbering majority of citizens and residents of the castle. But to Lorna and Maria it signaled the impending beginning of the final chapter. A horror story with a happy ending. Attired in her satin *robe de la toilette* and mules, Lorna circled her room impatiently, urging the minute hand to speed up, pausing frequently in passing the vanity mirror to peer at herself and picture how she would look in the uniform of a dragoon. Hilarious was the first word to come to mind, too foolish to even hope to pass muster. But as Maria had said times beyond totaling, "Captain Torzzini knows what he's doing."

Out of the dying echo of the twelfth ring of the town bell had come comment from her fellow uninvited guest, the cricket, its stridulations determinedly insisting that it, not the bell, nor the wind, nor the guard calling the changing, owned the silence of the night to break when it wished. Lorna had developed a one-sided friendship with the squatter in the wall. She wondered if anyone in or outside the castle other than she, Maria, and Paul even realized it was there. For of all the sounds of night, its song, though perhaps the most distinctive, had to be the most determinedly ignored. One heard it, and knew what it was, but paid scant attention to it. Undaunted by human indifference the cricket continued night after night lifting its voice to the stars. It was so very sure of itself, so very confident of its mission in life. Lorna admired that; if only she herself were imbued with such enviable cocksureness. She sorely needed something like it to bolster her spine and her hopes.

Lately, in spite of all the activity, the demands constantly being made upon her, the fact that she was rarely left alone, when she had been she couldn't resist letting her thoughts slip back to Hanover and home, her father and mother and her brothers. Spring had come to New Hampshire and Vermont—when the air warmed, when the land came back to life, when the slopes of the Green Mountains and the White Mountains burst forth with wild flowers, armies of daisies and black-eyed Susans and red and white clover. The asters and violets and Queen Anne's lace were mustering along the roads and trooping down the green banks of the Connecticut River drifting lazily by, a stone's throw from their front steps. The field she had lain in on the way back from Conflans had dusted off memories of the meadow behind their house, the flowers different, but the colors the same, as was the intoxicating perfume of the grass, so green, so clean that it sparkled . . .

Maria came into the room done up in her nightdress and cap, carrying a candle and looking bleary-eyed.

"It's after twelve."

"I know."

"He could be coming anytime now." The girl glanced about the room. "You aren't taking anything?"

"What do you see here that a soldier would carry on him? That wig stand. A silken bed sheet for a handkerchief? Powder? Rouge?"

Maria laughed. "It's so good to see you smiling, not all bundled and bound nerves and worry lines burrowing into your beautiful face. Still, you mustn't count your chickens . . ."

"Never fear. I've told myself a dozen times that getting out of this place undetected will be a small miracle. Getting out of Savoy another. I really am avoiding optimism like the plague."

"He loves you, I can tell." Maria set the candle down in front of the mirror, doubling its light, and smiled warmly at her, in what struck Lorna as motherly fashion—overlooking the fact that the girl was at least four years younger than she.

"I guess he does, I don't know."

"Modesty, modesty." Maria stared at her fondly. "You're so lovely, how can he help himself?"

"I don't feel lovely. Not with this wispy excuse for a head of hair. Thank God for wigs." She paused and studied the girl. "I wish we could take you with us, dear Maria," she said, clasping her hands, squeezing them affectionately and kissing her on the forehead. "You've been so marvelous, so loyal and helpful."

Maria blushed. "Nonsense . . ."

"I mean it. Without your help I'd never have gotten this far."

"What far? You haven't even started yet."

"You know what I'm saying." She hesitated, releasing the girl's hands. "You're the dearest, sweetest friend I've ever had, Maria, and I shall miss you, terribly."

"I shall miss you, Lorna." Tears glistened in both their eyes. The cricket stopped singing, the wind rose softly, as if to fill the gap, then the cricket resumed its song. All the while they talked and waited and wondered when he would come.

An eternity passed and there came a subdued brief rapping at the door. Maria put her finger to her lips and padded to it, her nightgown swishing, her fat little body all but rolling as she walked. Opening the door a crack, she turned and beamed at Lorna and nodded. In he came, closing the door and leaning against it. Maria picked up an ivory-headed cane that had been leaning against the wall and started out the door.

"I'll be down at the end watching and listening. There's always somebody prowling about at all hours looking for something to tattle about. If anybody passes me coming this way, I'll drop this stick. If you hear a clatter, Captain . . ."

"Under the bed I go," said Paul smiling. "Just in

case it's your jealous husband, my darling," he added, taking Lorna in his arms.

"That's not funny."

"*Faux pas,* sorry." Maria left. Holding Lorna close, he brushed her cheek with his lips, sending a tremor through her body. He kissed her eyes, as gently as breath touching them. Then their mouths met, working slowly at first, then faster and faster, furiously, setting her heart thundering! She could feel her nipples harden touching the coarseness of his jacket, his buttons pressing against her flesh under the robe. How she ached to have him, here, now, his member thrust deep inside her, her sex overflowing with a great rush of rapture, her soul drowning in it!

Their mouths parted and for the first time she noticed that he had come empty-handed.

"Maria said you'd have a uniform for me . . . a disguise . . ."

His finger against her lips stopped her. "There's been a change in plans."

"Oh, dear God, no!" Backing away from him, she dropped onto the bed, staring in disbelief, unwilling to accept what her mind racing ahead warned her had happened; it was over before it had even started.

"Lorna, for God's sakes, let me explain! Yes, I intended to bring you a uniform, walk you out of here, down to the postern gatehouse where our horses would be waiting, and from there it would have been a ten-minute fast ride to the old Roman Station and our encampment."

"What happened?"

"This morning, while you were at Mass, orders came through that our squadron would be one of those leaving at three this morning for Modane and the Frejus Pass on the border of Piedmont. But since I last spoke to Maria—luckily I got a chance to after I came to say good-bye to Caroline-Louisa. Oh, Lorna, what an unbelievably slushy leave-taking that was. A fly on the wall would have fallen off laughing."

"Never mind her!" she snapped. "What about me?"

"My squadron was to be stationed at the border to reinforce the permanent guard against a possible invasion by Piedmontese insurgents. But early this evening Ascoyne, the commander-in-chief, countermanded the order. We're to stay where we are until further notice."

"Good God!"

He flung his hands out helplessly. "Had the damned thing gone according to plan, I would have brought you your uniform, a lieutenant's, whisked you out of here back to camp, passed you off as a transfer from the 117th or some other battalion, and you would have ridden out with us. It's better than sixty miles over the mountains: we wouldn't be getting there until well into tomorrow night—you'd have a dozen chances to get away and head anywhere you pleased. Of course your best chance would have been when we stopped for supper . . ."

"So you're not moving out, can't you sneak me into camp the same way?"

"And risk being spotted? Don't be ridiculous."

"It's no riskier than being on the move."

"It's ten times the risk. Who can say how long we'll be hanging about now? Besides, you've a big schedule ahead of you this week. If DeLeone and Caroline-Louisa don't find you here tomorrow, they're certain to send out search parties. They'll comb this whole corner of Europe looking for you. You're far too valuable to let go running off."

"So now there's no chance at all, is that it?"

"That's not so! It just doesn't make sense to try tonight . . ."

"Then when?" He shrugged. *"Damn it, don't do that!"*

"Shrug?" He looked at her as if she'd suddenly lost her senses.

"Just say you don't know, that says it all!"

"Lorna, will you please stop? You're coming apart. It's a postponement, not the end of the world. Your friend Adelbert and General Ascoyne panicked when they got wind of a possible uprising in Piedmont. Just our luck it turned out to be a vastly overblown rumor."

"What?"

"A handful of peasants got mad at a certain Baron Giozzo, the lord high linchpin in Chivasso. They tried to take over his castle and throw him out. They failed, naturally. But a few big mouths turned the whole thing into a full-scale revolution."

She shot to her feet, slipping from his grasp, backing against the vanity, clutching the edge of it and immolating him with her eyes.

"And where do you get 'postponement' out of that?"

"Delay, then. Call it what you like."

"I fail to see how a handful of outraged peasants trying to throw some pig out of his stone sty has any connection at all with your precious revolution, Captain!"

"Every time you get mad at me, I stop being Paul and start being Captain! You're ridiculous, do you know that?"

"I'm also desperate!"

This he took as a slap in the face, self-administered. "Forgive me, I know I've let you down. Crushed you with disappointment. It was all set; we could have pulled it off as easily as turning your hand over. I . . . I guess I wanted it to happen for you so much, so badly, it never dawned on me that the order could be changed. So I went overboard. . . ."

She softened her tone and managed a smile. "You tried, I'm grateful, I am, honestly. It was a first-rate idea . . ."

"It still is. We'll be on our way any night now, probably in that same direction. We could get away, perhaps to Turin, then on to Asti, and down the Tanaro River. Once we reach the Ligurian Sea . . ."

"We?"

Once more he took her in his arms. "Do you think I'd let you go alone? Not now. Not ever. I love you,

Lorna. It's gotten so I hate even letting you out of my sight."

She kissed his cheek in sisterly fashion. He tried to hold her and kiss her, but she broke from him, gently, wanting more time to talk. About when and where and other things. Details. She told him what DeLeone had told her regarding the *carbonari's* hiring a paid assassin. This he discounted as utter nonsense.

She nevertheless pressed the point. "What if one of the other factions hired him?"

"Oh, I don't doubt that he's been hired all right, but not by us, not by any anti-monarchists. DeLeone and his friends are the ones bringing him in."

"I don't understand."

"Because you don't understand politics, particularly as practiced in Savoy by our esteemed prime minister and his cronies. You've gotten to know him, try to think like he thinks. Hire a paid assassin to come in and shoot you. Yes, you, the imposter." Gasping, she shook her head rapidly. "Perhaps wound you, or maybe even kill you. Can you imagine the sympathy such an act would generate for their cause?"

"That's stupid, it makes no sense at all. I'm not their queen!"

"You know that, they know that, the *carbonari* knows it—though let's be thankful DeLeone doesn't know *that*. The people know nothing. Only what they're told."

His gray eyes gleamed. "It's really very clever, my darling. The best thing would be to wound you, perhaps not critically, but at least fix you so you'd have to be confined to bed. Think about it, Savoy's king, Savoy's queen, both incapacitated. Her Majesty ruling from her pillow, poor brave soul. Taxes, tyranny, all the other black deeds are suddenly shoved to one side in the mind of the man on the street. First things first, pray for Her Majesty, both their majesties. Given such a situation how can the *carbonari* appeal to the public to support a revolution? Have you ever seen a shrewder way to buy time? And time is the monarchists' most precious commodity. The longer they keep their grip on the little man, the more they can squeeze out of his pockets; and ironically, the more difficult it becomes for us to win him over. That's why an uprising next door in Piedmont would be so helpful, and why its failure to come about is so disappointing. Oh, your friend Adelbert is clever, he is, clever as they come."

"The bastard," she rasped. "The creaking, old, hypocritical, lying snake!"

"My, my, such language. Is that any way for a queen to talk?"

"He tugged at my heartstrings for a solid hour this morning before we left for the Mass. And every word out of his mouth was a lie! Can you imagine actually warning me to be wary of a hired assassin, assuring me I'd have all sorts of protection . . ."

"His" hired assassin. Some poor fool who thinks he'll be paid and helped over the border. Not a chance. Better to let him get in his shot, then catch him like a fly in a bottle and keep him locked up incommunicado. A long-drawn-out trial before they hang him would be ideal for their purposes. Get him to confess he was a *carbonari* or at least that we hired him, smear us and our 'traitorous ambitions' with a wide tar brush for as long as they can, and leave us looking like a collection of fanatical rabble-rousers."

"Who cares about any of that," she muttered. "I don't."

"You ought to, you're in the middle."

"You still can't make me believe that DeLeone or Caroline-Louisa would want me killed!"

"Why not? Who are you? What are you but a foreign piece of meat that happens to look like her?"

"Thank you!"

"You know what I'm saying. Besides, the people don't need a queen, they still have their king."

"About as fit to rule as the cricket in the wall!"

"Be realistic, Caroline-Louisa could very well prefer

that you die. Can you think of a better cover for her getaway?"

"Getaway?"

"A way for her to drop out of sight. She'd love to go home."

"You're wrong, Paul. She's too puffed up and pleased with herself giving everybody orders. She hates everything but her job, and that she loves."

"Maybe not. It could be getting to be a bore. Think about yourself being married to a madman, confined to this castle, ruling over a duchy that could be a former duchy and the newest republic in Europe before the end of this month. Lorna, she could fill her bags with jewels and florins and be back in Germany with her family and all the gentlemen friends she left behind in a few hours. Leaving everybody back here mouring her untimely death. Not everybody, but a good number."

"You do have an overactive imagination."

"Put the pieces together. Then tell me I'm not making sense. Oh, that part about her is fairly wild, I'll admit, but DeLeone's bringing in a paid assassin to make us look bad is as true as we're standing here."

"Archbishop Umberto Falcone," she began.

He nodded, anticipating her question. "Yes, our Colonel Falcone is his son. They haven't spoken to each other in twelve years. There's a lot of that in Savoy. Families split down the middle politically."

The clock in town tolled three and his eyes drifted to the porcelain clock on the vanity. The times matched exactly.

"You'd better go, Paul."

"You want me to?"

"Of course not! I'm just worried somebody will see you and tell her."

"If that's fated to happen, what time I leave doesn't make much difference, does it?" He turned toward the windows. "It's better than two hours till sunup. Why should we waste a loyal lookout?"

Taking her in his arms he kissed her passionately;

so ardently and so overcome was she by anticipation
of what the next two hours would bring, for an instant
she felt as if she would dissolve. Then she caught herself.

"The door!"

"I turned the key after Maria left. Come." Leading
her to the bed he eased her down, loosening the knot
that held her robe closed at the front, opening it.
Standing over her, he leaned down and caressed her
eyes with his lips, her mouth, her throat. Parting her
robe, he brought his mouth down upon her breasts,
their nipples emerging above the lace edging.

The touch of his tongue drawn slowly over and
around first one then the other set her thighs quivering,
nearly driving her to orgasm then and there. Her hands
gripped the back of his head, holding his mouth and
his gently striking tongue upon her now fully exposed
breasts. He continued working her toward an aching
urge to hurry the foreplay and as he did so he began
undressing. At length, he ceased his soul-rousing assault
and straightened up. Naked.

His tawny flesh seemed to pulse with the fire smoldering beneath its surface. She could feel her own flesh
glowing with ever increasing fervidity as he stripped her
of her nightgown and lay her back upon the downy
comfort of the bed. Sitting beside her, he drew her
mouth to his, thrusting his tongue inside, thrashing her
tongue, sending her blood racing through her veins,
her heart growing larger, fairly bursting with hunger for
him. A sort of madness came over her as he took her
in his arms and their flesh closed in exhilarating contact,
an uncontrollable urge to be ravaged, to be wantonly
and beautifully abused by this god-man, this Adonis
with his marvelous eyes gazing deep into hers. The
sublime torment of foreplay continued, his hands and
mouth besieging her with a tenderness she could never
have imagined possible, as if she were being stroked
with flowers.

His member became enormous; in her wildest girlish

fantasies she had never imagined a man's thing so huge. Feeling it throbbing full length against her thigh, the sight of it erect as he rolled her over on her right side to again devour her breasts with his hot kisses, filled her with dread as much as uncontainable desire to feel it sliding up her thighs, its great pulsing head finding the lips of her sex, entering her. He sensed her fear and immediately slowed the pace of their foreplay, becoming even more tender, biting gently, fanning the flames of passion to blistering heat.

He was huge! Immense! No wonder the queen practically held him captive. No wonder she envied any other woman's mere glance in his direction.

He would hurt her entering, she knew, but she would not cry out. He was over her now and lowering, still without a word, but with the unspoken language of love filling her senses, honing them to needle sharpness, setting her mind whirling. Between her trembling thighs he eased and pressed into her. The pain was exquisite. Philip in the dingy room in the Gray Dragon a lifetime before was a boy in comparison to this magnificent man. She opened her eyes to fill them with his, the sight of his lust seething in them, glazing them. Feeling him enter, the immensity of his member stretching the walls of her sex, touching every point of passion without movement, with the size of him only, she marveled.

Then having captured him, imprisoned him, she wanted him to move, to pry and prod and probe, savagely, brutally, hammering her relentlessly, filling her, forcing the fountains to release in the incomparable ecstasy of climax.

"My darling, my darling, my darling . . ." she moaned.

He moved, driving; deeper, faster, bucking wildly, bringing her own hips thrusting upward, her sex slamming at the marvelous, enormous head throbbing mightily within her. Driving her delirious with joy. She dug her nails into his shoulders, causing him to wince, but she held her grip, hanging on, bucking, taking it all, more and more and more . . . Faster, harder, more wildly until the room swirled and whirled with the speed of light above her head.

"My darling, Paul, I love you, love you, love you, love you . . ."

Her sight dimmed, her brain engorged with the sheer and utter ecstasy of the act. Now together they had abandoned the room and the world and the heavens, the black infinite, cloaking themselves in the rapture of their oneness, driving to glorious climax. Repeated a second, third, and fourth time. Then exhaustion, his beautiful body falling away, their limbs entangled, their chests heaving, fighting to refill their lungs, both wringing wet with perspiration.

She moaned aloud, the wordless rhapsody of absolute contentment.

He had said "we." We will leave together. We will get to the Ligurian Sea. Ligurian Sea, any sea, anywhere. In this world, any world, as long as they were we, together, one. For here was a man who could make love as no other man alive.

And he was hers!

V

His visit ended, however, on a disturbing note. It was impossible for him to set a date when he might return for her. Their flight was completely dependent upon his unit's orders. When word came from headquarters to break camp and move, providing it ever did, only then would he be able to sneak her into the squadron that the two of them could flee at the first opportunity.

Even after he'd kissed her good night and departed, and Maria had returned to go off to bed, Lorna, lying wrapped in the silence of the room, imagining him still inside her, began worrying. About little things, the seemingly insignificant factors that suddenly became all too significant in a crisis, and could collapse their escape plan and land the two of them on the gallows. Paul was right not to take her back with him to the campsite. Someone would be certain to discover her, particularly after word got out in the morning that a certain young lady, easily recognized by the condition of her hair, was missing from the castle. On that same naked head, the prime minister would doubtless place a reward of five hundred florins!

When it came to that, how in the world was she supposed to disguise her head, with her hair only just beginning to grow back, still under an inch long? She couldn't wear a female wig, blond or auburn. She'd have to keep a hat on day and night. If that didn't raise somebody's suspicions, what would? And in those tight-fitting jackets the dragoons wore, how would she conceal her bust? Perhaps flatten herself with a sash of some sort. Also she'd have to cleanse her face of all makeup . . . perhaps even wear a false moustache. No! There was a limit. She'd look and feel totally absurd.

One important thing was in her favor. Thanks to her father's dedicated instruction, and plenty of practice, she was capable of sitting a horse like a man and she could ride with the best of them. Better than Clothilde, who was too hard on a horse to be a first-rate rider. A horse had feelings like any other creature; make friends with him, get him to like you, and he'll do his best for you. Bully him and he'll do what he's told, but don't look for him to extend himself.

Dawn was rosying the slits between the window drapes when she finally got her thoughts in order, temporarily cached her fears behind hope and faith in Paul, ceased teasing herself that he was still making love to her, deluding herself that it was too marvelous ever to end and never would, and dropped off to sleep.

The day brought nothing in the way of news from Piedmont, although at Lorna's insistence Maria covered the entire castle in quest of the latest word. Her mistress spent the day well guarded, wheeling about in the victoria handing out little silver crucifixes to loyal Savoyards who had distinguished themselves in some small way, in time forgotten by all save the recipient and his immediate family. Men and women who had saved people from drowning, couples who had produced twins, people who had attended church every day for two years, farmers who had raised the largest flock of sheep in their neighborhood, or who owned the cow with the largest annual milk production, raised the most rye or oats or barley—all received their tiny rewards. Their benefactor, however, received a touch of vertigo from the unabatingly unreasonable, seasonable heat and came back to her apartment carrying a headache that threatened to split her skull.

So Sunday and Monday of Holy Week came and went with no attempts on her life, although the way she glared at DeLeone out of the corner of her eye, had he seen her, she reflected, he might have been tempted to the deed himself. Tuesday and Wednesday passed, with visits to local hospitals and convents and ceremonies at schools and churches.

Now it was Holy Thursday bringing with it word from Maria that surprised neither of them, that His Majesty Felix would be in his bed all day. He had been out hunting the day before, chasing hares, spotting one, wounding it, and rashly dismounting to chase the poor thing on foot. The hare got away, but Charles Felix had tumbled into a thicket, turned his ankle, and would be confined to bed at least until Easter Sunday.

"He's some hunter, that one," went on Maria. "Do you know how he hunts?"

"I have no idea, I'm not the least bit interested, but I know you're going to tell me anyway."

"Men go out an hour before he does, round up all the crippled chamois and ibexes, hare and ermine, or find healthy ones and hamstring or blind them and strew the poor things along the path he plans to take. He never fails to come home loaded down with trophies."

"Poor Charles Felix, he's not only mad, he's ridiculous."

As a liturgical rite for Holy Thursday, Mandatum, the rite of the washing of the feet, is first found in the canons of the seventeenth Synod of Toledo, in Spain, early in the eighth century, some three hundred years before the founding of the House of Savoy. The rite was to be performed in the inner ward of the castle under the paternal eye of Archbishop Falcone and to the accompaniment of the beautiful hymn *Ubi Caritas* sung by the cathedral choir.

The pomp and sacred beauty of the occasion were lost on Lorna, for the most obvious of reasons. Her nerves were so tightly strung, her heart so weary from constant pounding, she was fleetingly tempted to either fall on the knife she wore under her skirt or throw herself out a tower window.

Twelve poor men, their impoverishment visible in their eyes and in the slackness of their faces as well as their cheap and tattered clothing, had sat quietly waiting during the mass preceding the rite; now they stood in a double line, three of them leaning on crutches, all waiting patiently for their feet to be washed and their palms warmed with coins.

The archbishop spoke in his reedy voice in Latin, extolling, according to Count DeLeone whispering into Lorna's left ear, the charity of the Mandatum and reminding the faithful that in the Old Testament it was a sign of hospitality for a man to wash the feet of his guests:

" 'Let a little water, I pray you, be fetched and wash your feet, and rest yourselves under the tree.'* At the Last Supper blessed Lord Jesus first washed the feet of His Apostles, and, as His servants and ambassadors, they were instructed by Him to continue His work by imitating His example of humility.

" 'After that He poureth water into a basin and began to wash the disciples' feet and to wipe them with the towel wherewith he was gird.' "**

The archbishop continued quoting and elaborating on the history of the rite. Then a basin filled with clear water was brought out with towels and set near her. A chair was placed directly in front of her. Archbishop Falcone then beckoned the first man to approach.

She washed his wrinkled, but already well-washed feet, and a priest standing beside His Holiness handed her some coins which she in turn gave to the man. Somewhat overawed by all the attention focused upon him, he blushed, mumbled his thanks, and backed away bowing. His place was taken by a tall, emaciated, Christlike figure. He wore a full beard and his hair

* Genesis 18:4.
** John I: 13:5.

long, reaching to and resting on his shoulders. His eyes were the saddest she had ever looked into. As if he had been collecting sadness and banking it in them for half a lifetime. Or as if he had seen his own death that very hour and was mentally preparing himself for that eventuality. He seemed only remotely aware of what he was taking part in and when she touched the cool water to his instep, he flinched and cried out. Evidently the sensation had jolted him out of his melancholy reverie, bringing realization of where he was and what was happening to him. She washed his feet, he was given his supper money; he thanked his queen and the priest who had passed the coins to her and the archbishop, and withdrew.

The third man in the front line had taken two steps forward in response to the archbishop's beckoning when a disturbance broke out at the rear of the gathering. What followed happened with incredible swiftness. A shout went up, and another, and breaking away from the group assembled behind, came Philip. He hurtled by the priest who had been handing her the money, all but knocking him off his feet. Confusion reigned, the archbishop sputtered indignantly, and Philip's foot struck the basin overturning it, sending the water sloshing over the stones.

A shot whistled by her ear, followed by a second one which would have hit her squarely in the chest had Philip not thrown himself in front of her, catching the ball in his shoulder and collapsing onto the empty chair, shattering it. For a moment frozen in time the crowd stood immobile in stunned silence. Then came a loud gasp and cries of "Assassin!" At once, crowding the inner ward was no longer an assemblage of the faithful, but a panic-stricken mob, women screaming, men shouting, everyone rushing for the gates. Philip lay at her feet, blood gushing from the wound in his shoulder darkening the red of his uniform.

The first shot had struck a young priest standing behind and to the right of the one who had been passing Lorna the coins. The ball had found his heart, driving him down on his back with the force of a shovel slammed against his chest. He was dead before his head struck the stones.

Turning from the sight of him to Philip lying at her feet, she knelt quickly, but the blood pouring out of him, the hysteria surrounding her, enveloping her, the suddenness of the attack in such striking and horrifying contrast to the peaceful holy atmosphere of the ceremony, were too much for her. She fainted.

VI

Philip was painfully wounded, but in no danger of dying. DeLeone felt constrained to remind her that Philip had risked his life to save hers. At the prime minister's direction, without so much as a glance of approval from his Holiness, the Mandatum had been terminated on the spot.

Details regarding the incident came from witnesses outside the castle wall; these were coupled with logical assumptions. Apparently, moments before the rite was begun, out of sight of the crowd and the participants, the man had entered the gatehouse tower overlooking the ward. He was disguised as a guard. He had knocked the guard on duty senseless, fired his two pistols, dropped both where he stood and, availing himself of a coil of rope evidently previously hidden in the tower, had thrown a loop over the nearest merlon and begun scrambling down hand over hand. It was thirty-five feet from the merlon to the rock base below, where his horse waited. According to the outside witnesses, the killer had descended less than a third of the way when his rope snapped and down he fell breaking his neck. Thereby cheating the hangman out of the two silver florins he would have received as payment for breaking it for him.

DeLeone and Captain Crespi had brought Lorna with them to Caroline-Louisa's salon in response to Her Majesty's summons. She demanded an explanation:

"All we're getting is jumbled nonsense from the silly little bitches who wait on us. It would do our nerves a world of good if every single one of them wore their tongues around their necks like dear little Teresa!"

DeLeone, assisted by Crespi, related the incident. The queen listened rapt, lounging on her *méridienne,* eating pecans in oil from a silver dish set on a curule stool.

"What about the colonel who saved her life?" asked Caroline-Louisa, staring at Lorna, giving her the uneasy feeling that Her Majesty was imagining she had only just returned from the dead.

"Major Sasso, Your Majesty," said DeLeone, emphasizing Philip's rank.

"*Colonel* Sasso, Minister." The queen smirked and popped a nut into her mouth, chewing it like a chipmunk, thought Lorna. "It seems the least we can do for the man who saved our life. Don't you agree, Mrs. Stone?"

"Yes, Your Majesty."

How she despised this vixen! Sometimes, just slipping briefly into a thought or two about her, seeing her haughty, eternally miserable face in her mind's eyes, hearing the deliberate contempt in her tone; her captivity by the creature rendered Lorna as limp as seaweed. At times it so infuriated her that when she had shaken it off she had found deep nail marks in the palms of her hands from unconsciously clenching her fists.

"Sasso . . ." began DeLeone.

"*Colonel* Sasso," interrupted Caroline-Louisa.

"Colonel Sasso has a painful shoulder wound, but Doctor Brabossi assures us that it is not serious. The ball has already been removed."

"That's a relief."

Lorna sensed that DeLeone disapproved strongly of Philip's sudden elevation in rank. Perhaps because it hadn't occurred to the old man himself to suggest it. Watching and hearing about egos clashing up and down the ranks was one of the few sources of amusement for Lorna. As to Caroline-Louisa, the only amusement she inspired was the maids' and ladies-in-waitings' gossip detailing her excesses and more infantile abuses. Her Majesty had a talent as well for imbuing those around her with the poison of her bitterness and chronic self-made discontent. She seemed to delight in hurting people's feelings, in embarrassing them, in grinding their pride under her heel. Lorna had early decided that the most sensible way to deal with her was to ignore her sarcasm. Let it strike and roll off her like rain off the leaves. Trying to shield her self-respect in such a manner may have been sensible, but it was far from easy. So the less she saw of the queen, the better for her.

It was hard to believe that Caroline-Louisa and Clothilde were sisters. Clothilde was vain and stupid and made an effort to be overbearing, but she couldn't begin to compare with the queen in those respects or any others similarly disagreeable. No one, male or female, was quite like Caroline-Louisa; no one Lorna had ever met.

DeLeone and Crespi were dismissed, the latter commanded to "find Clothilde and send her to us."

"Also," Caroline-Louisa went on, "this insanity this morning is extremely upsetting to us. We want more guards assigned to castle duty. We'll feel safer. Captain Crespi, see that Captain Torzzini and some of his men are brought back."

DeLeone cleared his throat and studied the floor. "Your Majesty, Captain Torzzini's squadron is awaiting orders . . ."

"We don't need his whole squadron, just him and two or three of his best men. If you're worrying about Piedmont, Adelbert, forget it. Some of our most loyal subjects are in firm control there."

"As you wish, Your Majesty," said DeLeone, his tone subdued.

"You," said the queen, spearing Lorna with a stare, "will stay. We haven't talked in ages."

"May I sit?" asked Lorna. This brought gapes of

isapproval from both DeLeone and Crespi as starting
ut the door, they turned to look.

No, shouted Lorna at them silently, I never will learn,
ill I! Get it through your heads, I'm just not the
ibservient sort. I've never met a Yankee who was!

"I still feel a little shaky," she said turning back to
'aroline-Louisa.

"Of course you do," said the queen. DeLeone and
'respi left. Caroline-Louisa motioned her to the *chaise
ondole* set against the wall between the *méridienne* and
window bench upholstered in scarlet velvet as were
ie other three pieces. "Eat a pecan. They are ex-
:llent for the complexion and the liver." To Lorna's
irprise, the queen picked up the dish and offered the
uts to her. Lorna took three.

"Thank you, Your Majesty."

"Were you terribly frightened?" asked Caroline-
ouisa, eyeing her intently.

"Terribly. I've never been shot at before."

"Nor we. It must have been exciting though." Her
uestioning look gave way to one of discouragement.
Still, it's horrifying, and unfair. We love them so, every
ie, rich or poor, young and old, the ill, the well.
/e've given them our hearts. We look to their needs
ke doting parents. How could any one of them even
ceam of harming us? It had to have been an outsider,
course."

It was all Lorna could do to beat back the tempta-
on to suggest she ask her prime minister for the
etails on that. Lorna smiled inwardly. How she'd love
poke a hot stick into the hive of the House of
ivoy and stir up the hornets against each other. As
she dared!

Caroline-Louisa went on and on about her subjects
id the love she lavished on them and how painful
was to have to confine herself!

"Just because a handful of maniacs are running
ound threatening us, telling lies about us . . ."

Lorna quelled an urge to yawn in her face. When

moments later the door opened and Clothilde walked in; it was all Lorna could do to keep from jumping up and embracing her out of gratitude for interrupting her sister's boring excursion into self-pity.

Clothilde was in a sour mood. Her favorite horse, an Arab stallion "that could outrun the wind down from the Pennines," had been killed an hour earlier.

"That dim-witted tramp of a stable master had him destroyed! Emir was sick with glanders, just sick, not dying, and he, the fool, ordered him shot! He should be discharged and beaten out of Chambéry." She turned from Caroline-Louisa to Lorna. "Have you ever heard anything so stupid in your life?"

"He did the right thing," said Lorna mildly, realizing as she spoke that she was deliberately courting an argument. But she was unable to resist commenting, particularly since Clothilde was openly looking to her for corroboration, although totally wrong. The effect of her words on the girl surprised her. Instead of biting back she appeared to shrink into herself, thoroughly discomfited.

"Glanders is terribly contagious," went on Lorna. "And incurable. The horse would have died whatever was done for him. Killing him probably saved half the stable."

"Contagious?" asked Clothilde mystified. "What does that mean?"

"It means it spreads and everything catches it, Clotee," interjected Caroline-Louisa, pleased with herself for being able to contribute.

"Oh," said Clothilde in a little girl voice.

"We've more important things to talk about than your silly horse."

"Emir was not a silly horse, Carrie! He was a pure-bred Arab as fast . . ."

". . . As the wind down from the Pennines; we know." The queen offered both of them nuts from the dish and rang for wine and filled Clothilde in on wha had happened in the inner ward during the Mandatum. Clothilde gasped.

"That's terrible!"

"We agree. And we think Mrs. Stone deserves a respite from her duties."

Lorna loved the choice of word, coughing into her hand and excusing herself, all to cover a smile.

"Since you've lost your favorite horse we don't suppose you're in the mood for riding," continued the queen. "What else can the two of you do?"

"Go through the shops in town!" exclaimed Clothilde. "You'll adore the shops. They're ten times more fun than hanging about this boring old place. And they'll take your mind off what happened."

"Perhaps, but I'd really rather make it another time," said Lorna. "What I need now is a nap. This business this morning . . ."

"She's right, Clotee. She's been through a nerve-racking experience. Just to think it could have been us out there makes us tremble. Perhaps later this afternoon?" She arched one eyebrow inquiringly at Lorna.

"Say yes, Lorna," said Clothilde.

"Another day, please."

"We leave it up to you," said Caroline-Louisa. "Have some lunch, take your nap, and settle your nerves."

"We'll have lunch together," said Clothilde, getting up. "Come." She reached for Lorna's hand. "Let's storm the kitchen."

VII

So there were to be good and bad in fairly equal balance, at least for the remainder of a Holy Thursday that in seconds had turned into an unholy brush with tragedy. Paul would be returning to the castle. Her Majesty would feel safer with additional guards. And safer and satisfied under her silken sheets.

Lorna sat with Clothilde over lunch in a small dining area off the kitchen. The meal consisted of a nondescript broth, a salad of cold breast of red-legged partridge, a berry tart, and tea. Clothilde rambled on and on, nimbly jumping from one dull subject to the next, so absorbed in her own words that she failed to notice that Lorna wasn't paying the slightest attention.

After last Sunday night, a span of darkness encompassing the most glorious two hours of her life, she was dying to see him again. And she would, when he was able to slip Caroline-Louisa's leash. To think that shortly the queen would be in his arms, feeling him, luxuriating in him, infuriated Lorna, but there was little to be gained by displaying her feelings for Clothilde's amusement.

At least he was back, or coming back shortly. They would be able to resume their clandestine meetings. To be sure, he dare not come to her rooms again, much as she would have wanted him to. Were he to suggest it, for his own protection she'd forbid it. But in spite of the nettles in the stew, mere knowledge that he would be back inside these four forbidding walls cheered her.

If he hesitated to meet her in the chapel, there must be some other place no one frequented late at night, perhaps one of the tower rooms, anywhere except the torture chamber. Recollection of that dank and dreary place with its hideous instruments all but panicked her.

"You look pale," said Clothilde, "are you ill?"

"Just nervous, and tired."

And worried, as usual, not only over the possible recurrence of the morning's incident, or perhaps another explosive device—this one attached to the victoria— nor even how long Paul and she would have to bide their time before attempting to flee. What troubled her above all of it was Maria. Whether they left as planned when Paul's squadron moved out, or tried to sneak out and head for the nearest border, they'd have to leave Maria behind. Visions of Teresa Zuccola, her tongue cut out and the frightful noises issuing from her mouth crossed Lorna's mind. Left behind to face the fury and brutality of the queen, Maria would be so vulnerable. Loyal, to be sure; they could beat her, even torture her, but she's never betray the Yankee and her captain . . . Yes, Your Majesty, mine!

She couldn't let that happen to Maria, she wouldn't have the heart. They would have to take her with them. If Paul objected it would be up to her to persuade him. She owed it to the girl. Without Maria's willingness to risk her all out of friendship, this Lorna Singleton could be stone dead.

Stone. It occurred to her that when she got back to her room after lunch there would be a note waiting, an order disguised as a suggestion from DeLeone that she go to Philip and thank him for risking his life to save hers.

Sitting nibbling at her salad, closing her ears to Clothilde's chatter, she could almost compose the contents word for word. It would, of course, include an appeal to her conscience. How outrageously ironic. As if either Philip or DeLeone had the slightest acquaintanceship with conscience. Though that wouldn't keep the old liar from nudging hers.

Still, she'd been relieved to hear that Philip's wound

was not fatal, and would not be crippling. Had he been on his deathbed, her sense of fair play would have forced her to go to him. But in light of the circumstances she could be flint-hearted and not bother. Besides, she had suspected from the very first that DeLeone had planned Philip's courageous gesture as surely as he'd planned the attempted assassination. As dangerous as it was. They were all mad, the lot; Charles Felix's insanity was as catching as glanders. Caroline-Louisa had it, DeLeone, Philip, even Clothilde a touch. If she herself stayed around the place much longer surely she'd come down with it!

Thank God for the saneness of Maria and Paul, now that she thought about it, the only two people she could trust and count on within a circle nearly nine thousand miles in diameter! She could scarcely trust Clothilde, not with her so clearly defined allegiances and her unstoppable mouth. This reflection sparked an idea. Questions and answers was a game that worked both ways.

"What's all this about Piedmont?" Lorna asked.

The question, interrupting Clothilde's babbling, coming out of a blue nowhere, jarred the girl. Nevertheless she seized on it.

"What about Piedmont? Have you heard something?"

"They say there's to be an uprising there . . . Something much more serious than that business about that handful of peasants and the castle."

"There could be an uprising. Charles Felix and Adelbert are always worrying about Piedmont," rejoined Clothilde, lowering her voice to the customary range of intimate gossip. "Mostly because it's on the other side of the Alps. They have all sorts of spies running around over there, but they don't really trust any of them."

"Is there a person breathing that Adelbert does trust?"

Clothilde thought this over briefly, knitting the inner

ends of her eyebrows together in a frown, then shook her head. "Turin's the bad spot. Nine years ago when Charles Felix's brother, Victor Emmanuel, was king, there was a mutiny there."

"The army?"

Clothilde nodded. "And there've been lots of little squabbles since."

History began pouring out of her at an impressive rate. She may not have known what glanders was, and the definition of contagious had somehow escaped her education, but she knew Savoy, probably, mused Lorna, listening attentively, because it and its politics were practically the only subjects of conversation among her sister, her bother-in-law, Adelbert, and the other high-ranking and influential Savoyards.

When the Restoration of 1815 returned the rule of Savoy to the House of Savoy, including all the territories previously annexed by Napoleon; back to Piedmont from seventeen years' exile on Sardinia had come Victor Emmanuel. His re-emergence, and the fact that he set about at once dutifully dousing the lingering brush fires of liberalism, triggered a kingdom-wide re-examination of political perspectives, initiating a whole new era. The king's campaign had an effect entirely the reverse of that he intended. It created a situation that ultimately spawned the *carbonari* who promptly announced their intention of championing the cause of unity and independence. The Piedmontese wanted not only liberty, but a constitution, as well, not to mention immediate war against the despised Austrians.

The mutiny in Turin was put down, with the help of a German army. The leaders were court-martialed and shot, and an uneasy peace settled over the land. But the idea of Piedmont-Savoy-Sardinia in its entirety becoming a republic had been born. Despite the monarchists' earnest efforts to uproot and destroy this idea, it had thus far proven ineradicable. Thanks, in great measure, to the *carbonari*'s nettlesome activities, as much as the taxes and tyranny of Victor Emmanuel, Charles Felix, and Caroline-Louisa.

"There's bound to be more trouble in Piedmont," said Clothilde. "There's always something happening there. But what do you care about that?"

Lorna wrinkled her chin and tossed one shoulder. "Just curious."

"There won't be any war. Just uprisings, put down as easy as stamping on an ant."

We shall see, said Lorna to herself, we shall see.

VIII

The remainder of the week ending with Easter Sunday was filled with events for the Savoyards. Lorna obligingly continued in her role, going through all the motions required of her. DeLeone set the tenor for her conduct with one of his patronizing observations: "We mustn't let that unfortunate affair in the inner ward cast a pall over the week."

She was seeing more of Clothilde now, little of Her Majesty, and not so much as a two-second view down a corridor of Paul, although, according to Maria, he had returned to the castle the previous Thursday afternoon. Climbing the spiral staircase leading to the northeast corner tower of the inner ward directly above the kitchen, she and Maria walked along the top of the inner wall discussing the situation.

"I have to talk to him, Maria."

The maid's response to this was a sympathetic frown, an effort to share some of the discouragement Lorna was feeling.

"I don't think he's been out of the queen's bedchamber since he came back."

"That's good news," she said sarcastically. "Can you get a note to him?"

"While he's with her? That's dangerous, mistress, for him. Worse than ever now. She's so jealous; if she ever even suspected the two of you, you know . . ."

She paused, lowering her eyes as two guards approaching passed them and vanished around the corner. Lorna sat down in the corner of a merlon and looked out over the green landscape fastened to the world

225

by pines and chestnut trees. Beyond, the Alps climbed gray-green to their snow, dazzlingly bright with sunshine.

"She's such a devil," continued Maria.

"What has she done now?"

"She simmered down during Holy Week, the bullying, the shouting, the insults, all of it. She spent most of her time with Father Asquino, but now that Easter's past she's back at the maids and her ladies-in-waiting worse than ever. Ranting and raving and accusing everybody of spying on her."

"She's as sick as Charles Felix."

"She is, but please wait till Captain Torzzini contacts you. It's safer."

"They way things poke along around here God only knows when that will be." She looked up at the girl and smiled affectionately. "Maria . . ."

"Yes?"

"There's something very important I want you to do."

"If I can."

"For you, not us. I haven't talked about it with him, naturally, not having seen him since Sunday night, but when we get a chance, I intend to tell him that you're coming with us when we leave."

Maria gasped. "Oh dear, I . . ."

"You want to, don't you?"

"I hadn't thought about it." Maria avoided her eyes and her voice suddenly assumed a fearful tone.

"You'll come; it's not safe for you to stay."

"But I can't . . ."

"Of course you can!"

"How? I wouldn't fit into one of their uniforms; I'm frightened to death of horses; I've never ridden one in my life. Besides, the two of you are taking a big enough risk as it is. With me along you wouldn't stand a chance."

"You mustn't worry about us."

"He wouldn't want me, mistress; you wouldn't need me."

"What are you afraid of, Maria?"

"I wouldn't want to make it harder for you, and I would. Besides, I don't mind staying, really I don't. Life isn't so hard here for me. Not since I don't have anything to do with Her Majesty."

"You've got to come with us. Once I'm out of here, you'll be back waiting on her, with Teresa and the others. But that's not what's worrying me. The big thing is she and DeLeone will have to suspect you helped us to get away."

"I'd never tell them a thing."

"They'd make you!"

"What could I tell them? I don't even know where you're going."

"That doesn't matter. All they have to do is think you're holding something back and they'll torture you. I've seen that place, and believe me, you wouldn't want to. One look and you'd pass out from fright."

The girl gasped and looked away. Lorna had never realized how very young she was, in many respects a helpless innocent, in spite of her courage and spirit. "They wouldn't" she said, "I'd tell them the truth, that I don't know where you've gone."

"Maria . . . Maria . . ."

"I don't want to wreck your chances. I'd only slow you down."

Lorna didn't want to say it, but it was the only thing she could say. "They'll kill you if you stay."

"You mustn't say that, please. It frightens me so."

Lorna stood up, gripping her by the shoulders. "You're coming and that's that. We'll talk no more about it now. It's very simple, dear. Paul will agree to take you. If he doesn't, then I won't go!"

This burst of straightforwardness had all the impact she could have wished for. Maria threw her arms around Lorna's waist and hugged her tightly. She began sniffling.

They parted company at the foot of the stairs, Maria summoned by Clothilde along with twenty other maids to begin preparing the great hall for Her Majesty's birthday party the following Sunday.

Lorna had little to do with what remained of the day but ramble through the corridors and think ruefully about Paul. That evening after dinner, after tumbling deeper than usual into the well of discouragement, she decided to retire early. It was still dusk, not yet time for her friend the cricket to begin chirping, but better to sleep than sit around moping.

She avoided Philip, even the thought of him, with fierce resolve. She told herself she would almost be willing to subject herself to another scalping if that would ensure that she never lay eyes on him again. Paul she missed, however, enormously, achingly. Memory of his embrace sent a tingling sensation through her body. But Maria was right as usual; better and safer to let him contact her. The fact that he had yet to in no way signified any lessening of his love for her, she assured herself. Dear Caroline-Louisa's relentless possessiveness was the culprit.

Disrobing, putting on her nightgown, making her toilette and taking care to slip the knife under her pillow, she locked the door, snuffed the candles one by one blending the shadows into total darkness, and got into bed. Within minutes she fell asleep, the disheartening gloominess she'd brought to bed with her displaced in her mind by a pleasant dream. Paul and she were together in a green and glorious place that looked suspiciously like Grafton County, Hanover and home. They made love in a lush and lovely field walled away from all but angel eyes by tall timothy and taller loosestrife raising its purple proudly for the gentle caress of the passing breeze. Lying close, touching, feeling the warmth of his flesh and his sweet breath on her cheek, was making love. And when after a beautiful interlude of foreplay she took him into her, it was so marvelous, she felt utterly transported.

Then, inexplicably, the dream shattered like glass, leaving a pale gray void. Something was touching her right side, the length of her arm, and her thigh down her leg. Body warmth, alien contact, unwanted closeness; instinctively she recoiled from it. Masculine odors, unfamiliar to her nostrils and the sound of heavy breathing quickly aroused revulsion and fear as she came awake. She shuddered, her mind silently shrilling warning of the horror that was to come, paralyzing her voice. A clammy hand ran over her thigh and stomach, over her heaving breast, and closed over her mouth, cutting off her scream as in desperation she found her voice.

His eyes glowed Satanically in the velvet darkness, his disgusting breath burning her cheek as his lust intensified. She could hear him lick his lips in anticipation . . .

His touch, his eyes, his breath . . . Charles Felix! His wet mouth came down upon her cheek to sneak beneath his hand cutting off her breathing. She struggled with all her strength, gripping his wrist, straining, pulling away his hand. She screamed, a piercing cry of horror mingled with dread. It so unnerved him he pulled back, his eyes widening. Then the instinct to ravage, to satisfy his demanding lust prevailed, sending his hands to her hips, tearing away her nightgown, exposing her sex. She screamed and screamed as he mounted her. Writhing, she strained to slip from beneath him, her arm twisted beside her head, her hand digging beneath the pillow, locating the knife, pulling it out.

Manhandling her naked breasts, panting furiously, he positioned himself, rammed his throbbing member between her thighs. But locking her ankles, she pressed her thighs together tightly—exerting every ounce of strength she had, vising his organ—and raised the knife above his back.

All the while screaming, screaming.

The door burst open, lamp light flooding the room eerily. Two men. One she recognized as Philip, standing in his shirt-sleeves, his left arm hanging stiffly at his side. The guard with him lunged forward, seizing her wrist, stopping the knife's downward plunge barely an inch from her attacker's spine. In the grip of the guard her fingers lost their strength instantly, as if the cords to the muscles had been cut like strings. The blade tumbled harmlessly onto the king's upraised back and was recovered by the guard, even as Philip took hold of Charles Felix's shoulder with his right hand and pulled him off her.

A loud groan escaped her lips, the long, drawn-out, heartrending wail of the helpless saved, pulled back from the brink of the chasm.

IX

Caroline-Louisa looked strangely pale and drawn, as if an illness were beginning. She lay on her *méridienne,* her slender neck resting against the sharply scrolled asymmetrical arm, the curving back of the lounge sweeping down behind her resembling an ocean wave gathering its bulk, preparing to break. She wore a velvet robe as black as obsidian, its cuffs and shawl collar trimmed in ermine. The black against the scarlet of the lounge and the other pieces in the room only heightened her pallor.

Two maids were in attendance, and Paul, deliciously dashing in his dress reds, thought Lorna, his saber dangling by his side. He was pretending as well as he was able to show as little interest in her as possible, concerned at that moment with working a loose thread out of one cuff.

On the curule stool lay her knife, like a scepter on a pillow. Her Majesty had said nothing whatsoever to her, not even deigning to nod as she entered and bowed. Before, that was demanded of her. Lorna watched Caroline-Louisa in silence as the queen beckoned to one of the two maids who hurried forward. The queen fixed her gaze on the knife, and picking it up gingerly by the tip, the girl handed it to her. Caroline-Louisa examined it, thumbing the sharp edge as skillfully as a pirate, thought Lorna, standing, watching and still seething.

She didn't need the mad king of this mad kingdom in her life, in her bed, in that part of her mind where peace was entitled to reign! The fact that he was Caroline-Louisa's husband, that evidently she didn't need him either, preferring Paul instead, more than rankled Lorna. It made her wish with all her heart that it was her own thumb testing the blade edge preparatory to driving it into Her Majesty's heart!

Only slightly less annoying was the coincidence interjected into the incident. Though not for a moment would she consider it such. It was the fact that of all the nearly three hundred guards, servants, and persons of rank occupying the castle, it had to be Philip whom fate had placed close enough to her door to hear her screams. Saving her seemed to be becoming a habit with him. He and the guard had performed their heroics and left, taking the knife and Charles Felix with them, His Majesty babbling semi-coherently, remonstrating with them about the situation in Piedmont.

Abandoning even the idea of attempting to get back to sleep, she had aroused Maria, with no little difficulty, confirming that the girl had been drugged. Lorna had then examined herself, decided that she had come off better than the first time, having suffered no ill-effects other than the fright of her life, and with Maria alternately stuffing her fingertips into her ears and crossing herself, had embarked upon a string of invective that all but wrinkled the drapes.

She was nobody's fool, least of all DeLeone's. He had made certain Philip would be within earshot, as well as assigning some underling to drug Maria and another to steer Charles Felix to her rooms.

She cast a sidelong glance at Paul, who continued to ignore her. Caroline-Louisa held up the knife.

"Where did you get this?"

"I found it."

"You're a liar!"

"I'm a liar, Your Majesty."

"Hold your insolent tongue, bitch! Or I'll have you hung by the thumbs until your nails drop out." She flung the knife back onto the stool, glaring at her malevolently. "Listen, and do not interrupt, as you usually do. Not one sound!" The queen's pallid complexion was fast altering to pink as her anger rose. "You amaze us, you really do. We have never known such ingratitude. We give you the best of everything, clothes, jewels, rooms, everything." I live like a queen, thought Lorna, clenching her teeth and digging her nails deep into her palms, battling to restrain herself. "We give you free run of our castle. We treat you as a sister, and this, this obscene behavior is the thanks we get."

Lorna's jaw dropped. Stunned, she stared at the queen, unable to believe her ears.

"Are you saying . . ." she began.

"*Silence!* Captain Torzzini . . ."

"Your Majesty?" Paul turned from the window, striding swiftly to them.

"You . . ." Caroline-Louisa pointed at Lorna. "Turn toward him." She did so. "Captain Torzzini, face her directly." Clicking his heels and bowing, he did as commanded. "Draw your blade." The sound of the saber being unsheathed sent a chill twisting through Lorna's heart. "Now, if she so much as parts her lips, you will open her throat!"

His jaw muscles tautened as his eyes lowered to avoid Lorna's. "Yes, Your Majesty."

"Yankee, upon your head we place full blame for what happened in your rooms last night. We are forbidding you to speak for a very good reason. All your denials, all your lying, cannot disguise the truth. You lured Charles Felix to your bed, to your arms . . ."

Lorna stepped back, preparing to interrupt, to deny. But sight of the tip of Paul's saber coming up to within half an inch of her throat gave her pause. Of all the twisted, baseless, insane accusations she had ever heard in her life! Clenching her teeth so hard she feared she would crack them, closing her eyes and praying she might do the same for her ears, she stiffened and began to die slowly, from the sheer and utter frustration of being forbidden to defend herself.

"Don't fancy for a moment that the motive behind your shameless lechery escapes us. You're not the first to attempt to take advantage of his Highness's unfortunate condition. To use your body to win his favor, to turn him against us, knowing well the advantage you have over the others. In his present state, with your resemblence to us, it's not in the least surprising that he mistook you for us. You used that, you slut, you gutter baggage, you whore! *Whore!* That's what we've so graciously and charitably taken into our circle, Captain Torzzini, a devious and scheming whore.

"For your unspeakable conduct, for taking advantage of a confused and helpless man, you will pay!" Her voice was like flint, the last three words carved, shaped, and sharpened, a dagger of stone. She paused, her face now scarlet, plunging into thought, angling her head sharply and eyeing the ceiling. "Precisely how, in what coin, we have yet to determine. But pay you shall. Now get out. Before we lose our temper and order him to run you through! *Out!*"

Lorna fled, joined by two guards outside the door. Clothilde came around a corner.

"Lorna, I just heard. Colonel Sasso told me . . ."

"I beg your pardon, Miss Von Schuppe," interposed the shorter of the two guards, "our orders are to escort her back to her rooms."

"In a moment."

"Which version did you get?" asked Lorna in a small voice, leaning against the wall, shaken to her heels by the confrontation.

"Charles Felix attacked you."

She nodded. "I was asleep. The door was locked. I know; when I got back I called for Maria and when she didn't answer, I locked it myself. I was dreaming. I woke up, and there he was . . ."

"How awful for you! It's a wonder you didn't die of shock!"

Lorna sighed. "I thought he was going to murder me."

"He wouldn't have, never . . ."

"Miss . . ." interrupted the guard again, casting a worried look at his partner.

"Just a second," said Clothilde.

"Your sister has the whole thing turned inside out," said Lorna wearily.

"I know. I could hear her all the way down the corridor, even through the closed door. Half the castle heard her."

"Clothilde, you must help me."

"She knows you didn't do anything. What do you want me to do, remind her?"

"She doesn't know!"

"She does. She knows him. She's just covering up for the sake of her pride."

"You mean for the sake of her pride I'm to be shot or hanged or thrown off a tower?"

"No, not a bit. She'll cool down."

Lorna shook her head. "Not this time. With that knife lying on the stool I was lucky to get out of there alive . . ."

"What knife?"

"Never mind, it's nothing."

"Lorna, it's not as bad as you're making it out . . ."

"It's worse. Talk to her, please."

"I wish I could. Nobody can talk to her, about anything. Except him."

"Charles Felix?"

"Torzzini. The one in there with her. He knows how to wrap her around his little finger. Apart from De-Leone, he's the only one in the world she will listen to. Too bad it wasn't he who broke in and saved you."

If you only knew, thought Lorna, and thank the Lord you don't! Paul saving her would have been far worse than Philip. The first question Caroline-Louisa would have asked would have been what was he, of all people, doing near her rooms that time of night?

For one thing, she could be grateful. Evidently, at least according to Clothilde's version, Philip had told the truth.

Unfortunately, it wasn't the truth Caroline-Louisa wanted to hear.

X

Still groggy and complaining of a _kopfschmerzen_* that felt as if a hammer locked in her head was pounding its way out, Maria greeted her at the door. By the time Lorna had finished a brief recapitulation of the event and Caroline-Louisa's reaction, the pain in Maria's head had gotten so intense that she had to lie down with a cold towel across her brow.

"What are we to do? What are we to do?" she complained anxiously, wincing in punctuation to each repetition of the question.

"There's nothing either of us can do," said Lorna glumly, "except await her pleasure. Her pleasure, my misery." Lorna removed the towel from the girl's forehead, dipping it into the basin half-filled with cold water sitting on the night stand. Wringing out the cloth, she laid it back in place.

"Ooooo . . ."

"You were drugged," Lorna said.

Maria grimaced and stuck out her heavily coated tongue. "It tastes like I bit into a rotten nut. Somebody must have put something in the tea I brought back from the kitchen after we all finished working at the great hall. Finished for the night, that is. It's such a monstrous big place, we've barely started."

She studied Lorna. "Have you had any breakfast?" she asked.

"I'm not hungry."

"I could get you something from the kitchen." Maria

* Headache (German).

237

started to rise. Lorna stayed her with her hand to her shoulder.

"Don't bother, I need rest more than food. You just lie there and take it easy; your headache'll go away. I'll let in some fresh air."

"Would you? That's what I need." Maria managed a thin smile between winces. "Anybody walking in will wonder who is the mistress and who is the maid."

Lorna patted her cheek, squeezed her hand and, getting up from the side of the bed, drew the drape rope at the single window and opened it. Then she went out, closing the door, lying down, burying her face in her pillow in the hope of driving out the jumble of loathsome and humiliating thoughts entangled in her mind.

What would Caroline-Louisa do to her, she wondered? Certainly not order her killed. Nobody, not even she, stayed mad indefinitely. Her anger had to cool, and with so many other things on her mind, punishing her imposter could hardly take precedence. Luckily, Paul was with the queen. Bright and clever and able, as Clothilde had put it, to twist her around his little finger, he'd calm her down. Hopefully.

She gasped aloud as she recalled how close she had come to killing Charles Felix. As frightened and furious as she was she would have. Holding the knife above his back as he struggled to separate her thighs and enter her, the fear and revulsion flooding her brain drowned any apprehension she might have had over the consequences of such an act. Better she kill and be killed than continue this cruel and horrible farce.

But now in retrospect, strangely, perhaps because Caroline-Louisa had been so wretched to her, she no longer felt prepared to exchange her life for that of either monarch, or both. No, damn them, all of them, from now on she'd defy them all, Caroline-Louisa in particular! Why not? She certainly had nothing to lose. If she betrayed their duplicity the next time she posed as the queen, they'd dispose of her. If she continued to cooperate, she'd come off no better; when they were done with her, they'd still get rid of her. They'd have to.

Maria appeared in the doorway, holding the cloth to her head, reeling slightly. "I forgot to tell you . . ."

"What?"

"His Excellency, the prime minister, sent word he wanted to speak with you in his rooms as soon as you got back. I'm sorry, I forgot."

"Don't worry about it."

"Go at once, he's waiting."

"Let him wait."

"He'll be furious!"

"Good. Perhaps he'll give himself apoplexy, or a heart attack."

An insistent knock rattled the door. "Oh, no!" burst Maria. "Pray that's a guard and not him."

Hesitantly she opened the door a crack, then pulled it wide, beaming broadly. "Mistress . . ."

Paul came rushing in, slamming the door, covering the distance to the bed in four great strides.

"Are you mad!" exclaimed Lorna. "If she . . ."

"I had to see you." He sat on the edge of the bed, holding her close and kissing her tenderly. Her heart pounding in panic in concern for his safety, she tried to speak, but his kiss stopped her words while Maria discreetly withdrew, her florid face filled with worry. At last their lips parted.

"You *are* mad," she said, her voice soft, submissive.

"I had to chance it. I have to explain."

"That's not necessary; I know you couldn't do anything for me with her standing there."

"You'll never believe how close I came to swinging around and running her through. I never knew I was capable of such self-restraint."

"Thank heaven you were."

"You, I never would have hurt. I'd have turned the point into my own stomach first."

"Don't talk that way, please. Oh, my darling, hold

me and kiss me and go. You must. DeLeone will be coming," she explained.

Paul got up, lifting her to her knees on the bed, his arms still encircling her, his kiss beautifully burning her mouth, his glorious presence consuming her with joy. With an enormous effort of will, she gently freed herself, pushing him away. He sighed in defeat.

"You're right. If I'm seen here with you it won't do either of us any good. I'll talk to her, nothing'll come of it."

"I don't care about that."

"You should. She's livid. But she'll get over it, she always does."

"Go quickly, my darling."

A knock sounded.

"Damn!" His teeth found his lower lip and he glowered, his eyelids stretching to slits. Maria appeared, waving him to her. He went into the other room, closing the door softly. Maria answered the second knock. It was Crespi.

"Mrs. Stone. His Excellency wishes to see you immediately!" he snapped, clicking his heels and bowing. "He's been waiting patiently. Let us go . . ."

"Captain Crespi, you may inform His Excellency that I have a severe headache, that I am in bed, and that I have no intention of getting up."

"But you are fully clothed."

"I was just about to begin undressing. Now, if you have my message straight, would you mind giving me a little privacy?"

Standing up, she began unbuttoning her dress.

Crespi colored, sputtered something under his breath, bowed again, and removed himself. No sooner had the door clicked shut than Paul reappeared.

"Meet me tonight, my darling," he said. "Midnight."

"The chapel?"

He thought a moment, then shook his head. "The blacksmith's shop."

"Where's that?"

"I know," interrupted Maria. "I'll give you the directions."

"Midnight," repeated Paul, "or as soon after as I can make it." Lorna nodded. He turned to leave, stopped short, and came back to her. Taking her in his arms he kissed her again, soulfully, sending a tremor of excitement spreading through her body.

"Oh Paul, Paul . . . it's so discouraging."

"Don't let it be. We'll work it all out; we will."

"We will, dearest. Go."

Maria had opened the door and was peering out and down the corridor, cocking one ear for the sound of footsteps.

"Hurry . . ." she rasped.

And he was gone.

XI

A full moon scrubbed bright by a passing cloud gazed down upon the castle, like an absorbed and disapproving eye. There was so very much anyone could disapprove of in this Castle Mad of the House of Savoy, she mused. A chill had seized the night air, the wind wailing as it swirled about the battlements and the towers. She drew her cloak more tightly about her as she hurried across the inner ward toward the blacksmith's shop, out of sight around the east inner gatehouse tower.

Her defiance of DeLeone's summons had brought unpredictable results. To her surprise His Excellency had let the matter drop, ostensibly accepting the excuse she had given Crespi. Nor had Caroline-Louisa as yet decided what form her punishment was to assume.

Of all the hypocritical idiocy, she thought! To top matters off, irony of ironies, the king himself had no doubt completely forgotten the incident.

From out of the shadow of the well housing, a guard emerged, confronting her.

"Mrs. Stone?"

"Yes . . ." She answered hesitantly, her voice cracking slightly, her heart in her mouth.

He was an ugly man of medium height, with a mass of red welts scarring his complexion and a number of moles scattered about his neck and left cheek."

"This way . . ." He glanced warily back the way she had come and gestured her toward him. The shop door was ajar, a faint orange glow visible inside.

"Is he here yet?"

'No, but he wishes you to wait inside." The man was whispering, but he stopped abruptly and his glance shot

upward. She froze as she heard footsteps directly over
their heads, the corner guard walking his post in the
machicolation above. Easing the door open, she slipped
inside. The odor of burning coals met her. The fire in
the forge had been reduced to a miniature galaxy of
bright orange stars separated by the coals. It was the
only illumination in the shop, cut off from the light of
the moon as it was by the tower rising alongside it. A
window directly opposite the door looked down upon
the town, itself reduced to a few flickering torches, over-
lorded by the cathedral tower importuning itself upon
the night sky.

With the aid of the feeble light, her eyes gradually became accustomed to the gloom. The smith's tools, tongs,
hammers, and leather bellows lay about. Two anvils,
one twice the size of the other, squatted in front of the
forge. Filling one corner of the shop within a foot of
the low ceiling was a pile of coal. The shop and everything in it appeared to be coated with a layer of coal
dust. There were a number of three-legged stools filthy
with it. Dusting the seat of one with her hanky, she disposed of the cloth in the bed of embers, actuating a
flame consuming it in an instant.

She waited and waited. Thinking back on their brief
relationship she had yet to have a planned meeting with
him at which he showed up even reasonably close to the
appointed time. She estimated that at least an hour had
gone by before she heard voices, having left the door
slightly ajar for him. Approaching the side of it, she
listened intently. It was not Paul talking to the guard,
however, but another guard who presently went on his
way.

Time crept by, taking the minutes one by one, using
them, discarding them. Her eyelids felt leaden, and sitting on the stool, she dozed, leaning forward, catching
herself, straightening, yawning . . . waiting.

He came at last, hurtling in, taking her in his arms,
kissing her passionately. Then he eased her away at

arm's length, went back to the door, spoke briefly to the guard, and closed and latched the door.

"A lot has happened since this morning, darling. Unbelievable things."

"Piedmont?" Hope leaped in her breast.

He shook his head. "Not yet, everything but. I talked to her about you."

"Oh, Paul, I wish you hadn't. I thought about it after you left this morning. She thinks we hardly know each other; that the last time I'd even seen you was at that funeral!"

"Don't worry, I was careful. I took the tack that even though you were nothing but foreign baggage, to get rid of you now she'd only be spiting herself. Your filling in for her during Holy Week alone proved how valuable you are to her." He smiled grimly. "I figured I'd start out by saving your life, then work down to a slap on the wrist. You know, take away your wandering privileges, restrict you to your rooms when you aren't posing as her. Unfortunately, she wouldn't listen."

"Did she throw another tantrum?"

"No. I said she wouldn't listen; it's more she couldn't . . ."

"I don't understand."

"She's ill, Lorna. She complains of a sick stomach, but it looks to me like it's no ordinary stomachache. She's paler than she was this morning, listless, no appetite. She's usually as strong as an ox, and very quick-listening, understanding, responding. I've seen her keep up with three conversations at once. But this, whatever it is, is not just her stomach, it seems to be affecting her mind." He wandered to the window framing the sleeping city below. "I was with her early this afternoon. She was lying on her couch and fell asleep. She began talking in her sleep. Brace yourself, Lorna, you won't believe this. I didn't, and I stood there and heard every word. But it's got to be true."

"What?"

"Charles Felix, the attempt on his life? I'll give you one guess who hired the would-be assassin."

"*No!*"

"Ssssh."

"She admitted it?"

"In her sleep. I swear. Is that incredible? I thought at first I was imagining I was hearing it, but I got to thinking about it . . ."

"Why would she own up to such a thing if she didn't do it?"

"Exactly, nobody would. Besides, it all makes sense. With Charles Felix out of the way, she would be sole ruler of Savoy for as long as she lived. She thought . . ."

"Thought?"

"According to the constitution, Savoy can never be ruled by a woman. Oh, the lady's bright, perceptive, and totally ruthless, all right; her only problem was she acted too hastily. Better she'd taken the time to read up on Savoy law. Then came the second twist."

"Charles Felix survived," said Lorna, thinking aloud. "Although he's incapable of ruling. So she rules temporarily in his stead. It's weird."

"Isn't it?" Moving to the forge and picking up a pair of tongs, he stirred the coals aimlessly. "If Charles Felix had been killed she would have had to relinquish the throne; in fact she never would have been able to assume it. But DeLeone came to her rescue and arranged matters. In defiance of the constitution, perhaps, but Charles Felix, having survived, wasn't completely mad, not then, not yet. During his rational periods he's the sole ruler. So it isn't breaking the law, it's only bending it. Of course nobody outside the castle, except our people, knows how rapidly his condition is deteriorating. At that, he's only going completely mad, he's not dying. How many mad kings have we had in this world?"

"She sounds like she's going mad."

"The doctor's with her now. More on that tomorrow."

It was becoming clearer and clearer to Lorna, all the

loose ends coming neatly together. "No wonder she lit into me so," she said. "If I'd stuck that knife into Charles Felix . . ."

". . . She would have been shoved right out of the picture. You really staggered her. She'd have had no more power left to her than Clothilde."

"If he goes completely mad and she dies, or doesn't; if she's just rendered powerless, who takes over the throne then?"

"Ask your friend Count DeLeone. He'll still be manipulating everything and everybody. It would be no setback for the monarchists. The only problem would be that Charles Felix has no male heir. Neither of the two kings preceding him, Charles Emmanuel IV or Victor Emmanuel I, had any sons. Charles Felix is the youngest of three brothers."

"The last of the line?"

"Not exactly. Here it gets a bit complicated. According to the law, when he dies without an heir, family rule would have to pass from the direct line to the cadet, another branch of the family. A younger branch, the Carignano line. Adelbert would handle the whole changeover, naturally."

"It's all very confusing."

"You very nearly lit the fuse on a keg of dynamite, with that pig-sticker of yours. You could have turned this kingdom upside down!"

"I wish I had." She stared at him, then took hold of his shoulders, pressing her cheek against his chest. "What are we to do, my darling?"

"Make love, beautiful love. Love glorious, the other night all over again."

"Be serious, this whole situation is getting worse and worse. Every time we meet, it's slipped further downhill. And every time we see each other you risk . . . Darling, you could be shot on the spot."

He smiled. "That part of it I'd rather not think about. You're the only part that interests me." His voice assumed a serious tone matching his expression. "We've got to get you out. Preferably before sunrise."

"Us out."

"You first."

"Not without you, Paul. And Maria. Leaving her behind would be leaving her to pay for what I've done."

"What in the world is that?"

"You know what I'm saying. Everything Caroline-Louisa's holding over my head."

"I understand how you feel about the girl, Lorna, but your situation is much more dangerous than hers. You have to come first."

"You're not listening. I said I won't go without you and Maria."

"You'll go, and I'll join you. With her, if I can possibly work it."

"Is anything happening anywhere, Piedmont, Sardinia, even Austria? Anything threatening that might get you recalled to your unit? Your original plan was good; it could work."

"Nothing is happening, Lorna."

The door slammed open, the latch springing loose, arching through the air between them. In the doorway, his dark eyes burning, an evil smile twisting his mouth, his saber drawn and held straight out in front of him, stood Philip.

"Well, well, well, what have we here?"

Paul threw himself backward, pulling his saber, the ember glow of the forge bursting from the blade as he brought it up to defend himself.

"*No!*" shouted Lorna, stepping forward to intervene.

"Stay back!" snapped Paul, "well back, against the wall."

"You give my wife excellent advice, Torzzini," said Philip, chuckling, kicking the door closed behind him. "A pity if the prize in the contest were to accidentally become the victim."

"Don't do this, don't, I beg you both!"

But neither one paid her the slightest heed. Blades up,

each with his fist firmly planted in the small of his back, they began circling. Philip lunged, but Paul drove his blade aside with a hard stroke, and, forcing an opening, attacked. His point slipped under Philip's right arm, missing his rib cage by a hair and bringing a grin to his stormy features.

"Excellent, Captain," he said, quickly regaining his composure and returning to the offensive. The expressions of pure hatred on both their faces, the determination in their eyes and the set of their jaws, the clicking of their blades as they exchanged, flooded her heart with fear. Standing with her back against the wall, she watched in horror as Philip beat lightly on one side of Paul's blade, dropped his point quickly under it, then beat violently on the other side in an effort to force the way open to his heart.

They were evenly matched, Philip smaller, quicker in attack, and in recovery. But Paul with his great strength handled his blade with the deftness of a foilsman, standing his ground, parrying Philip's thrusts as the latter began slowly circling him. With each lunge Philip drew a counter. There was no more talk now, the grimness of each man's resolve demanding complete concentration. A terrible thought flew through her mind; Philip was wrong, she was not the prize, merely the cause. The prize was life, the winner standing over the loser sprawled on the floor, his heart slowing, stopping, the flow of blood pouring out of his wound abating. And death.

"Stop it! Stop it!"

Not the flicker of an eyelid betrayed that either heard her, that they even remembered she was still in the room. Taking advantage of a careless lunge that threw Philip momentarily off balance, Paul executed a riposte, thrusting quickly forward, aiming for the colonel's chest. But Philip quickly recovered and parried. The tempo grew furious; hopefully, she thought, neither one would be able to sustain the pace and both would give it up exhausted. But for such a reason, only a miracle would make them quit simultaneously.

On and on they dueled, each drawing blood from the other's upper left arm, neither cut seriously. Then it happened; Paul attacked, lunging past the anvils toward the door, forcing a retreat. Philip managed to avoid contact, his point and his hand describing small circular movements giving him the momentum to follow up with a thrust aimed squarely at Paul's stomach. She screamed, but Paul's blade had already come down upon his adversary's, forcing it low. With an audible click Philip's point struck Paul's belt buckle, denting it visibly, but inflicting no injury.

"Dear God in heaven," she whispered. "Will you stop this insanity!" she burst. "Stop!"

The words were barely out of her mouth when Paul, in backing away from a short lunge, turning to let the point pass him, tangled one foot in a hammer lying on the floor. He lost his balance, flailing the air with his arms and saber, falling backward.

In an instant Philip was on him, a triumphant leer stretching his mouth and brightening his eyes. He kicked Paul's saber well out of reach and drove his point straight at his throat.

"*No!*"

It touched the flesh and stopped.

"I will count to ten, my unfortunate friend. In a whisper. So you'll be able to say your prayers aloud. It's more than you deserve."

"Get it over with," declared Paul.

Lorna had rushed forward, but Philip stayed her with his free hand.

"Philip, please . . . Don't do it, don't."

"My darling, I have every right to kill him. He's been caught in the act of seducing my wife. The law is very clear. A husband . . ."

"Please, I'll do anything you say, anything! But let him live."

He turned to stare at her, the brightness in his eyes

vanished, displaced by the hard look the victor reserves for the vanquished.

"Will you indeed, my love?"

"Anything, I swear it. But if you kill him I give you my word you'll pay . . ."

He laughed with false hilarity. "You hear that, Torzzini? My own wife threatening me. Your reputation does you justice. You do have the most extraordinary effect upon the ladies, especially other men's wives. My darling," he said turning back to her. "If I let him live, will I be able to trust your word?"

"I'll do anything you say."

"Come, come, mustn't overplay your role. There's very little I'd ask." He ticked them off on his fingers. "Reinstate me in your affections, move in with me, begin behaving like a dutiful wife, resume our marriage. To pick up where we left off in Boston would be nice. Would that be asking too much in exchange for his life?"

"No."

"So do we have a bargain?"

"Yes."

"You're looking at the floor, your tone . . . You seem somewhat less than enthralled at the prospect. Come, let us both see a smile on that beautiful face. Such a face should never wear unhappiness. Don't you agree, Torzzini?"

Paul ignored him. Angered, Philip deliberately pricked his throat, drawing a single drop of blood. She screamed, but sighed relief when he stopped the blade's downward motion just in time, then freed his point, pulling an inch away from Paul's throat.

"Let him up, Philip, please. I've agreed, I'll live with you as your wife."

"And love me as before? Only even more ardently now, seeing as I'm giving him his life. Right?" She nodded. "Excellent." He lifted his point a few inches more and grinned at Paul. "Captain Torzzini, you may get up."

Paul started to, but down came the point again. "One moment. I have a question."

"What is it?" asked Paul.

"The obvious question: Do you really think I'd let you off so easily? You steal my wife practically out of our bed, I catch you and defeat you in fair combat, and, I'm to let you get up and walk away? Does that make sense? Shouldn't you at least have something to mark the occasion, something for you to remember me by?"

"Philip . . ." she began.

"I'm not talking to you, wife, I was addressing your friend here, the champion of all seducers."

"Let him up."

"Sorry, I can't do that, not just yet."

"You're a monster!"

"On the contrary, I'm only an outraged husband."

"What do you want? What more?"

"Satisfaction, my love. Think about it, everything I've, asked of you, you've agreed to give me, correct?"

"I swore, I'll swear again, I'll do anything you ask. Just let him live."

"I intend to." His eyes, no longer grim, were suddenly glowing like Charles Felix's had glowed the previous night, smoldering with consummate evil. "But, everything you agreed to you'd have to in any case. You're my wife, remember? All legal and sanctified. I've asked you for nothing you don't already owe me by virtue of your marriage vows. Enough explanation, we're wasting time. Kneel down beside him, so you can get a good look."

"I don't understand."

"You will do as I tell you." She knelt at Paul's knees as Philip indicated the spot. "You, Torzzini, unfasten your trousers. Open them all the way. And open your underclothing. Lorna, my darling, take hold of the hem of your dress; I'm afraid there's going to be a lot of blood."

"I ask you to kill me like a man," whispered Paul tightly. "Get it over with."

"He's not going to kill you; and I won't let him do this."

Philip disregarded her completely. "The buttons, Torzzini. Unless you'd like me to cut my way in."

Paul's hand started down his chest, prompting Philip to lift his saber. So absorbed was he concentrating on what he was about to do, so obviously taken with himself at having reduced the two of them to such humiliation, he seemed no longer conscious of Lorna's presence. Kneeling beside Paul she tensed, straightened, and threw herself across him, turning her body, her shoulder smashing against Philip's legs, sending him crashing to the floor, his saber clattering loudly as it struck the stones. Paul was on his feet like a cat, snatching up Philip's blade and readying it even before he had pulled himself up to full height.

At which point, the previous scene was resumed, with the players' roles reversed.

"Paul, don't do it . . ."

"If I let him live, we're both done."

"That's not so," she said. "Only if you kill him."

"Take a look outside."

"What for?"

"Just do it!"

She complied, returning a moment later. "There's nobody, nothing."

"Vorcese, the guard?"

"Gone."

"Damn!"

"Torzzini," said Philip, with admirable calmness, "I'm a sporting man, I'll give you one chance."

"You're in no position to give me anything, Colonel."

"I'm serious. Let me up, let me go, and we'll wipe the slate clean."

"I'm apt to let you up . . ."

"Explain it to him, Lorna, he's obviously too dense to figure it out for himself. Paul, old friend, you're the queen's pet. If you let me up and I run to her and ac-

cuse you of stealing my wife, she may very well find
ropes for both of you. For you, my darling, for stealing
her lover on the heels of attempting to steal her husband. Naughty, naughty. Now, I wouldn't mind losing
you, Torzzini, but you, Lorna, I've grown very fond of,
very fond indeed."

"Even if you were foolish enough to tell her, I
wouldn't have to be hanged for you to lose me forever,"
said Lorna. "I'd shun you like the plague."

"As you have up to tonight. First-rate shunning, too."

"You've lost me in any event."

"Pity."

"You have, unless . . ."

"What?"

"Don't give him dirt, Lorna," interjected Paul heatedly. "You do and you'll be as sorry as you were the
first time."

"Please, Paul, let me handle this. Philip, if you want
me on your terms, you can have me."

"What the hell . . ." began Paul.

"With this provision," she continued calmly. "You
must accept my terms on resolving this business."

Paul touched her arm with his free hand. "Lorna,
don't bargain with this filth."

"You're still being dense, Torzzini, she hasn't any
choice."

"None of us has," she said evenly. "As I was about
to say, *my* terms are these: he leaves the castle. Your
orders, Colonel Sasso. And there'll never be so much as
a whisper about what happened here tonight."

"Fair enough," rejoined Philip, smirking.

Paul stiffened. "Sasso, you'll be a dead man before I
let that happen."

"Darling, be sensible, kill him and you'll put ropes
around both our necks! Let him live, and you leave,
he's reassigning you . . ."

"It's no good," said Paul wearily. "Look at his face,
he knows as well as I do she'd have his hide if he sent

me back. Besides, he can't, he's not my commanding officer."

"Problems, problems," said Philip, chuckling.

"Keep your mouth shut, Colonel. I'm in no mood for your sarcasm; it just might pull this steel into your craw!"

She pondered the situation, the two of them staring at her expectantly, Paul's point still hovering over Philip's throat.

"I don't know what to do," she confessed at length. "Other than for you, Paul, to get back to her and I . . ."

". . . Resume living with your adoring husband. In exchange for my guarantee of silence," said Philip triumphantly.

Paul's eyes bored into her, his face gray. She nodded.

"No!" he shouted. "That's no good!"

"Let him up," she said quietly.

"Lorna . . ."

"Trust me, please."

Muttering, Paul sheathed his saber and put one foot down on Philip's, lying on the floor. "You can pick up your saber in the morning, Colonel. I'm not about to trust you tonight. Get up and get out."

Philip got to his feet smiling, dusting off his sleeves and his trousers. At the door he turned. "My darling, I shall send a man to your door first thing in the morning. Be packed and ready for him. I'll be waiting. You keep your part of the bargain, I'll keep mine. You can finish this night in the arms of the queen, Torzzini, no need to worry."

She stayed Philip with eyes narrowed to slits. "If anything about this gets out we'll know who let it out. Then you and I will separate, Philip, for the second and last time. Only this time there won't be any play dead."

"If I lost you, I'd kill myself," said Philip, smirking. "Seriously, though, you're being very sensible. I detect a trace of bitterness in your tone, but keep in mind you loved me once. I promise you, you'll love me again. Good night to you both."

Out he went, Paul closing the door behind him. He exploded, his voice filled with frustration.

"This is wrong, completely! There's no way we can trust him. He knows damned well you're not capable of killing him, no matter how much you despise him."

"Don't delude yourself, my darling."

"How can you do this? How can you let him touch you, let alone sleep with you? You can't stand to be in the same room with him!"

"I'll do what I have to, if it means saving you, and our chance for escape."

"What chance? He'll never let you out of his sight."

"We'll see."

"Oh, we'll see all right." Bending, retrieving Philip's saber, he flung it clattering against the wall and began carrying on, a small boy balked and reacting with a fit of ill temper. At any other time she would have burst out laughing. But at the moment, laughter was the furthest thing from her mind.

XII

Returning to her rooms, she closed the corridor door with her hands behind her back, feeling the coolness of the brass knob, then touching her palms to her forehead to drive away the heat of the nervous strain binding her head and neck. She lit a single candle, setting it on the vanity. Kicking off her mules she sat on the edge of the bed, noting the time: five minutes before four, less than two hours till dawn. The steadily recurring muffled sound of Maria's snoring worked its way through the inner door. She consciously let her body droop, her shoulders sagging, her head falling forward. She had never before felt so physically and emotionally wrung. Turning toward her vanity, she appraised her reflection in the mirror, touching one cheek with the tips of her fingers. That she had to look like a queen, like this queen, had already brought her more misery than she would have believed possible. With the promise of much more to come. To love a man, as passionately as she loved Paul, and live one's hours knowing that he was in someone else's arms while you yourself were consigned to the arms and the bed of one you heartily despised, had to be grounds for suicide.

How she loathed this existence, this nightmare carousel ride whirling on and on through one mad crisis after another, spinning faster and faster, dizzying and sickening her! And rapidly approaching the limits of her tolerance.

Troubling her at the moment was her decision. Go back to Philip to save Paul. If she didn't, Philip would destroy him, would likely destroy them both, in spite of his professed love for her. There was no love, there never had been. He had needed her, he had used her; the pretense of love had only been a mask for his deceit. Thinking of Philip, his towering ego, his total insensitivity and his lies, all but inspired a wave of nausea. To be his wife once more, to be forced to lock up her heart and wall in her emotions in defense against his advances, to let him fondle her while he whispered his lies, to feel him inside her, to see the exultation in his eyes at climax would be unendurable. But endure it she must, for the sake of the man she loved.

She shook her head and addressed her face in the glass: "What have you done? What have you brought on yourself? Is he so egotistical he really expects you to forgive and forget? How can you possibly pretend with any conviction whatsoever that you can tolerate, much less welcome, what he'll do to you?"

The most gifted actress in the world would be unable to effect such a pretense. The very first time he so much as touched her with the tips of his fingers she would resist. He would be more repulsive than Charles Felix, as loathsome as the brute who had raped her aboard the *Anselmo*.

How she hated him, in part because she loved Paul, so deeply. Maybe her decision wasn't the best alternative after all; maybe Paul was right, better that he kill him and be done with it. Outside the blacksmith's shop, Paul's friend the guard was nowhere to be seen when she'd opened the door. Dismissed, they both assumed, by Colonel Sasso. Would they have been able to kill Philip and get away with it? Probably not. The guard had talked to another guard while she had waited inside for Paul; who knows what they had said to each other? And Philip himself, had he followed her to the shop? Had he stood hiding on the other side of the tower waiting for Paul to appear so that he could catch them together? Had he known about Paul and her previously? He must have, but how could he?

"Use your head, girl, you know by now there are few if any secrets in this awful place!"

Bone weary and totally depressed, she readied herself for bed. But when she slipped under the covers and put her head down upon the pillows, as she had suspected, she was unable to clear her mind for sleep. She lay staring at the ceiling, helpless to prevent the events and circumstances of the past few days from tumbling through her mind, arranging themselves in their continuity, and one at a time offering themselves for examination, and secondguessing. What if . . . If only . . Why didn't I . . .

What next?

Philip next. As if the two of them could ever pick up the Gray Dragon Inn pieces! Can sweet well water fouled by poison ever again be imbibed and enjoyed? It can't even be tasted! . .

As exhausted as it was, her mind wanted no part of sleep. She did not even doze; instead she lay there sinking deeper and deeper into the black pit of despair. If only Paul could get out of the castle, routinely, on the legitimate orders of his commanding officer, for whatever reason. Once he was outside, they would stand a chance. Even if his unit remained at the Roman Station he'd be able to help her and Maria escape. Then the three of them could make for the nearest safe haven. It sounded so easy; a pity attempting it appeared next to impossible.

The blackness thick against the ceiling and walls softened perceptibly giving way to slate, then light gray, and eventually a wan yellow, almost flesh color, the spiritless effort of the rising sun to light the world.

Maria appeared sleepy-eyed and yawning, surprised to see her awake. Before either of them could utter a word a fist thumped the door, the sound so long anticipated by Lorna, so frightening as she heard it, she gasped before groaning in capitulation to the inevitable

"What's the matter, mistress, and who on earth could that be at this hour?" queried Maria. She moved to the door. "Yes?"

"Open the door."

An unfamiliar voice, one of Philip's men, thought Lorna gloomily.

"Let him in," she said.

"But you're not dressed."

Lorna pulled the covers up to her neck. Maria opened the door revealing a squat, red-faced guard, all chest and belly, resembling an enormous red egg with limbs and head attached.

"I will be ready in thirty minutes," said Lorna. "We haven't started packing."

"My orders are to tell you to come right away, madam. To Her Majesty."

Punishment time, as if being forced to resume her so-called marriage wasn't punishment enough!"

"Give me time to dress."

"At once. Her Majesty is waiting. His Excellency, the prime minister, gave me a direct order."

Maria fetched her robe. "Go mistress, it will be all right, it will."

"It won't be, and you know it."

"Wait and see . . ." said the girl, helping her on with the robe.

"I don't have to."

Maria smiled, a curiously self-satisfied grin. Had she been a cat, thought Lorna, she'd surely have emptied the saucer of cream. What wasn't she telling her?

Count DeLeone greeted her soberly at the door to Caroline-Louisa's bedchamber. Her Majesty was in bed, sleeping or resting within the confines of her curtain. Others were present, all men.

"Mrs. Stone, I would like you to meet Doctor Brabossi," said DeLeone in a subdued tone. She was hurriedly introduced to each man in turn. Their names were meaningless to her, but most of their faces she recognized. They had been among those assembled in the throne room on the day the queen had introduced her to Clothilde.

Brabossi drew her eye. He was a bear of a man, compactly built with a head the size of his chest lodged neckless between his shoulders. He wore pince-nez spectacles with a slender blue ribbon trailing down to his breast pocket. He seemed agitated and she noted that his bag lay open on a marble-topped Regency table at the foot of the bed. He wiped his glasses and his face, with his handkerchief and turned to His Excellency.

"I shall be in my rooms," he said in a troubled tone, stuffing his stethoscope into his bag and snapping it closed. He hurried out the door. DeLeone closed and locked after him, as he had when she had come into the room.

Her glance straying back to Caroline-Louisa's prostrate form, she noticed, through the curtains the dim outline of a figure standing on the other side of the bed. Whoever it was was mumbling. Straining her ears, she thought she recognized Latin. Father Asquino, she wondered? What was going on? Why had she been summoned even before the queen awoke. Could it be possible . . .

"May I ask . . ." she began.

DeLeone cut her off. "Mrs. Stone, a great tragedy has befallen us. I regret to say that Her Royal Highness has passed away. About two hours ago. Doctor Brabossi attributes death to a heart attack."

Father Asquino finished and came padding around the end of the bed into view, his hands clasped in an attitude of prayer. Passing the two of them, he glanced at her with somewhat of a surprised look, and crossed himself.

"You've met Father Asquino," said DeLeone. "Father, Mrs. Stone."

The priest stopped and nodded, affected a twisted suggestion of a smile, and resumed his progress toward the door. One of the others opened it for him. Watching him leave, Lorna's mind began hurling up all sorts of conjecture. Caroline-Louisa was dead, the House of Savoy without a queen. How very careless of her!

The look in DeLeone's eye confirmed her next supposition; he was staring at her, the same look in his eyes she had seen when they had first met on board the *Iphimedia,* satisfaction, approval tinged with a gleam of surprise at recognizing Caroline-Louisa's face with a New Hampshire accent coming out of the mouth. She had come immediately, as the guard had insisted, wearing only a robe and no makeup, but DeLeone obviously approved now, as he had on board ship, of what he saw.

Because he had no choice but to approve. For she, Lorna Singleton of Hanover, New Hampshire, Grafton County, New England, U.S.A., was his queen, his only queen, the precious surety of his position and his power.

Taking her by the arm, he walked her to the bed, pushing aside the curtain revealing Caroline-Louisa, the sheet drawn over her face. He pulled it down. Lorna swallowed and looked away. He replaced the sheet.

"To paraphrase the words of the British on an occasion such as this, Mrs. Stone." He touched her chain, easing her face around so that their eyes met. "The queen is dead, long live the queen."

XIII

The shoe, as the saying goes, was now on the other foot. To be specific, the royal golden slipper. DeLeone had lost little time getting to the point Lorna had already arrived at. In His Excellency's haste, however, he negligently lost sight of the obvious. A substitute he had, a remarkably similar-looking counterfeit queen. But the self-complacent expression on his face assured Lorna that he was reckoning without consideration of the power he was thrusting into her hands.

"We must have a long talk, Your Majesty," he said warmly. "There is no end to the things you must be brought up to date on," he said, lowering the bed curtain. "How do you feel?"

"Tired. I didn't sleep well last night."

"There'll be plenty of time to rest later. We must begin your indoctrination."

"Of course," said Lorna in a voice steeped with self-confidence. "I shall be in my rooms, properly dressed and made up in one hour. See that you don't keep me waiting."

His face tightened, his jaw muscles stretching, his dark eyes suddenly smoldering.

"Mrs. Stone . . ."

"Correction, Count DeLeone, Queen Caroline-Louisa. Long live the queen, remember? Or has Her Highness died? Has Charles Felix been informed? Will there be an announcement to the people? Will there be a state funeral, seven days of mourning, or will she rise from her bed today and tend to affairs as usual? Will she sleep tonight in this room, in another bed, to be sure, at least a new mattress and sheets and pillow and curtains. Will she, or won't she?"

His voice was brittle, his irritation increasing by the second. "One hour, in my rooms."

"My rooms," she said quietly.

He hesitated, his eyes burning through her. But he neither nodded nor shook his head in refusal.

Turning, she walked off, reaching the door, letting herself out. Pausing, she looked back to him.

"Adelbert," she said in attempted imitation of Caroline-Louisa's haughty tone. He bristled, seething, his whole body tensing like a heavy spring coiling. "One other thing, please see that Colonel Sasso continues to keep his distance."

"Sasso?" he asked, mildly perplexed.

"Ah, you do remember the name." The others in the room stood speechless and mystified, staring at them, their eyes switching back and forth like the spectators at a tennis match. "The colonel mistakenly believes that I'm planning to move in with him. You will inform him that Her Majesty is much too busy for any dalliance, certainly with the likes of him. Charles Felix would never approve of such disgraceful goings-on."

With this she closed the door on the group of astonished faces and marched off down the corridor.

Maria closed and secured the door behind her, standing with her back planted firmly, her palms flat against it as if she were expecting a squadron of cavalry to come charging into the room. Paul appeared in the doorway to Maria's room. Lorna rushed to him.

"What do you make of this?" he asked in an incredulous tone, a stunned look on his face.

"It's the whole world turned right side up!" she exclaimed gleefully. "No more Caroline-Louisa, no more Philip, you go back to your regiment."

"This morning, ten o'clock. Colonel Haproux has already told me."

"Marvelous!"

"Maybe. Maybe not." He sobered slightly, releasing her, and turning away. "It's the break we need, certainly. Still, it doesn't sweep away all our problems. I return to my men, fine, but there we'll sit until something in the way of trouble crops up."

"We don't have to wait for that, darling. Once you're back you can get what you need, horses, food, a gun, hide them somewhere outside of town, come and get us and off we go."

"Just like that." He snapped his fingers.

"Why not?"

"You've got to carry it further. What happens when I show up at camp with you two?"

"You don't go back. We leave here, we head for France, for Switzerland, down to the sea, whichever way you think safest."

"That would be very risky. By the time we reached any border it could be sealed off."

"We have an expression back home. I don't know whether you've ever heard it; it has to do with the feet getting cold . . ."

"Damn it, Lorna, I'm not turning coward on you! I'm trying to work this thing out the safest, most sensible, most practicable way. Don't you see, if there were an uprising, the whole duchy would be in an uproar. It would be the perfect cover for us. We could walk out of Savoy. Besides, you're queen now, I mean their version of the genuine article. DeLeone and his cronies, everybody with anything like a twinge of sentiment for the monarchists, will be watching you like a hawk. You're their survival."

"That's it!"

"What?"

"You sneak me out, hide me, let out the news that the queen is dead, spread the word, rouse the populace, and you'll have your precious revolution! Don't you see?"

"I see. But you're overlooking something; you're forgetting Charles Felix. Caroline-Louisa can be dead or alive, he's still king, in spite of his health. She . . . now you are simply covering for him."

His playing devil's advocate, so glibly, so determinedly, was becoming unnerving.

"So what are we to do, sit on our hands and wait?"

"For the present, yes. You wait; I'll contact you."

"When, approximately?"

"How can I say, even approximately? It's useless for me to get in touch until the time is ripe."

"The time couldn't be riper."

He took hold of her hands and searched her eyes for understanding.

"My darling, I love you more than any words can describe. You own my heart. You're far and away the most precious thing these hands have ever held. Because of that, because of you, I cannot countermand my instincts. I'll risk my life in this thing gladly, but your life, your future, never. Nor the girl's. We've waited this long, we'll wait a little longer. I'll leave here in less than two hours. That's our first step right there. Be patient, there's light at the end of the tunnel. Just squint, and you'll see it. You're the queen of us all now. Why not enjoy yourself while you're waiting? Just be careful of old Adelbert. You've underestimated him before."

"He underestimates me. You should have seen him steam when I put him in his place."

Maria listening in the other room showed herself, pursing her lips and crinkling her forehead worriedly.

"You shouldn't have, mistress. You should never cross him."

"She's right, Lorna," said Paul. "Yes, he needs you, they all do, but don't overplay your hand. Push him too far and he'll order your throat slit and get Sasso to volunteer for the job."

She shook her head. "DeLeone wouldn't, he needs me, now more than ever."

"He only needs you to back up Charles Felix; he won't trust you, he won't confide in you as he did her, and when you're no longer useful to him, when he's completed arrangements for operating the government with somebody legitimate and healthy on the throne, he'll dispose of you. But don't worry, we'll be out of here long before then."

"How can he legally, or illegally, dethrone Charles Felix? Without throwing everything into chaos?"

"There has to be a way. If there isn't he'll devise one. Being on top of the world he'll do everything in his power to stay there."

"Lady Jane Grey ruled England for nine days, and ended up beheaded. Paul," she said, touching her neck gingerly, "we've got to get out as soon as we can."

He nodded. "Absolutely. Safely. The least possible risk."

"I don't have to go, not now," interposed Maria. "That will make it easier for you."

"You do have to go," said Lorna.

The girl shook her head. "She's dead; life around here is going to be much different from now on, much more pleasant."

"Not after the monarchists are overthrown," said Lorna.

"What would the *carbonari* do to me, an insignificant maid? Bother the monarchists and the *carbonari*, all of them, I'll just go on doing my work."

It occurred to Lorna that the smile seemed to be securely fixed on the girl's face since the guard had come to the door earlier with word that DeLeone was waiting. And what was it that Maria had said to her just before helping her on with her robe? "It will be all right, wait and see." And that self-satisfied grin . . .

"Maria . . ."

"Yes, mistress?"

Freeing herself from Paul's embrace, she went to the girl.

"How did you hear about her death?"

"Captain Torzzini told me."

Lorna looked at Paul for confirmation and he

nodded. But her curiosity was aroused, awakened by intuition, and she was not about to be put off. "You knew before, though, isn't that so?"

"How could I?"

"You knew before the guard came here, before I found out. How?"

A guilty look seized Maria's features and she shifted her eyes to stare past Lorna.

"I don't know what you mean."

"Maria, I'm your friend, we both are."

"I know."

"Tell us what you know, all of it."

"I can't; I'm afraid . . ."

"The doctor says a heart attack. But what did she really die of?"

Maria shook her head and studied the floor, biting her lip nervously and withdrawing into herself.

"I must go to work at the great hall. They'll be calling for me."

"There won't be any birthday party, Maria," said Paul gently, "not now. Do you want to talk about it?"

"I can't, I just can't!"

Lorna took her by the shoulders, kissing her affectionately on the forehead. "Then don't. We're just being nosy; it'll all come out anyway."

Maria relaxed and nodded. "She's dead, that's the main thing. She'll never slap us or scream at us or tease us or watch us being punished or cut out our tongues and make us wear them around our necks, none of it ever again!"

XIV

As a skeleton hangs in a corner of a doctor's office, His Excellency, Count Adelbert DeLeone's glory, fitted snugly to a seamstress's dummy, occupied a corner: his uniform jacket resplendent with his collection of decorations. The office itself was windowless and intentionally drab, decided Lorna, affording any visitor all the more encouragement to concentrate on the vulgar display in the corner.

She sat in front of an early Empire pier table in service as a desk, its cumbersome mahogany platform resting on the floor, its double columns on either side topped by ormolu mounts, and its work area, a rectangular piece of plain gray King of Prussia marble, cluttered with countless papers. DeLeone sat back in his chair eyeing her over the tips of his index fingers forming an inverted Vee in front of his nose. He had won the verbal tug of war, sending a burly officer to her rooms well before the hour she had demanded had elapsed. Luckily Paul had departed by then and she had gotten dressed but there was not time for makeup, let alone the meticulous handiwork taught her by René Tallot created to perfect her resemblance to Caroline-Louisa.

DeLeone seemed not to notice, nor did he take exception to her behavior earlier in the bedchamber. Evidently there was too much to discuss to be bothered by such trifles as bruised egos.

"The queen's body will be secretly interred, of course, probably tomorrow, but you will be taking over immediately. I trust we can depend upon you to give us your customary satisfactory performance. A little extra effort wouldn't hurt; we're all of us already beginning to feel the strain and if we can rely on you, have full confidence in you, it would bolster everyone's spirits. It will only be for two or three weeks."

She stiffened. "Two or three weeks?"

His reaction left little doubt that he wished he hadn't added the last sentence. Clearing his throat, he smiled his icy smile.

"I mean of course there'll only be two or three weeks during which you'll have to attend events and functions outside the castle."

"Then what?"

"Then government, well, actually that doesn't concern you."

"What happens to me at the end of 'two or three weeks,' when you no longer have any need for me?"

"Did I say that? I'm sure I didn't."

He picked up a letter opener and, holding it by the blade, cleared space among his papers and began tapping the handle against the marble top annoyingly. "Why don't we cross that bridge when we come to it?"

"You have to get rid of me, don't you. Make it look as if I never arrived, never even existed."

"Come come, Mrs. Stone."

"*Miss* Singleton."

"Why not Your Majesty? As I was about to say, we Savoyards are not savages. We're decent civilized folk."

"So I've noticed."

Voices could be heard outside through the double doors, his servant, Joseph, and a woman. Clothilde.

"Either you announce me or in I march!" she shouted.

"But His Excellency is with someone. A private discussion . . ."

DeLeone had come around the table and opened the doors. Lorna turned and saw Clothilde, her hair in disarray, a wild look in her eyes. She rushed into the office, pulling the doors together so hard they bounced apart. DeLeone closed them.

"Carrie's dead, *dead!*" she shrilled, ignoring Lorna. "You knew hours ago, why wasn't I told at once? Answer me!"

"There's no need to get upset," said DeLeone firmly. "It all happened very suddenly."

"Never mind about that. What I really want to know is when you intend to begin?"

"Begin what?" he asked mystified.

"Preparations, of course, for my coronation. I've already spoken to Charles Felix, and he agrees. Why shouldn't he, what's right is right!"

He pulled a chair away from the wall and set it beside her. She sat.

"It was very unwise of you to speak to His Majesty."

"What are you talking about? How dare you! Such impertinence. It may interest you to know, I intend to discuss marriage with him. He's ill, he needs a woman's care."

"Let's discuss it, shall we?"

"What's to discuss? She dies, I'm her only sister, I take her place, naturally. Charles Felix . . ."

"Forget Charles Felix!" he snapped. "You may be her sister, but let's get one thing straight, you have no ties to the throne. Through marriage or blood."

"Is that so! Well, now we know where you stand. You're going to try to block me, aren't you? *Aren't you!*"

"Are we finished?" asked Lorna of DeLeone.

"No, please wait outside."

He let her out while Clothilde continued to rant, her voice clearly audible through the closed doors. Joseph frowned and shook his head as he indicated a chair for Lorna by the window. Clothilde's highhandedness was obviously netting her nothing. DeLeone was rapidly becoming livid. The double doors threatened to rattle in their frames as the two of them went at each other. Astonishing as it seemed, Clothilde actually believed she was entitled to the crown. DeLeone denied it, shouting her down in an effort to get through to her.

Browbeating her into temporary silence, he explained in acrid tones that for a woman to become ruler of the House of Savoy was entirely contrary to constitutional law.

Clothilde would have none of this, and once again began arguing and threatening. She couldn't have picked a worse time to attempt to beard the lion in his den, mused Lorna, listening to them, but she refused to back down.

"You dare block me, DeLeone; you try to pass her off as Carrie and I'll wreck you, all of you! I'll spread the word from here to Leman. There won't be a man, woman, or child in all Savoy who won't know what you've been up to, you conniving old fool, you fourth-rate Metternich!"

"Get out of here before I throw you out!"

The doors slid open, DeLeone showing his face, nearly as red as his uniform standing in the corner.

"Joseph!" His servant came into the room so fast, he created the impression he was fleeing a roomful of explosives about to detonate.

"Call the guards, I want her out!"

"At once, Excellency." He flew to the door, shouting up and down the corridor. Her neck bowed, she followed DeLeone back and forth as he paced, blistering his eardrums with threats and invective.

"Charles Felix will support me, so will the generals, every single one. You're finished! Pack your bag and get out. You'd better, the first order I'll give when I take over will be to have you thrown into prison. I'll see you tried for treason, you contemptible old fool, you devious swine!"

Three guards came thundering in; two dragged her out kicking and screaming. DeLeone, wiping the sweat from his neck and face with his handkerchief, got a grip on the reins of his anger and addressed the third man.

"Lock her in her rooms under guard until further orders. My orders only, understand?"

The guard saluted. "Yes, Your Excellency."

"See to it." He kicked the door closed after the man, shutting out the fading din in the corridor. He turned to Lorna.

"Shall we resume?"

He talked of many things, mostly about Caroline-Louisa, her ways, her faults, her aptitude for matters of state. He made no reference whatsoever to Clothilde. It was as if she had never even come in, almost as if she didn't exist.

"Matters of state will, of course, be no concern of yours. All you'll do is continue playing your role."

"And if I refuse, if I cease to cooperate?"

"You're too intelligent to jump off that cliff."

"We shall see."

He was back behind his table, his elbows planted on it, his forearms upward, the tips of his index fingers restored to their prior position at the end of his nose.

"Let me recount for you a little bit of my early life. I entered service at the age of eighteen. I was to be trained as a cavalryman. Even at that tender age I was, if I may say so, a superb horseman. They gave me a horse, a young mare, coal black except for a white, diamond 'so big' "—he held up his thumb and fore-finger spaced—"on her forehead. She was as wild as the winter wind chasing down from Mount du Chat. No one, not the best horseman in Savoy, could ride her. Many had tried. It was a joke, you see, the veterans were having sport with the green recruit. That horse was incredible; she bucked furiously, reared, kicked, bit . . . She threw me nine times. I broke seven ribs and my wrist and nearly broke my neck."

"But you tamed her."

"Ah, you've snatched my proudest claim to fame right out from between my teeth. But seriously, she was the most spirited animal I've ever encountered. Yes, I broke her. You, Your Majesty, remind me of Ribelle;*

* Rebel.

you are extraordinarily spirited, plucky, and mettlesome in light of your situation. Many a woman would cry herself to sleep every night; not you. Tears don't come easily to one with your backbone.

"You showed your spirit with your sarcasm in the queen's bedchamber earlier. You anticipated my offer and practically threw it in my face. You made me very angry, Your Majesty. You embarrassed me in front of my inferiors and my friends. Very thoughtless, very inconsiderate. But gifted as I am with Spartan self-control, I held my piece. Not that I wasn't furious.

"You remind me of my mare. Difficult to break, but not impossible. I can tell you, the joke was on those potbellied idlers who gave her to me when I rode her in dress parade two weeks to the hour after I'd been given her. You should have seen their faces." A knock sounded. "What?"

Joseph opened the door. He held a silver tray; on it, an envelope.

"Your pardon, Your Excellency, this just came from Doctor Brabossi. The guard who brought it said it was urgent."

"Give it here." DeLeone drew out his monocle and adjusted it over his eye. Reading the note to himself, he reacted shocked, his monocle dropping. "Thank you, Joseph, you may go."

Joseph bowed and withdrew. Five seconds reading and DeLeone's face had become as grave as a parson's, thought Lorna.

"Disturbing news," he said quietly. "Dr. Brabossi's initial determination as to the cause of her death was heart failure. Now he strongly suspects she was poisoned."

"Was she now? What do you know, we have a viper in the royal womb."

"It's not funny, Mrs. Stone.'" He blew out his breath and clucked discouragingly. "Though I must say it's apt. Who could have done such a thing, and how?"

"How many people in the castle?"

"The question is who was closest to her, who was with her most of the time? Opportunity, you see. Torzzini? Mmmm . . ."

Her heart froze. He restored his monocle to his eye, and reread the note, crumpling it, and disposing of it in the basket.

"I must go at once to discuss this with the doctor. Oh, yes, there is to be a ceremony the day after tomorrow which you will be attending. You'll be presenting medals to soldiers at Lémenc."

"The Roman Station north of town."

"You know it?"

"I've heard about it. But really, this whole thing's absurd. How can I possibly continue posing as the queen? Once word gets out . . ."

"That's the point, Your Majesty, word will not get out. It will be shut up inside here like a nut in its shell for as long as is necessary, just as His Majesty's lamentable condition has been kept a secret?"

"He's completely mad, isn't he? There hasn't been any such thing as temporary periods of normalcy. Not for weeks."

"Which, if you think about it, measurably enhances your value to us."

"A madman in power."

"Other madmen have ruled, George the III. . . ."

"As long as your madman is supported by men mad for power . . ." He silenced her with a scowl.

"Speaking of Charles Felix and my spirited mare, I don't for a moment take your conduct this morning lightly. If you ever do that again, you will wish you had never been born. Once again you appear to be in need of proof of the seriousness of your situation."

"Am I to have my head shaved again?"

That's it, you fool, the voice inside her shouted, put the idea in his head!

"Not at all. Nor will your tongue be cut out. Nothing quite as ruthless as that. No, what I had in mind is in a way, somewhat of a favor to you. It includes an ironclad guarantee that Colonel Sasso won't come anywhere near you ever again. It's this: Your Majesty, your husband, the king, will be looking forward to welcoming you back to the royal bedchamber tonight and every night from now on. Since the attempted assassination, as you're aware, Caroline-Louisa has been sleeping alone in the royal bedchamber, but now we shall see Savoy's monarchs reunited in holy wedlock."

"You wouldn't . . ."

"I am."

"He raped me once, he tried a second time."

"He feels affection for you." He leered at her.

"If you force me to lie in the same bed with that . . . I give you my solemn word I'll kill him before he so much as lays a finger on my arm."

"Tsk, tsk, you wouldn't, and you know it. Life is too precious to you for you to reduce yourself to martyrdom. Besides, you're upsetting yourself unnecessarily; he won't hurt you. Oh, he'll lapse into babbling once in awhile, he'll bore you, and his breath is foul, but he's harmless. He'll only want to . . . you know."

"I'll kill him," she said. "I swear to God I will!"

"If that's the case, I'll have to see that somebody is seated in the room at all times, with guards outside the door. Should you be so foolish as to attempt to carry out your threat, you'll be stopped before you can do any harm. As to the girl sitting in the room, she won't be playing Peeping Tom. The bed curtains will assure you privacy for your lovemaking.

"Well, now that that's settled, did I remember to thank you for coming to see me, and being so prompt? I do thank you. You may go along now, there's a good girl. You're a queen now, Mrs. Stone, lift up your head, square your shoulders, look proud, haughty, imperious." Standing, clicking his heels, he bowed. "Good morning, Your Majesty."

BOOK FOUR

DESTINY'S YOKE

I

The rest of the day and into evening she lived on tenter-
hooks anticipating her first "voluntary" meeting in bed
with Charles Felix. Mere sight of him in her mind's
eye repelled her so she shuddered. She debated confronting DeLeone and absolutely refusing to go through
with it. But that, of course, was exactly what he wanted,
and if she put her foot down, he would simply force her
to. As easily as he forced her to do everything else,
she mused morosely, as she lay stretched out on the
méridienne examining her dilemma. Forcing her would
set the sadistic old fool glowing with satisfaction; but
forced or otherwise, the thought of once again submit-
ting to the king's clumsy advances, permitting him to
satiate his lust, the odor of his vile breath, his endless
slavering upon her mouth and face and breasts and
other intimate areas, his entering and abusing her, was
enough to send her hurrying back to her rooms where
she locked herself in.

Maria was nowhere about, having, she assumed, already been assigned other duties.

She sat at her vanity in a royal blue silk gown
trimmed with Mechlin lace, wearing the imperial dia-
dem of pearls and brilliants and rose diamonds, looking like a queen, but feeling more like a concubine summoned and pressed into service to appease the royal
sexual appetite.

The hours flew by, sundown, twilight, dinner, which
she shared with Charles Felix—to her disgust—and
nightfall following in rapid succession. At 10:30 two
guards, who from the worried looks on their faces had

ostensibly been searching the castle for her, arrived at her door to:

"Escort Your Majesty to the royal bedchamber."

"I'm not going; I'm sleeping here. You may inform the prime minister."

They were prepared for this response, probably, she thought, by Adelbert himself. She was right.

"Your pardon, Your Majesty, but if you refuse to accompany us, our orders are to persuade you," said one.

"Failing that, we are to bring you regardless," announced the other. "If we have to carry you."

Luck was with her. Charles Felix had been drinking most of the day. At the dinner table he had imbibed copious amounts of wine and when she was ushered into the bedchamber it was to the sight and sound of him fast asleep.

The woman assigned to watch over the proceedings arose from her bench set against the wall opposite the as yet unoccupied right side of the bed. She bowed. Sight of her sparked an idea in Lorna's mind. In the darkness, in his condition, Charles Felix would hardly be able to differentiate between one female body and another.

"What is your name?" she asked.

"Felicity, Your Majesty."

Lorna cast about, settling on a small but exquisite jewel-encrusted pill box on the vanity.

"His Highness is asleep, I see," she said.

"Yes, Your Majesty, he fell asleep right away."

Her cow eyes, indolent tone of voice and a lower lip that protruded absurdly suggested that she was not overly endowed with brilliance. Wandering to the vanity, Lorna picked up the pill box and pressed it into her hand.

"Beautiful, isn't it?"

"Very beautiful, Your Majesty."

"Would you like to keep it?" Down came the lower

lip revealing yellowed teeth. The cow eyes bulged. "It's yours. All you have to do is change places with me. I'll sit on your bench, you undress and get into the bed."

The woman's response to this was delivered in a monotone that suggested that she had been coached and had rehearsed all afternoon. She set the box down upon the bench.

"His Excellency, the prime minister's man, Joseph, warned that you would try to bribe me to change places with you. But I won't. I am forbidden to. And I must, say no more."

Lorna persisted, adding other items to the bribe, cajoling, wheedling, even, in desperation, bullying the woman. It was useless; sealing her fat lips she thrust out her chin defiantly, cast her eyes at the floor and, held them there and refused to say another word.

Lorna gave it up, undressed, made her toilette, dressed for bed and, pushing aside the curtain, eased herself slowly and carefully under the coverlet, silently praying she would not disturb his slumber. She lay wide awake, tensed like a fist and prepared to leap out should he awaken. Listening to his disgusting snoring, she decided that involving the woman, even the attempt, would have hardly been fair. At that, even had she been able to talk her into it, with this Yankee's luck something would have surely gone wrong. They would have caught and severely punished the two of them. So once again she found herself between the proverbial rock and hard place. With only the king's drunken stupor saving her from his lust.

She did not sleep, did not dare to close her eyes, and when the first telltale gray of dawn began filtering in between the partially drawn drapes, she got up, dressed, and sat at the vanity, waiting for the sun to clear the horizon. It had been the longest night of her life and on top of not sleeping, the nervous strain, the fear filling her in the realization that he lay a mere three inches away, had left her exhausted.

Would her luck hold, she wondered? Would Charles Felix continue his heavy drinking? Did the poor mad creature even know that his wife was dead? Or was he as much a dupe as his subjects, with Adelbert orchestrating the entire charade? She couldn't care less about that aspect of it, not with a second night and a third and only God and the count knowing how many more ahead of her in the royal bed!

She took breakfast alone in the salon, yawning, rubbing her eyes and wanting nothing in the world so much as bed and sleep, though not that bed! She wondered what DeLeone was doing about Clothilde. Certainly something had to be done. She had been practically dragged out of his rooms screaming about her right to the throne. He couldn't keep her locked up indefinitely. Although why not? People had been locked up in far less luxurious surroundings than hers for years. Nevertheless, she was proving a thorn in Adelbert's side, and for that alone Lorna applauded her. Anything to discommode the detestable old fool!

One of the guards outside the door knocked timidly and opened it revealing Philip. As if apprehensive that she might immediately order him out, he came rushing in.

"What do you want?" she asked icily.

"We must talk . . ." He hesitated, raising his eyes from her and glancing at first one maid then the other. "May we be alone?"

She was tempted to summon the guard and order him thrown out bodily, but her resentment at his intrusion as well as her feelings for him in general were temporarily overridden by her curiosity. With Caroline-Louisa dead and Paul dispatched to his regiment, Philip no longer had any hold over her. Now that she thought about it, DeLeone needed her considerably more than he needed this or any other colonel.

"You may go," she said to the maids. "Five minutes."

"Ten," said Philip in a voice so hopeful sounding it bordered on begging.

"Five minutes. Get a breath of air, then come straight back. Colonel Sasso will be leaving."

They bowed and withdrew. Closing the door behind them, Philip rushed back to her.

"I have a proposition for you, my darling."

"You're up to your ears in bargains and propositions these days. What is it now, your friend DeLeone's sash in exchange for helping me get away? I doubt if that's possible, even with your conniving mind manipulating things."

"Please listen. Adelbert told me about disciplining you, forcing you to sleep with Charles Felix for talking out of turn and treating him like a footman. You'll never learn, will you?"

"Has he sent you around to teach me?"

"Lorna, why don't we stop fraying each other's nerves. I've been frantic with worry."

"Poor Philip, how distressing." She yawned, covered her mouth and, getting up from the couch, crossed to the window.

"I realize you couldn't come to me as you promised what with all that's happened. Nevertheless, it doesn't change anything, it's only temporary. I'm not one to give up so easily."

"You're wasting your breath, Philip. We don't have a bargain anymore. The captain's long gone."

"I wasn't thinking about Torzzini. It's Charles Felix." His eyes took on a sly look as he continued. "I don't like the idea of any man sleeping with my wife, even the king. Oh, I know some husbands would be flattered, but I'm not one of them. If you come back to me, on my terms, you'll be spared that horror."

He had moved to where she was standing. He touched her forearm. She recoiled, pulling away, facing him, her eyes blazing.

"Don't do that!"

"Come, come, my dear, are you trying to tell me you

don't enjoy my lovemaking? That I failed to come up to your expectations on our wedding night? You're joking, of course."

"My devoted husband come to save me from a fate worse than death. What an appropriate cliché."

"Wouldn't I be saving you? Be practical, the man's not only repulsive, he's mad and dangerously unpredictable. You may wake up tomorrow morning, you may not. And who in Hanover will ever know what happened?"

How she hated the sight of him, his self-assured tone, his conceit, his egotistical smirk. Unfortunately, he was absolutely right; to deny it would be ridiculous. His bed in exchange for Charles Felix's. What a choice. The bed of the man she despised more than any other in all the world as opposed to that of a lunatic. There was, unhappily, no other alternative; it was like being trapped in an alley two feet wide with the sheer side of tall buildings rising on either side. At one end a tiger waited, at the other, a lion. While somewhere up at the top of one of the buildings Paul waited with a rope. Down tumbled the end, she'd grab hold, and he'd pull her up to safety. She pictured herself, her feet firm against the knot at the end, clutching the rope for dear life, looking down at the two beasts charging headlong at each other.

There was only one difficulty. There was the alley, the beasts, and Paul; there was the rope. *When* would he toss it down?

"I'm supposed to be posing as Caroline-Louisa," she said wearily. "I can't very well move in with you. I doubt if Adelbert would approve."

"We're man and wife. We'll meet at eleven o'clock every night, in the royal bedchamber."

"Really . . ."

"Why not? Her Majesty got away with turning the entire castle into her bedroom; it'll be a lot simpler for you. For us." He placed his hand on her shoulder and she fought off the urge to shrug it away. "I love you, Lorna, with every source of feeling in my body. The long days and nights between the Gray Dragon and here and now have made that clear to me. I can't live without you; I can't function. You despise me for what I did, for that I can hardly blame you."

"How very generous of you."

"But you can't hold a grudge forever."

"Try me."

"Think about it, your hatred replaced your love. Why can't that work in reverse? It can. You'll see, you'll love me again, even more than before."

"If you only knew, if you had the vaguest idea of the measure of my depth of hatred for you."

"Words, mere words, nothing more. You say them, but deep down in your heart you don't mean them. How can you? I'll go now and square things with His Excellency. Eleven tonight it is. We'll have a bottle of wine, just like the Gray Dragon."

And he was gone.

II

She lunched alone, missing Clothilde's company. Lately they had been dining together more and more frequently. She seemed to be losing her appetite as the days slipped by; she blamed her nerves, continually aroused and overly abused by the swift concatenation of events, in particular the latest turn in her fortunes which saw her returning to Philip's bed.

She ate in the salon, a wedge of Beaufort, a softly textured Savoyard Gruyère with the delicate taste of Alpine flowers, freshly baked rolls, and Hyson tea.

Philip amazed her; he bulldoggedly persisted in belaboring the point that she had loved him before and would love him again because of it, because, he insisted, she "knew how." Never mind all that had happened to her; dust that away like a cobweb from a corner.

She could never love him again, what woman with pride and self-esteem and memory could? It was like being brutally raped, only to have your assaulter satisfy his lust, then turn around and propose marriage. Philip's logic, his love-supplanted-by-hate-which-in-turn-could-be-supplanted-once-again-by-love idea was that false. Absurd, as far as she was concerned.

There was only one course open to her. Go to bed with him if she must, yes, but close her eyes and ears, mind and heart to his presence. Substitute Paul in the darkness, Paul darling, Paul passionate, tender, considerate; her love, her only love.

That afternoon she journeyed with General Ascoyne, the commander-in-chief of the army, to the rock of Lémenc, the Roman Station of Lemincum north of the town. Here, under Colonel Etienne Haproux, the 11th

Calvary was encamped, prepared, according to the general, on an hour's notice to move in any direction to secure one or another of Savoy's borders.

The area was striped with neat rows of gray-white tents. Spirals of smoke climbed out of cooking fires, and the officers and men sat astride their mounts in row on row on parade, awaiting the arrival of their queen.

Ascoyne proved a garrulous sort, regaling her with tales of the 11th's glory against the Austrians and the French. He was a huge man gone to fat around the waistline and under the chin; his hair was fiery red and he wore it short, standing straight up Prussian-style, while his untrimmed, untamed moustache, half the size of two red foxtails, flourished at the center third of his face, effectively hiding the source of his words.

The ceremony was mercilessly long and boring, each recipient's name being called out, the man dismounting and standing beside his horse, while she pinned his decoration upon his pocket. In all there were forty-six awards. Occasionally, between the drone of the sergeant major's voice announcing the name and presentation of the award, she sneaked a sidelong glance about the camp. She finally caught sight of Paul astride his horse in the rear of a group of officers drawn up behind Colonel Haproux. Paul looked so handsome, she said to herself, his gray eyes shadowed under the peak of his shako, but the rest of his features clearly seen.

When? the voice inside her shouted as her heart quickened! No longer was it the prospect of escape alone that beckoned like a hand reached out to a drowning man, it was being reunited with him, the two of them never to be separated again. If only the fates were that cooperative! If only she could blink her eyes and cause everyone to vanish, except the two of them. Off they'd ride in the victoria, his horse trailing after them, a soldier and his girl on their way to a picnic. Across the nearest border!

The heat was brutal, the air more stifling than any day in recent memory. What she wouldn't give for home and the pool in the meadow. Closing her eyes she envisioned it on a summer night dotted with stars surrounding the image of the full moon. And she and Paul swimming nude in the cool clear water, standing waist-deep, embracing, kissing passionately, feeling his marvelous member firming against her sex. Dissolving in his arms, her heart sledging her breath, her mind dizzying, reeling as their mouths and tongues met.

Paul. She almost shouted his name out loud, then wresting herself free of her fantasy, accepted the round and beribboned piece of silver presented to her in its velvet-lined box, pinning it onto the jacket of the lanky corporal standing self-consciously in front of her and congratulating him.

It was nearing four o'clock by the time she returned to the castle. As usual, DeLeone wanted to see her right away. The man seemed to have a predilection for piling up reasons for monopolizing her company. He came pounding into the salon, worry bunching his wrinkled features.

"Bad news, most unfortunate news, Your Majesty. Miss Von Schuppe has had an accident." He tossed up his hands. "What am I saying, how can I call it that? The poor creature has committed suicide."

"Clothilde?"

He nodded. "Jumped from her window. Killed instantly on the rocks below. What a pity, she was so young. Her whole life ahead of her."

"I don't believe it!"

"I've seen the body with my own eyes . . ."

"I believe she's dead, I don't believe she killed herself. She was pushed, she had to be."

"How can you say such a thing?"

"Easily, Your Excellency. Suicide doesn't fit the pattern of events around this perverted paradise of yours; murder is much more like it."

"Suicide! Obviously she was distraught over being denied the throne. You know how headstrong she was."

"Headstrong, yes, impulsive, yes, but hardly to the point of taking her own life because you denied her the crown. Not her, never!"

"Have it your own way."

"She's not the suicide type."

"Enough!" He was suddenly furious, the veins in his neck all but popping through the skin, the redness spreading across his throat rushing upward, flooding his face. "She committed suicide! And that is that." Clenching his fists and pounding his thighs, he got control of himself, softening his tone. "Forgive me, but your obstinacy, your argumentativeness really do bring out the worst in me."

He crossed to the curule stool, slumping tiredly down onto it. "Her body will be prepared for burial and sent back to her family in Germany."

"A pity both of them couldn't be sent back. The House of Savoy could wash its hands of Von Schuppes."

He smiled grimly. "We could hardly send back the queen's body. Your Majesty is in such enviably good health. Tell me honestly, don't you feel the slightest, smallest twinge of pride, even conceit, in being able to delude an entire regiment into accepting you as their queen?"

"It never crossed my mind."

"It must have."

"It didn't, Your Excellency. Probably because I have such little respect for royalty in general. And what I've seen around here only re-enforces that feeling."

"I'm sure. Oh, something else happened while you were at Lémenc. Doctor Brabossi and I had a long talk and he's more convinced than ever that Her Majesty was poisoned. I'm telling you to put you on your guard."

"I don't follow you."

"Obviously what I've been cautioning you about all along still holds. There are, unfortunately, those who prefer the queen dead. You dead. Brabossi insists that all the symptoms of arsenic poisoning were in evidence, stomachache, loss of appetite, a general malaise. True, her heart failed, but that was the means of death, poison the cause. The questions remain, who and how? He and I discussed that at length. Not surprisingly, he too mentioned Captain Torzzini who, as you know, spent a great deal of time with her. Which afforded him better opportunity than anyone else. Still, the doctor and I agreed that Paul is not stupid. He has to be aware that he would be the logical prime suspect."

"Have you questioned him?" she asked.

"Not yet. I feel it might be preferable to let sleeping dogs lie. At least for now. After all, it comes back to the obvious, does it not? You're not really dead, Your Majesty."

"Not yet. That we leave in your capable hands, Your Excellency."

"General Ascoyne tells me that you performed flawlessly this afternoon. My congratulations. You see the sensibleness of cooperation? You see how much easier life can be?"

"Will I get a medal?"

He sighed in exasperation. "There you go, slipping back into sarcasm. No, I was thinking of something more practical. Possibly discontinuing your punishment? What would you say if I forbade you to sleep with Charles Felix tonight?"

"I'd be very grateful."

"I'm sure you would be," he said jauntily.

Wonderful! Marvelous! She wouldn't be needing Philip after all to escape the king's clutches. She could turn her back on him, snub him completely, perhaps even return to her old rooms.

"No . . ." went on DeLeone, screwing in his monocle, bending his head back and studying the ceiling, "why continue subjecting you to his excesses? It's plain you've learned your lesson. Besides, your husband has been badgering me to give you back to him. No, no, that's putting it too indelicately. Forgive me. He wishes to be reunited with you, and I've given him my blessing. I give you both my blessing. Once before I told you I thought you were judging him too harshly. Now that your enmity has had a chance to cool, perhaps you don't feel quite so bitter toward him. He loves you deeply. I know, he's told me so."

"He's told me so, Your Excellency. Unfortunately, I can't stand the sight of him. That business with Charles Felix, when he climbed into my bed while I was sleeping. I could have killed him with my knife. In self-defense, mind you. It wouldn't be self-defense with Sasso. I would jump at the chance to murder him!"

"You'll get your chance tonight."

"Don't make me sleep with him. If you want me to, I'll get down on my knees and beg. But don't do it, please. I've never really asked you for anything, I've done everything you've asked of me."

"You have."

"Please don't make me sleep with him."

He smiled, tilting his head slightly, releasing his monocle, letting it drop into his hand. Then he studied her in fatherly fashion, and patted her gently on the shoulder.

"You mustn't beg. I won't have it. Besides, you'd be wasting your breath. I've already given you my decision. You will sleep tonight with your husband. Good day, Your Majesty."

III

Shortly before dinner she was walking a corridor alone, heading toward her rooms, when around the dogleg corner came Maria, beaming at the sight of her, and running to her.

"Mistress, mistress, I've been so worried about you. I imagined all sorts of horrors . . ."

"I'm all right, dear, as good as can be expected. Where are you going?"

"To the kitchen. They put me back there. I worked in the kitchen when I first got here, before I came upstairs."

"Come back to our rooms with me, can you? We've so much to talk about."

Maria ignited her gap-toothed smile and nodded. "Of course." She seized Lorna by the hand.

Behind the locked door, each one gushed forth everything that had happened to her during the past few days of separation. Maria was shocked and saddened by Lorna's disclosure that she and Philip were to resume "playing at man and wife."

"That's the cruelest thing I've ever heard!" exclaimed Maria bitterly. "What can you do?"

"I have an idea. There was an older woman who lived on our street back home in Hanover. She had the reputation for being the coldest, most unfeeling bedmate in all of New England, though how the gossips ever determined that I'll never know. The story was that her husband took her virginity on their wedding night and from that hour forward she never let him near her again. The last I heard they had been living together, man and wife, for thirty-nine years. Separate beds, separate rooms." She grinned grimly. "As for Philip . . ."

"Get him angry and he may hurt you."

"I have no intention of getting him angry; I'd much rather make him miserable. Best of all would be to see him crawl. Plead and beg . . . It should be an interesting night, Maria. Did you hear about Clothilde?" Maria nodded. "And DeLeone says that Doctor Brabossi insists Caroline-Louisa was poisoned." Maria looked away. "You knew that before Brabossi did, didn't you? Who did it, Maria? You know, tell me."

"I . . . can't."

"DeLeone suspects Paul."

"No!"

"Sssssh. Yes, because they were together so much, just the two of them. The old fool doesn't have a motive for Paul, of course. Thank the Lord he doesn't suspect he's a *carbonari.* Anyway, with everything so up in the air, DeLeone isn't about to stir up that bed of coals. Besides, he's too busy making arrangements to crown Charles Felix's successor."

"How can he do that?" asked Maria.

"Charles Felix is mad, dear, and, I expect, completely unmanageable. His Excellency, your esteemed prime minister, doesn't need complications compounding complications. He had no love for Caroline-Louisa, but he needed her, and he could trust her. Charles Felix he can't. So he intends to replace him."

Maria's eyes strayed to the door, and the key in its hole. Moving to it she made doubly certain it was locked and coming back took Lorna by the arm and walked her to the window.

"You think I poisoned Her Majesty?"

"I didn't say that. But I think you know who did."

"I could have, maybe I did."

"What are you talking about?"

Abruptly, as if the God of Confidence had touched her vanity with his magic wand, Maria's mind changed. She had a story to reveal and suddenly no power on

earth could keep her from blurting it out. Reading her
eyes, Lorna sensed that if she didn't unburden herself
she might very well explode.

It turned out to be a tale so bizarre Lorna could only
gape in astonishment.

"It was poison, yes. One of the girls, I can't tell you
who, stole it from the stables. They use it to kill vermin;
a white powder. They say it has no taste."

"Arsenic . . ."

"That's it. There are forty-two maids and ladies-in-
waiting in the castle, counting the kitchen girls. The
other night, in the dead of night, forty-two teaspoons
were laid out in a row on the long table in the kitchen.
Forty-one were filled level with sugar. The forty-second
was filled with arsenic, with a topping of sugar to cover
it. So all the spoons looked the same. One of the kitchen
maids prepared them. When she was done, she left the
kitchen. Another kitchen maid came in and not knowing
which was the poison spoon rearranged the whole row.
Then she called the first girl and all the rest of us in.
We passed the table one by one, each picking up a
spoon, dumping it into the queen's sugar bowl, and stirring the bowl. You see, every morning like clockwork,
her coffee is brought to her and she prefers it very
sweet, so she always takes three sugars from her bowl.
Even if someone else is with her, they have another
bowl, you see, and another pot of coffee or tea. That's
what gave us the idea; we didn't want to make a mistake and kill the wrong person."

"And by the second morning she had taken enough
arsenic to kill herself," said Lorna in an awestruck tone.

"Clever, don't you think?"

"Very. Brilliant. Who's idea was it?"

"I can't tell you. I can't tell you any names. You understand. They're not important anyway, since we're all
guilty."

"All forty-two."

"All guilty of murder, which is exactly the way we

want it. I mean, how could any one of us hold her head up in front of the others if she didn't take part?"

"How indeed. . . ."

"You must cross your heart and swear by the Holy Virgin you'll never tell anyone. Not a living soul."

"I won't."

"Not even Captain Torzzini when you're miles and miles from here."

"I cross my heart and swear by the Holy Virgin I'll never tell your secret."

"We shall have to tell it ourselves, though."

"Why?"

"At confession. Murder's a sin, even if you kill the devil. And that's what she was, the devil with a crown."

"You won't have to confess."

"But we do."

"Do you think she confessed to Father Asquino that she hired the man who tried to assassinate Charles Felix? Confess that she made her own husband insane."

"She hired the man?"

Lorna nodded. "As sure as we're sitting here. There's another reason you can't confess to murdering her, the best reason of all. You don't know if you did. That business about all forty-two of you doing it is nonsense. You said yourself only one spoon had arsenic in it. Which means the chances are forty-two to one in your favor you put sugar in the bowl. Maria, you haven't murdered anybody."

"Perhaps you're right."

"Of course I'm right. When you die and go to heaven, you'll know it."

"Not really. I mean that's no proof. The girl who put the poison in is certain to go to heaven, for giving the rest of us a whole new life!"

IV

Late that afternoon, Lorna having spent most of the remainder of the afternoon at her salon window looking wistfully out in the direction of the Roman Station, DeLeone came to her door. With him was a strutting little sparrow-man bearing a battered briefcase and wearing an expression of holier-than-thou disapproval. At first glance he looked to her as if he had bitten into a persimmon, so strained and knotted looking were his features. He stood just inside the door, clutching his hat in his free hand, bowing low and freezing in position, as if his spine had locked. DeLeone came forward, clicked to a halt and bowed.

"Your Majesty," he said quietly, "may I present Counselor Innocent Marisanti, Chambéry's foremost attorney. He arrived . . ."

"Would you please straighten up?" she asked, interrupting. "You make us nervous."

DeLeone gestured the man, now standing six strides behind him, erect. The count then reduced his voice to a whisper. "He's come at the head of a delegation. The others are waiting in my chamber." He paused and scratched his cheek thoughtfully.

"What's all this?" she asked.

"A problem, a very serious charge. Counselor . . ."

Turning back to the man a second time, he snapped his fingers. Marisanti unstrapped his briefcase and digging into it brought out a sheet of vellum, what appeared to be a document of some kind. Bowing his way forward, the look of disapproval still firmly fixed to his face, he handed the paper to DeLeone and backed off. The prime minister adjusted his monocle and held up the paper.

"What is it?" she asked.

"A confession," he whispered. "By one Ignacio . . ." He hesitated.

"Crotienne," called out Marisanti.

"A wastrel, from what I can gather," said DeLeone in his normal voice. "He confesses that he was hired to assassinate your husband, Highness. More to the point he accuses you of paying him two hundred gold florins to do so."

"Does he really?" she asked, feigning exaggerated innocence, her tongue rounding her cheek.

DeLeone turned back to Marisanti. "Counselor, would you mind rejoining the others in my chambers? I shall be back shortly."

"As you wish, Minister." Another bow, heels clicking loud enough to cause an echo in the corridor, and counselor Innocent Marisanti was gone. DeLeone dropped into the gondola chair, studying the paper in his hands, temporarily oblivious of her presence.

"It appears to be authentic. If it is, and he and his friends insist it is, it could put us in serious difficulty."

"Us? I'm sorry, I see no reason why you should include me."

"It's all here, chapter and verse. He claims a lieutenant acted as go-between. No name, but he shouldn't be hard to find. Though why we should find him, so that he can substantiate the allegation, makes no sense." He turned the paper over on his lap. "I must caution Your Highness that Marisanti is a very important man, a specialist in constitutional law. Scrupulously honest, and a great patriot, the type who wears the flag on his tongue. And zealously protective of the House and of his king. One of those who raged to the mountaintops when Charles Felix married her. He despises the Germans, continually citing their inferior blood. As far as that goes, he hates everybody and everything that is not Savoyardian."

"This is all very interesting, but I fail to see . . ."

DeLeone had turned the confession over. He began folding it neatly, reducing it to the size of a ruler, and thrusting it into his inside jacket pocket.

"You, Your Majesty, are the queen."

"Don't be ridiculous. You can't possibly accuse me of . . ."

He cut her off with a swipe of his hand. "Be still. We need this"—he tapped his pocket—"about as much as we need another war with France. But it's a bit late, to nip it in the bud. The word is out all over Chambéry, you can be sure; by this time tomorrow it will have spread from one end of the duchy to the other. That means we can't shove it under the carpet, so we'll have to go along with them, we'll have to cooperate. You will be brought up on charges."

"You're out of your mind!"

"*Silence!* Although I don't profess to be a lawyer, I would imagine that on the basis of this confession alone, not to mention the testimony of the officer who actually put the money into this Crotienne's hands, it will go against you. I see no reason why it shouldn't, do you?"

"Against the queen, not me."

"Ah, but who is the queen? Everybody accepts you, but you." He chuckled. "You certainly fooled Marisanti."

She eyed him intently. "I'm beginning to understand. Very neat, very clever. Suddenly into your lap drops the perfect means to eliminate the sacrificial lamb. Of course, first you must get rid of Charles Felix like you did Clothilde. Perhaps murder him and put the blame on his queen? It's all very logical, hasn't she already tried?"

"As usual, your imagination is smothering your common sense."

She turned from him and walked toward the window, in her mind's eye again seeing Paul astride his horse. When would he come for her? When! This waiting would soon shatter her nerves completely and send her screaming out a tower window if she had to, put up with it much longer. Every day, almost every hour a new problem cropped up, piling upon the others like the faggots piled around Joan of Arc at the stake. Still, whatever had happened, whatever was to come, this Yankee was no martyr; come what may she was not about to be a human sacrifice on the altar of this old man's insatiable ambition. A pawn in his game, perhaps, but only until she could turn the play around and checkmate him.

"It won't work, Adelbert, I won't let it. I'll play along until they're just about to declare me guilty and pronounce sentence. Then:"

Snatching off her wig, she flung it at him. It struck him in the chest, tumbling into his lap. "Your honors, ladies and gentlemen, see for yourselves, I am not Caroline-Louisa and never have been! Caroline-Louisa is dead, murdered! Picture their faces, Your Excellency, their eyes saucering, their mouths hanging open."

"Then of course you'll point your finger at me and accuse me of being the principal machinator." He laughed and tossed the wig back at her. She stepped aside and let it fall. "Do you think for a moment you're telling me anything I haven't already anticipated? Use your head, child, you don't seriously believe that I would go to all this trouble to end up letting you or anyone else subvert my plans for Savoy? Not likely. It's very simple, you continue to play along, and you'll have my protection. You cross me on the stand or anywhere else and you will be dead before you get the second word out. Assassinated, Your Majesty, by a fanatical monarchist supporter who will jump to his feet, his smoking pistol in hand, and shout some singularly memorable phrase that will eventually find its way into all the history books. Something like: Death to the German murderess, long live Savoy!

"What a bore. Pick up your wig and put it on, Your Majesty, and let us go to dinner. We'll give Marisanti and his friends an hour or so to get a rein on their umbrage, then blithely announce our willingness to stand accused."

V

She sat at the vanity in the royal bedchamber conscious of a stone lodged in the pit of her stomach, the result of dinner forced down against the will of her appetite. Counselor Marisanti's accusation fell neatly into position in a predictable pattern that saw each event occurring as more calamitous than the one preceding it. That DeLeone ultimately wanted her dead she did not doubt for a moment, the only question was when? How far along was he, she wondered, in his arrangements for supplanting Charles Felix on the throne? With Caroline-Louisa dead, it was obvious that he had no choice but to remove the king. Charles Felix was in no condition to rule his hunting dogs, let alone the House of Savoy. Erratic, unpredictable, by his prime minister's own admission, wholly unreliable, wresting the scepter from the queen's lifeless fingers and handing it back to him would invite catastrophe.

Lorna stared at her image in the mirror and Clothilde's description of her sister came back to her: "She's not pretty and fresh looking anymore. And those lines around her mouth . . ." Living under the sword of Savoy certainly appeared to be taking its toll on her, Lorna mused, touching her chin and sighing. And her failure to sleep the night before certainly didn't help.

Teresa Zuccola, another maid, and two ladies-in-waiting stood stiffly and silently by watching her, awaiting orders.

"What time is it?" she asked.

"Almost nine o'clock, Your Majesty," said one of the ladies-in-waiting, a tall, flaxen-haired, scrawny-looking girl. At first sight of her earlier, Lorna had

301

decided that her bones had been assembled too hastily, in somewhat the manner of Ichabod Crane. "I'm very tired," she answered. "I think I'll go to bed. You may all go, except Teresa."

They nodded in unison, bowed, and backed away, playing their roles to the hilt, the door clicking softly in front of them as Teresa bustled forward.

For the first time Lorna noticed that the small bulge, the sachet holding the dried remains of her tongue, under the girl's neckline, was missing. Around her neck in place of the slender black ribbon was a delicate silver chain holding, of all things, a tiny silver spoon.

Surely the most appropriate thing, Teresa's way of announcing to all who knew about it her part in disposing of the queen. Lorna wondered if the girl was aware that Doctor Brabossi had guessed that Caroline-Louisa had been poisoned. Had she, she might hesitate to flaunt the spoon. On the other hand, it could be that Her Majesty's death had imbued Teresa, imbued them all, with spirit and daring.

Teresa noticed her staring at the spoon and began fingering it self-consciously, a trace of concern in her dark eyes. She must reassure her that she was in no danger of being told on from this Yankee, mused Lorna. Swinging about on the bench she stood up.

"Come closer, Teresa, I won't bite you." The girl nodded and smiling thinly inched toward her. Lorna examined the spoon. "Very pretty. It's the symbol of a silly lover, did you know that?" Teresa relaxed and nodded, beaming. "Are you a silly lover?" Teresa shook her head. "Then you have a silly lover." She blushed and hid her face behind her fingers.

Lorna laughed. "Dear, I'll get myself ready for bed. I want you to run an errand for me. Go and find Maria, my maid, the German girl; I don't know her last name. She's probably in the kitchen." Teresa nodded, and went to find her.

Left alone, Lorna lay down fully clothed on top

of the bed and began wrestling with her most immediate problem. In less than two hours Philip would be standing at the door. Did he really intend to sleep with her in the royal bedchamber? Possibly; matters had reached a point where she would put nothing past either DeLeone or him. The two of them seemed to make up their own rules as they went along, Philip answering to the count only and DeLeone treating him more like his favorite nephew than his subordinate.

Merely going through the motions with Philip in bed, imitating a life-sized wax doll, would frustrate him, even infuriate him, but discourage him? Never. He seemed tenaciously dedicated to winning her back, body, heart, and mind. The latter two, it was safe to say, were well and permanently beyond his reach, though that he would never accept. His vanity wouldn't allow it, which promised nothing but trouble for her. The problem reduced itself to "if I can't have you nobody else will," meaning Paul, of course.

She yawned wearily and closed her eyes, but her mind refused to jettison the problem. There'd be no more sleeping this night than there had been the last. She could well imagine what her mirror would present to her tomorrow morning.

If only Paul would come, if only she could get word to him that her situation was worsening by the hour. If he knew that, he just might drop everything and come running, whatever the risk. Still, he had to know what was going on, at least the substance of it. Why didn't he come! Whatever the odds against them, if they had to gallop a hundred miles, lathering the horses and all but bursting their lungs, then so be it. Once up on a horse's back all the Savoyards in Christendom would never catch them. They would ride and ride and never look back.

A gentle knock sounded and the door opened. It was Teresa with Maria.

"Mistress, what is it? Has something happened?"

"Something may be going to, Maria." Lorna hesitated. "Teresa, dear, you may go for the night." Teresa nodded and Lorna let Maria in closing the door.

She placed her hands on her shoulders and held her eyes. "I want you to go back to the kitchen and get me a small knife, like the one she took away from me."

"What are you going to do?"

"Prevent a rape."

"Colonel Sasso?" Lorna nodded and explained. "I'll need it to protect myself. I tell you this, and I mean it with all my heart, I'll see him dead before he touches me."

Maria sighed and began pacing, wringing her hands. "If you kill him you'll be signing your own death warrant!"

"They intend to get rid of me regardless. If Paul doesn't get me out of here first. Don't you see, DeLeone can't possibly let me live, any more than he could Clothilde. If I don't hang for conspiracy to assassinate Charles Felix, I'll have an 'accident' just as she did. He's as much as admitted that."

"Really?"

"The expression on his face tells me I'm doomed more clearly and honestly than any words. Just go and get the knife."

"If I must."

"You must."

"Captain Torzzini will rescue you long before any of them can do anything to you. Kill Sasso and you'll be throwing your life away!"

"It would be self-defense, Maria."

"You don't believe that, nor will His Excellency, not for a minute."

"Then put it this way; I'd prefer to die rather than submit to him."

"Mistress . . ."

"Don't misunderstand, I'll do my best to prevent it. The knife will be my last resort. Unfortunately, pessimistic as it sounds, I feel it in my heart it'll eventually come to blood. If not tonight then tomorrow or the night after. We're both stubborn mules pulling in opposite directions. Go."

Maria sighed and left, dragging her feet reluctantly.

She lay ensheathed in a deliciously soft pink silk nightgown trimmed with lace and so light and airy she felt as if she were wearing nothing at all. Her robe lay across the foot of the bed. A single sconce continued burning in anticipation of his arrival. Under her pillow was the knife. She slid her hand to it, gripping it where it lay. If he failed to listen to reason, if he forced her to submit, if she became too exhausted to struggle and he overpowered her, she would kill him. Could she? Did she have it in her to deliberately take a life? She had had it when Charles Felix attacked her, and that night for him she had only fear, nothing like the contempt she felt for Philip. Comparing one with the other, Charles Felix invited more pity than anything else and pity was the last thing she could ever feel for Philip.

He had cheated her in the most heartless and despicable way possible; he had lied to her; out of jealousy and nothing else he had tried to kill Paul, worse, emasculate him, and would have, had she not intervened. Still he persisted in pressing his campaign to retrieve her affections and clearly he would not be dissuaded until she gave in.

Turning the situation over in mind like an apple in hand, she wondered would it be better to submit, endure his advances until Paul came to her rescue? How on earth could she? In her present state of mind and body, where would she find the steel to firm her resolve, to screen off that part of her mind overflowing with hatred for him? How could she possibly give him the satisfaction, the triumph he so eagerly sought? Better she kill him and herself!

No, not that far. That she didn't deserve, nor did Paul, nor the promise of enduring love that the two of them found; the very last thing she would destroy would be their future. Dear God, as if they had one!

The knob turned and without knocking Philip strode into the room, closing and locking the door, setting a bottle of red wine and two glasses on the cabriolet table against the wall.

"Lorna, my darling . . ."

At the sound of the knob turning she had sat up, snatched up her robe, put her feet down on the floor, and was getting into her robe when he came in. Walking away from him, she sat down at her vanity.

"Colonel, before you come near me, before you start anything, I want you to be very clear on one thing."

"How you feel about me, I know; why bother picking over those old bones? There's something else, something I have to get off my chest. I've thought about us a great deal since the other night in the blacksmith's shop. I confess I behaved very badly, but you know my temper, and you have to understand that I was jealous."

"Really?"

"Worse than jealous, I could have strangled him with my bare hands. It was such a shock to me; I never dreamed there was anybody between us."

"Colonel, *you* are between us. You've created an abyss a mile deep that you'll never be able to cross, that I would never even attempt."

"I know, you're absolutely right."

She reacted surprised, not only at the words, but the humble tone in which they were spoken. For a moment she half-imagined that the next thing out of his mouth he'd be begging her forgiveness.

"Nevertheless," he went on, "in the face of this whole unfortunate business, and your feelings toward me, I still can't get you out of my mind. Or my heart. If anything, I love you more now than ever before. My darling, I'll do anything under the sun to make it up to you, just give me the chance."

"Anything?"

"Name it."

"Very well, get me out of here and on a ship home."

"Lorna, be reasonable!"

"That's unreasonable?" She eyed him coldly in the mirror. He was standing behind her, stiffly postured, his face drawn looking, his eyes as mournful looking as a beaten dog's.

"It's eleven now," he said quietly. "I'll be leaving here in a few hours. At least two hours before dawn. I've been given a regiment, the 22nd, camped near Chapareillan, an hour's ride from here. We'll be breaking camp one hour before dawn; I have no idea when I'll be able to get back to Chambéry."

"What's going on?"

"Some trouble, nothing terribly important, at least not at this stage. But you never know; one thing leads to another. I may be back in a few days, a week or more, or never come back."

"Colonel, when or even if you come back doesn't interest me in the slightest."

"What if I'm killed?"

"With my luck, that would never happen."

It had been a clumsy effort on his part to find and touch a sympathetic chord. But she had no feelings for him even vaguely resembling sympathy, and his humble, resigned approach in no way encouraged such a reaction. On the contrary, the news that he would be leaving in a few hours and be away from the castle for an indeterminate time inwardly cheered her so, she couldn't resist a smile of relief. Let him do his foulest tonight, she thought, come four o'clock or thereabouts he would be up and out and she rid of him, hopefully forever.

"Be specific, what is this business that sends you flying off in the middle of the night? It sounds serious."

"Ah, so you're worried about me after all."

"About as much as I worry about Adelbert's health."

"Lorna . . ." He took a step closer, hesitated, and

placed one hand tentatively on her shoulder. She shook it off.

"Don't."

"Oh, come now!" he snapped in exasperation. "Aren't you carrying this a little far? You'd think I was attacking you."

"I'd rather you didn't touch me, Colonel. I have good reason, it makes my skin crawl."

He didn't like that. He reddened slightly, clenching the hand that she had shaken off into a fist and tensing his body, as if preparing to strike her.

"What am I supposed to do?" he asked tightly. "What do you want of me?"

"Nothing. Just go away and leave me alone. Leave early for wherever you're going, get acquainted with your new troops before you dash out into the cannon's mouth."

"Enough!" A sharp hissing sound struck her ears as he sucked in his breath through his teeth. "I've taken your nastiness, your sarcasm. . . . I've swallowed my pride, catching you with that toadying bastard Torzzini, I've poured out my heart to you, practically groveling at your feet, and all I get is rejection."

"I wonder why?" She began toying with a perfume vial, tapping it gently against the vanity top, and staring at him in the glass.

His hands shot out, taking her by the throat, holding in position without tightening. "I could break your neck so easily . . ."

"Why don't you?"

"You're driving me to it! You are . . ."

"So go ahead, you'll probably be the one he'll have kill me one day soon anyway. Don't tell me you don't enjoy doing his dirty work."

He didn't hear a word; he was too concerned with rationalizing his choler, and mollifying his outraged pride.

"I could kill you because you've made me so crazy

I can't see straight. I pour out my heart and get nothing in return but contempt, every other word out of your mouth a slight, a sneer."

"Philip . . ."

"What do you want! What?"

"Stop shouting, you're hurting my ears!" She wrested free of his hold, rising and glaring at him. "What I most certainly don't want is you. Try and get that through your head once and for all. For the first time in your life take no for an answer. Accept the obvious; you are the last man on the face of the earth I'd let touch me!"

"You don't 'let' anything, wife." His voice was suddenly husky, his eyes blazing with anger, his mouth curling viciously. "You behave like a wife, you do as your husband tells you." He began unbuttoning his jacket. "Everything your husband tells you. Into your bed, wife. *Move!*"

"That's all you really want, isn't it? With honeyed words, with trickery or by force. It doesn't make the slightest difference, does it?"

"You're my wife. I don't have to play games with you. I can do as I damned well please with you. I can make you crawl and beg me to take you; I can beat you bloody to bring you into line!"

Gripping her head between his hands, he pulled her mouth roughly against his own, kissing her savagely, forcing her teeth into her lip.

"Bitch, you dare taunt me! I'll break you if it's the last thing I do! *Into the bed!*"

He began wrestling her over to it, throwing her down, whipping his belt free of its loops. A loud knock sounded; he froze, lowering the belt.

"Whoever that is, get rid of him," he rasped, "if you know what's good for you!"

"Your Majesty," said a voice she recognized as one of the guards. She broke away from Philip and raced for the door, unlocking it, pulling it wide. He followed

her, hurriedly restoring his belt to his trousers, then
reaching out to stop her, but she was too fast for him.
The door opened, stopping him gaping in his tracks.
There stood Charles Felix in shirt and trousers, wearing
a silk smoking jacket, the jet black lapels gleaming in
the light of the single sconce overpowering his diminu-
tive frame. Absent from his eyes was the usual maniacal
gleam, and his expression was one of innocent curiosity.

"Colonel Sasso, what are you doing here?"

"I . . . ah, was just leaving, Your Highness," blurted
Philip, bowing and fumbling with his jacket buttons.

"But why are you here?"

"I came to report my reassignment; His Excellency,
the prime minister's orders, sir. I'm leaving for Chapareillan shortly."

"Godspeed."

"Thank you, Your Highness."

Charles Felix stood aside, letting him pass. Outside
Philip turned to say something to her, his expression
betraying his boiling frustration. Then he thought better of it, sighed, bowed once again, and fled. Charles
Felix closed the door. A chill sped up her spine, reaching the nape of her neck and circling it, tightening
about her throat. He saw the look of fear spread down
her face.

"Calm yourself, relax." He indicated the vanity
bench. "Sit."

"Yes, Your Majesty."

He was not Charles Felix. He was a different man
entirely, as lucid as she, although behaving as if he
had just emerged from a closed room wherein he had
been shut off completely from the world around him.
As a man long stranded on a desert isle is rescued
and craves water, he, rescued from the demons that
possessed him, wanted only to talk. She let him. He
confessed to being dumbfounded by the rush of
events swirling about him, and wanted very much to
catch up on everything. It was astonishing, weird, see-

ing, hearing, politely conversing with him, a madman bereft of his madness, gone, apparently, completely sane. For how long, she hesitated to guess, but for now, sane he certainly sounded.

"I was napping," he said in an awed tone. "I woke up about an hour ago and to my surprise, the pain was gone." He touched his forehead. "Like magic. As if I was one of the Galileans Jesus touched and healed. Everything came back to me clearly, all the things that had been hazy, that I didn't fully grasp. Carrie . . . She's dead, and you're supposed to be posing as her. That's the only new thing I know for certain. Your playing her was Adelbert's idea."

He shook his head, assuming a hangdog expression. "Poor Carrie, I shall miss her. Do you know that four years ago when she came here we had never even met, never even heard of each other; and yet up she popped with Clothilde and their entourage and two days later Carrie and I were married. Two days; of course all the preparations had been made weeks before. But, and this you won't believe, the oddest part of it all; we fell in love." He slapped his knee and beamed. "I called her my beauty back then and she called me Carl, German, of course. Those were the happiest days of my life. Every morning I awoke with a song in my heart. When the weather was warm we would take endless rides about the duchy, and when it was cold and snowing, we would have a roaring fire built in the great hall and have gay parties and laugh and dance and drink until sunrise.

"We were so content, and she was beautiful and loved me, and now she's dead. I woke up Adelbert just before I came here and I asked to see her, but she's been buried. He didn't even know where. Do you?"

"No, Your Majesty, I'm sorry."

"Adelbert knows, he just isn't saying. He knows everything. I want to find out where she is so I can go and pay my respects and put flowers on her grave. She was very fond of yellow roses. I'll miss her so; She was my right arm. She had a vile temper, and she could be as stiff-necked and imperious as Mother, but she . . . I loved her. Dearly.

"It wasn't easy for her here. De Boigne, Adelbert, and the others don't like Germans very much, because they hate and fear the Austrians so. And they're pretty much the same stock. But Savoy needs Germany's protection, you see, so the marriage made sense. Carrie understood the reason for their prejudice, and never let it bother her. After a time they came to respect her, Adelbert especially. He had great respect for her. She was very bright, very perceptive, and strong—the strongest woman I have ever known. I myself am not very strong, none of us were, Charles Emmanuel, Victor Emmanuel. Mother was. You women are almost always strong, and immensely clever about when and how to use your strength, hiding it until you need it. When I was almost assassinated, and I began getting those terrible headaches, Brabossi put me to bed. I lay there nearly a month as useless as a cracked stick. That's when Carrie took over the affairs of state. Oh, Adelbert guided her, and of course he influenced her, but she made all the decisions."

She was tempted to interrupt and quietly explain that in her view, Adelbert was not prepared to rest until the two of them had followed Caroline-Louisa to the grave, but she might as well be realistic. Charles Felix would never believe her. His faith and trust were those of a small child. She let him ramble on, offering monosyllabic responses where he wanted them, agreement, confirmation of an assumption and the like. He was so unlike his other self, the animal Charles Felix, she could hardly contain her astonishment. And so unlike a king. He was instead a decidedly common, ordinary soul in the clutch of a heart-wrenching sadness, a husband who had lost the wife he worshiped and now found himself wandering down the lonely corridors of his mind in quest of peace or something like it, anything that promised comfort and perhaps understanding. He was so openly earnest, so candid, so human, her heart went out to him, this troubled, strange little man treading so uncertainly upon his newly found and perilously narrow and circuitous pathway of sanity.

He was yawning more frequently now, covering his mouth politely with the back of his hand and excusing himself. She helped him to the bed and he lay down atop the covers, falling asleep in seconds. How she wished she might sleep, even a few hours, just long enough to allay her exhaustion and revive her strength. Would she dare lay down beside him? And chance his waking suddenly as mad as ever to ravage and perhaps even murder her? Never! Better she steal back to her own room. A sound came at the door.

"Your Majesty," said a muffled voice.

"Paul!"

She flew to the door, unlocking it, jerking it open, throwing herself into his arms.

"Hold me, my darling. I was beginning to think you'd never get here."

With him were two guards whom she had never seen before. He spied her staring at them curiously. "Corporals Avodaine and Nuscio. They're from my squadron, here to relieve your guards." The two men exchanged glances and laughed. "Enough gawking, men, to your posts." They saluted and obliged.

"Isn't that risky?"

"Not at the moment. The barracks below is in an uproar; half the men are leaving on detached service for camps in the area. If things run according to form, they're down there having the devil's own time figuring which half." He glanced behind her. "The only risky part was our bursting in on you. Thank God he's asleep and that it's he; I was expecting your beloved husband."

"He's on his way to Chapareillan."

"That's good to know; we'll give him a wide berth."

The man he had introduced as Nuscio, a slender blond fellow in his thirties, handed him a large drawstring sack. Out of it Paul produced a uniform.

"Get this on, and hurry."

She went about dressing behind the bed curtain while he stood at the door open a crack peering out.

"Hurry!" he rasped.

"I'm doing the best I can. The trousers are too tight."

"Or your hips too big. Rip the seams if you have to, but for God sakes get them on!"

"I am, I am . . ."

"When you put the cloak on, make sure you tie the strings tightly. Hold it closed with both hands, and cover the lower part of your face with your scarf. The brim of your shako will shade your eyes."

"Where are we going?"

"I'll fill you in on the way. There's been an uprising."

"Piedmont?"

"Sardinia. Cagliari, in the south." He turned from the door to study Charles Felix lying sprawled on the bed, snoring lustily. As Paul looked at him, the king stirred, stopped snoring, smacked his lips, and rolled over on his right side. Lorna stiffened, as did Paul. The snoring resumed and both relaxed.

She came around the bed, out from behind the privacy of the curtains. She pirouetted, showing off her uniform. He shook his head disapprovingly.

"Much too revealing. You wouldn't fool a blind man. Tilt your shako forward a little; get the full benefit of the brim. Tighten your scarf around your face and whatever you do, keep your cloak closed in front like I said until we get you up on a horse." Holding her by the shoulders, he pulled down her scarf and kissed her. "This is it, darling, the hard part. Through the castle, down the stairs by the great hall, across the inner ward, past the barracks, into the outer ward, and out the postern gate. The horses are waiting. Don't walk fast, don't show your face, and don't utter a sound.

"Take a deep breath, say good-bye to this lovely madhouse, and let's go."

VI

Leaving the king sleeping and the door without a guard, they made their way through the maze of corridors outside, across the inner and outer wards to the postern gate. She had brought along the knife, easing it out from under the sleeper's pillow and shoving it into her belt. At the gate, with stout oak and iron winches the last barrier blocking their way to freedom, a voice suddenly bellowed at them from out of the darkness, sending her hand instinctively to the knife.

"Halt and be recognized!"

A lantern emerged from the left tower door, a hulking, hatless man, his jacket unbuttoned, his boots sorely in need of polishing, holding it high and peering at them out from under lids laboring determinedly to stay open.

"Ah, it's Captain Torzzini . . ."

"And three men of my squadron. We're returning to camp at Lémenc. Open the gate."

"C squadron, isn't it, sir?"

"B, the 22nd Cavalry."

The guard held the light up to Paul's face, revealing his own in its entirety, bulbous and ugly, his mouth smeared with grease, as if they'd interrupted him halfway through a leg of mutton.

"Yes, sir, Captain, all the lads will be on the move this night, so they say. Except us gate guards. The rebels has took both towers down to Cagliari and are defending them fiercely." As he poured out his information he shifted the lantern from one face to another pausing in front of Lorna. She held her breath. "Let's have a look at you, lad." Reaching for her scarf,

he was about to pull it down when a stubby curve of
steel arched downward upon his head, the grip of
Corporal Avodaine's handgun striking his skull with a
sickening thud. He fell heavily to the stones in front
of her.

"You've killed him!" she burst.

"Not a chance, his skull is two inches thick."

"Better you had killed him," murmured Paul.

"He called you by name," she said.

"Exactly. Get at the timber, men, open the gate and
let's get out of here."

"Halloo down there, Lucien. What is going on?
Who do you have there?" A second lantern showed
at the top of the right tower, a guard leaning out, his
musket aimed downward. "Lucien . . ."

"Damn!" snapped Paul, "in thirty seconds this place
will be crawling with guards!"

A sibilant rush of air, a flash of light, moon on metal,
and a loud groan followed in rapid sequence. Down
fell the musket rattling to rest upon the stones, after
it the man, his head smashing like a ripe melon. Corporal Nuscio, who had thrown the knife, bent to retrieve
it, jerking it free of the dead man's breastbone. Lorna
turned from the sight, stifling a gag. Paul and Avodaine
sprang to the gate, removing the cumbersome timber, opening it and gesturing her and Nuscio forward.
Even before the gate was completely closed behind
them, the sound of voices and running feet could
be heard coming from the barracks.

Her horse was a bay mare, a fine, muscular animal,
its mane wild, its eyes wilder, rounding huge at sight
of the cloaked stranger climbing up on its back. Off
they flew, thundering up the dusty road. Leaning forward gripping the reins so tightly they cut into her
palms, she glanced back at the castle, its forbidding
immensity stark against the blue velvet sky. Hades
raised from the core of the earth, she fancied, walled in,
towered and turreted to stand locked to the land forever, a solitary ugly blot on the otherwise magnificent

landscape. Her prison, but no longer, thanks to the three men surrounding her. Now, like the wind that played about the battlements, she was free, to multiply the miles separating her and the recent hideous past, and reduce Hades to a rectangle of stone no larger than her thumbnail.

"Good-bye, Maria," she whispered, "and good-bye, little cricket. Keep singing."

Paul drew up alongside her. "Are you all right?"

"I'm fabulous, darling, never better," she shouted, above the wind and clatter of hooves. "I love this, I love you. I've only one regret.'

"Regret?"

"That Adelbert isn't roped to our saddles and dragging along behind."

"You're a terror, Mrs. Torzzini."

"I like that, Paul. Say it again and again . . ."

"We're a good three miles from there and they'll have no idea where we're heading. Let's pull over to the side. I'll send the men on, we can find a pleasant litle spot . . ."

"You're quite mad, Captain." She glanced back, but made no move to slacken her pace.

"I love you!" he bellowed.

"And I love you, Paul, I do. So much that meeting you, being with you now and forever smudges out all the misery back there. It really does balance the scales."

"I must remind you to write Sasso and DeLeone and thank them for kidnapping you. I certainly mean to."

"Be serious, where are we going, Lémenc?"

"St. Jean-du-Marienne, the rest of the regiment is already headed there."

"Won't you be missed? Who is leading your men?"

"Lieutenant Mario Abroza. An excellent man; one of my closest and dearest friends. Mario is Colonel Falcone's cousin. Don't worry, we'll be back in time for the battle." He laughed.

"There will be fighting."

"Not for a while, and not where Adelbert, Ascoyne, and the rest think. That's our whole strategy."

"Tell me."

"Our people in Cagliari know we're on the way. We'll be taking ship at Menton sometime tomorrow. We'll land at Sarroch on the southern coast of Sardinia in two or three days, then head straight up to Cagliari."

"I don't understand."

"There's no need for you to." He winked and grinned impishly.

"Tell me, I've a right to know. If there's danger . . ."

"For you there'll be no danger. Long before Sarroch you'll be on your way to Port-St.-Louis-du-Rhône."

"Not without you I won't!"

"Without me . . ."

"But you promised!"

"I know, and I meant it when I said it. But I can't leave now. I can't desert my men when they need me most. Everything's set, you're to wait for me in Port-St.-Louis. I'll be there in a week, less with a little luck." He patted his pocket. "I have your papers and money, florins and French francs. We'll stick together until we get to the coast. I have friends where you can stay in Port-St.-Louis; you'll be safe there."

She straightened up, pulled off the road and reined up, the mare snorting and whinnying loudly, as if in protest at the sudden break in its powerful stride. Paul was unable to stop until a dozen yards past her, swinging about and cantering back, great clouds issuing from his horse's nostrils. His men had pulled up even further on, turning in their saddles and staring back questioningly. He waved them on.

"We'll catch up!" he called. He turned to Lorna frowning. "Darling, this isn't the time or place to discuss it. I told you, everything's arranged."

"Obviously without consulting me."

"How in heaven's name could I consult you? Lorna, do you want to get out or don't you?"

"Not without you."

"I give you my word, I swear by all that's holy, I'll meet you in Port-St.-Louis!"

"What if something happens to you? What if you're captured or wounded or, God forbid, worse?"

"I have to get on that ship out of Menton. It's absolutely imperative. We're going to take it over."

"You and your two corporals? Three men against Colonel Haproux's entire regiment?"

"A and B squadron's only, and more than three of us. Every man in our unit is on our side, all one hundred twenty-eight, and the other squadron has a score or more ready and willing to lay down their lives for the cause. We're going to take over the ship and attack the other ships on the open sea."

"That's insane. How many ships will there be? Dozens, I bet. . . ."

"We won't be one ship, we'll have our own fleet. A hundred armed fishing boats will be hiding inside Cape del Falcone." His eyes gleamed fanatically. "There won't be any battle in Cagliari. The monarchist troops will never land."

"You hope . . ."

"I know. Why do you think it's taken us so long to work out a feasible plan? Not just because so much depends upon the outcome. Also because we only get one chance, so our strategy has to be perfect. Drawing troops away from the mainland, leaving skeleton forces all over Savoy is precisely what we need, not a mutiny in Turin that can be put down in two hours, that tears the heart out of our hopes and disillusions and discourages our people from any future attempts. Lorna, after fifteen years of waiting, this is it, the dawn of a new day for Savoy. It's here, with liberty, and justice at last! With no Germans to come riding to their rescue, like the last time. In six days it'll be all over, a practically bloodless coup. Darling, the Lord built the world in six days; in six days, we're going to build a new Savoy on the broken dreams and battered hopes and frustrations of the old one!"

"When you come to power, what will you do with the monarchists?"

"We'll give them a choice, something they've never given us. They can join us or get out."

"No bulging prisons, no hangings?"

He glared at her. "I prefer to be serious about this. It happens I dearly love my country. I would die for her. But until she's free she is not my country. She belongs to DeLeone and his gang, to be abused and plundered and reduced to abject servility in the name of their version of patriotism. Oh, we'll have a king, to be sure. We Savoyards, like the English, dearly love a lord, but whoever sits the throne will answer to a parliament, republicans all."

"No opposition party?"

"Certainly there'll be opposition. The setup will be no different from your own country's. Look what your revolution gained you, and you'll see what Savoy hungers for, what we're willing to fight and die for. All revolutions are the same, from the Athenians' rising and overthrowing their tyrants five hundred years before Christ, to this one: the same motives, the same yearning for liberty and justice. The keystone is the strategy."

"And yours is perfect."

"It can never be perfect. Let's say it appears eminently workable."

"I hope it does work, darling, for your sake."

"For all our sakes. No nation in history ever deserved freedom more."

They rode on, catching up with the corporals, climbing into the mountains, heading single file toward a col at the top of a winding pathway cluttered with loose stones that rang and rattled under the horses' hooves. She fell to wondering. Suddenly divested of her dilemma and pointing the way to Port-St.-Louis-du-Rhône and passage home, a new worry flung its shadow across her mind's eye. To leave him, to wave him away toward

Sardinia and the inescapable violence and bloodshed, sickened her at heart. He could so easily be killed and she'd never even hear what happened. Who would there be to tell her?

She could not break with him like that, a final embrace, a good-bye kiss, her heart pounding, both of them murmuring Godspeed. It could too easily be the last time they saw each other. You simply don't love someone, you don't pledge your heart and your life for good and always, then deliberatively break it off. There was, she decided, only one way to deal with the situation. When the time came to part, she would refuse to leave. She would board ship with him, even if it meant stowing away. She would fight alongside him, stay with him night and day, never let him out of her sight.

That she might be killed seemed a possibility unworthy of serious consideration at this point; what mattered, all that mattered, was that they never again be separated.

VII

The four of them caught up with the squadron an hour after sunrise. Readjusting her scarf to conceal the lower half of her face and falling into ranks, she rode slowly along watching Paul take his place at the head of the column. The road to St. Jean-de-Mauriénne crossed the Isère snaking its length through the Alps. It was hard country, a land of austere beauty, the rye climbing halfway up the slopes seemingly firmed in place by immense belts of grapevines. Above, the larches and dark green-leaved arollas heavy with nuts assembled and ascended toward the glistening peaks.

The rendezvous point where the entire regiment along with the 9th and 19th were to assemble lay some fifteen miles distant in the basin of the River Arc, but the approach was so rugged, the footing so perilous, the twisting and turn of the way so devious, it took the better part of all day to bring the river basin under hoof.

The men of B squadron were ordered to eat as speedily as possible and continue on their way southward. According to Colonel Haproux's aide, they had been selected to act as the vanguard of the main troop. Paul was further instructed to post outriders to scout the terrain where the road broke away to the west of the river in search of possible ambushes.

They ate salt pork, biscuit as hard as the tin it came in, and drank coffee boiled over open fires and as thick as gruel. A far cry from the castle fare, she thought, grateful, nevertheless, for the coffee and the way it dusted the cobwebs from her weary brain. She sat on her saddle on the ground in imitation of the others, washing down the last of her biscuit with the coffee. This accomplished, she moved her knife from her belt to the calf of her right leg, fixing it in place with a strip of cloth torn from her hanky. She was restoring her scarf to the lower part of her face when she spied Corporal Avodaine. Beckoning him over, she gestured him close and whispered.

"When do we stop for a real rest?"

"This is it, ma'am, for us."

"No sleep tonight?"

"In the saddle, if you know how. This is a forced march, the ships are waiting."

"I haven't slept in two nights."

"Take off your belt, bind your wrists together under your horse's neck. That way you'll catch a few winks on the move without falling off. It's against regulations, but everybody does it. Take heart, it won't be long till Menton." He winked and smiled reassuringly and went away. Minutes later the order was given to mount up and ride out, leaving the rest of the regiment to dawdle over their meal and catch two hours' sleep.

They rode into the gathering gloom of a starless night, the moon, as well, erased by a thick blanket of bluish-gray clouds. The darkness when it came was like a lap robe thrown over them, smothering them in its folds. Riding on the right flank halfway down the column, she could barely make out Paul's head and shoulders rising above those of his friend, Lieutenant Abroza, a pace behind him. Paul had scrupulously avoided her at the St. Jean assembly point for obvious reasons, though she would have welcomed the chance to try and talk him into letting her board ship at Menton instead of continuing on to Port-St.-Louis-du-Rhône. It was absurd; he would never agree to her coming along. She would have to stow away.

Over the rocky path under the shadow of the Maritime Alps they passed, the steady hammering of hooves, the occasional audible whistle of the wind worrying about the peaks overhead, the clacking of saber scabbards against the horses' flanks the only sounds. According to Corporal Nuscio, from St. Jean to the coast was 125 miles as the crow flew. As the narrow route wound its way, rising, and falling into little valleys, following slender streams flinging themselves wildly through the rocks, it stretched nearly fifty miles farther. What she would not give for sight of the Mediterranean, its turquoise waters lapping gently against the shoreline. She tried to sleep, but was unable to overcome the fear that she might tumble out of her saddle and snap one tightly belted wrist in falling, or the mare's neck.

One thought gave her solace, assurance that never again would she see the Castle of La Bathie et de Monterminod inside, or out. More than a castle, worse than prison walls heavily guarded round about, that house of horror was a state of mind, an infection of the imagination, surely the most wretched and terrifying she had ever contracted. From one hour to the next she had never known what would befall her. The whole dreadful experience reduced itself to a nightmare, from first sight of the castle's outer curtain and towers gilded by the setting sun to its night-shrouded massiveness slowly shrinking against the blue velvet heavens. Recollection of it vanishing in a wink as the mare had rounded the first turn in the road sent a shudder coursing across her shoulders.

Pulling her cloak more tightly about her against the chill night air, she squinted ahead into the darkness as the tireless mare thundered forward. They came upon a lush meadow stretching between two almost perpendicular cliffs, the sharp sound of hooves against loose stones giving way to a dull, rhythmical thumping. Then abruptly, like the dragon's teeth sown by Cadmus, up sprang row upon row of dragoons, familiar red uniforms clearly recognizable by the light of torches held high in front and in back of B squadron.

"Captain Torzzini!" roared a voice from behind the

solid wall of mounted men in front of them, an all-too-familiar voice, one that struck fear into her heart and sent her hand to the knife under her trouser leg, firm against her calf. The voice was that of Colonel Philip Sasso.

VIII

The trap proved both ideally sited and springable with ridiculous ease. Not a shot was fired, not an inch of steel shown. Paul, Lieutenant Abroza, and the men were ordered to dismount and the front rank of their captors parted to permit Philip and his aides to pass through.

"In the name of His Majesty Charles Felix, I hereby place you all under arrest," he announced. "You will drop your weapons to the ground, remove shakos and jackets, and ready your persons to be shackled. Any attempt to resist or to flee and you will be shot."

"Sasso, what is the meaning of this idiocy!" exclaimed Paul heatedly.

Philip ambled up to him, smirking, his dark eyes burning with triumph. "Yours is the idiocy, Torzzini. Your simpleminded blundering has destroyed your little mutiny before you could even start it. Such a pity. Colonel Haproux insisted we round you up and spike your guns before Menton. Had it been left to me, I would have let you trek all the way there, board your vessel, run out to sea, get halfway to Sardinia, and blow you to bits with broadsides!"

"Sorry you're disappointed, Colonel, you have my sympathies."

"And you mine."

"I'm curious," continued Paul. "Since you have us clearly, perhaps you'll be so charitable as to tell me how the colonel found out about us."

"Ask Abroza, why don't you?"

Lieutenant Abroza strode forward bristling. "Colonel . . ."

"Forgive me, Mario, this is hardly the gratitude you're

entitled to. Unfortunately, I don't happen to consider that gratitude is called for; it was your duty as a loyal Savoyard. Yes, Torzzini, your long-time friend the lieutenant here did the deed." Philip's hand disappeared inside his jacket, emerging with a small sack. He held it up, jiggling it. "Your silver, Judas." He tossed the money to Abroza who let it thump against his chest and fall without any attempt to catch it.

"You gave me your word as an officer . . ." he began.

"And a gentleman," interposed Philip. "Did I really? Tsk, tsk, it must have slipped my mind. Still, I actually shouldn't call him Judas, Torzzini, his motive was more than greed. As you undoubtedly know, he's a disasterously inept gambler, heavily in debt. Pick up your money, Lieutenant, you've earned it. Stoop, pick it up, think of your creditors. All right, we haven't all night, bring up the irons. Sergeant Roloyne . . ."

A massive-shouldered older man, his face all but concealed behind his bushy beard, stepped forward saluting. "Sir?"

"Pick a dozen men to round up their horses, arms, jackets, the lot. By the time you're done we'll have their jewelry on them. You and your men will then march them back to Albertville. Turn them over to the jailer immediately, whatever the hour, and see that you get a complete list of names and ranks for Colonel Haproux. There'll be passage waiting for you at Menton. Don't dally. Report to me as soon as you get back. We mean to crush the rabble in Cagliari and anywhere else on the island and stop the poison from spreading back to the mainland, so get them to Albertville and quickly march back."

"It's too late to stop anything, Sasso," said Paul mildly. He seemed unperturbed, taking it calmly, she thought, now that the initial shock wave had passed. Not so Abroza, though. He stared about, a wild look in his eyes, his breath coming in gasps, his face furrowed with fear, as if he were conscious that 127 pairs of eyes were burying daggers into his back.

"Whether it is or not, you'll never know," responded Philip. "Your fumbling attempts at high treason are over. Farewell, Torzzini, and the rest of you patriotic souls. When next we meet every one of you will be looking down at me from a gallows!"

"What are you doing!" burst Abroza, "You're not sending me back with them, you can't!"

"Don't talk rubbish, Mario, of course I can. And I am. Sergeant . . ."

"*No!*"

She gaped in disbelief as Abroza lost control completely and threw himself at Philip's throat, his fingers closing on his windpipe. A saber flashed, catching the light of the nearest torch down its guttered length. Straight into the lieutenant's side, the hand gripping the hilt drove the steel. Then jerked it loose, dark with blood a third of its length, releasing a freshet of blood. Abroza's throat closed, sealing off his scream, reducing it to a pathetic gurgling sound as he slumped to the ground.

"Tsk, tsk," said Philip in a tone barely above a whisper. "What a needless loss. His creditors will be so disappointed." Kneeling, he retrieved the money sack and set about stuffing it into the dead man's trouser pocket.

IX

The acrid stench of putrid straw mingled with that of
the decaying carcass of a fat black rat snugged into one
corner and the musty smell of the mildew staining the
cracks in the walls and ceiling. The cell was a cramped
little cubicle with a single eight-inch-square barred window; had she been four inches taller she would have
been unable to stand upright. As it was, she had no
wish to stand at all, preferring instead to slump into a
ratless corner as far as possible from the disgusting
straw. She began massaging her wrists and ankles only
recently relieved of their shackles and the painful chaf-
ing they produced.

For the first time since René Tallot's cabin aboard
the *Iphimedia* and sight of her head stripped as clean as
a ball by his razor, she could be grateful for what he
had done, what DeLeone had ordered him to do. She
ran her fingers over her hair, yet to reach its full inch
and standing as straight as a porcupine's quills. It was, if
ironically, a regulation haircut for recruits and, despite
her delicate feminine features long since washed clean
of makeup, it helped her pass for a man, providing one
did not look too closely. Mercifully, none of Philip's
men nor he himself had given her a second glance in
the flickering light of their torches when she, with the
others, had complied with his order to divest themselves of their shakos and jackets. She could thank the
Lord they had been permitted to retain their cloaks,
which she took pains to keep wrapped not too tightly
about her. Leaving the site of the ambush. Paul had explained that dragoons without shakos and jackets were
marked as deserters or traitors.

Chained in single file, they had been marched north to Albertville by the sergeant and his men, though so tired was she, on the verge of collapse after the first mile, Paul had been obliged to carry her in his arms, like a bride over the threshold. His words came back to her:

"I carry you in my heart as lightly as a feather, my love. In my arms just as easily."

She had been too exhausted to acknowledge his tenderness, to talk at all. The shock to her already beleaguered system when Philip and his men had surprised them, the chilling dread that he would recognize her and the realization that all was suddenly lost for both her and Paul, as lost as Abroza's life, had all but extinguished the last spark of hope.

As lost as their own lives shortly, she thought. A crushing blow to her dream of returning home, examining it now, the final blow. Philip was right, he would see them all dancing at the ends of ropes, if one or another of her jailors didn't discover her sex and destroy her in satisfying his lust before the hangman took them. At the moment Abroza appeared to be the luckiest of the lot; his death had at least been swift, spared of anticipation.

How could he denounce his friend, all his friends and comrades? For money for gambling debts? Inconceivable. On the contrary, terribly true. Philip's disclosure had stunned Paul, shattered him. The expression on his face had touched her heart, his eyes fixing on the lieutenant, staring in disbelief, the word "no" forming on his lips, but unuttered when he saw Abroza's face. On it there was no shame, nothing like it, only a caught-in-the-act uneasiness at being betrayed in front of his victims, fear that those close to him would fall on him and beat him to death.

The march north had been interminable, but Sergeant Roloyne had proved humane, taking pity on his prisoners, letting them rest often. That morning outside of Necudy, within sight of Mount Bellachat, he had sent three of his men to nearby farms to collect food.

They had reached Albertville after dark, the town lying close to Conflans to the west and the landscape surrounding it similar in apearance to Conflans and to the area where the coach had blown up. The Albertvillians, for the most part farmers and shepherds and therefore early risers, were asleep, their cottages in darkness, the streets deserted. The fortified church of Clery rising into the night mutely proclaimed sanctuary for some, she had thought discouragedly, as they had shuffled by it. Beyond it stood the prison, as depressing and dismaying a sight as she anticipated it would be, its lofty crenelated walls and heavy double gate shutting away all sorts of imagined atrocities, cruelty, degradation, filth, and wretchedness. Punish and humiliate the mind and heart before you take the soul. They had been led into a yard cut off from the street by a high brick wall. Their names and ranks had been taken down and each individually examined. An old man with, luckily for her, failing eyesight and hearing very nearly as weak, from the way he cupped his hand over his ear, had been assigned to her. He looked her over as disinterestedly as she could have hoped for, ordering her to turn out her pockets. She carried no money, to his disappointment, though out of the corner of her eye she could see Paul dejectedly turn over the florins and francs and false identity papers he had been holding for her. She heard him explain to the man searching him that the papers belonged to a friend now dead and once more she thought of Abroza. Worried that the old man examining her might demand that she disrobe as some of the prisoners were already beginning to do, she voluntarily turned over the knife, an effort to underscore her willingness to cooperate. Reluctant though she was to give it up, knowing she might very soon need it to defend herself. Doing so proved wise. He smiled toothlessly, nodded his head in approval, and satisfied that she had no money and nothing else of value on her he passed on to his next prisoner without even asking her to open her cloak. Whether it was negligence on his part or his

way of showing compassion she had no way of knowing;
the important thing was it had kept secret her sex, for
the time being, at least.

Now here she was, alone, so weary she ached all over,
so frightened she was unable to quiet her pounding
heart, so dejected and dispirited she hadn't the energy
to raise her head. But still alive, and comforted by
Paul's presence somewhere close by. She resolved to
fight on, whatever the odds, whatever fate held for them.

She refused to concede that Philip had won. On second thought, that seemed ludicrous: the cards were all
his, all that was left to be done would be slip the nooses
around their necks. As to the glorious revolution, it
would soon be put down, just as the Turin mutiny had
been nine years earlier. If the towers in Cagliari had not
yet been retaken, they would be shortly. Even Paul,
briefly discussing their plight on the way north, picking
and probing for favorable possibilities, had to concede
that the uprising there was doomed without additional
strength with which to forestall the advance of the monarchists. A hundred freedom-loving fishing boatmen,
even a thousand, likely poorly armed, certainly un-
trained for battle, would be no match for the monarchist forces.

Her eyes by now accustomed to the darkness, she
stared at the dead rat in the corner. Had she the stomach, she would have picked it up and forced it between
the window bars, but just the sight of it set the juices
churning, whipping up nausea and she turned away.
She could not possibly sleep on the straw, and the stones
of the floor were badly laid, making it impossible to lie
flat without feeling as if one were stretched out on a pile
of rubble. So she continued to sit slumped in the corner
ignoring the foul odors, the rat, the situation, and the
dread prospect of execution. She tried to sleep. It came
at last, stealing over her, a soft woolly coverlet easing
the taut bindings of her muscles, assuaging the torment
in her mind.

She fell to dreaming, of home and the meadow in

early summer, the timothy, the daisies, clover, and sea of grass rippling over the ground all the way to the red spruce and balsam fir beyond the brook. The brook burbled musically, the sunlight scattering diamonds down its length as Paul took her in his arms, his beautiful eyes luring her into their depths, his flesh warming hers, thrilling her, his lips searing her mouth with kisses, their tongues driving, thrashing, drawing the burning broth of excitement from the crucible of their passion. An irrepressible desire to abandon all control engulfed her, sapping her strength as his strong arms lay her down upon the lush green grass. Above his sinewy nakedness, his neck and shoulders glistening with golden beads of perspiration, a swallowtail butterfly silently beat the warm air, the sun brightening its colors, black and yellow, blue and the twin red dots above the slender appendages thrusting downward from the trailing edge of its wings. She watched it circle daintily and lift itself toward the azure sky. Then losing it in the sun, she turned her mouth back to his, to the exhilarating fire of his kisses, feeling his tongue again and his gentle hands tenderly stroking her breasts. Down came his mouth upon her breast, his tongue sliding over the nipple, and circling it, teasingly. She squealed and seizing his head with both hands pressed his mouth harder against her, at the same time feeling his member enlarge and stiffen against her inner thighs. She trembled and sucked in a breath of air through clenched teeth, tasting its sweetness, moving his head, giving her other breast to his tongue, surrendering to its glorious stroking, drowning in the sensation of sheer wantonness raising the fires within her. They played, his tongue and lips and fingers finding their separate ways about her flesh. An eon passed, the earth tilted and whirled and sped onward in orbit, tides rose and fell, stars were born and died and by the billions glowed unseen in the cloudless blue heavens, and still they played, his caresses sending slender rivulets of liquid fire coursing up her spine from all directions to her throbbing, hungering sex. His member was now

fully erect and enormous, its velvety head gliding slowly between her quivering thighs, finding its way unerringly, easing forward, touching, entering, moving into
her, thrusting onward, filling her. Taking him inch by
magnificent inch she formed around him, engorging his
massiveness, devouring it. Without withdrawing he began to move within her, angling, touching everywhere,
sending shards of exquisite agony lancing through her,
dissolving her, driving her to climax . . .

I love you, Paul, love you, love you, love you, my
darling, my marvelous Paul, my own. . .

The planet trembled and the sky, the sunlight shimmering, separating into slender swaths of gold, twisting,
winding about them, tightening, binding their bodies together, her sex clenched about him, her hips driving
wildly, her teeth biting deep into his shoulder, her eyes
glazing with ecstasy, awareness vanishing of everything
save his manhood pulsating, throbbing mightily within
her.

The dream carried forward to completion and she
slept, the deep and weighty slumber of sheer exhaustion,
the screen of her mind blank, her body relaxed, her
breathing sonorous. A sound woke her, a loud metallic
clacking and the groaning of the door to her cell as it
was pushed open. Her eyelids parted; she winced, her
pupils struck by the strong white light flung through the
window. Keys jangled, a voice muttered unintelligibly.
Her eyes clogged with sleep, she blinked and recoiled in
fear at sight of the straw moving. A small rat emerged,
casting about with its beady red eyes, scampering for
the open door, running out.

"Bastard!" A loud thumping, a boot heel coming
down, hammering the creature's skull out of her sight
around the corner, crushing it with a loathsome crack-
ling sound. A man came in carrying a plate with a crust
of bread and a cup of what she could not guess, holding
it as he was above the level of her eyes. His face was
the red of ripe watermelon pulp, bloated, damp with
sweat, unwashed, unshaven. His clothes were wrinkled

and soiled, all the buttons but one missing from his coat. His right cheek was swollen, the blue cast of a bruise emerging from the redness. Above it his eye was black, puffy, struck by a fist, she imagined, as his cheek had been. Over his eyebrow a trail of blood newly dried and forming a scab inched up his forehead. He stared at her, his eyes glued to her chest; her heart froze as it dawned on her that in waking and straightening, her back against the corner, she had carelessly let her cloak fall open, revealing the roundness of one breast under her blouse.

"My, my, what have we here?" he muttered, licking his lips lasciviously and setting down the plate and cup, the latter gently sloshing a cloudy, watery-looking liquid onto the floor.

Clutching her cloak tightly about her too late, she pushed to her feet, sliding her back up the wall.

"Stay away from me . . ."

"It's a slip of a girl." He slammed the door behind him, the echo rattling down the corridor, and started toward her.

"Don't touch me."

In three strides he was up to her, blocking her escape from the corner with his arms outstretched, his palms flat against the wall on either side of her. She tried to duck under his left arm, but he lowered it catching her, forcing her to straighten.

"Pretty as a picture."

Her mind swirled, grasping at lies, seizing one. "Don't you dare lay a hand on me. I am His Excellency, Count DeLeone's mistress. Touch me and he'll kill you!"

"DeLeone's mistress, are you?" This intelligence momentarily confused him, drawing the center of his brow together in deep grooves.

"These traitors kidnapped me in Chambéry and forced me to go with them to St. Jean. Their leader planned to exchange me for safe conduct to Switzerland . . ."

"DeLeone's playmate, eh? You lie in your pretty

teeth." Seizing her jaw roughly, he jerked it back and forth. "And pretty teeth they are. Pretty lips, lovely, give us a kiss."

He kissed her wetly, full on the lips, a loud smacking sound, his breath stinking of stale rum, his eyes glowing fiercely with his mounting lust. She wrenched free.

"Stop it, leave me alone! It's the truth, they kidnapped me!"

"And when you were stopped and rounded up, you never said a word . . ."

"I didn't dare, I would have been killed on the spot. One of them held a knife to my back the whole time . . ."

"All the way back to here. Ah, now I understand, you're the one their captain carried back. Roloyne told me about that. You don't fool me, pretty slip, you're the fellow's whore."

"I am His Excellency's mistress! Return me unharmed and I promise you you'll be rewarded."

"He dressed you in uniform and sneaked you into the squadron, his little playmate. What better way to wipe out the weariness of battle, than with a piece of candy within reach. Nothing new about that idea."

"I'm warning you for the last time, touch me and His Excellency will slit your throat. Even now he has men out searching for me."

He laughed and, gripping her by the back of the neck with one hand, slid the other down her blouse, fondling her breast, then jerking open her blouse revealing it and rubbing it clumsily.

"So soft and so white. As white as snow, only so much warmer . . ." Lowering his head, he covered her breast with his wet mouth, taking it into his mouth, sucking, hurting her, sending pain knifing through it to her heart. She winced, cried out, and tried to pull free, but his left hand held her fast by the neck. He raised his head, wiping his mouth with the back of his hand and leering.

"Take off your clothes . . ."

"No!"

"Take 'em off, or I'll rip 'em off, blouse, trousers, every stitch. Then what'll you have to put back on when we're done, eh? Strips and dustrags? Take 'em off!"

"Don't hurt me, please . . ."

"Hurt you? Don't be a ninny, I wouldn't hurt you, you're too pretty. Off! Let's have a look at all your lovelies."

Sighing, her shoulders sagging dejectedly, she began to disrobe starting with her cloak, letting it fall and pile at her feet, then slowly unbuttoning her blouse. Too slowly for him; seizing one side he yanked, ripping down the row of buttons, loosening and scattering them about the floor.

"You got me all wrong, little slip. Mustn't let this eye and cheek deceive you. A little difference of opinion, that's all. I'm a gentle soul, I am, tenderhearted. You do for me what I want, as best you can and I'll treat you nicely. I'll bring you good food, the fresh fruit and vegetables and good meat we guards eat, cooked at home. None o' this rotten prison fare, loaf heel and goat's milk. I'll bring you fresh cool cow's milk and maybe some sweets. You like sweets? 'Course you do, every little slip likes sweets. And I'll bring you a kitten, too, a cute little bundle. He'll keep the rats out o' here. This whole cruddy place is crawling with rats, some big as dogs. Looky that fat boy in the corner. Phew, it stinks in here; that straw and that carcass. What this place needs is washing out top to bottom. Can't get enough air in here, that's the trouble. It stinks, really stinks . . ."

As he carried on his hands roamed her body, examining her breasts, her hips, her thighs, her sex, his filthy fingers resting on her lips. At last she stood naked and trembling before him, crouching in embarrassment, her forearms over her breasts, as cold as ice in the stuffy heat of the cramped little cell. Shaking so, she could not keep her teeth from chattering. He leered and chuckled and rolled the tip of his tongue over his lips, smacking them loudly. Then he opened his belt buckle and undid his trousers. Pushing her down and holding her there by the throat, he began . . .

X

He was gone, with a promise to return shortly, the door clanging shut behind him. She lay in the corner, totally inert, numbed all over, conscious only that she had been brutally ravaged, forced to do things to him, for him that sickened and repelled her. She had survived it, but whoever he was, he would be coming back again and again, probably until he put an end to her life, breaking her back or her neck in a fit of rage when she was too slow to comply with his demands. He hadn't believed for a second that she was DeLeone's mistress; who would? Who swallows any wild tale so obviously conjured up to prevent disaster?

No, he would be back again and again. To do with her as he pleased, abuse her, hurt her brutally, make fun of her appeals for mercy, shout with her screams, and roar with laughter. Slowly, painfully, she pulled on her clothes, and was drawing up her left boot when again she heard keys jangling outside, one thrust into the door, turning the lock. She stiffened.

"Dear God in heaven, not so soon, no . . ."

The door swung open groaning loudly. It was not him, but the older man who had so casually examined her in the yard the night before. His face fell at the sight of her.

"A woman. I knew it . . . I suspected, I did."

She sighed, unable to respond, too weary to try, slumping back against the wall. He hurried forward, his keys jangling from the ring on his belt.

"Here, here now, are you hurt?"

"I thought you were him," she whispered weakly.

"Who? Who was it?" He paused, pondering a moment, stroking his stubble-strewn chin and eyeing the plate, the butt of black bread untouched and the cup of goat's milk sitting on the floor near the door wall. "Guinard. He brought breakfast around this floor. He saw you were . . ." She nodded. "Oh, blessed Saint Pierre." He crossed himself and kissed his fingers. "He's an animal."

"You don't have to tell me."

"I'm so sorry, child."

"He's coming back."

"No, you'll be spared him, at least for a while. He went off duty a few minutes ago. He's leaving for Monthion. His eldest son is being married tomorrow."

"When exactly will he be back?"

"Who can say? Cheer up, by then . . ." Once more his face fell.

"What?"

"You'll probably have left here with the others."

"For where?"

"Chambéry."

"No!"

He nodded. "They say all of you are to go on trial there." She had tensed at the mention of Chambéry, then fell back against the wall, smiling enigmatically. "Is that funny?" he asked.

"Not really. Ironic. My life seems to be coming full circle."

"What are you, a woman, doing here? Posing as a dragoon. You're much too feminine to fool anyone."

"So it appears." She explained briefly. Why shouldn't she? The man was obviously a human as humane and goodhearted as Maria, sympathetic, understanding, though he certainly couldn't help her escape no matter how sorry he might feel for her. Still, he could make her confinement more comfortable, and he offered to do so at once.

"We must get this disgusting straw out of here," he said, moving to the rat's carcass, picking it up by the tail and stuffing it between bars. "Phew! Best be careful of fleas; you get bitten, you could become very sick. There's an extra bed in the guard room; I'll sweep this out of here, and bring it to you. Maybe I can find a pillow and a clean mattress." He studied her, tilting his head, his eyes earnest with compassion. "I am sorry . . ."

"It's not your fault."

"It's everybody's. There shouldn't be this unrest in this lovely land of ours, son against father, brother against brother. We should have peace and happiness for all. Of course, you don't have to worry. Once you get to Chambéry and they see you're a woman, they'll let you off."

"I wouldn't be too sure."

She had explained her presence by telling him only that she had been abducted by a high-ranking army officer, brought from America to Savoy, and was in the process of being rescued by another officer who had planned to see her to the coast where she could board a ship for home. Then the roof had tumbled in. She saw no need for more detailed or more honest explanation; that wouldn't help her with him, and might even make him hesitate to make her life a bit more comfortable if in doing so he chanced inviting the ire of the first officer.

"Where are they holding Captain Torzzini?"

He pointed overhead. "Two floors above, the north block. I don't know which cell exactly. Why do you ask?"

"Just curious."

He disposed of the straw and brought her the bed and a mattress and pillow. The bed proved a ramshackle, poorly constructed affair, barely able to stand, all four legs badly in need of tightening, but as welcome as the queen's own. He also brought her fresh veal cooked in Jacquere. It tasted delicious and revived her strength. After she'd eaten he insisted she lie down, "test the bed, see how comfortable it is." She did so, resting her head on the goose-down pillow, reminding her that it had been ages since last she'd slept cleanly and comfortably.

In their conversation she confirmed that he did not know for certain exactly when they were to be taken to Chambéry, hopefully, for her sake, before Guinard returned from Monthion. She would take Chambéry and reunion with Adelbert, Philip, Charles Felix, and the others in a wink before chancing a second encounter with Guinard. She shuddered; sight of him stepping inside again, his evil leer, his tongue stroking his lips would be enough to stop her heart. Still, Chambéry would be no solution to her problem, her increasingly pressing problem of staying alive and keeping Paul in the same condition. Philip wanted him dead, there could be a little doubt about that, just as De-Leone eventually wanted, needed her. Probably as soon as the uprising was quelled, which it surely had to be by now.

Sitting on the edge of the bed, she stared upward at the old man and smiled.

"You've been very kind to me, and I'm grateful. There's one thing more . . ."

He shrugged. "Name it, if I can get it, it's yours."

"The small knife I gave you out in the yard."

His face darkened and he shook his head slowly. "That you can't have, I'm sorry."

"But I'll need it to protect myself. When he comes back he'll come straight here, you know he will!"

He sighed and shook his head again. "I know. All the same, I can't give you a knife. The captain of the guard knows I examined you. If you killed Guinard with it, he'd know for certain where you got it. I have a wife and two unmarried daughters. I need this job. I just can't. I'm sorry."

She nodded. "I understand."

He smiled thinly. "Don't look so forlorn. Actually, you don't have to have a knife to protect yourself."

"Oh, but I do."

"Not really. I'm going now. When I lock the door behind me, go to the window and look out at the yard. When you do, grab hold of the bars." She shot to her feet and started for the window. "Not yet," he cautioned, "wait till I've gone."

He left, locking the door. She gripped both bars and felt the right one give at the base, the mortar dust disturbed rising in a little puff. She began working the bar back and forth easily, loosening it more and more with each push, each pull. The window, only eight inches square, would never permit her to squeeze through it and drop down into the yard, but if she continued working on the bar she would be able to free it.

It was cast iron, as solid as the candlestick with which she had knocked Rudolf Crespi unconscious in her room at the Croix d'or in Montélimar.

XI

The confidence gained by discovery of the bar, freed and left standing upright in position, did not linger long after the old man had departed. Guinard was so powerful, so bull-like; if she hit him and failed to knock him out, she'd never get the chance for a second try at it. He'd get hold of her and break every bone in her body. Better to be sent to Chambéry with Paul and the others and take her chances with DeLeone. Better? Hardly. If they were removed to Chambéry, Paul and his men would hang as surely as the sun set. She herself would be back where she'd started, pinned under His Excellency's thumb waiting for him to settle affairs of state to his satisfaction, wondering all the while as to how precisely he intended to dispose of her. She was left with one avenue of escape only—with Philip beckoning her down it. Oh, he would be delighted to rescue her, on his terms, to be sure. The harshest imaginable. Marriage to him would be little more than penal servitude; life without Paul, hell on earth!

Three days passed, days spent eating, sleeping and thinking, about many things—wondering about Paul, and how he was faring; Philip, where he had gotten to, what he was presently busy destroying; the fate of the uprising; DeLeone's progress in disposing of Charles Felix, replacing him with a younger, somewhat saner royal blood from the cadet line. Would he, she wondered, be able to replace Charles Felix? Surely not if the king continued as rational and coherent as he had been on the night she and Paul had fled the castle. What difference did that make, anyway; it was Adelbert's problem, not hers, though if Charles Felix did remain on the throne it was possible that DeLeone might decide to continue passing her off as the queen. At least until her trial and conviction for attempted murder. Her running away with Paul so soon after the accusation was tantamount to admission of guilt.

It was uncanny; everything seemed to be against her and Paul. As if they were stuck in a sinking rowboat bailing with thimbles. Going down was inevitable.

One thing she could do, she must do, was to keep the cumulation of threats in perspective, concern herself with the immediate dilemma, and relegate the others to their proper positions down the line. These thoughts brought her back to Guinard. The sun had vanished below the top of the yard wall, gilding the underbellies of the clouds, purpling the sky, and filling the cell with the dingy, depressing color of tombstone granite. Intuitively she sensed he would soon be returning. She pictured him arriving in Albertville in the public diligence, getting out bag in hand in front of the prison, striding up to the gate, activating the spring bell bringing the gatekeeper out to let him in. He would go straight to the guard room to change into his uniform, perhaps get a bite to eat, then go on duty. The shift changed at eight o'clock, the clock in the steeple of Clery punctually tolling the hours. But the fact that the new shift did not take over until eight was no assurance that he would not come to her before then, even directly from the front gate, without dropping off his bag.

She could imagine the thoughts that intermingled in his mind, the three days' accumulation of lust, the feverish anticipation of ravaging her, the uncontrollable craving to vent his sadism upon her, to humiliate and abuse her. She winced and shuddered and swallowed, her throat suddenly as dry as sun-bleached sand; and cool beads of perspiration glistened on her cheeks and forehead. She pictured him thundering in like a charging bull, his eyes suffused with lust, his voice an obscene guttural sound chilling her to the marrow, his huge hands seizing her . . .

She would kill him; she had to. If she did not, if she hesitated even for a moment, it would be all over; he would kill her then and there, or take her and kill her after he had sated his lust. That she had lived through it the first time amazed her when she thought about it.

She sat on the edge of the bed, her face buried in her hands, torn between fear of the consequences of attacking him and those of failing to. Twilight was blotted out by night, the stars burning through the darkness, the moon drenching the world with a blue-white cast. The heat of the day lingered in the cell, a block of stifling discomfort confining her in its center. Closing her eyes she saw Paul sitting in his cell two stories above, pondering his situation, his thoughts centering on her and his men, furious with himself for leading them into the ambush. As if it were humanly possible to prevent it, once his outriders had been taken. Poor darling, he seemed shackled to misfortune, just as Philip was to luck, with, to be sure, DeLeone's support and protection. But it was all so blatantly unfair; everything fell neatly into place for Philip; everything fell to pieces for Paul—and her. At least there was some satisfaction in knowing that she had frustrated Philip, pricked his shameless ego, and greened him with envy. His eyes when he first saw the two of them together in the blacksmith's shop were like those of a small boy seeing his hated rival accepting a prize he himself coveted. It was good for Philip, and deliciously satisfying to her to take him down a peg. Had he discovered her with Paul at the ambush, had she not been back in the shadows, he likely would have gone berserk and run them both through on the spot.

Footsteps. Far down the corridor a muffled, heavy tread. She stiffened, rising from the edge of the bed, her hand instinctively going for her blouse, gripping both sides tightly together. Her knees felt like water and her heart was suddenly hammering. The steps drew closer. Keys jangled on their ring, one inserted in the door, turning, drawing the bolt, the door whining open, a feeble yellow light spreading across the floor.

His red face appeared almost purple by the light of the lantern. Having risen, she backed toward the window, feeling for the wall with one hand, the other still clutching her blouse.

"Little slip, little slip, here I am, back at last." The door clanged shut, propelled by the sole of his boot. "Did you miss me? 'Course you did, what a question. I missed you, little slip, your softness, the sweet smell o' you. Delicious. Don't back away. Come here, come . . ."

"No . . . please."

"Yes! Down on your knees, bitch, and crawl to me. I want you to lick my boots. And something else. *Down!*"

"*No!*"

"You dare defy me?" His rage was instantaneous, exploding from him, overwhelming his seething lust. Bristling, his fat lips quivering with anger, he bolted forward, dropping his lantern, reaching for her with both hands. She had backed against the wall, her free hand swinging over her right shoulder, her fingers closing, groping for the bar. Her knuckles touched it; sliding her hand up to the top of it, she gripped it, pulling it free, swinging it right side up. Down it came squarely against the front of his head. It stopped him, his eyes widening with wonderment, his disgusting mouth agape. A crimson stripe leaped from the flesh running vertically from above his hairline halfway down his forehead. His head began to gyrate. Swerving to one side, and swinging about facing his side she struck again, putting every atom of strength behind the blow, smashing him across the eyes, cracking the bridge of his nose loudly like a walnut crushed between the heels of the hands. Down he went, his face hitting the wall with a sickening thud, his great shoulders rolling over, spinning him, his weight pulling him down to a sitting position.

The blood from the cut on his forehead trickled

down upon his broken nose; his eyes filling with it and closing, the lids coming together, blood beading and slipping out between them, staining his cheeks. He did not move. He seemed to have stopped breathing. Kneeling, she pressed her ear against his heart; there was no beat, or if there was it was so faint as to be inaudible. Straightening, she shuddered, throwing off the terror that had seized her. Then gritting her teeth, she got a firm hold on herself and removed his key ring from the clasp on his belt. He did not move, but his chest appeared to be rising and falling. Casting about, she sighted the tin lantern lying on its side, its candle still glowing. Retrieving it, she then changed her mind and, blowing it out, set it back down on the floor. To get up two flights of stairs and locate Paul's cell would be difficult enough without announcing her presence with the lantern to any guard ahead or behind her. The sconces lining the walls would give her all the light she'd need.

Clutching the key ring, she left the cell. She tried to find the right key to lock the door, but after six unsuccessful attempts, gave it up and hurried down the long corridor to the corner. There the stairs ascended to the second floor. She was about to start upward when she heard footsteps overhead freezing her where she stood, one hand grasping the railing. She glanced about fearfully, then circled the stairs, crouching under them in the shadows. Just in time. Down came two guards talking jovially, swinging their lanterns, flinging eerie shadows up the walls. They ambled slowly down the way she had come, continuing to talk and laugh. Her heart in her mouth, she watched them pass her cell door without looking through the slot, reach the corner and disappear around it. Once again she started up the stairs, reaching the second floor and ascending the second flight to the third floor.

The kindly old guard had not known exactly where Paul's cell was located, only that it was in "the north block." Standing in the narrow corridor at the top of the stairs she couldn't tell north from south, east or west. She started down the corridor, whispering his name into one door slot after another. From the seventh slot came a voice.

"The north block. Around two corners, second cell on the right."

A voice from the tomb, she thought. What were these stone-and-iron boxes but tombs, at best the next-to-the-last stop before the grave. She must free them all, but not until she found Paul. Letting them out as she neared his cell would only precipitate a rush to get out which could see them cut off before they reached the front gate and shot down like wolves in a pit.

One thing was certain; she must find and free him before she ran into another guard. In the corridor there was no place to hide, nothing but walls and doors on either side from one corner to the next. She'd been lucky to hear the two guards at the top of the stairs before they heard her and manage to get out of sight before they came down. Her luck would have to hold. God forbid she turn a corner and come face to face with one, or even see the glow of a lantern preceding his appearance.

Running, she made it to the far end and around the corner, down the shorter way to the rear of the prison and around the second corner. To the second door.

"Paul . . ."

His eyes came to the door slot. "Lorna! Good Lord! How . . ."

"Later, let's get you out!"

Fumbling, fighting to keep her hands from shaking, listening with one ear for the sound of steps, she tried key after key, all fifteen of them. None fit.

Paul swore and slammed his fist against the door, then got hold of his frustration. "The guard'll be coming by. He's due. You'd better find a place to hide."

"That won't get us the right key."

"To hell with the key!"

"He'll be carrying it, won't he?"

"What do you plan to do, politely ask him . . ."

"Get his ring away from him."

"Lorna . . ."

"It's the only way. Damn!"

"What?"

She told him hurriedly about knocking Guinard over the head with the window bar. "I thought for a minute I killed him."

"You'd better hope you did."

"It's too late to worry about that now. What I'm trying to say is I should have brought the bar with me. It was lying at my feet. All I had to do was pick it up."

"There's nothing you can do, Lorna."

"There has to be something! Shhh . . ."

"What?"

"I think I hear somebody."

"Get away, fast as you can . . ."

She ran, clutching the keys tightly in her fist to keep them from jangling, rounding the corner at the end, casting an anxious look back around it in time to see the guard's lantern swing into sight and out again and his left leg. Pulling her head back, she leaned against the wall, her breath coming in short, nervous gasps. An idea came to her. Listening intently, she could hear him open Paul's door, close it, then move on the next cell. He evidently took his duties seriously, which meant that instead of merely looking in through the door slots, he would be opening each cell. He would work his way down the line, around the corner where she stood, and back to the stairs. Then what? Would he go up to the fourth floor, or down to the second? Which way was important. If down to the second, she could conceivably sneak up behind him, let him descend four or five steps, jam her foot squarely between his shoulder blades and send him tumbling down, hopefully to land on his head and knock himself cold. But if he started up to the fourth floor, gravity and the fact that he had his back to her would no longer be her allies.

She would have to wait for him to come down and start down to the floor below.

Luckily, both flights faced in the same direction, the top step of the lower one separated by about four feet of floor from the first step of the upper flight. She could hide behind it, as she had below when the two guards had come down. There was only one problem. He was presently coming the way she had come, shortening the distance behind her. There was no way she could crouch behind the stairs without his walking by and seeing her all too easily by the light of his lantern.

She ran to the end and the stairs, turning the corner, flattening against the wall. What she wouldn't give for the bar, or even a stone the size of her fist! Her eyes fell to the keys in her hand; relaxing her grip on them she curled her fingers around the ring, swinging the keys easily to avoid jangling them. The fifteen keys were large, each one weighing at least two or three ounces, with the ring perhaps two pounds in all. Swinging them freely would give them added weight. But nothing like the window bar; nor anything like the effect.

She waited breathlessly as the guard's steps grew louder and louder. He was, she judged, almost up to the corner behind her. She chanced a glimpse and sure enough, the glow of his lantern yellowed the wall directly ahead of him. Clutching the keys again, filling her lungs, and firming her resolve, she pushed away from the wall to the ascending stairs. Rushing up them. Turning, at the top and backing out of sight, she looked down, waiting, listening as he approached. His light came into view below. She stiffened and crouched, balling her body as tightly as she could, cutting off sight of the stairs. He stared up; she slipped the key ring over her wrist and counted . . . two, three, four, five . . . and sprang forward, flattening her left hand against the wall, seizing the railing post with her right and driving one foot forward. It caught him full in the chest, sending him toppling over backward, his head thudding down the last two steps, coming to rest on the floor, his lantern bouncing all the way down to the bottom of the flight below. Down she rushed, snatching up his keys and running back the way she had come, thanking the benevolent goddess luck for having started him up instead of sending him down. Perhaps more luck was in the offing. Perhaps he would remain unconscious long enough for her to free Paul and between them and others every man in the squadron. And get out.

XII

"You could have tried to get away without bothering about me," whispered Paul, staring at her admiringly.

"I wouldn't have gotten as far as the yard," she replied. "Besides, it never occurred to me to go without you."

"You've a lot of grit, Lorna, so much that sometimes it scares me."

"It's either try or curl up and die."

Half of the squadron, more than sixty men, crouched and knelt flattened against the dry, crack-infested wall in a line in the third-floor corridor awaiting the return of two of their number dispatched by Paul to recover the unconscious guard at the foot of the fourth-floor stairs. They returned with him in his underwear, one almost finished buttoning on his uniform. The other held up his lantern.

"She's out, sir."

"A good reason for you to go back down to the guard room," said Paul. "Bring back the keys to the second- and fourth-floor blocks and if you can a couple of handguns. On second thought, I'll go with you.

"Paul . . ." She took hold of his arm.

He pretended not to hear her. "Corporals Avodaine and Nuscio."

They came running up. Paul explained his plan. "You come, too." He turned to the private wearing the guard's uniform. "Whoever we run into, Private, you pretend that the three of us were creating a disturbance, tearing up our cells or whatever. You're bringing us down for punishment."

"Won't whoever it is see that I'm not a guard, sir?"

"Stay in the shadows. He'll believe your uniform, if he can't see your face. Avodaine . . ."

"Sir?"

"How many men would you say are on night duty?"

"Probably two for each floor. They seem to be spelling one another making the rounds." Others near him nodded.

"That makes eight," said Paul.

"At least one extra for back-up," continued the corporal, "the officer of the guard, and two men on the front gate, with the gatekeeper."

Paul frowned and scratched his shoulder, his forearm angled across his chest. "Thirteen in all. We'll have to take them as they come. We can lock them in separate cells."

"Yes, sir."

"When we locate the keys, we need one of you three to go back upstairs and give Sergeant Damasso the ring for the fourth floor. Corporal Nuscio, you'll see to opening up the first floor."

"Yes, Captain."

"Whatever happens, whatever we have to do, we do it as quietly as we can. We'll take their weapons, but there'll be no shooting if we can help it. Corporal Avodaine."

"Sir?"

"Is your uncle still in Conflans?"

"Yes, sir. He's on our side; he has been from the start."

"Good. Pay attention, everybody: When we get out, we'll split up into the four troops. Each will be on its own. We'll give the locals twenty-four hours to beat the bushes looking for us. If we can lead them a good chase they'll soon be ready to give it up. Luckily there's no price on our heads, so there's nothing in it for anybody. We'll get together at midnight tomorrow outside of Bénétant, in the walnut grove west of the village. Now, when you get out, don't just run. Find horses; get them from the military if you can. You should run into plenty of troops on the move. Just be careful you see them before they see you. You'll be armed, you can waylay patrols. We need those horses; we can't do a thing for the cause on foot."

"Is there still a cause, I wonder?" asked Nuscio morosely.

"We'll find out."

She stood by, taking it all in, studying Paul, recognizing the glow returning to his eyes. Whether she liked it, accepted it or not, the war was about to resume, and he would be in the thick of it. She sighed inwardly. Hanover, suddenly it seemed less an ocean and more like worlds away.

"Paul, be careful."

"Don't worry."

"When we leave, where will we go, Conflans?"

He nodded and grinned. "Back to the scene of your early triumph."

"I hope you don't think you're going to deposit me there to sit and wait while you run off and get yourself shot."

His expression gave him away. She'd read his mind. "Lorna . . ."

"Forget that!" she snapped. "Where you go, I go. I'm not letting you out of my sight."

"Let's get out of here before we start in on that?" He smiled grimly. "If we don't make it, that's one less problem we'll have to worry about."

"And if your precious revolution has died aborning, we won't have to worry about that, either."

XIII

The room was carefully, devotedly furnished, a dark red velvet upholstered rococo chair, the intricately carved confusion of C- and S-curves and scrolls of its straight back obscured by the bulk of its occupant, a priest, leaning on his forearms set upon a bulky mahogany flattop desk well knotted and nicked and taking up fully a third of the space in the room. Behind him on the wall hung a large, somewhat gaudy oleograph of the *Sacred Heart,* and, as if to balance the spiritual with the temporal, opposite it on the mantel over the fireplace stood a modern, slender-handed, rosewood shelf clock displaying on its supporting lower casing a glass tablet of the madonna and child surrounded by delicately painted flowers and shells.

The walls were decorated with small Spanish and Roman reproductions of good quality, Murillo, Velazquez, El Greco's dramatic conversation between Saint Andrew and Saint Francis, Tiepolo's absorbing *Immaculate Conception,* and Raphael's nameless cardinal, his eyes a study in reserve, his lips sealed as if worried that he might inadvertently betray his identity.

The hands of the clock stood at six minutes before four in the morning. Out the window looking westward across the sluggishly moving Arly, La Belle Etoile rose against the starry sky. Framed by the casement, the moon hung as pale as a pearl, its glow feebly assaulting the darkness.

"Once you had taken the guard room, the rest must have been easy," said the priest, his serious tone oddly out of character with his round face and ready smile brightening it. Reaching for the decanter of Marestel and refilling two glasses, he was about to fill Lorna's when she raised a hand.

"No more for me, thank you, Father. One picks me up, a second at this hour and I can't keep my eyes open."

"That's your nerves, child. Playing the heroine can be as exhausting as four masses in one morning."

"We got their guns and sabers and the keys, of course," Paul went on, "then locked them up separately."

"I'm curious, what about the other prisoners?" asked Father Avodaine, "Those who were already incarcerated when they brought you and your squadron in?"

"I thought we should have let them all out," interposed Lorna, looking at Paul seated beside her.

"We couldn't do that," Paul said. "Some could have been murderers. Besides, we had to get out. It went off surprisingly smoothly."

"How many came with you?"

"Thirty-one, Father. One quarter of our strength." Paul explained his planned rendezvous with the other three troops.

"You have arms," said the priest, "you'll need more, and horses, of course."

"The men are out after them now." Paul shook his head, his expression disconsolate, his eyes fastened on his fingertips slowly revolving his glass by the stem. "I do hate the idea of getting out now, running away with our tails between our legs . . ."

"Why would you do that, after all this trouble?"

"What is left for us?"

The priest brought the flat of his hand down so loudly on the desk Lorna flinched.

"What's left? Savoy, my friend, our country, our future. *Dei Gratia!* Your short time in that pigsty has knocked the props out from under your optimism. It may surprise you, but the *risorgimento* is very much alive, your revolution proceeding at a great rate!"

Both stared at him in astonishment, the glow of a

developing smile slowly raising the corners of Paul's mouth.

"Yes indeed, you and your squadron may have been taken, but what makes you think our side is beaten? If anything, we've gotten the upper hand."

"Tell us," said Paul.

The priest spread his hands. "Where to begin . . ."

"What about Cagliari?"

"Both towers have been held, and when last I heard it looks like the entire city is falling to the *carbonari*."

She and Paul exchanged glances. "But the monarchists with all their firepower, the 11th, the 19th, the 22nd; they must have wiped out the fishermen hiding inside Cape del Falcone!" he snapped.

The priest's face sagged into a sorrowful look. "Indeed they did. I have heard that the turquoise waters of the Gulf of Asinara became ruby red night before last."

"How could you find out so soon?" asked Lorna.

"My pets." The priest held up one finger, winking past it at her. "I get all the news from all over within hours. Excuse me a moment." Rising, he gripped his skirts with both hands and vanished through the narrow archway behind them leading into the other room. They heard a door open and close.

"It's a miracle!" burst Paul. "We're still in it, fighting, winning. Our bunch can get . . ."

". . . Back into it, I know," she said tiredly. "Of course the *carbonari* can't possibly win without your personal involvement."

"Would you rather we stand on the sidelines watching?"

"I'd rather you and I get out altogether, and as soon as we can. Your side is winning, darling. They've as good as won."

"Not yet we haven't."

The door out of sight opened again and Father Avodaine reappeared in the archway, a pigeon perched on his wrist, its head jerking, its dark red eyes peering about inquisitively.

"This nervous fellow is St. Stephen. A heart full of courage, like his blessed namesake. All my pigeons are saints." He indicated. "See the quill attached to his tail-feathers, hidden in there? It can hold one gram in weight, fifty words or more written on rice paper. I have twenty-eight tireless workers like this one. They fly all over Savoy."

He flattened his hand on the desk and the pigeon walked off his wrist, strutting about pompously and cooing.

"You say the fishermen were massacred and yet Cagliari is still in our hands?" asked Paul. "There were at least three thousand monarchist troops . . ."

"Word of the fishermen's heroic stand reached Cagliari before the troops. It may have been a massacre at Cape del Falcone, but it also turned out to be a successful delaying action, not to mention the fact that the fishermen's courage fired up the citizenry so they're battling the troops like seasoned veterans. And winning, as I said."

"Philip," she said quietly.

Paul nodded. "He's run into action he certainly didn't expect."

"I beg your pardon?" Father Avodaine looked from one to the other.

"Someone we know with the monarchists," explained Paul.

"Whoever he is look for him to be coming back," said the priest, "all of them will, all who survive. After Cagliari and Sassari, Porto Torres and Algherro, there won't be a bush or a rock on all of Sardinia where a redcoat can hide." He smiled at Lorna. "It's interesting, my dear, the Sardinians are more bitterly opposed to the government and its policies than those of us here on the mainland. A pity it took a bloodbath to wake everybody up. It so often happens that way. A whole-sale slaughter on top of Charles Felix's taxes, the straw that breaks the camel's back. There's not only blood and taxes down there, but starvation. I have heard that the peasants are eating grass to stay alive. The price of bread is sky high and with the salt tax added to it, the poor are cooking their *polenta** in sea water. It is said that a poor child in Algherro, if let loose in the kitchen, runs to the salt cellar rather than the sugar bowl."

"You said the revolution is moving forward at a great rate," said Paul, "you mean only in Sardinia."

"Not at all! In Piedmont, in Turin, in Cuneo and Asti we are battling and winning battles in the streets. The monarchists' forces are spread too thin. In Savoy, in Aosta and Beaufort, even Chambéry."

"Chambéry!" she exclaimed, vaulting from her chair, unsettling the pigeon strutting about the desktop, causing it to ruffle its feathers and eye her indignantly.

"Yes, Chambéry," said Father Avodaine quietly.

"Any idea exactly what is happening there?" asked Paul.

"As elsewhere there has been fighting in the streets for the past two days. Rest assured, Captain, your power-hungry friend DeLeone is running about like the proverbial headless hen. *Mirabile dictu!* It's rumored he's furious with General Ascoyne for failing to stem the tide and that he himself intends to take over command of the army."

"Wonderful, let him!" exclaimed Paul. Setting his glass down, he rubbed his hands together gleefully and rising, began pacing up and down behind it. "This is the best news we could possibly hope for . . ."

"Now, now, now," interrupted the priest. "It's good and getting better by the hour, but let's not rush things. Only Cagliari is actually falling, and even that news is unconfirmed. Everything else going on from border to border is still up in the air. The next forty-eight hours should tell."

"It's the trend, Father. In Sardinia alone. And that'll

---

* Corn gruel.

be the yardstick. The massacre of the fishermen was the low point, but as you say it lifted everyone up. Taking and holding Cagliari is sure to lift them even higher."

"Hopefully. But what about you two, what are your plans?"

"To get back into it, of course."

"How, where?"

"That, you and I should discuss."

"That, both of us should discuss with you, Father," said Lorna evenly.

"It's a question of where you can do the most good," said the priest, corrugating his brow and considering the dregs in his glass thoughtfully.

"Why not head back the way we came?" she asked. "If Colonel Haproux and Philip and the others are being routed in Sardinia, as you said, Father, they'll be coming back to take up the fight here, or in Piedmont. The question is which."

"My instincts tell me here," said Father Avodaine, "Chambéry. If there's to be a last-ditch stand it would have to be in Chambéry, the castle, Charles Felix's person . . ."

"Have you a map?" asked Paul.

The priest nodded, excused himself, disappeared through the arch and returned with a large wall map of Europe, spreading it on the desk, holding it down with the decanter and his fists. Paul indicated a spot on the coast of the Ligurian Sea.

Father Avodaine nodded. "Menton."

"They left from there. They'll probably come back in the same place. If we hurry perhaps we can get down there and set up before they land and be ready to welcome them."

The priest drew a line with his fingertip from the northern coast of Sardinia to Menton.

"It's only two hundred miles. With favorable winds they could easily cover it in a day and a night. You'll have to get your horses and ride like fury. Getting horses won't be a problem, but the distance . . ."

"I'm going with you," she said.

Both men lifted their eyes from the map and stared at her.

"Lorna . . ."

"Father, is there somewhere Captain Torzzini and I might argue in private?"

"Here in this room, if you like." He rolled up the map, tucked it under one arm and offered his wrist to the pigeon, which had discreetly wandered to a corner of the desk to avoid trespassing on Europe. The bird climbed onto his wrist. "I shall be in the kitchen. You must be hungry; I am." His face burst into a broad, beaming smile. "What a glorious day this is for Savoy! How I envy you and your men, Captain, your youth, your strength, your zeal, your courage. To be able to open up a whole new world for us all. *Gloria Tibi Domini!*"

He left them alone. Paul took her by the hands, filling her eyes from the depths of his own.

"Darling, please understand, I must go . . ."

"Of course. Don't confuse the issue. I'm not about to stand in your way; far from it, I'm going with you."

"No, not this time. It's too damned dangerous. We were lucky at the ambush, lucky we weren't slaughtered. I want you to stay here, with him. Give us a week; by then it should be all over and the dust settled. We'll bring Charles Felix down with such a crash they'll hear it in Hanover. In China! I'll come back here for you, or send a man to bring you to Port-St.-Louis. Once we're back together no one or nothing will ever separate us again, I swear to you."

"Forget it, Paul, I'm not staying here. There's no need to go into the reasons. They haven't changed since the last time."

"You're not coming, and that's final!" His face reddened, his gray eyes narrowing, boring into hers.

"Nothing is final, darling, nothing concerning this Yankee. Unless I say it is."

"Be reasonable . . ."

"I'd rather not, and I don't want to argue about it. I'm much too tired. Take me or don't; run away if you want, but I promise you, I'll follow. You can ride to Menton and across the water to Africa, depend on it, darling, I'll be right behind you. It'll be that or we can ride side by side. I want a horse, I want a gun, and a beret to cover this hideous scalp of mine. I want a change of underclothing and a change in your thinking. It's really very simple; all you have to do is ignore me; pretend I'm not even there. Until it's all over, until we're free to head for Port-St.-Louis and home. You can do it, just put your mind to it and try. Now, let's go into the kitchen; I smell bacon and eggs, and I'm famished."

XIV

Seizing the initiative created immediate problems, chiefly the delay. Paul had no option but to wait until the following midnight to rendezvous with the rest of his squadron near Bénétant. His and Father Avodaine's chief concern was that the returning monarchist force would land at Menton and scatter before the squadron could arrive. Unable to rendezvous earlier, there was little Paul could do throughout the day other than heed Father Avodaine's advice and pray that the enemy would be slow in returning from Sardinia.

The three of them sat together in the study that afternoon while the troop under Lieutenant Chalfaunt, who had replaced Lieutenant Abroza as Paul's aide, waited impatiently in the woods outside of Conflan for darkness and the evening hours to pass, occupying the time preparing their weapons requisitioned in the area and added to those taken from the guard room at the prison.

Father Avodaine's housekeeper, a tiny creature who talked constantly to herself and floated about the house like a ghost on the haunt, now and then peeked around the archway corner at them, her snapping black eyes alternately curious and concerned. A staunch monarchist the woman was not, according to her employer; it was merely that strangers upset her.

"Anything out of her ordinary routine, like three sets of dirty breakfast dishes instead of one, is hard for her to cope with," explained Father Avodaine. "To change the subject, before you reach Menton, or later when it's convenient, you'll want to stop in Villars."

"I know Villars," said Paul. He turned to Lorna.

"It's high in the Maritimes, a natural fortress. If we could only get there before they pass through we could stop two thousand men in their tracks from such a place. They'd never get by. What's more, I'll bet that'll be the route they'll take; what do you think, Father?"

"I wasn't thinking of them, Captain, but of you two. I have a friend from seminary days in Villars, Father Jean Lessipe. An extraordinary man, really remarkable. He'd be a monsignor, perhaps even a cardinal if he were less of a firebrand and more in keeping with the Mother Church's ideal, the paragon servant—dutiful, obedient, apolitical, a scrupulous shunner of controversy, open heart, closed mind and mouth. Jean is just the opposite of all those things. Is he ever!" He laughed and shuddered. "Very supportive of the *risorgimento*. You can count on him to give you all the assistance you'll need, money, whatever papers you may require . . ."

"The two things we never recovered back in Albertville," commented Paul, shaking his head.

"I have some money . . ." began the priest.

"No," interrupted Lorna, "you've done enough already."

"Nonsense, my dear, no one can do too much in times like these. You'll also need my map, Captain, and this . . ." Opening the center drawer of his desk he brought out a small box, a folded piece of paper protruding from beneath the cover. "'Matches." He opened the box and showed one.

"I've never seen a match like this," said Paul, taking it from him and examining it.

"They're called friction matches. Invented a couple years back by an Englishman. Very handy. You don't have to dip them into sulphuric acid, so you don't need a bottle. Watch . . ." He took back the match and pulled it through the tightly folded paper. It burst into flame. "They're coated with sulphur and tipped with a mixture of sulphide of antimony, chlorate of potash, and gum."

"They'll come in handy," said Lorna. "It must be freezing at night high up in the mountains."

The two men exchanged smiles. "Handier even than that, darling," said Paul. "Father Lessipe doesn't know me and I don't know him. To prove to each other we are *carbonari* I'll have to show him I know some of our secrets, the handshake, the sign, and a burnt match."

"The Charcoal Burners."

"Right," said Father Avodaine. He winked at her. "Now that you know, it makes you one of us. You must keep it to yourself."

"I shall."

"Now I have a good-bye gift for you, Miss Singleton." He stood up, closing the drawer. "Come, both of you."

Her gift was a beret which fit her nicely and for which she couldn't have been more grateful. He also gave her a heavy wool sweater, protection against the bitter cold of the high Alps.

They started out for Bénétant at ten o'clock, having whiled away the remainder of the afternoon and early evening napping in preparation for the arduous journey ahead. They took along food—bread, wine and Reblochen and Tamié cheese. At the rendezvous in the walnut grove outside Bénétant all three men checked out their arms one last time and mounted up. Paul and Lorna were told that at least one rumor had managed to assume reality. According to Lieutenant Chalfaunt, DeLeone had indeed exchanged his ministerial sash for his uniform standing in the corner of his office. Once again burdening his chest with his shining and colorful collection. Father Avodaine was right, commented Paul, the tide must be turning. Whether the prime minister, temporarily General DeLeone in Ascoyne's stead, would be able to rally the redcoats, time alone would tell. As the priest had advised shortly before they had ridden away from his back door:

"The night will tell you which way things are going.

Watch for the fires in the mountains. If you see any you'll know that all is going well. If you don't see any, take it for granted that our cause is in jeopardy, if not altogether lost. Myself, whichever way our Father turns his hand, I will be philosophical. Win or lose, one thing is certain; *Omnia mutanter, nos et matamur in illis.** *Dominus vobiscum.*"

They rode in force from the walnut grove down the winding country road toward the Isére, to follow it southward through the rugged high country. She had bathed and washed out her underclothing and blouse, drying them in the sun before nightfall. Riding by night at a lope, resting frequently so as to break in their horses for the difficult miles ahead was, at least for the first few hours, exhilarating, a downright pleasure. But when dawn sent the stars fleeing and rosied the heavens, it signaled the advent of a typical July day. A broiling sun appeared, firing the land, setting riders and horses dripping with perspiration. The air soon became so hot it hurt the throat to breathe and even the ascent out of the river valley into the mountains failed to bring relief. The sweat lathering the horses caught and held the dust roiled and raised by their thumping hooves. Brick red and as dry as desert sand it collected upon her face, against her teeth, sneaking into her mouth and down her throat setting her choking. Forcing her to mask her mouth and nostrils with her scarf, in spite of the heat.

On and on they pressed, pushing the horses now, stopping every third hour for ten minutes to desert their saddles, fling themselves into whatever shade they could find, eat, and water the animals. At length their continuing ascent brought a welcome coolness. But when the sun dropped below the horizon and the wind rose wrapping them tightly in its bluster the temperature dropped nearly forty degrees within minutes. Here, where the southernmost reaches of the Graian Alps

---

* All things are changing and we are changing with them.

thrust their massiveness up against the Maurian as if intent on dislodging and tumbling them into the Rhone Valley, impressive stands of tall slender larches assembled on the slopes, trooping up to hardier Siberian fir and mugho pine. Far below, their tops swirls of green, their trunks hidden under their foliage, stood the less adventuresome oak, beech, ash and sycamore, while scattered up the slopes and down were pink and red flowered rhododendron, blue whortleberry, and dwarf willow. On the crags and outcroppings perched above the squadron, Lorna spied edelweiss, delicate alpine campion and Eryngium, with its dense blue heads. White-tailed ptarmigan rustled the sparse ground cover, bustling through it in search of food while overhead swifts swooped and darted under the watchful eye of an occasional golden eagle, its seven-foot wings spread majestically, its body hanging motionless in the air, riding the high winds.

The same winds herded together premonitory-looking clouds into one enormous black-bellied menace. The effect of the upward thrust of the mountains upon the prevailing winds was to lift the warm air of the lower regions into the upper zone. There it rapidly expanded in volume, losing its heat and creating moisture, the air holding it in a widespread layer under the storm clouds. The wind rose, shrilling defiantly, swirling about the peaks, loosing the glistening snow, sending white wraiths whirling down onto the trail. Murmuring thanks to Father Avodaine for the sweater, Lorna clutched her cloak over it tightly about her, clenching her teeth against the bitter cold, the wind flapping and clapping the hem of the cloak. The cold was rendered even more intolerable by the suddenness of its arrival, and the sharp contrast with the earlier suffocating heat.

Frozen rain began falling, and the squadron, stretched along the road in a single line nearly a mile long, obeyed the order passed down it to halt. Everyone dismounted to find cover to wait out the downpour.

Paul and she huddled in a narrow crevice, partially

roofed by the exposed roots of a fir spreading octopus-like six feet above their heads. The rocks around them took on a skin of ice, glistening brightly, eerily. She was shivering now, biting down hard to keep her teeth from chattering out loud, her cloak soaked through, a limp rag descending from her shoulders. So narrow was their refuge it was impossible for one to lie down or even sit without forcing the other out from under the protection of the roots. Their horses stood side by side shivering near the mouth of the opening, the rain rattling loudly off their heads and flanks and the saddles, like small stones flung into a pan.

"Is this really the way wars are fought?" she asked.

"Ask Hannibal. Your cloak is soaked through," he said, placing his hands on her shoulders. "Let me get your blanket." He started to squeeze by her.

"Let it be," she said. "It's dry in its sack. I'd rather it was dry when we stop to sleep tonight."

"I doubt any of us will get much sleep this night," he said, eyeing the sky.

"How much further will we be traveling this high up?"

"Nearly a hundred miles, I'm afraid."

"This high?"

"Even higher when we get to the Maritimes. We'll have to circle Mount Viso; it's over 12,600 feet."

"How far to Villars?"

"Too far. We have to find and tend to Philip and the rest before we can think about Villars. Which shouldn't be hard, providing they didn't land yesterday and have already run away to Piedmont. Though that I doubt. As hard as moving through the mountains is it puts one thing in our favor. This route is the best, the only really dependable one. With any luck, they'll straggle right up to us. If our pickets manage to spot them coming and give us the luxury of an hour, we'll be able to set up over them and sit and watch them wander up below."

"An ambush," she said, thinking out loud.

"One we owe Philip, wouldn't you say?"

She covered his hands on her shoulders with her own, watching the pattern of glistening rain angling downward break momentarily buffeted by a passing breeze. "I wonder what would have happened if they hadn't stopped us, if we'd boarded ship to Sardinia?"

"Do you seriously think I would have let you?"

"Do you seriously think you could have stopped me?"

He sighed. "Probably not."

"Definitely not."

"We would have gone after them at sea as we'd planned. As General Falcone ordered us. We'd have weakened them so, with the fishermen joining us, they'd have been a sorry-looking lot of rescuers by the time they got to Cagliari. No match for the *carbonari* down there."

"Where is General Falcone now?"

"Chambéry, unless we've already taken it and our high command has sent him to Piedmont or even south. You're trembling all over." Leaning over her shoulder, he kissed her on the forehead. "And running a fever. I knew it! I knew I shouldn't have let you talk me into . . ."

"Nonsense, I'm perfectly all right," she lied, feeling the flush in her cheeks and a sudden dryness in her throat.

The freezing rain persisted, rendering the route too dangerous to negotiate. Paul cursed the rain and the darkness and the monarchists, reserving his choicest expletives for her friend, the prime minister. But the hard-working elements blissfully ignored his invective and it was not until nearly midnight that the squadron was able to resume its journey. She slipped four riders behind him, deliberately, so that he might not hear her hacking cough as her fever rose and an achy feeling seized her chest and muscles. Getting out her blanket, she folded it, tripling it in thickness, and arranging it like a shawl under her wet cloak.

She had been depressed before in her life, many times, though rarely plunging so far down as to flirt with despondency; as she had shortly after the doctor with no name had informed her of Philip's "death." Even so, she could never recall feeling quite so miser-able before. Physically, mentally, absolutely, thoroughly wretched. Her thoughts flew back to Conflans and Father Avodaine's comfortable little home, imagining a roaring fire in the grate under the madonna and child cloak. She pretended to feel the warmth radiating throughout the room, seeping into her pores, gently massaging away the aching discomfort. She pictured herself in bed, her eyelids fluttering, discreetly stifling a yawn as blessed, beautiful sleep, without disturbance, without dreams swept over her. What she would not give for a snug bed, clean sheets, a wooly warm coun-terpane, her hair and skin dry, the sweet scent of perfume rising from the powder covering her body after a piping hot bath.

The horse shuddered beneath her, shattering her reverie. Bowing its head, it plunged forward into the gloom and her imagination fled Father Avodaine's house, the fire, the bed and all its regal comforts, re-turning to the man she loved. What new barriers lay ahead of them, she wondered, what obstacles between this wind-ravaged, nameless, godforsaken alpine reach and Port-St.-Louis and their ship? What dangers, what misfortune, what changes in the emerging pattern of the revolution that would affect them directly? Which there was no way they could avoid.

The next few days would tell; they would bring the climax to the incredible and relentlessly unpredictable chain of events that linked together her life and love and destiny in this madman's mad duchy.

XV

They slept for four hours that night, the men weary
and bedraggled looking, but infused with nervous energy mindful that they would soon be coming upon the
enemy and despite their fatigue eager to press forward.
Lorna had no such enthusiasm. Her fever had climbed
and her cold worsened. She was beginning to suspect
it was determined to become pneumonia. Paul insisted
that they head straight for Villars so that she might
see a doctor and be put to bed.

"To hell with Philip and the rest of them; they're
beaten, that's the main thing. Avenging ourselves with
an ambush has no military value whatsoever."

"Who are you trying to convince, you or me? You
know perfectly well it does. Those you capture will be
taken out of the fight for good. Making that many
fewer you and Colonel Falcone and the others will have
to face."

"Have it your way. The point is, you are out of it.
You're heading for Villars, and I'm going with you."

"Yes, Captain, yes, sir. Whatever you say, sir."

His threat posed a problem; the last thing she wanted
was for the two of them to be separated. But to drag
him away from the promised action he and his fol-
lowers had ridden so far and put up with so much to
engage in would be distressingly unfair. This was one
burden she had no desire to support with her conscience.

Mid-afternoon of the following day found them within forty miles of Villars, beyond it lay the descent
onto the coastal plain, Menton and the Ligurian Sea.
At times the road widened as the rocky eminences

rising around them allowed; at other times it narrowed
to a path barely two feet wide, an almost perpendicular
wall on one side and a chasm a mile deep or deeper
opposite it. St. Sauveur lay to their left beyond a long,
narrow abyss that appeared to plunge to the very core
of the earth, its bottom vanishing into pitch blackness.
Its far side, studded with quartz along its visible rim,
caught and reflected the dark orange rays of the drying
sun. She looked down once, gasped, and refused to
look down again. On and on they rode, picking their
way carefully, watching for loose stones that if stepped
on could sprain a horse's fetlock joint or pitch him
and his luckless rider over the edge. Dazzlingly bright
snow-shrouded peaks, shadowed slopes holding them
aloft, upward thrusting inverted cones in series, in pairs
and alone, like stalactities lifting from a cavern floor,
rose before her eyes. Around a curve about sixty yards
ahead the way widened, according to Paul. Within a
quarter mile the abyss ended in a ridge, raised a
thousand feet above the neighboring peaks. They
rounded the bend and saw two of their pickets riding
back toward them, waving their muskets and yelling.
Announcing the good news. Less than two miles ahead
the first stragglers had been sighted.

"Fifteen or twenty men," said the first picket to rein
up. "Some riding, most of them on foot. They're beaten
and they look it; it's Napoleon's retreat from Moscow!"

The group was disarmed and taken without an ambush, without a shot. They appeared to Lorna not only
relieved, but pleased to be captured, as if they had been
looking forward to it and were grateful that they had
been made prisoners rather than being cut to pieces.
Their ranking officer was a lieutenant, a callow- and
consumptive-looking individual, who by his haughty
tone and manner suggested that he would have felt
more at ease at a ball with a pretty girl on his arm
than dragging the remnants of his command through
the mountains under the burden of a shameful defeat.
Unlike his men, however, he personally did not ap-

preciate being captured by a band of jacket- and shako-less turncoats and said so.

"What do you intend to do with us?" he barked.

"Drop you over a cliff, if you don't behave your-selves," said Paul.

"Take us back the way you came. To Guillaumes."

"I will give the orders, thank you. You can turn around and head back the way we're going."

The lieutenant swore and whipping off his shako dashed it to the ground. "Damn you, you traitorous swine!"

"*Enough!* Listen closely, my unhealthy-looking friend. You will take your places and move ahead of us in tight formation. When we run into your com-rades you had better pray to Saint Gregory that they'll not be so foolish as to attempt to defend themselves. If they try it, you'll be the first to die. We'll climb over your corpses and wipe them out."

"Don't bet your last florin on it," sneered the lieu-tenant, bending and retrieving his shako. "I have news for you, relief is heading this way. You'll be the ones who'll be praying to Saint Gregory."

"You're a liar."

"Am I? Don't be too sure. A full regiment is coming from Monferrato, traveling by barge down the Tanaro River. By now they're probably past Fossano and onto the Stura. It won't be long."

"Shut up! Fall your men in in front of us; those mounted will walk their horses. When I give you the order to quick march, see that you do, if you don't want half an inch of steel opening up your neck. Move!"

By twilight they had picked up nearly one hundred men, but hesitant to chance an encounter with a fresh force—the relief regiment claimed by the lieutenant to be heading their way—Paul kept the squadron and the prisoners moving. Men were assigned to guard them while the pickets to the east were doubled in number and ordered to ride three hundred yards apart from two miles ahead back to two behind. The prisoners, now all on foot, soon began dropping from exhaustion, however, and like it or not, Paul was forced to call a halt alongside another vast and seemingly bottomless abyss at a point estimated to be less than thirty miles from Villars. The stragglers were herded into a cut, a heavy guard posted for the night, and those men not on duty were permitted to scatter and find shelter against the threat of a renewed downpour.

Paul found a ledge twenty feet above the way, with a convenient overhang. There, some distance from his men, most of whom had moved farther up the line, he made Lorna as comfortable as possible. He built a small fire over which she might warm herself and together they ate.

"I have to go," he said. "I'll be back shortly."

"What is it?" she asked worriedly.

"I have to make rounds. Make sure the men are in good shape and check on the prisoners." Bending, he kissed her lovingly. "It won't be long now, my darling. Tomorrow morning early we'll be in Villars and you'll be in a nice warm bed, with hot food, gulping down some foul medicine, and on the mend."

"It sounds wonderful, except the part about the medicine."

He hugged her and kissed her again. "Don't fall asleep. I'll be back before you know it."

She could hear his boots send loose stone sliding down the twisting approach to the road below, the whinny of a horse, and silence broken only by brief laughter in the distance. The breeze high above the overhang lazied about the peaks, then sped away to the south, and the night closed in around her. She yawned and surrendering to her weariness, fell asleep in spite of herself.

She had no way of judging how long she had been asleep, but when she awoke she noticed that the fire had reduced itself to brightly glowing embers. The rain or snow had not yet arrived. Below she could hear voices, Paul's and another man's, a voice she thought she recognized. Throwing aside the blanket, she crept to the edge and, supporting herself between two boulders, peered straight down. Both men had drawn their sabers. She gasped. . . .

"Good Lord," she whispered hoarsely, stiffening with fear.

Philip! Watching them angle their sabers upward, touch edges and prepare to attack, she wanted to shout down at them, but fear clutched her voice, her heart wrenching in her breast in one wild leap. Their battleground was less than six paces long between their horses at their backs and two paces wide to the edge of the abyss. At a glance she could see that it was far too narrow to permit them to circle to seek an opening, as they had in the blacksmith's shop. Her hands flat against the two boulders, she continued to stare down at them, transfixed. Just beyond them yawned the abyss, its opposite wall bathed in a soft bluish light by the moon.

Philip was talking, Paul refusing to, instead concentrating full attention on him, moving about to define the limits of his position, moving toward the edge, coming within a foot of it sending her hand to her mouth to stifle a gasp. Then moving back.

"This time you won't have her to help you, Torzzini. This time you're mine. Better say your prayers, traitor, you're a dead man. There's your grave, ten thousand feet down."

They flew at one another, parrying, their sabers ringing. Philip lunged, Paul neatly sidestepping his thrust, beating his blade vigorously to prevent a remiss. Then he pressed the attack, forcing Philip's blade aside in a try for a riposte. Philip skillfully avoided his point, speedily countering, pressing the attack. In a hectic and furious flurry, he drove Paul to the edge once, then a second time, twisting her heart within her. He would have driven him a third time had not Paul turned away his advantage with a swiftly executed stop-thrust, forcing him to parry.

Now it was Philip forced to the edge and nearly over, saving himself at the last instant by ducking under Paul's closing blade and leaping to one side. Caught off balance in lunging forward, nearly carried over by his momentum, Paul stopped himself, by dropping to one knee, losing his saber. Roaring exultantly and kicking him in the ribs, Philip sent him over! She screamed. Miraculously, Paul's descent seemed to halt in mid-air, the visible right side of his body hanging suspended for a split second. Then his legs and trunk dropped from sight. With his right hand he had grabbed hold of one of a number of small bushes growing out of the wall three feet below the edge. Getting both hands around it, digging his toes into the wall, he struggled frantically to pull himself back up.

Her scream from out of the darkness above him had distracted Philip. He froze, saber in hand, turning away from Paul and peering upward. She drew back from the rocks out of sight, then moved back as he turned again to Paul. Moving to the edge and raising his saber high like a broadsword, he was about to bring it down full force on Paul's head when he suddenly lost his footing, falling over backward. His saber slipped from his grasp, landing beside him, clattering to rest. In that moment, she saw that Philip had not lost his footing; Paul, gripping the bush with one hand, had grabbed his ankle and pulled him down.

Flat on his back, Philip tried to push himself up, cursing viciously.

But he did not make it, even to a sitting position. Down out of the blackness over his head came a large stone. Landing squarely on his chest, crushing his breastbone and heart beneath, killing him instantly.

XVI

She hurried down to the road, past the dead man, the stone cratered by his chest, rushing up to where Paul was hanging, dropping to her knees.

"I can't reach the edge," he said tightly, fear filling his eyes.

"Grab my arm . . ."

"No, you're too weak. I'd only drag you down with me. Damn, if we only had a rope."

"Hang on, I'll get help."

"I can't, not much longer."

She cast about helplessly, then her eyes brightened. "Your horse . . ." Up on her feet, she ran down the way to the horse, pulling it clopping up to where Paul hung. Over the side went the curb reins.

"Can you reach them?"

She lowered the horse's head, dropping the reins lower. "Grab them . . . I'll back him up."

"It won't work."

"It can, I know. I know horses. Do it!"

She watched the reins tauten as he took hold with first one hand, then the other. The horse's head bowed perilously low, threatening to snap its neck, and it snorted in protest. Quickly she was at its chest, pushing with all her strength and talking soothingly to it. Instinctively it set its forelegs, then slowly began backing away. Moving alongside it, gripping the reins, she pulled and pulled. Paul's fists appeared, one, then the other letting go, grabbing the edge. He pulled himself up, collapsing on the ground, gasping for breath.

Down on her knees, she began kissing his forehead, his eyes, his cheeks, his lips . . .

"You shouldn't do this," he said quietly.

379

"What?"

"You're getting yourself into a rut, saving my skin. This is the second time." He got to his feet, heaving a prodigious sigh of relief and whisking the mud from his trouser legs.

"Which only makes us even. You saved mine, getting me out of the castle, and on the way back to Albertville."

He swept her into his arms, kissing her soulfully, then lowering his lips and nuzzling her neck. "My darling . . ."

"Oh, Paul, Paul. . . ."

"Will you do one more thing for me?"

"Whatever you want."

"It's not much really, trivial compared to saving my life."

"What?"

"Will you marry me?"

"In a minute, my dearest darling. In the wink of an eye."

Again they kissed, the wind coming to life over their heads, whining in ostensible disapproval. Gently, touching his cheeks affectionately, with her fingertips, she broke from him to turn and look at Philip. Paul crouched beside him and removed the rock. His chest was covered with blood.

"His heart's burst."

She turned from the sight, then slowly brought her eyes back. "I had to . . ."

"Thank God in heaven you did." He closed Philip's eyes.

Slipping off her wedding ring, she knelt beside Paul and prepared to place it on the dead man's lips.

"What are you doing?"

"It's an old Gypsy curse." She explained as Maria had explained to her, then started to set the ring in place but hesitated and finally drew back her hand. "I can't," she said quietly. "Whatever he was, whatever he did, I haven't the right."

XVII

Father Jean Lesippe wore a face seemingly capable
of but one expression, displayed with only slight,
barely discernible variations. It reflected all his many
moods with the result that he appeared to be scowling
even when he laughed. Only the sound of his voice
betrayed departure from seriousness. He was an impressively large and broad-shouldered man, displaying
the fitness of an athlete, but for the suggestion of a
paunch threatening to develop at his beltline. Sitting,
listening, nodding, sweating, he inserted his index finger
inside his collar, circling his neck with it. A futile effort
to ease the itching caused by the mild rash presented
him by the heat wave. Again and again his finger
went to his collar, in between excursions by his free
hand to his glass of Pinot.

The three of them shared a corner table in a
bakery, the interior immaculate, noisy and redolent of
the sweet smell of freshly baked bread. They had
arrived in Villars, located Father Jean Lesippe, and
Paul had introduced them, asking for a place where
they might talk. When the priest hesitated, he had
drawn him into a nearby alley, produced the burnt
match, and exchanged the secret handshake.

The lack of privacy in the bakery, the proximity of
others, had at first unsettled Paul; she could see
it in his eyes. But Father Lesippe seemed not at all
concerned that they might be overheard. When they sat
down, practically the first words out of the priest's
mouth were a string of questions, unbroken to permit
responses, regarding Father Avodaine—the state of his
health, his parish, his part in the uprising. Begging a

chance to answer, gesturing with upraised palms, Paul assured the priest that his friend was well and sent his fondest regards and answered all his other questions.

"He obviously told you about me," said Father Lesippe.

Paul nodded, "He spoke very highly of you."

"He exaggerates, he always did." The priest's eyes drifted to Lorna, his scowl softening to its permissible limits into a smile. "Excuse me, miss, but being one who never hesitates to speak his mind, I must say that you look poorly. Are you ill?"

"Not very. Getting better," she said grinning in amusement at his whimsical candor.

"She's in the first stages of pneumonia," said Paul grimly, "possibly the last. We really must get her to a doctor."

"Of course." Father Lesippe stood up, his stool scraping the floor loudly, drawing curious stares from others in the room.

"That can wait," insisted Lorna, "one other thing first." Paul stared inquisitively. She smiled at him, holding his eyes relentlessly with her own. "Father, would you be so kind as to marry us?"

"Now?" asked the priest, sitting slowly.

"Now, here. This minute." She took Paul by the hand.

"Is she serious?" asked Father Lesippe.

"She is. We do want to be married, as soon as possible. First, darling, we must clear up this business."

"Coward . . ." she snapped with mock irritation.

"Father, let me fill you in on what we've been up to, then if you wouldn't mind, I'd like to hear what you know. Even the rumors. To some extent you'll be dictating our next move."

"Go ahead."

Paul's recapitulation of events prior to the ambush and leading up to the squadron's mid-morning arrival in Villars was as brief as he could make it. "Our problem is, we've been out of the action for better than a week. Has anything important happened, good, bad? Oh, before I forget, my men are guarding prisoners, but we have reason to believe that a monarchist regiment is headed this way, coming from Monferrato."

"Nonsense," said the priest, "there's no such regiment. There can't be. The monarchists are in flight from one end of the kingdom to the other. It'll be all over in the next few days. Your commander, Colonel Falcone, has taken Chambéry with less than a hundred men, every brick but the castle. The people are coming over to our side in droves. The prime minister knows he's beaten."

"Has he replaced General Ascoyne . . ."

"He has, though he would have done better to leave him in command, and have himself a scapegoat for this glorious disaster. We can thank our Holy Father for old Adelbert's monumental ego. Ego or not, he knows he's through. Last night word arrived that he's rescinded the *mascinato*." Father Lesippe lifted his glass and broke his scowl with a genuine grin. "My friends, it's over, it really is. We've won! *Won!*"

"Ssssh," cautioned Paul.

"What's to sssh about? There isn't a monarchist left in Villars. If there is, he'd best keep his tail between his legs, his mouth shut, and get out while he can."

"You say DeLeone did away with all the taxes?" asked Lorna.

"Every penny."

"Obviously a last-ditch effort to hang onto support," said Paul.

"Last ditch is right. Talk about grasping at straws . . ."

"Do you think there's a chance it'll work? That out of gratitude the mass of people will stick with him and Charles Felix?"

"Never, he hasn't a prayer. His time's run out; we've rendered him and his politics obsolete. The monarchists are finished. Viva Savoy!"

An uproar arose in the street. Other patrons in the room began rising from their stools and moving to the windows. Two bakers, their ankle-length aprons and their arms and hands white with flour, came pounding out of the kitchen. Outside people were shouting, a large crowd gathering. Inside, stools clattered to the floor as the patrons rushed for the door. Father Lesippe threw open the nearest window and stuck his head out.

"Viva Savoy! Viva Savoy! Viva Savoy!" The chant rose from the street. A seedy-looking man ran by the window, a batch of flyers hanging over his arm. Out shot the priest's hand, grabbing him by the shoulder.

"What have you got there, Desozo?" Without waiting for the answer, he snatched away one of the flyers, reading it, turning slowly, dropping heavily onto his stool, his perpetual scowl tinged with surprise.

"Mother of God, can you believe this? He's declared a general amnesty. Full pardon for every *carbonari*, every sympathizer."

"Wonderful!" exclaimed Lorna.

Whipping the flyer out of his grasp, Paul scanned it. "The bastard!"

"Paul!" she burst, as Father Lesippe stiffened, swallowed, and crossed himself. But Paul neither saw him, nor heard her.

"The devious pig. He's totally incredible. He must be out of his mind!"

"Devious, totally incredible, reprehensible, foul, but never out of that mind. To him, a soldier, a general, amnesty is merely a fallback position."

Paul stared at him. Slowly his face relaxed into a grin. "Just one more straw grasped at, is that what you're saying?" His head began bobbing agreement. "You're right, you are . . ."

"The act of a desperate man," said the priest. "He's fascinating. I wonder what his next move will be?"

"I wish we knew for certain what was going on," said Lorna. No sooner had she gotten out the last word than her eyes rolled up into her head and she slumped forward, her face coming down on her forearms, her half-filled glass of Pinot toppling over, drenching the tablecloth. Paul leaped to his feet.

"I knew it," he muttered angrily, "we sit here drinking while she should be in bed being taken care of."

"Bring her along," said Father Lesippe. "Follow me, we'll head straight for Doctor Galuto's."

XVIII

She awoke in a small room with a menacingly low ceiling and whitewashed walls that fairly gleamed, sending darts of pain into her eyes until they became used to the brightness. The sun poured through the single window, a low sun, painting an almost horizontal shadow against the inside of the wall supporting the window frame. It was late afternoon. She stirred and stretched, reveling in the freshly laundered sheets and down pillow. But her cold and the fever still gripped her, her chest heavy with phlegm, her throat dry to cracking—she feared trying to swallow—and still sore. A fist rattled the door and it opened. A small, ascetic-looking, bald-headed man wearing pinch glasses above his flat, pale cheeks leaned in smiling.

"Did you sleep well?" he asked solicitously.

"Yes, thank you."

"I am Doctor Galuto, resident *Æsculapius* in this little aerie."

"Lorna Singleton. May I ask, is it pneumonia?"

"Not quite. I diagnose it as a heavy cold with bronchitis. That glass on the night stand. Drink a little, and every so often." Anxiety seized her. To mind came the doctor in the room at the Gray Dragon Inn, the gold-rimmed spectacles instead of pinch glasses, the entirely different face, but the same drinking glass, with, she noted, almost the same color liquid rising three-quarters of the way to its brim. "It's all right," said the doctor, reassuringly. "It's only cough medicine. It'll relieve the soreness and dryness. Take a sip."

It tasted like strawberries, in spite of the color, and seemed to relieve the dusty feeling and the discomfort.

"Your friends are here. Do you feel up to seeing them?"

"Yes, thank you."

Paul and Father Lesippe came in, Paul with a small bouquet of bud roses and fern that looked funny in his fist, strangely out of character for one who always seemed to be holding a saber. The doctor nodded to both men and went out closing the door. They took chairs on either side of the bed.

"Feeling better?" asked Father Lesippe.

"Achy and weak as a kitten, but I'll be all right. This bed is fabulous, like a warm cloud."

Paul handed her the flowers. "May we get on with it?" He produced a silver ring, holding it up between thumb and forefinger for her approval. "It's the best I could find on short notice. I'm sorry it isn't gold."

"I don't care if it's brass. It's the most beautiful ring I've ever seen."

"You did say you'd marry me."

"I did. On my feet or off."

Father Lesippe got a well-thumbed, somewhat abused looking Bible out of his pocket, opened it, found the passage he wanted, and lay the place ribbon down the inside of the binding. "Are we ready?"

"Don't we need a witness?" she asked.

"In my wedding ceremonies, Almighty God and all his angels bear witness. Mortal interlopers we don't need. If you please . . ." He read, they exchanged their vows, Paul placed the ring on her finger, sliding it as far up as it would go, to the second knuckle. They were then solemnly pronounced man and wife and they kissed. And the music in her heart swelled to a crescendo, filling the chapel surrounding her, the setting sun beaming through the stained glass windows.

"Congratulations to you both. May you live in happiness and good health, raise a dozen children, and never hear a gun or see a saber again," said Father Lesippe.

"Amen," said Lorna. She squeezed Paul's hand,

stroking his cheek affectionately with the other hand, unable to take her eyes off him. "Give me three days, darling, I promise I'll be on my feet and able to travel."

"To Port-St.-Louis." He turned to the priest. "You'll never believe how frustrating it's been getting there. Every time we start out, something gets in the way."

"Not this time," she said determinedly, "nothing or no one. Promise?"

"I promise."

"You don't need me anymore," said Father Lesippe, "why don't I wait outside for you, Paul."

"That's not necessary," she said.

"Let's say it's preferable." He got up, pocketing his Bible. "May I kiss the bride?" She smiled, nodded, he kissed her on the cheek and patted her hand. "Get well very soon, and be happy as a child. It's a proven preventive to old age. Take your time, Paul, I'll be with Alphonse."

They talked. He made no mention of the maelstrom surrounding them, but talked enthusiastically about the future. Nevertheless, she felt constrained to ask the obvious question.

"What about the revolution?"

"What about it?"

"Well, if it's over and you've won, there's nothing more you need do, is there? You can just hang up your uniform, can't you?"

He laughed somewhat thinly, she observed. "What have I done, actually? What has anybody in B squadron done? We started out from Leménc, got ourselves ambushed and taken prisoner; Albertville, Conflans, and back down to here. What can you point to in all of that that could earn us medals? Nothing."

"You took prisoners."

"Nothing. All we've done was to mop up after the fighting."

"I'm sorry you're disappointed, darling; let's be happy it's all over."

"It's certainly beginning to look like it."

"What will happen to Savoy now? The government will change hands . . ."

"You bet." He chuckled. "The irony of it is the new regime will probably follow through on Adelbert's original idea, and replace Charles Felix with someone from the cadet line. There'll be elections, a parliament formed, old laws junked, new ones enacted . . ."

He paused and turned his head toward the window. From some distance away, what seemed to her to be the other end of town, came a rumble, like restless rather than booming thunder. It was a moment before they both realized that it was the noise of a crowd. The door flew open banging against the wall and Father Lesippe and the doctor came barging in.

"You won't believe what's happened!" exclaimed Father Lesippe. "I don't believe it myself."

The doctor nodded vigorously, his glasses' ribbon jumping up and down on his lapel. "Austrian troops have come over the Öztal and Rhaetian Alps, and from Milan and Venice. Heading for the Piedmont border. A full-scale invasion."

"No," groaned Paul.

"Oh, yes," said Father Lesippe. "No rumor, my friend. That old war horse, General Rudetsky, is leading them. The news is coming in from all over. The government is pulling all remaining troops out of the field and rushing them north. Adelbert is waving the flag and screaming for volunteers."

"First the tax rescinded, then the amnesty, now this," snapped Paul irritably, on his feet and gesticulating. "Don't you see, don't either of you understand? It's DeLeone's latest and biggest trick out of that damned bag of his!"

"Is it possible . . ." murmured Father Lesippe in a bewildered tone.

"Of course! What better way to rally all patriotic Savoyards to the colors? In defense against an invasion by our most despised enemy! Who can ignore the call to rise up and throw back the greencoats? Who would dare? What are we liberals to do but drop our principles, our victory, everything but our arms, and rush to the rescue!" He was livid; she had never seen him so upset.

Father Lesippe turned slowly to the doctor. "He's right. This has to be Adelbert's doing, the devil. He stops at nothing."

"It's ridiculous," she said quietly, raising her voice as she continued. "Insane. You're all being stupid. Who do any of you know who'd be taken in by such an absurdity?"

"I, for one," said Paul resignedly.

"You're joking . . ."

He walked to the window and stared out, talking to the glass, reluctant to meet her eyes.

"Yes, it's his doing, deliberate, contrived for the obvious reason, no doubt of it. It's what he's been up to the past few days, an exchange of notes with Vienna, a secret covenant, promises made on both sides. A handshake with Metternich's envoy sealing the bargain. You invade, but you let us stop you at Locana and Novaro. Give us a month, thirty days, time to pull our divided kingdom back together. All we ask in return is your support of the monarchy. Give me that and I'll give you all the territory north of the 45th parallel."

"I don't believe it," she said between teeth clenched in anger.

He swung about, facing her. "Believe it. He's bartering sovereign territory for his hide."

"You don't understand what I mean. What I don't believe is that you know that it's all a fraud and yet you're willing to drop everything, me, our marriage, our future, and run up there. You do intend to, don't you?" He sighed and extended his hand helplessly. "I knew it! You're incredible, totally. You make no sense at all. This is fantastic, that's the only word for it."

"Perhaps you'd rather talk in private," said the doctor, taking Father Lesippe's arm.

"What? Oh, of course," said the priest.

"I'd rather not talk about it at all," she rasped. "Please leave, all of you."

"Lorna," Paul began.

"Please. I can't talk. Not now. Get out and leave me alone."

"Mrs. Torzzini," said Father Lesippe, his voice subdued. "Would you be so generous as to grant me one small favor? Would you give me five minutes? I feel I must explain something to you."

"I wish somebody would explain what I'm doing here. Why I stuck with you, Captain. I must be simpleminded . . ."

Paul and the doctor withdrew. Father Lesippe sat down beside her, covering her hand with his own, lending her his warmth and a smile, a seemingly painful alteration to his customary glower.

"You are angry and bitter and you have every right to be."

"Thank you, Father."

"I mean it. One minute you're in heaven, married to the man you love, the future before you, home and friends and all of it. The next we drop you down to the bottom of the pit. We, not just him. We, because we're all three Savoyards, and Alphonse and I understand what Paul was trying to say. He's right, of course."

"Of course."

"Please. I don't mean about his wanting to go back, although I can hardly dispute him on that. Don't look so shocked, hear me out. What I'm trying to say is before we are revolutionists, he and I, we are Savoyards. Austria is about to invade us, placing our beloved country in serious peril. Contrived or not, the danger is still there. Suddenly it's no longer important whether that mad marionette Charles Felix sits on the throne with Adelbert pulling the strings or we take over. First, the greencoats have to be stopped. We must drop everything, alas, even love and marriage, to do that. When we have stopped the invaders, then we can get

rid of the monarchists and form the kind of government the people are entitled to. It's monstrously unfair
to you, and to him. The timing couldn't be worse. It's
enough to make you bitter the rest of your days. But
he has to join the fight. If he does not; if instead he
waits out these days for you to recover and the two of
you leave for America; if, that is, he turns his back on
his country in her hour of need, he'll regret it as long as
he lives. You'll see it in his eyes, even when he holds
you in his arms. He may never talk about it, but it will
always be at the back of his conscience, like some loathsome creature gnawing at him. Now I ask you, is that
the way you want him? Is it?"

"Better that way than running off and being killed.
Playing right into that monster's hands. Much better."

"Believe me, Lorna, there'll be very little killing in
this farce. It'll be nothing like the real thing." He shook
his head. "No man in Savoy detests Adelbert DeLeone
more than I, but I have to admit there's no shrewder
conniver alive, more unprincipled, more ethically de-
praved. The man has absolutely no stopping point; he
sinks as low as he can, then begins digging with his
bare hands to get even lower."

"I wish he'd die. Why doesn't somebody kill him?"

"What would that do for Savoy? Evil perpetuates
itself on this earth through people like Adelbert. More
skillful at it than most he may be, but as a practitioner
of malevolence he's hardly unique. Rid Savoy of him
and along will come another. There's always another
one waiting in the wings."

The door opened. Paul leaned against the jamb, his
hand on the knob, his expression enigmatic.

"Father, would you excuse us?"

"I don't think we have anything to talk about, Paul.
We'll only argue."

"Father. . . ."

Father Lesippe got up from his chair and gestured
Paul to sit. He left.

"I mean it," she said, turning her face to the wall. "It's useless."

"Will you please let me speak? Without interrupting."

She shrugged and closed her eyes. He began. He talked about Savoy, about his love for his country, and his hatred for those in power who abused its ideals, dissipated its resources, tyrannized its people, and bankrupted its future.

"I hated the idea even more than you, of leaving you to run up there. But I said to myself, what choice have any of us? Then outside in the other room, sitting alone, staring at the wall, I thought about Savoy and how I feel about it. I've said I love my country and I do. Slavishly. But what precisely is love of one's country? How do you define it? I see the flag, my breast surges with pride, my pulse races, I tingle all over. I hear drums and see redcoats, I swell up, I want to cheer my lungs out. You may not know it, but the House of Savoy is the oldest ruling house in Europe, in the world. The longest, unbroken rule in all civilized history."

"So I've been told," she said, staring at the ceiling.

"Pride, loyalty, patriotism, love. But a curious kind of love. Of ideals, of a . . . concept, if you will. Admittedly nebulous. I mean I can't embrace my country. I can't touch it, smell it, taste it. Pride isn't love, nor is patriotism.

"You are love. That's as different as night and day. I can touch you, feel your warmth, smell your hair, your skin. I lose myself in your arms; feeling your closeness my heart lifts inside me. Your kiss brings me to life, makes me glow. When I look into your eyes, when I feel your breath on my cheek, when our bodies touch, just . . . just our hands, it's beautiful. Glorious! I can hold you; I can't hold Savoy. That's it in a nutshell," he said, as if he'd suddenly uncovered a hidden truth and was holding it up and seeing it clearly. "Loving you I look ahead and see us as the weeks go by, the months, the years. In America. I close my eyes and picture you big with our child, my seed in you growing, the baby being born, a boy; my face looks up at me, squalling. Little legs kicking. Red and hairless or wildly hairy as they tell me I was. Me born a second time. You making it possible. Has there ever been another miracle to compare with that? All thanks to love. Then I see a little girl with pigtails and pinafore. A small you. To have the three of you to love. To hold, to touch. Solid, substantial, lasting. Oh, my darling, that's love, that's it. That's what you give me, and what you promise me with your eyes. The only kind of love for me."

"Do you mean it?"

"Look at my face and ask me that."

"Paul . . . Paul."

He threw his arms around her. "Savoy doesn't need me."

"Certainly not like I."

"Like we need each other. They won't miss me up there. Only in my pride, and then only if I'm so thoughtless and stupid as to let it. You're the last person to say it to, but Savoy really is a remarkable country, in odd ways. Perhaps that's why it's survived for so long. Like Switzerland, most of it is so high up it's too troublesome to bother trying to conquer. Napoleon found that out, and the Austrians before him. Every new generation of Austrians learns that hard lesson. Oh, I tell you, the would-be conquerors line up as far back as our history goes. But we've outwitted and outwaited them all and held this piece of Europe for eight hundred years. Even added to it. Eight hundred years, and we'll hold it for eight hundred more. Without my saber." He laughed sardonically. "If I did go up there I'd probably contribute just about as much as I did to the revolution. No, my place is with my wife."

"Come close to me."

She held him and kissed him.

"Three days, my darling," he said, "and no more than three after that before we board ship."

"Which only leaves one loose end."

His cheek pressed against hers, he smiled grimly. "Isn't there always?"

"The revolution . . ."

He held her at arm's length, absorbing the look in her eyes, then glancing down at the sheet drawn over her lower body.

"It's over, it's won." His tone seemed earnest, but his words held little conviction.

"Not now; he's snatching your victory right out of your hands. Even supposing he doesn't, it still has to be secured. You have to get rid of him, Charles Felix, the lot."

"We will, we will."

"We?" She began aimlessly smoothing the fold at the end of the sheet.

He got up from the side of the bed and began pacing. "Once the Austrians are pushed back, he'll be thrown out. The *carbonari* will simply pick up where we're leaving off now. It's not even a 'leaving off,' only an interruption."

"You'll come back to help, of course."

"They won't need me."

"Ah, but you'll need them. You've been waiting for this. You wouldn't want to miss the coup-de-grace."

"Lorna."

"I'm not teasing you, darling. I'm serious. We'll come back together. That's the only condition. We must never be separated again."

Elation filled his eyes, flooding his face. "You mean it, don't you!"

"I do. You gave in on Austria, fair is fair. Besides, I've become involved in your revolution. I see it as just as important as you do. As far as I'm personally concerned if all it accomplishes is to bring down Adelbert, it will serve its purpose."

He rushed to her, sweeping her into his arms.

"Please," she protested, "you're breaking my back! I can't breathe . . ."

He kissed her and kissed her again.

"I love you, my wife. Now and forever." She smiled, moved by his sincerity, seeing him through gathering tears. "Here, don't cry . . ."

"They're tears of joy, Paul. From my heart to my eyes."

EPILOG

Although massing no fewer than twenty regiments along the border, Austria failed to invade Piedmont. Within forty-eight hours it was disclosed that Austrian Prime Minister Prince Klemens Wenzel Nepomuk Lothar von Metternich had changed his mind. The Greek revolt, having already dragged on for nine years, had abruptly begun to inspire revolutions in other countries, threatening to overthrow the entire fragile structure of 1815 in the West. But events which at the outset appeared to presage total ruin for Metternich's system of government paradoxically gave it, in effect, a new lease on life. Informed of the July revolution in Paris, the prime minister dropped all plans for extracting DeLeone's monarchical chestnuts from the fire ignited by the *carbonari*. Instead he recalled General Rudetsky and his troops and himself hastened to meet Count Nesselrode, the Russian diplomat, at Carlsbad. It was a simple case of priorities, with the preservation of Austria's status among the nations of the West taking precedence over the acquisition of a mountainous region that was of little strategic value, hardly worth settling, and a waste of manpower to police.

Count Adelbert DeLeone was turned out of office and forced to flee for his life. King Charles Felix was replaced on the throne by the first representative of the Carignano line in Savoy's long history, Charles Albert the Magnanimous, descended from the younger son of Charles Emmanuel I.

Three days after recovering from her illness, Mrs. Paul Torzzini and her husband arrived in Port-St.-

Louis-du-Rhône and boarded ship for Marseilles and eventually America.

*"Vincit qui patitur"**

My true-love hath my heart, and I have his,
By just exchange one for another given:
I hold his dear, and mine he cannot miss,
There never was a better bargain driven:
    My true-love hath my heart, and I have his.

My heart in me keeps him and me in one,
My heart in him his thoughts and senses guide:
He loves my heart, for once it was his own,
I cherish his because in me it bides:
    My true-love hath my heart, and I have his.
            Sir John Philip Sidney—1554-1586

---

* He who endures conquers.

THE STORM AND THE SPLENDOUR

Jennifer Blake

SHE WAS A SLAVE TO PASSION ...
AND A MASTER IN THE ART OF LOVE

Julia Dupré had had a charmed childhood, a sheltered youth, and could have the pick of the eligible gentlemen who courted her — but she wanted to have excitement and adventure.

When she first met Captain Rudyard Thorpe, handsome and eligible, she never dreamt that her life would change so dramatically. Instantly repelled but magnetically attracted towards him her heart was torn in two. And then fate stepped in. Her father died, propriety necessitated marriage and before she knew it, Captain Thorpe had taken her for himself ...

HISTORICAL ROMANCE   0 7221 1744 2   £1.85

And don't miss Jennifer Blake's other historical romances:

LOVE'S WILD DESIRE
TENDER BETRAYAL

- Also available in Sphere Books.

SPHERE BRING YOU THE BEST IN WOMEN'S READING...

FICTION

GOLDEN LOTUS	Janet Louise Roberts	£1.75 ☐
LOVING	Danielle Steel	£1.50 ☐
TARA'S SONG	Barbara Ferry Johnson	£1.75 ☐
INNOCENT BLOOD	P. D. James	£1.50 ☐
WIFEY	Judy Blume	£1.25 ☐
SPECIAL EFFECTS	Harriet Frank	£1.25 ☐
THE BLEEDING HEART	Marilyn French	£1.75 ☐
THE WOMEN'S ROOM	Marilyn French	£1.95 ☐
CRASHING	Enid Harlow	£1.25 ☐
BARE ESSENCE	Meredith Rich	£1.35 ☐
STEPPING	Nancy Thayer	£1.25 ☐
REVELATIONS	Phyllis Naylor	£1.50 ☐

NON-FICTION

EMMA AND I	Sheila Hocken	£1.25 ☐
A NURSE'S WAR	Brenda McBryde	£1.25 ☐
LOVE SCENE	Jesse Lasky Jr and Pat Silver	£1.50 ☐
COME WIND OR WEATHER	Clare Francis	£1.50 ☐
BOOK OF CHILD CARE	Dr Hugh Jolly	£4.95 ☐
GREAT DISHES OF THE WORLD	Robert Carrier	£2.95 ☐
A TASTE OF DREAMS	Josceline Dimbleby	£2.95 ☐
WORLD OF SALADS	Rosalie Swedlin	£2.75 ☐
DEEP FREEZING	Mary Norwak	£1.50 ☐
PEARS MEDICAL ENCYCLOPAEDIA	J. A. C. Brown	£3.50 ☐
THE BREAST BOOK	Anthony Harris	£1.50 ☐
A GUIDE TO PAINTING IN OILS	Barbara Dorf	£1.25 ☐

All Sphere books are available at your local bookshop or newsagent, or can be ordered direct from the publisher. Just tick the titles you want and fill in the form below.

Name _____

Address _____

_____

Write to Sphere Books, Cash Sales Department, PO Box 11, Falmouth, Cornwall TR10 9EN

Please enclose a cheque or postal order to the value of the cover price plus

UK: 40p for the first book, 18p for the second book and 13p for each additional book ordered to a maximum charge of £1.49.

OVERSEAS: 60p for the first book plus 18p per copy for each additional book.

BFPO & EIRE: 40p for the first book, 18p for the second book plus 13p per copy for the next 7 books, thereafter 7p per book.

Sphere Books reserve the right to show new retail prices on covers which may differ from those previously advertised in the text or elsewhere, and to increase postal rates in accordance with the PO.